TETRIS TRILOGY #1

THE TETRIS EFFECT

AN URBAN FANTASY THRILLER

COLIN CARVALHO BURGESS

OTHER WORLD BOOKS

First published in Great Britain in 2018

Paperback ISBN: 978-1-9998184-0-1
.epub eBook ISBN: 978-1-9998184-1-8
.mobi eBook ISBN: 978-1-9998184-2-5
Hardback ISBN: 978-1-9998184-3-2

@CarvalhoBurgess

www.otherworldbooks.com

Cover design by SpiffingCovers

For Graeme

ACHIEVEMENT UNLOCKED

LEVEL ONE

1

Hotei sprang into a defensive Kung Fu stance. White wires snaked through flowing hair, leading to the tiny device in the palm of his hand. He had just been startled by the piercing sound of a guitar chord.

It was magic to him how so much energy could be summoned at the simple touch of a button. Looking to his immortal family for reassurance, they smiled, bowed politely, and urged him to continue with his experiment. He began to express a variety of conflicting emotions. At first he seemed serious, then cheerful, and then utterly confused. He appeared briefly elated before being overcome by what they presumed to be a deep sadness.

Tears formed in the old man's sunken eyes as he experienced the frenetic energy of rock and roll.

2

Drop a frog into a scalding pot of water and it will instantly leap out, but leave the frog in cold water and slowly raise the temperature − then it will boil itself alive.

The doctor had succeeded with a profound achievement while in the clutches of the otherworld. This made him different from the beings that inhabited this strange place; the shadows with vacant faces and absent expressions. After an incalculable amount of time, and with incredible persistence, he had fought against the gravitational pull intent on stealing his memories, and managed to maintain a sense of self. The state wasn't permanent, however. Sometimes he would be up, like when he remembered how to roll a mandrake joint, sometimes he would be down, like when he forgot how to walk.

His joint extinguished with a fizz as he submerged in the tin bath. He opened his eyes underwater and was somewhere else entirely. He could see beyond the leaves, spider webs and trees. He was drifting high over hills and deep into valleys like a fly-by cut scene. He could focus in on the sound of every insect as they maintained their perpetual chorus. He could detect the shadow animals as they crawled in the corners, ready to strike like deadly sentinels.

A spasm shook his body. He repressed the desire to breathe and instead concentrated on the name of the avatar that he'd just reset to level one; Izanagi.

Dr Vegas was the chain smoking, hair growing, free thinking know-it-all of the afterlife, but he was also the frog and the temperature was rising.

3

Never forget; nineteen eighty-three — the year when two video games were blamed for sending the entire home console industry into meltdown. America announced a recession and called it the great video game crash. The Japanese gave it a more stylish twist by branding it — Atari Shock.

Over-confident in the arcade success of Pac-Man, twelve million cartridges had been manufactured for the Atari 2600, despite having only sold ten million consoles. It didn't port well, it didn't play well, and the kids began queuing up for refunds.

Thirty million dollars were paid for the rights to E.T., rushed out in five weeks to accompany the Spielberg film. It was openly branded as the worst video game ever.

Five new consoles were launched the following year, and despite Pac-Man and E.T. taking the fall, the market had become flooded with bad titles that no one enjoyed playing. The second-generation market peaked, over extended, and plummeted in the years to follow. Atari made a loss of five hundred million dollars in a single financial year.

In a landfill site near Alamogordo, New Mexico, millions of unsold cartridges were made to disappear in the dust overnight. When news of the desert dumping ground hit the local papers, the kids arrived in their hundreds to resurrect the cartridges, and they found way more than just E.T. and Pac-Man. The plastic graveyard hid a catalogue of buried treasures; Centipede, Warlords, Defender, Space Invaders, Berzerk; all were buried in the dry desert dirt. What followed was digital grave robbery on a massive scale. It was an 8-bit appreciation flash mob, a spark that ignited the digital piracy flame and inspired the attitude that the fun stuff should be free.

The Alamogordo authorities declared the site a bio-hazard, at risk of unearthing mercury covered pigs or dislodging a vat of nuclear waste from this former desert dumping ground. It was sealed under concrete. The cartridge tomb became urban legend.

Thirty years later, the site was excavated and the games began appearing on eBay. Lars paid almost a grand for his copy of E.T. and didn't understand why he was compelled to do so. Physically holding a piece of computer gaming history, despite it being just a rectangle of time-worn plastic, touched him to the very core of his soul.

4

The bar at The Dunes Hotel & Oasis Casino popped, fizzed, and ordered one more. Crushed velvet curtains cornered off VIP areas where the lighting was dim enough not to betray the age of its more glamorous clientele, but just bright enough to catch their jewellery.

Professor Van Peterson and his new assistant, Tadashi Finjoto, sat patiently, having ordered a pair of Whisky Sours that now looked like an advertisement on silver doilies. The professor wasn't interested in his drink. Whenever a tuxedo approached he would look up. On realising that it wasn't who he was waiting for, his gaze would return to the mirrored table where he would quickly become lost in his own reflection.

Tadashi stubbed out a cigarette in the crystal ashtray. 'Twenty years is a long time,' he said.

'I imagine that my little conference is being monitored from all over the inquisitive globe,' explained the professor.

'He was your boss?'

Van Peterson sat up, finally admitting to himself that the wait would be much longer than expected. 'He was a fund manager of sorts. They call it risk assessment these days. We would be tasked with challenges and invited to discuss possible solutions, before he would file his report on the likelihood of a successful outcome. Convince Jimmy and you had the money, that's what we used to say. We would meet to discuss projects designed to test the very boundaries of science. We were like a club and he became, well, just like one of us really, but we knew he wasn't. He was there to observe. That was how it worked back then. Much more civilised. None of this dirty stage business.'

The assistant was surprised. 'You're not looking forward to the conference?'

'The Universe has decided that I must sing for my supper, Tadashi, but I am not a fan of public karaoke.'

'With respect, I am excited to witness the regression first hand.'

The old man laughed. 'That is kind of you. I will allow you to make your judgement after the conference.' Van Peterson tried to focus on a small group that had entered the bar. He looked disappointed when he realised that his contact wasn't in the crowd.

'Were all of your projects funded by Mr Carlton?'

'Of course. We had plenty of work. We were busy. We were necessary.'

Tadashi moved in closer, just as he'd seen in the American espionage movies. 'CIA?' he spelled out in a whisper.

Van Peterson wasn't sure if he should be talking about his work at The Office, or if twenty years were enough to pass the government embargo. He checked over his shoulder and replied in equally hushed tones, just to be safe; 'CIA – DST. The Central Intelligence Agency Directorate of Science and Technology, and there's really no need to whisper, I think.' He tutted, annoyed by something that had happened a very long time ago and was now consigned to a nagging memory.

Tadashi watched a diamond necklace cling tightly to a low-cut top, on its way for a cocaine refresher in the bathroom. 'Professor,' he asked, 'tell me about the Stargate?'

Van Peterson laughed and tasted his whisky, savouring the flavour before he replied. 'Bless you for being so curious, but we're not living in a movie about a little lost extra-terrestrial.'

Tadashi was humbled to have been invited to document the spiritual science conference, let alone chat informally to the man he admired so much. He didn't want to risk the opportunity by coming across as naïve. 'I am sorry,' he said, lowering his head. 'I ask you too much.'

The professor let out a deep sigh. Despite the constant questioning, Tadashi's enthusiasm was actually quite welcome. Discussing past endeavours had brought them closer. It had just been so long since he was the focus of as much attention. 'No. It's me who should be apologising. Maybe it's the thought of seeing him again after all these years. Those days were cold and calculating, my boy, but it was a very long time ago. Times have changed. There's nothing wrong with a little curiosity. And the Stargate, didn't work. Ah!' He laughed to himself as if enjoying a private joke and reached out to pat his young assistant on the shoulder. 'Which reminds me of the last time I would have seen Jimmy. Operation Acoustic Kitty.'

Tadashi's eyes brightened at the prospect of an anecdote. Van Peterson indulged with a reassuring smile.

'Implant a radio microphone in a moveable and yet inconspicuous object...' he explained in an authoritative tone, 'such as a cat, and you may well believe that you have designed the perfect cold war spy; adaptable, portable, cute.

But expect your kitty to stay within earshot of the target and exactly where you want it? Disaster.' He cradled the tumbler in the palm of his hands and leant in. 'We had reams and reams of tape, Tadashi; recordings of angry hotel kitchen staff, valets ushering our kitties out from under parked cars, firemen climbing ladders to rescue them down from trees. One lady even took a kitty home. Technically that's theft of government property.' There was a spark of mischief in the old man's eyes. He was enjoying himself. 'Did you know that tomcats make a very husky growl when mating? It's really quite vigorous.'

The assistant felt it appropriate to take a slug of whisky.

'That project turned out to be a little too unconventional for our friends in the suits. Jimmy said the results were unsatisfactory. So The Office and I parted ways before too many little cats lost their tails in the name of science.'

Tadashi pulled a face and made a note to look the case up later. 'Then you joined the Accademia del Cimento?'

Van Peterson rolled the ice cubes in his tumbler and didn't answer. He was deep in thought.

The hotel bar spun in a twisted carousel of silver drinks trays; the constant popping of champagne corks, long blonde hair and longer black dresses. They had been waiting for almost an hour. There was still no sign of the man from The Office.

Tadashi finished his whisky in a few large gulps and considered ordering another but the old man had hardly touched his. He took a moment to watch the decadence of the room, allowing time to pass, and couldn't resist exploiting the opportunity one more time.

'Tell me about Project MKUltra? Did you manage to harness the power of the psychotropic?'

The professor looked uncomfortable. Tadashi bowed his head and waited, unsure if he was going to be denied the story.

Van Peterson made a point of shifting in his seat to reset the conversation. 'Of course. I used to séance with Andrija Puharich. The Office were particularly intrigued by his achievements in extrasensory perception. I had the privilege of being in the search party that found the amanita muscaria. You are familiar?'

'The fly agaric; a most powerful psychoactive hallucinogen.'

'He called it the sacred mushroom. Now that, Tadashi, was a thing of pure fantasy. Such a beautiful thing to observe. It had a bright red bulbous dome and tiny white spots. If it wasn't right there in front of me, I would never have believed it even existed. The mushroom was growing in the woods so close to Andrija's laboratory, as though it had been planted there just for us to discover.' Van Peterson set his tumbler on the silver doily. 'Occasionally, Mr Huxley would join us. We would perform meditation, both under the influence of psychotropics and of sober mind.'

Tadashi bowed in thanks but the professor wasn't finished. A flicker of mischief flashed across his face. He was about to reveal more than he knew he should. 'Once, Aldous wanted to borrow my bicycle for an LSD trip, but I had ingested a rather significant dose of the Peyote cactus so I refused.'

'Still talking about drugs, Malcolm?' asked a low, southern American drawl.

They looked up to see a man in a grey suit; squat figure, hair combed abruptly to one side, and a smile that wouldn't go amiss on a great white shark. Special Agent Carlton stood, waiting to embrace with arms outstretched. He hadn't changed in twenty years.

'Hello, Jimmy.'

Tadashi watched them wrestle a hug and pat each other on the back. They seemed relaxed, like they had parted only weeks before.

'Now, will you have a whisky?'

'I'm still not drinking.'

'Tell me, what else are you still not doing?'

'I'm still not funding you,' he laughed.

'Indeed, and how is Mrs Carlton?'

'And I'm still not going to tell you anything about my personal life,' he joked, but was in fact perfectly serious.

Carlton sat on the leather armchair and casually unbuttoned his jacket. He pulled out a pack of Old Gold cigarettes. No one spoke as he lit up. Soon, he too appeared to be waiting for someone like himself to arrive.

Tadashi keenly anticipated the conversation.

'Oh,' spluttered Van Peterson. 'This is the new assistant. We can talk in front of him.'

Carlton took his time before turning to face Tadashi. 'I don't believe that I have had the pleasure, young sir?' He allowed smoke to rise between them.

'Where are my manners? Mr Tadashi Finjoto, from the Tokyo University of Science, may I introduce Special Agent Carlton,' he hesitated, 'a very old friend.'

Tadashi bowed. Carlton tapped his cigarette in the ashtray. They both leaned forward in their chairs and firmly shook hands, neither of them standing.

'Mr Finjoto will be documenting my work at the spiritual science conference tomorrow.'

The agent appeared to relax as much as a stiff could. 'So, Malcolm,' he said, 'what exactly should Mr Finjoto expect to document?'

There was a pregnant pause. The room buzzed with chic dinner jazz and wealthy conversation.

'What would you say, Jimmy, if I were to tell you that I have made a discovery that will profoundly contradict the very nature of humanity?'

The agent stubbed out his cigarette. 'I would say that you had my full attention, Malcolm.'

5

His parents were concerned. As a young boy, Lars appeared to have school friends, he was eating well, would do his chores when asked, but instead of going out with the other kids he would sit in front of his gaming console all day.

He was hooked to the virtual interaction offered by the pixelated screen and grew up with an obsession for arcade computer games. His personality evolved by fight or flight instruction as he lived these real-time adventures over and over; repeat play, repeat experience, repeat adventure. He became many people, solved many puzzles, and lived many lives. He spent more time in front of the screen burning gaming imagery into his tired, wide eyes, than he did simply growing up. It was this that his parents put down to a lack of engagement with the actual physical world.

Doctors were unsure how to help. Most of them recommended pills. One insisted that Lars be given the opportunity to develop an emotional attachment to a pet. This just made his parents worry about why this emotional attachment couldn't have been to them.

When Lars was ten years old he was given a goldfish. It was orange, plump, insignificant, and much like any other goldfish. He called it Mr Chips. Of course, the life expectancy of a common goldfish barely allowed him the time to form any kind of relationship before he found it floating dead, upside down in the cold tank. The young boy sprinkled fish food but it just bobbed, drifting rigid. He left it for three weeks until the flakes turned brown, convinced that it was looking at him, waiting for him to do something.

One evening, as the landing light broke through a crack in the door, revealing Mr Chips floating at an angle, he positioned a chair so that he could reach into the tank. He took a net and prepared to scoop it into the bin. Just as the net hit the water, the goldfish flapped into life.

This game of resurrection would be re-played, repeatedly, for the rest of Lars' otherwise average life.

On the morning World of Warcraft was launched, Lars waited in the rain outside his local games shop. There wasn't a queue but he had arrived an hour before opening anyway. As he felt the sacrificial chill of the weather, he vowed to become a committed resident of Azeroth.

He raced home and abandoned arcade gaming for good, creating his own cardboard box Alamogordo landfill, to be buried at the back of a cupboard and deep under the bed. It was a short step to the hyper fantasy world of the deep web, browser based, massively multi-player online role-playing game named after the great crash of eighty-three.

Atari Shock was a pop culture phenomenon. The lifestyle blogs called it "a twisted top trumps for Generation Z – a place for enemies" which showed how little they really understood about what the players were getting up to online.

It was a war zone in a virtual world, pure nonsense to the untrained eye, but pure poetry to the hundred thousand players who were permanently logged in and fighting to survive. Set in an arena where points prevailed, the aim was to stay alive and stay in the game. Every move was life threatening. Every decision had impact. To play, you needed a credit card, a connection, and a complete disregard for face-to-face social interaction.

Once an avatar is created, the player uses their power-up tokens to launch nukes, exchange dirty drugs, seduce inexperienced players into traps and sneak up on friends to send them back to the beginning of the game. The geeks, the misfits, and the over-complicated were instigating gang warfare in a simulated reality overrun by bruised egos, high stakes gambling, and a whole lot of pissing on virtual territory.

The game operated in real time so endurance was essential. Gamers that went without a break always had the advantage. It took commitment and stamina. The console kids were having their heads bitten off and shoved up their asses before they could trade a single nuke. The bingo queens were lambs to the slaughter and barely progressed beyond level one. Playing under the influence led to mistakes. Energy drinks tasted like chalky water after around thirty-six hours of continuous play.

Since its creation, office worker, energy drink slurper, married man who should really know better, Lars Nilsson, had appeared consistently at the top of the league. It came naturally to multi-task tactics while chatting with his forum followers. He would speak as though to an old friend, while simultaneously setting elaborate traps.

'You're not taking those co-ordinates, SkullMonkey. They are reserved for the professionals.' He performed a hot key operation as calmly as an air traffic controller, and the weaker player was vapourised to permadeath. A nauseous excitement swelled in his stomach, and the real world faded into insignificance every time he got lost in the game. Lars played ruthlessly to maintain overlord status in his virtual world.

Amassing an infinite number of power-up tokens was essential to long term survival. This was possible either by excessive game play, or by players teaming up to form a gang known as a super clan, and travelling together around game space like a constantly feeding whale shark. When a super clan showed any kind of weakness, there was a high chance that it was a multi; a single player with multiple accounts, a peacock splaying its feathers in an attempt to appear bigger than it was. Lars knew all the tricks.

'This game takes commitment. You have to feed it like one of those virtual pets, otherwise it'll die.' He stole a glance at the fish tank. Mr Chips was swimming at a sideways angle. He vapourised a small clan of low-ranking players in an aggressive attack manoeuvre. Followers spilled emoticons and absurd comments in his forum feed. The chat room lit up like a stream of consciousness brain tap.

He was logged in for up to eighteen hours a day. He played hard and fast to earn his secret status. His method was to keep playing until he heard the dawn chorus, and then snooze between regular cigarette breaks at work. His wife hoped it was a phase. She didn't know the half of it.

'No, GreySkull, a plus twenty nuke attack is pointless. Try harder, dumb ass.' The player was sent to the bottom of the leader board in a swift hot key attack combo.

He heard the familiar sound of the bedroom door slamming. This was Claire's warning shot. Lars thought about the neighbours, then wondered how long it would be until the door fell off its hinges.

The small room at the top of the stairs was his gaming cockpit. It was lined with Ikea shelves crammed with old files, books that he'd never read, photo albums documenting the life and unfulfilling times of the Nilsson's; manuals, old stationery, used coffee mugs, boxes of papers, a couple of old printers, rotting banana skins, five monitors — only two that worked — plates of unrecognisable half eaten somethings, the sacred E.T. Atari 2600 game cartridge that no one was allowed to touch, Mr Chip's tank and plenty of old skool wires and cables that no longer had a use but he was reluctant to throw away. This was his mess and everything had a place, even the rubbish. There was a tiny window but it was easily forgotten and too high to see through without climbing on a chair. The clutter made the space seem much smaller than it was but also gave it a sense of purpose. It wasn't possible to do anything else in this room apart from sit still and stare at the monitors. It was the perfect place to host operations.

'Are you coming to bed?' Claire was standing in the doorway wearing the no sex tonight, oversized dressing gown.

He pulled off his headset. 'Sorry, honey, I didn't see you.'

'Is that Minecraft?' she sniffed. The bathrobe hung off her in a way that wasn't as flattering as she had intended.

'Yes. It's Minecraft,' he replied, barely looking up from the screen.

'Mr Chips is dead again,' she said, and closed the door without saying goodnight. This was a regular occurrence. She just wanted a hug.

Lars leaned over and brushed his fingers through Mr Chip's water. The goldfish sprang into life and hurtled around the tank like it had just taken a hit from a defibrillator. Moments after she'd left the room he'd forgotten that Claire was even there. He was lost in the livestream, and GreySkull was back.

'Ah, you buffed up, GreySkull. Got yourself a cheeky cash stash have we? Don't just shoot stuff. That tactic will get you nowhere. Heal and run. Dodge and build. Get some trap bait going. Hunter sets a baited cage, greedy monkey gets trapped. That's all the advice I'm giving you today.'

Forum followers spilled emoticons of bananas and monkey faces.

Atari Shock avatars came with free but limited inventory. Most new players bought a more powerful profile for a chance of lasting longer. Players could also collect and hide power-up tokens in-game, at the risk of them being discovered and raided.

It was the ability to give your avatar a unique identifier, however, which made you truly stand out from the crowd. Choosing your profile name was crucial. It was a shield and a spear, as well as a symbol. More than just a nickname, it was part of the gameplay strategy. It could protect and provoke. Casual players would typically choose an aggressive or violent name to try and intimidate their opponents; BoneCrusher. DeathWatch. Fuck-u-up. They would also use anonymity as a tactic and change their avatar name frequently for protection.

When on a winning streak, the mightiest of reputations would cut a path clean through game space. You got noticed and everyone wanted a piece of you. Virtual fame was just a few clicks away. The perfect choice of an avatar name was a statement of intent, a show of force, a colourful flag on the blood-spattered battlefield. Infamy would spread on the bounty hunter forums and blogs, causing opponents to use avoidance tactics instead of risking head-on confrontation. Lars knew that to maintain the presence of a consistently powerful avatar name − was to become immortal.

The player-feed flickered. He barely blinked as he expertly assigned instructions, grasping power-up tokens wherever he could. He was determined to maintain the status that he commanded. He didn't feel tired. He didn't feel anything.

The klaxon sounded imminent attack.

'Player-feed: GreySkull launches +100 nuke attack.'

'GreySkull, you fucking noob,' he laughed, instinctively taking evasive action. This was a typical transaction, fast and frenetic, the jostling of points, the push and shove of power, over in seconds. It was barely a challenge for a gamer of his skill, but just at the critical moment, his controls stopped responding. He tried to activate a teleport. The hot keys were frozen.

'Player-feed: The Immortal critical hit −100 life force.'

'Dammit,' he muttered, as he was thrust helplessly into a war zone of explosions; flashing nukes and multiple chat room windows opening and closing with bribes, trades, violent death threats and cybersex, occurring simultaneously in a melting pot of pure fantasy.

Lars watched in amazement as his game space filled with players, more than he had ever imagined possible; two hundred, five hundred, a thousand, five thousand, and they all began sniping away at the most powerful player on the server.

There was a crash of bins from the alley outside. A shrill and piercing animal shriek echoed through the tiny window. 'You!'

His co-ordinate counter was increasing with more players by the second. The community had ganged up on him, forming a super clan that blocked all exits, and somehow, someone had worked out how to render him helpless.

'You!' The creature howled for attention as the moon glowed through a fog of light pollution.

6

The professor made them wait, enjoying the scent of malt whisky in his tumbler. 'Tell me, Jim,' he eventually asked, looking the agent directly in the eye. 'Do you believe in reincarnation?'

Carlton cleared this throat. 'Now, if you are suggesting that I will come back as a flower or a monkey or something like that, then no sir I do not.'

'There are many faiths who believe that our lives are directly influenced by the choices that we make,' explained Van Peterson, 'even those choices made in a previous incarnation. They teach that in the event of death, we are re-born to live again with the consequence of those decisions. They call it Karma, Jimmy; where good deeds are spiritually rewarded, and bad deeds are forever haunting.'

'I know what Karma is, Malcolm,' he coughed, seeming impatient.

Van Peterson innocently raised his eyebrows.

Tadashi watched quietly, trying not to draw attention to himself.

'What if the soul could be cleansed of this karmic state, with the opportunity to absolve itself of its sins? What if it were possible to learn from our mistakes and to harness the opportunity to try again from the beginning, with the knowledge of experience passed down through generations? What if, ultimately, we had the chance to seek forgiveness for wrongdoing, and give life another go? What would you say to that, eh?' The old man sat back.

'Our Lord will decide who is forgiven,' Carlton stated, firmly.

'Does he give you the opportunity for a second life?'

'There is no second life.'

'Jim, there is,' said Van Peterson, excitedly.

'You're talking about Heaven and Hell?'

'There is no Heaven, no Hell, but there is the space in-between.'

Their eyes locked.

Tadashi didn't dare move for fear of interrupting the staring contest.

'Where are you going with this, Malcolm?'

He smiled sympathetically and to everyone's surprise he encouraged the assistant to speak. 'Mr Finjoto, would you be so kind as to enlighten us?'

Tadashi was humbled. He hadn't expected to say anything. He ducked his head in thanks. 'I will try my best.'

The agent scratched his nose and lit up an Old Gold. He wasn't going to let it slip that he was quite happy to be back in the ring with his old sparring partner. 'The floor is yours, young man.'

Tadashi spoke softly and with an assured confidence. 'The passing of life is the visible becoming invisible, the transference of the spirit from one cosmic plane to another,' he explained. 'Upon re-birth, the invisible return to our dimension and become visible once more. It is the darkness returning to the light. This is what I believe the professor is referring to as our second chance.'

'Claptrap,' shouted Carlton, just a little too loud for the room they were in. People turned their heads despite the chaos of chatter. There were hand signals. A waiter approached.

'Is there anything I can get you, sirs?'

Carlton was defiant. 'I am not talking to you. Please allow us some privacy while I talk with my colleagues.'

Tadashi took it as a personal victory that Carlton had just referred to them both as colleagues. The waiter retreated as quickly as he'd arrived.

'And who, or what, do you claim to worship, Mr Finjoto?' He was being deliberately provocative and settling in for the fight, trying to undermine the young assistant. 'Do you have a God?'

Tadashi was humble, but defiant. 'My faith does not celebrate the concept of life and death. There is simply harmony between humanity and nature. I practice kami-no-michi — Shinto. It is the native religion of Japan. I worship my ancestors who have passed on. They are my gods, my spirits, and they are what I too shall become.'

'Be careful what you say, boy,' Carlton grunted. He extinguished his cigarette and casually signalled to the exact same waiter that he'd just told to leave. The waiter hesitated, unsure if he should interrupt.

'I exist to become one with the many, 'continued Tadashi. 'My purpose is to join the collective ancestral being; a powerful force that exists everywhere and in everything. We all have the opportunity to achieve this enlightenment. It gives us meaning, during our time on this mortal plane.'

Van Peterson was cradling his tumbler. 'Just like old times, eh, Jimmy?'

The agent breathed heavily, trying to stop himself from saying something he'd already decided he shouldn't.

The head waiter arrived and Carlton ordered a spritzer with a twist of lime. Tadashi took another whisky. Van Peterson looked at the floor.

'This is big talk for such a small man.' He was almost laughing to himself as he said it. 'Think you're better than everyone else, huh?'

Tadashi looked to Van Peterson for reassurance but he just smiled. The assistant was on his own. 'I am simply in touch with my spiritual ancestors,' he replied. 'And this connection gives me the confidence to never fear life, or death.'

Carlton eyed Tadashi, suspiciously. The spritzer arrived and he took a large and unruly gulp. The drink seemed to calm him. 'So, you think this attitude of yours will bring you salvation, do you?'

'I do not require salvation, Mr Carlton...' Tadashi smiled, 'for I am already saved.'

The agent wiped his lips with a white napkin and prepared for round two. 'You deny that in death we shall be judged and offered a chance for eternal life in Heaven?'

'Judged by who?' Tadashi interrupted.

'By our Lord, Jesus,' he stated, matter-of-factly.

'And what happens when we have been judged?'

'We go to Heaven, or Hell, based on how well we follow the teachings of our Lord,' said Carlton, as if reading from a bible school pamphlet.

'You are almost correct.'

Carlton was shocked. 'What right does this ignorant boy have to question my faith, Malcolm?'

'Hear him out, Jim. Mr Finjoto has much experience in these matters.'

Van Peterson wanted them to fight their corners. The book was open and all bets were off.

The head waiter ushered new arrivals as far away from their table as possible. A woman sipped a bright pink cocktail topped with whipped cream and a maraschino cherry. The cream stuck to her nose and she laughed out loud.

Tadashi was just getting into his stride. 'If you insist on there being a Heaven and Hell, Mr Carlton, then where are they?'

Carlton lit another cigarette and clicked the Zippo shut. 'They are in the afterlife.'

'So, the afterlife exists?'

He nodded and smoked.

'And how might I find it? Do I take a tram?'

'It's not a physical place,' he puffed. 'It's spiritual, ephemeral, it's where we pass through.'

Van Peterson interjected. 'Come on, Jimmy, you can do better than that?'

'Look, I have faith, but I am not the most eloquent at giving lessons in redemption.' He shifted in his seat, uncomfortable at the provocation. 'I'm no preacher, I admit that, but I know what I know and I don't care much for your colleague's line of questioning.'

Tadashi leaned forward in his chair. 'Mr Carlton, if you would be so kind as to forgive me. I have been asked by the professor to contribute to this conversation, and I have no intention of upsetting you, but I will speak my mind.'

The agent tapped his cigarette. 'Go on, boy, state your piece.'

Tadashi smiled. There was one more vital move to play which would determine the result of the match. 'I believe that it is possible to travel to the high heavenly plain and reside with our ancient ancestors, and should the challenges presented to us in the afterlife be overcome, then we can be reborn on mortal Earth. This privilege has always been reserved for the most enlightened of souls, until now, until this man, until Malcolm Van Peterson.' He took a large gulp of his whisky to declare the fact that he had finished, and choked slightly on the fumes.

The Dunes Hotel bar was oblivious to the battle that had just played out under their cocaine fuelled noses. A champagne cork popped. There was an excited squeal from a dark corner that none of the bar staff wanted to investigate.

Carlton allowed the cigarette to burn in his fingertips. The conversation had taken a turn that he hadn't anticipated. He was now making up his mind whether to stay for the conference, or to file a report that would get lost down the back of a filing cabinet and never seen again.

Van Peterson cleared his throat to declare that it was his turn to reclaim the conversation. 'Through ancient regression techniques and some chemical enhancements of my own creation,' he announced, 'I am able to induce a transferential state in the subject where I believe them to be travelling to the space in-between life and death, and returning to our mortal plane.'

Carlton ran his tongue over his teeth and licked his lips in a gesture that was altogether unpleasant. 'You're making people die and come back to life?'

'Well I think that depends on your definition of dead now, doesn't it?' He smiled, allowing time for the concept to sink in.

The diamond-studded bar continued to dance an elegant, alcoholic waltz.

The agent had seen many strange things during his career at The Office, and heard his fair share of absurd claims. Most of them he had easily shouted down, some he had recorded in a file and tried to forget. He was an experienced professional sceptic and programmed to seek the truth in the ridiculous. He shook his head and shifted in the leather chair. 'So, what you're trying to tell me, Malcolm, is that you have worked out a way to travel into the afterlife, and back again?'

'The subject doesn't relocate physically. The mind becomes a platform; a vehicle for the conscious unconsciousness.'

Carlton laughed. 'This time you've completely thrown me, my old friend.' He stood up to leave and fastened a button on his jacket.

'Perhaps our point is best made with a demonstration? Van Peterson waved and a young girl drifted over to their table. 'My dear, please meet Special Agent Carlton. He will be observing your journey to enlightenment at the spiritual science conference tomorrow.'

She smiled, dreamlike and dazed; flowing hippy dress and tangled auburn hair. 'Hi, I'm Lotus Flower,' she said, considering giving him a hug.

'You really think I'm gonna stick around for your ridiculous light show?'

The professor swirled his tumbler. 'Don't tell me that you've come all the way to Las Vegas, Jimmy, and you're not tempted to take a little gamble?'

7

'Player-feed: GreySkull launches +500 nuke attack on The Immortal. Critical hit −500 life force.'

'Back off, asshole,' he shouted down the microphone.

Players in their thousands were populating the game space. He considered a hard reboot but it would leave his avatar completely unprotected. He didn't have an escape plan for this eventuality.

There was a scurrying of claws. 'You!' The animal yowled again, deep and low, from the yard. It had been calling out with increasing regularity, determined, like a scared child crying in the night. The sound sent physical shivers down his spine. It was an uncomfortable feeling. Every time it shrieked, a snaking detachment clawed deep in the pit of his stomach, pulling him into a cavernous and cold unknown. He'd even given the feeling a name. He called it spiralling. He hadn't dared mention it to Claire.

'You!'

He hit the keys but his controls were still frozen. 'I'm so dead,' he said, just as a new player teleported into game space range.

'Player-feed: Hotei raises shields around The Immortal +1000. Hotei launches +5000 nuke attack on GreySkull. Critical hit −5000 life force.'

GreySkull was obliterated. The Immortal had just been saved by an unknown player.

A private IGM popped up. The box began to scroll data at speed, so fast that it was impossible to read; numbers and images, blurred information, until eventually it settled to display a single message.

"Tengu is watching _._."

The cursor blinked.

Lars blinked.

The screen re-booted to black.

'You!'

Sudden recognition sent the spiralling sensation twisting to new depths as he realised that the creature was calling out a word. It was saying "You!" Lars climbed onto the office chair. It swivelled dangerously. He looked out of the window and directly into the shining eyes of a fox.

The animal stood by the bins and stared back. Piercing eyes illuminated deeply, fixed as fast as headlamps. It wasn't scared. It didn't move. It was totally aware of him. With a flicker of fur the fox raised not one, but nine bushy tails. They twitched individually in the moonlight.

Lars struggled to focus, trying to clear his vision, unsure what he was really looking at.

The fox lifted its head and screeched a long and conversational cry, telling tales that only foxes could understand. It looked at him and was gone. In the far distance, he heard it cry out once more. 'You!'

He didn't see her standing in the doorway. Claire was dressed and ready for work.

'Why are you standing on the chair?'

Hours had seemed like minutes. The night had

evaporated quicker than ever.

'I'm looking for my iPod.' The chair swung and he almost fell.

'Be careful!' she scolded, disappointed that he'd just lied.

He climbed down and checked the screen. The familiar logo of Atari Shock was back. He tapped the keyboard, trying not to appear desperate. To his relief the game space was operational. His controls were working again but there was still a problem, the super clan had hit one hundred and fifty thousand players and the numbers were increasing.

'Can you just leave that game alone for one minute, please? At least while I'm in the room.'

He raised his hands in a hostage situation. 'Did you hear something, just now?'

'Hear what?'

'Like a fox?'

'What does a fox sound like?'

Lars wondered how best to explain what he'd just seen. He could still sense the shrill echo of the call.

A klaxon sounded and an exit presented itself. This was his chance. He looked at her.

'Don't you bloody dare touch that keyboard, Lars Nilsson,' she threatened. 'I mean it.'

'I just need to do one more thing,' he pleaded.

'There's always one more thing.'

He selected the hot key sequence and The Immortal vanished into player-safe mode.

She snapped. 'Why do you keep doing this?' Her lip quivered on the verge of tears.

Lars and Claire had met at university, at a time when he imagined that anything was possible, when he was Captain of the indestructible Galaga. He had put more time into her pursuit than he did his economics degree, and he still managed to get in a solid twelve hours of gaming every day. He used to write her cryptic love letters, verging on the scientific, leaving her with no option than to meet him down the pub at eight. After a typical night out; couple of pints, packet of Cheese and Onion, when she went to sleep, he went to his keyboard. He was a serious gamer even then.

They shared a house in their final year. Claire fell in love. Lars fell into an online routine. At first she thought his obsession was cute, but she didn't realise the extent to which he was hooked. She expected him to change but he didn't. The attention to companionship, partnership, and their relationship that she longed for, he spent gaming. A year out of University and they were married. Nothing changed.

The real world came flooding back the instant he knew that his avatar was safe. 'What time is it? Shit. I'm going to be late.' He stumbled to the bathroom.

'I don't care about the games,' she shouted after him, 'or whatever it is that you're doing all night, but why don't we talk anymore?'

'Have you seen my iPod?'

'No, Lars,' she sighed. 'I don't know where you left your stupid iPod.'

'I'll book us a table,' came a mumble from behind the bathroom door. 'Dinner, tonight, ok?' There was the sound of the toilet flushing.

She had been rehearsing the conversation all night during uncomfortable bursts of sleepless exhaustion, but she hadn't expected it to go like this. She hadn't expected him to play the game until dawn and then just ignore her. She mouthed the words that were meant to inspire an altogether different encounter. 'Lars, I'm pregnant.'

A fin broke the waterline as Mr Chips began swimming at an angle.

Daylight shone through the grey bus window. It was raining. The top deck smelled of damp bodies and shower gel, wet hair and wetter shoes.

Lars watched the crowds push along the pavement, keen to get to work so they could count down the minutes until they would struggle in the opposite direction home. Everyone was staring at their phones; some head first in Facebook, some scanning the Atari Shock forums.

He opened the app and checked his life force. The situation was bleak. He'd taken a serious hit. The thief forums were discussing the super clan attack. One theory claimed that the game had become self-aware and was preparing to raid every single player to fund its own A.I. programme. Another thread suggested that The Immortal didn't exist after all, and was just part of the game mechanic to encourage players to spend more on micropayments. Lars preferred the A.I. theory.

In the light of day, the events of the night before seemed at a safe distance. He thought about the fox, and wondered if what he'd seen was just the result of tired eyes in bad light. Perhaps he should get his eyes tested?

He watched raindrops slide down the dirty bus window. As the lines of water spilled, they formed the familiar geometric shapes of Tetris; inverse skew, left gun, right gun, square and straight stick. He rotated them in his mind, clearing the way for more. A new theory occurred to him as he watched the rain streak the glass. What if he was exactly like his avatar, trapped in a game of chance that would never end? What was the point of trying if everything just re-set to make way for more?

The spiralling sensation twisted in his stomach. He swallowed back sickness. Something was changing. He felt like a diseased man waiting for the symptoms to show, convinced that it was learning how to manifest itself physically. He'd been getting stomach pains. It was just a matter of time. He felt claustrophobic, spinning in circles, drifting downwards, his defences weak. He had slipped through the cracks of life to become someone that he wasn't, a man who thought things that he didn't, a version of himself who was scared of the shadows.

He wasn't going to work. If there was anyone who could give him answers — it was Wiki.

8

Sugar; a quick hit of the unrefined, the cereal cerebral suspended animation − recreational drug of the hyperactive − lifesaver of the insomniac. You had to know what you were doing when it came to sugar, an uncalculated comedown could be painful.

She weighed out the granules on a small, hypersensitive scale, making sure that the exact amounts were strictly adhered to. Starting with an average bowl, she poured out a single serving of cereal. This was her baseline of thirty grams. She added a further two hundred and fifty millilitres of Hype energy drink, and exactly fifteen teaspoons of sugar. It was a tried and tested formula, the perfect amount to prevent the honeyed oats from sticking to the roof of her mouth.

Her metabolism was in overdrive. She thrived off this diet of dry cereal and sweets. Twelve minutes after consumption, Berry knew that she would feel fucking awesome. It was all she consumed, but despite the extreme sugar intake she looked fragile on first impression. She embraced the glucose overdose and became a shadow of her unsweetened self.

Her flat was a cocoon of the contemporary, a collection that would never be complete. Every available space was loaded with toys, icons and games. Her hunger was insatiable. She collected TV box sets and special edition DVDs like they were essential to saving the human race. Magazines and discs were scattered on the floor. At first glance you might ask where the checkouts were, then you might wonder how much the burglars had gotten away with. She was a consumer, a user and a pop culture leech. She had created a life that enabled some well-trodden agoraphobic and reclusive tendencies.

In her daydreams, she lived in a small cottage in the Scottish Highlands, where her interaction with the outside world was the fortnightly delivery of food and paint supplies, followed by a passionate night with the delivery girl. In another fantasy she lived in Paris, among the intellectual elite, where she lost herself to the depths of artistic melodrama, and engaged in frantic orgies with fellow bohemians. Then there was the one about a post-apocalyptic future, where zombies roamed the streets and going out after dark was a death sentence. This was her favourite. A survival bag was packed for the very eventuality, and she had already planned her escape route to the coast. When she wasn't dreaming, she lived in a small bedsit in Loughborough Junction, South London, and existed for her video games and perfect isolation.

Berry stood by the window, crunching on cereal, pulling the curtains to scan the early morning street for movement. The road was quiet.

Television filled the silence but she never watched. She was permanently logged in to Atari Shock. The player-feed spooled layers of information. War was raging online.

'Player-feed: GreySkull teleports into game space range. GreySkull launches +100 nuke attack on The Immortal.'

She was well into her second bowl, one hundred and forty five grams of sugar, when she was confronted by something more puzzling than any challenge presented by her virtual worlds. Her landline telephone rang.

She never received phone calls and took every precaution to protect her contact information. Any work request came through an agent and always in an email. She kept all interaction strictly non-verbal. Communication with the outside world was made through the safety of broadband.

She hesitated, picked up her phone, and instantly regretted it.

'Miss Butler-san?' It was a young woman. The line crackled with long distance static.

'She's out.'

'We have an opportunity.' The caller paused, following a pre-determined script where Berry was now meant to ask what the opportunity was. 'She will be grateful when she hears our offer.'

Berry considered putting the receiver down but didn't want to leave the caller with an option to phone back. 'I'll deliver the message.'

The caller sounded relieved. 'Miss Butler has been selected to join a new venture from a leading digital architecture company.'

Berry hesitated. 'Are you guys Nintendo?'

'No. We are not Nintendo,' replied the voice, matter-of-factly.

There was a momentary pause while Berry checked how The Immortal was doing, and accepted an IGM from GreySkull to join a super clan.

'I am an assistant of Dr Finjoto-shachō of The Foundation of New World Technologies. Miss Butler is invited to attend a meeting where she will be instructed further, once she has signed the confidential disclosure agreement.'

'You can trust me with details, if that's what you mean?' mumbled Berry, unsure if this kind of conversation was considered normal.

'Inform her please, that she will receive payment of one hundred and twenty thousand pounds GBP in advance of attending the meeting, and a further two hundred and fifty thousand pounds GBP on signature of a month's development work.'

Berry slipped into the imaginative safety of pretending that life was a film, and that this was just another thrilling scene, or perhaps a DVD extra.

'I trust by the sound of your breathing that you are taking notes,' said the voice. 'Dr Finjoto would not want her to miss out on such an opportunity.'

'She gets this kind of thing all the time.'

'Of course she does,' replied the caller.

Berry Butler had a gift, a talent that made her an asset to the companies that hired her and gave her the celebrity status that she shunned. Algorithms came easy. She saw her world in statistics and problem solved her way through the day. She was an incredibly fast coder, able to achieve as much as a small team in half the time, and development time was money. Some of the biggest gaming companies fought to have her on their books. She stayed true to the Indies and created worlds that were truly original.

She'd studied mathematics at college and could always be found in the I.T. room, locked into an action role-player hack and slash like Diablo on the communal PCs. She won a scholarship offered by a leading provider of serious games for major corporate and government clients, and with the cash, she'd bought her first laptop. Research kept her staring at the screen, computer on, burning game imagery into her brain. She lived through strings of numbers, patterns and puzzles, and as soon as she understood the rules, her Universe exploded, full of possibilities. Her imagination had walls to bounce off, engines that enabled a reality without limits; no boundaries, no rules. She had enabled a future in virtual spaces, and found her purpose in life. Her journey into a parallel existence online began.

'When's the meeting?'

'Tomorrow.'

She sat cross-legged on the couch and considered her reply. She wasn't used to this kind of directness. The woman wasn't asking, she was demanding. It was confrontational, like a veiled threat. She reached for her pack of Jujyfruits. This was her quick fix. She allowed the colours to speak to her, inviting her to choose an Asparagus Bundle; corn syrup, sugar, modified corn starch, natural and artificial flavours, white mineral oil, carnauba wax, caramel colouring, artificial colouring, red forty, yellow six, blue one. They lasted longer, according to Travis Bickle, and he was a man used to sleep deprivation. Sugar always made everything right. Jujyfruits were her saviour.

'What exactly do you want her to do?' she asked the conversational vacuum.

'Miss Butler-san will be developing a new gaming infrastructure, and be the first in the world to play.'

She rolled the gumdrop around her mouth. She didn't care about the money. The woman had just said all she needed to hear. 'How did you find her?' she asked, googling The Foundation of New World Technologies and new gaming platforms in two separate windows.

'We have it on good authority that she is the one.'

Berry laughed.

'Is something funny?'

'She's… the One. You know? I like my dystopian movie references.'

'I'm afraid I don't understand.'

Berry was convinced that this was all a set up. Someone had gotten hold of her direct number and published it on the thief forums. Whoever it was had done their research on what pushed her buttons. 'Surely there are other, more suitable candidates?' she asked, secretly chuffed that she was the one.

'Everything will be made clear on agreement of the project terms and conditions.'

The search brought up a corporate page for The Foundation: 'Architects of a New World Generation. Dedicated to bringing emerging technologies into hyper-reality.' New gaming platforms brought up adverts for Augmediated Reality and domestic VR consoles. Nothing new, nothing next generation.

The phone line crackled. There was a pause. The caller was checking something. 'If we are in agreement then confirmation will be sent to your inbox.'

'You've got my email?'

'The funds are insufficient?'

'No, no, it's not about the money.'

'Double payment has been authorised. Are we in agreement, Miss Butler-san?'

Berry was hesitant. She didn't understand why there was such a rush but the sense of urgency made the project seem all the more intriguing. 'You knew it was me?'

The phone line hissed static to no reply.

'I don't even know your name?'

The caller was silent.

'Hello? Ok. Yes. Of course, we're in agreement.'

At that precise moment an email arrived from The Foundation of New World Technologies.

'My name is Chieko. Your escort will arrive at six am. We look forward to receiving you in Toyko, Miss Butler. Domo arigato gozaimasu.'

9

The front door was locked, but between posters for Spider-Girl, Marvel Zombies and Scott Pilgrim, he could see a body slumped face down on the counter. He tapped on Spider-Girl's pert breast, then knocked harder on Scott Pilgrim's head and a Hulk zombie.

'Hey!' he shouted. 'This is an emergency.'

The body moved, raised its arm, and flipped Lars the finger.

'I'm serious. Wiki, is that you? It's...' he hesitated, 'it's The Immortal.'

There was a buzzing and the door clicked open.

Two screens simultaneously flashed Atari Shock data. The player-feed scrolled fresh information.

'What time is it?' moaned a moan.

'Ten-ish. How long have you been playing?'

'Thirty seven hours-ish,' mumbled the body, barely managing to raise its head from the desktop. Blood-shot eyes, skin as pale as an emergency milk chocolate bar; this was Zack, Wiki's right hand man and co-owner of The Amped Up Comic Book Store, "Where Creatures Come To Life."

Lars tried to smile at the dehydrated mess of a man before him. There was an over-long pause and the faint sound of snoring. 'Hey?'

Zack blinked and slapped his cheeks to try and wake himself.

'That never works,' said Lars. 'You need electrolytes and eggs, and a single shot of caffeine with a can of Hype, then keep eating Haribo until you feel full.'

'What time is it?'

'I just told you.'

Zack's eyes fluttered closed.

'Hey!' Lars shouted again. 'I need to speak to the Wickster.'

'Upstairs!'

Lars pushed behind the counter and the Atari Shock forums caught his eye. He saw the words, The Immortal, followed by a variety of imaginative insults on multiple threads. 'Not you as well, Zack?'

'This guy formed a super clan. We all get a piece of the immortal pie. Seen how many people are grouping? Hundreds of thousands. Quintillions even.'

Lars pushed the door with a fuck you and climbed the stairs.

Zack began tapping at the keyboard and was soon lost in the clutches of the game.

The flat above the Amped Up was an archive; boxes of comics and graphic novels were piled high next to framed superhero posters and bags of colourful t-shirts.

Wiki was locked into a laptop, a duvet over his head like a Jedi shawl, a piece of toast hanging from his lips.

'Pissed a few hundred thousand people off then, have we?' he crunched without looking up from the screen. Talking to Wiki was more like making a phone call. It rarely needed the punctuation of eye contact. Whenever it did, though, you knew that he was hooked.

'That's not why I'm here.'

'Start again. I can trade you a new buff, been working on her for a while. She's loaded and fucked.'

'How fucked?'

'Totally.'

Lars considered the offer while he moved a stack of t-shirts and slumped into an armchair. 'The Immortal is not for trade.'

'You'll never be able to use that avatar again if the super clan stay after you, and you know it. You should man up and make the sacrifice.'

'Never,' said Lars dramatically as he pulled out a blonde action figure that was jabbing into his back.

'Careful. That's a nineteen seventy-four, Dukes of Hazard, Bo Duke original. Very rare. Worth a fortune.'

Lars looked at the shit-eating grin of the plastic figurine. 'A tenner on eBay?'

'Excluding postage and packaging.'

He dropped it into a cardboard box, along with several other Dukes of Hazard, Bo Duke originals, that were equally as rare.

'How long have you been buffing up?' Wiki asked, nonchalantly.

Lars couldn't quite place a date. Had it been months since he'd first created the almighty avatar, maybe years already? 'Long enough to know that The Immortal is too precious to let go.'

'He's an Atari Shock god, right?' smirked Wiki, trying to look like he didn't care enough to be having the conversation.

This was another well-rehearsed act and Lars knew it. Whenever Wiki really wanted something, he either spoke with complete apathy or overstated sarcasm.

'You seen the forums?'

'Never read your own press,' replied Lars, considering reading the forums.

'They're all after you.'

For some reason the words made him shiver. He touched his forehead. He had a cold sweat. Perhaps he was coming down with something. 'I hadn't noticed,' he replied. He wasn't as good at playing the apathy or sarcasm game.

Wiki crunched on dry toast.

Lars didn't feel hungry. He couldn't remember the last time that he'd eaten. The nauseous spiralling sensation was hanging in the pit of his stomach.

'If you haven't come to trade, then what do you want?'

'At the time I got hacked…'

'Played badly.'

'Got hacked,' Lars repeated. 'I saw something weird.' The image of the fox was still perfectly clear, vivid and haunting; lean body and piercing eyes. 'I saw a fox with nine tails.' He stated the fact like he'd accidentally summoned the Stay Puft Marshmallow Man.

Wiki resisted the temptation to look up and instead took another crunch of toast to prove his absolute disinterest. He allowed the crumbs to dissolve in his mouth as he considered his answer. 'You saw a kitsune.'

'I saw a what?'

'Dude, Usagi Yojimbo, issue one hundred and thirty two.'

Lars was blank.

'Ok. Magic The Gathering? Jade Empire? Naruto?'

Still nothing.

Wiki became more frantic. 'Shippo from Inu Yasha? Sakura from Hyper Police? Fuck, you've never played Perfect Cherry Blossom? Ran Yakumo is the kitsune Shikigami of Yukari, the extra stage boss and the phantasm stage mid-boss.'

Lars shrugged.

'What about Ninetales? You know Ninetales, right? The Pokémon?'

'Well, what's a Pokémon doing in my bins?'

'Seek information and Wiki shall provide, but Wiki cannot be expected to explain that information,' he said with a touch of the Jedi master.

'Helpful, mate. Seriously, I appreciate it,' replied Lars, sarcastically, and this time really meaning it.

Wiki stared at the laptop and began typing. His eyes took on the glaze of someone who had no intention of saying anything for a very long time.

'Dude?' asked Lars, with a pained expression. 'Help me out here?'

Wiki paused, hit a few keys, minimised and maximised some windows, and put Atari Shock into player-safe mode. 'You saw a kitsune. Plain and simple. It's probably your spirit animal. Maybe someone close to you is about to die. Maybe you're about to die? Maybe it just wanted to say hello, who knows? But well done for having the awareness to allow yourself to be contacted by what is essentially a being from another cosmic dimension. It made first contact, and it will expect you to answer. It probably wants you to go on a spirit quest or something. Did it ask you anything?'

Lars shrugged. 'It said – "you."'

Wiki stroked the bristles on his chin. 'What, like… you look nice. I love you. You coming out to play?'

The more Lars thought about it, the more he realised that the haunting "you" had been echoing throughout the early morning for weeks. The strange sensation hit him that maybe the animal was trying to get his attention. 'Do you know a player called Hotei?'

Wiki had never looked him in the eyes like he did at that moment. 'Hotei is a bot. We have no more business to discuss.' He lowered his head and tried to feign disinterest.

'Hotei saved me at the exact moment when the fox was crying out, and then, he disappeared. It's like the game rebooted. I was sent a bunch of crazy IGMs. Look at this?' Lars pulled up the game history on his phone.

Wiki took a fleeting and overly disinterested glance. 'Remember your true self. Beware the shadow animals. This is bullshit, man. Return to Mt. Hōrai. Tengu is watching? What the fuck?'

'What's Tengu?'

'Tengu was a member of Lady Shiva's Circle of Six. It could kick Richard Dragon's ass, but didn't stand a chance against Batman.'

'OK, so one minute I'm top of the league, next I hear a fox say "you", and now I've got one of Batman's evil villains after me?'

'Exciting times, huh?'

'Someone got into my account and locked me out. Someone sent me a bunch of weird IGMs. It's connected. I know it.'

'You're saying that you had nothing to do with the poorly played decisions of The Immortal, and that a fictional animal made you screw up your game?'

'You were the one who said it was a kitsune!'

Wiki pulled the duvet higher over his head and retreated.

'You know something, don't you?'

'OK, just because it's you. So, I've tried tracing influencer I.P. recently and I came across a massive cluster of avatars in Japan, like, out of this world huge; thousands in one location. Then, just when I think I've cracked the GPS signal, they ghost, disappear, like they never existed. Perhaps Hotei is part of this ghost clan, somehow?'

'Hotei's a ghost?'

'How the fuck should I know.'

'This really isn't helping.'

'Just ignore it and be grateful for the assist. You've got more important things to worry about like an angry mob after your avatar and a Pokémon in your bins. That'll be twenty hot rocks if you please, oh, immortal one,' demanded Wiki from under his duvet with a sense of winner's pride.

Lars was more confused than ever. 'You don't deserve it. You've explained absolutely nothing.'

'Then perhaps you haven't been listening.'

Wiki's face was hidden from view but Lars could tell by the sound of his voice that he was grinning wider than the Bo Duke doll. He waited for more but there was only the sound of empty keys tapping in the cluttered room. He pulled out his phone and pinged the hot rocks into Wiki's Atari Shock account, and then jumped down the stairs realising that he was very late for work. He always came away from these meetings poorer and more confused. Today was no exception.

'It's a never ending battle against evil, dude,' Wiki muttered to himself, as he disappeared under the duvet like a creature retracting into its protective shell. 'Tengu is watching.'

10

M. V. PET RSON'S 10th SP RIT AL SCIENCE ONFERENCE

A young girl, waist too thin for her curvy frame and a dress sense that suggested this wasn't the only job she held down in Las Vegas, was pressing white plastic lettering onto a black pin conference board. Voluptuous Vampirella, as her more intimate friends knew her, shook the box and tutted. 'I'm missing letters!' She scrabbled inside the box. 'I'm missing an R, a C, an I, another C, and I'm missing a U.'

'Missing you too, baby,' boomed a distorted voice over the conference tannoy.

'Go screw yourself,' she hollered back.

'Be seeing you on stage tonight, darling,' the speaker breathed, lasciviously.

'It's double the price for you, sleazy old bastard,' she mumbled and stomped off, leaving the sign unfinished.

Elvis Presley sung Suspicious Minds as the cheap wedding rings were passed between the happy couple. The chapel organ reached a crescendo and rocked on a groove as The King of Rock and Roll acknowledged the absent crowd.

'Thank you very mush,' said Elvis. 'Now kiss her like you mean it.'

They kissed. They meant it.

'I now pronounce you, the man, an' the beautiful bride.' Elvis signalled for the cassette tape to play and he blared out a chorus of Glory, Glory, Hallelujah. The young newlyweds thought about laying their bodies down.

A palm tree rustled in the dry desert heat. Las Vegas was 104 degrees Fahrenheit and rising. It was a glorious day for a glorious wedding; frozen lime margaritas for breakfast, running hand in hand down The Strip in open necked shirts and short skirts, trying for luck at The Flamingo, a cheeky fuck in a stalled elevator at the Dunes, and then as the sun went down over the Nevada Desert, the happy couple had accosted two tourists of unknown origin to witness a blessing by the sweatiest ever King of Rock and Roll. Everyone was wasted and the champagne flowed.

'That's it. You're married!' sung Elvis, excitedly. 'Let's get Chinese food!' The King signalled for a drum roll. It came right on cue.

The happy couple collapsed into giggles.

'Now, a word of matrimonial advice from yours truly. You two have an incredible life, an' you man; you look after your incredible wife. And when you two beautiful people have beautiful babies, just remember that Elvis Aaron Presley said think with your heart and that "Elvis" is a wonderful start. You catch my drift?'

'Thank you, Elvis Aaron Presley,' said Sarah. She kissed him on a sweaty cheek.

'If it's a girl then you can call her Priscilla.' Elvis blushed behind his star spangled sunglasses.

The honeymoon suite at The El Rancho Hotel & Casino wasn't quite the luxurious penthouse that the two had imagined. It had a balcony that looked onto the car park, a television set powered by loose change — twenty cents for twenty minutes — and a bathtub that not only needed a clean, but also a plug. The bed, however, was huge, soft, and all that was on the couple's mind. The sound of the chapel organ still whirled in their ears.

Sarah was lying on her front, grinning through the warmth of a post-sex heat haze.

Mike traced a finger down her slender, naked body and then carefully placed his glass of frozen lime margarita on her arse.

'That's bloody freezing!' she shrieked, pushing him off the bed.

He necked the rest of his drink and hurled it across the hotel suite. It smashed into the wall and they laughed with reckless irresponsibility.

'Another margarita, Mrs... Hey, what are we going to call ourselves?'

She rolled over and kissed him deeply. 'Hmm,' she replied, sleepily. 'I got it, Mr and Mrs Vegas.'

He lit up a joint, took a toke, and handed her the rest.

'No, wait,' she said, excitedly. 'Mr and Mrs — Doctor Vegas.' She laughed. 'That doesn't sound right. I'm a bit drunk.'

He smiled. 'It's perfect.'

'Thank you spiritual science, whatever you are.' She reached for the room service menu. 'Club sandwiches?'

'I like to think that it was the Universe that brought us together,' he mumbled and pulled a toke on the joint.

She kissed him on the cheek as a reward. 'Club sandwiches and red wine,' she hummed, contentedly. 'A wedding feast.'

He rolled over and picked up the phone to dial room service. She threw herself on him before he could place the order.

Mike wrapped a towel around his waist just in time to answer the door. They sat on the bed, naked, eating fries and sandwiches, swooning in the thrill of elopement.

'I have lost all concept of time,' he said. He pulled the curtain to reveal Las Vegas in a comatose slumber. A pink neon Vacancy sign anticipated the sunrise. 'It's not even dawn.'

'What happens at dawn?' she asked with mock suspense.

'I turn into Michael Jackson and dance to Thriller.'

'Hah! Maybe I turn into Olivia Newton-John?'

'I'd like that.'

'I bet you would,' she pushed him away. He threw back a pillow. She caught it, and hurled it back in his face.

'Easy now, Olivia.'

'Don't tell me to get physical or I'll divorce you on the spot,' she laughed.

'I wouldn't dare,' he said, reaching for the fries.

They were silent, until Sarah opened up the conversation that they had both been avoiding.

'It's going to be ok, isn't it?' she asked, eating a French fry to keep it casual.

He poured himself another large glass of wine and breathed out. 'Honestly?'

'We're married now, so you have to tell me the truth.'

'We should have cancelled the tour. We should have found someone else.'

'I was thinking about papa, not her.'

'Your dad knows what he's doing. He's been through all of this before.'

'I suppose you're right.' She took a drink. He immediately topped up her glass without asking.

'Have you noticed how much she's changed since New York?' he asked.

'Lotus Flower?'

'Let's never call her that.'

'That's her name.'

'That's definitely not her name.' He laughed and stared out of the window at the rising glow of the sunrise. 'She's been getting worse. It's like she doesn't quite come back, you know, after each trip?'

Sarah used the soft pillow to cover her body and listened. She knew that he was anxious, but they had been so busy preparing for the conference that they hadn't discussed it. The avoidance tactics had been a little too successful. When the weekend had finally arrived, the stress found itself an unexpected release and exploded into a fit of passion the moment work was complete. She hadn't expected to be sitting, naked in the lotus position, eating club sandwiches in a cheap hotel room at four in the morning after a shot-gun wedding. Then again, she hadn't expected to meet Mike.

'She can handle herself,' she said.

'I don't like the way they're pushing her.'

'They?' Sarah sat upright. 'Is this because of the new guy?'

Mike put down his wine glass and sat on the edge of the bed. The intimacy was over.

'Don't you think it's strange that we get this far with the project and then he turns up? Your father takes him in, just like that?'

'He's here because he's an expert, and he has money.'

'I know we need the funding, I get that, but there are limits, Sarah. He's convincing your father to accelerate the program much quicker than we should. It's exploitation.'

'She's hardly being kept against her will, Michael.'

'Sounds like something your papa would say.'

'Isn't that what the people want? Why we're here in Vegas, for a show?' She took a bite of the club sandwich and spoke with her mouth full. 'Tadashi? He's just enthusiastic.'

'Why are you defending him all of a sudden?'

She re-positioned herself on the bed. 'Are we about to have our first argument?'

Mike laughed and pretended to look at an invisible watch on his wrist. 'We managed, what, three hours?'

'Well, it was good while it lasted, Doctor Vegas,' she said.

'It was the best, Mrs Vegas,' he replied, catching the smile in her eyes.

She touched his arm and they pushed the tray of food to the floor.

11

One joule of energy is all that's needed to lift a single piece of fruit exactly twenty centimetres into the air.

Her heart skipped as an executive limousine rolled into view. Berry put her unfinished cereal bowl on the window ledge and added a large beaker of water to the wooden tub that housed a white lotus flower. The bloom was incredible, with many curvaceous petals, fragrant and fertile. She tried not to think that it would be dead by the time she got back.

She closed her laptop just as a series of instant pop-ups littered the screen.

Remember your true self. Return to Mt. Hōrai. Tengu is watching.

The messages went unseen, lost in the white noise of her IGM history amongst the thousands of competing chats, flirts, bribes, temptations and game threats.

She switched her Atari Shock avatar to player-safe mode and hoped there would be Wi-Fi on the flight. Three travel bags were packed with last minute essentials, grabbed at random from her clutter. She was as ready as she could be.

Glasses on. Light off. Laptop in Crumpler bag. Pineapple flavour Jujyfruit in her mouth. Berry was about to leave her flat for the first time in months. She floated down the stairs, having consumed enough sugar to lift two hundred and thirty-six million, six thousand and fifty-two pieces of fruit.

Outside, she found herself face to face with a woman wearing a black power dress and a blonde smile.

'I thought for a minute that you'd changed your mind?' she said.

Berry turned to push the door and check it was definitely closed.

'I'm Sarah Clarkson.'

Berry smiled, embarrassed, suspicious, or both. They shook hands.

'This way, Miss Butler.' Sarah gestured to the car and the door automatically opened. 'We have a busy schedule once we arrive. You may want to sleep.'

Berry wasn't sure if she should explain that she hadn't really slept in weeks. A man appeared. 'Dr Finjoto?' she asked.

'Oh no, he's not important. He'll look after your bags.' Sarah looked at the three sacks filled with who-knows-what. 'You like to travel with a lot of stuff, don't you?'

'I don't like to travel,' Berry replied.

The man reached for her laptop. 'I'll keep this with me.' She clutched it to herself and avoided eye contact.

He bowed politely and put the rest of her bags in the limousine, returning to the driving seat without saying a word.

The street was quiet. There were no cars or people. Yellow streetlights reflected off the perfectly clean car bonnet.

'After you, Miss Butler, please?' gestured Sarah to the open door.

The car was impeccably clean and smelled of leather. There was a mini bar, a bunch of glossies and a small TV screen mounted in the dashboard between the front seats.

Sarah used the rear view mirror to make eye contact. 'There's a welcome pack on the table in front of you. I'd recommend that you read it. It has some background information on Dr Finjoto's outstanding work.'

The front cover displayed a logo for The Foundation of New World Technologies.

'Help yourself to the bar. It's all for you. Or we could stop for coffee, if you'd prefer?'

'I don't need booze or caffeine, ta,' said Berry as she crunched on the Jujyfruit. It occurred to her that no one knew where she was going. Even she didn't know where she was going. More upsetting though, was the sudden realisation that she had no idea who she would tell.

The car pulled away and she felt her stomach lurch as a piece of her soul was left behind on the cold morning roadside.

There was a scurry of claws as Kitsune lifted her nose over the fence and pulled herself higher to sniff the air. 'You!' she yowled, but the limousine was too far down the road. She cursed in annoyance and dropped to the dirt.

'There's an iPhone in the seat locker. It's yours for the duration of the contract.'

Berry slipped the phone into her bag. She took a deep breath and remembered her motivation. Everything would be ok. She was going to be the first to play.

'It's forty minutes to the airport. We're fast tracking, so I just need your passport.' Sarah caught her eye in the mirror.

'Your passport, please, Miss Butler? It'll save us time when we get to border control.'

She handed over her passport and watched Sarah zip it into a black flight wallet.

'Ok. I'll wake you when we get there.'

Berry sat back and watched the houses turn to motorway as they headed for the airport. A gust of wind twisted damp leaves in a spiral in the exact spot where Kitsune had just disappeared.

12

The BBP was a pharmaceutical company whose name was made up of the initials of the conglomerate of families that had founded it more than fifty years ago; Bishop, Banes and Price. Lars and his friend, Stu, had updated this to appeal to a more modern clientele and subsequently changed the acronym to Bigger, Better, Pills. This was abbreviated further by staffers in the loop to simply − The Pill.

It was eight am, a time when the real backbone of the company cleaned up the loose ends from the day before. They filed their reports, planned exec meetings, and brewed coffee pots ready for another day of slowly poisoning the world.

The offices were open plan, grey and blue fabric, the corporate colours of conformity. White-collar staff were arriving and opening their Facebook profiles, counting down the minutes to the next cigarette break or snack stop.

Julia Miller could taste the granules in her cup and was convinced that over consumption of instant coffee was giving her rheumatoid arthritis. Rain persisted outside. She'd worn the open toed sandals, a big mistake. She could make out her own bleary image in the smudged windows of a neighbouring high rise; repetitive strain injury, a thousand

Julia Millers watching the drip, drip, drip of their day. She noticed the flashing message light and routinely pushed the answering machine button, knowing full well that another of Lars' excuses would be cued up and ready to play.

'Hi, Julia. It's Lars…'

She reached for her nail polish.

'Just a quick message to say that I'm running a bit late today, so if you could make sure that the morning reports are filed, that would be great. Yeah. You know how it is. [A breath]. Buses. [Quick intake of air]. So please carry on with everything you're doing. Thanks for being brilliant [pause] and good luck [pause]. I'll see you in an hour or so. Ok then.' [Dead tone].

Working at The Pill was about as routine as it got. The fact that Lars spent most of his time absent, playing Atari Shock, chatting with Stu, or sleeping while pretending to be on a break, hadn't gone unnoticed by the woman who was supposed to be his junior colleague. When it came to professional reputation, Lars wasn't top of the league.

He suffered from terminal cycle syndrome where every hour of every day was exactly the same, to the second, to the millisecond, to the nano − Collate. Save. Sigh. Syndicate. Daydream. He would sit in the office, staring at the cheap plastic clock; a glorified librarian with nothing to read, a pen pusher with no pen to push, just an on button at the start of the day and an off button at the end.

Julia made it look like he was doing a reasonable job by taking on all of his responsibilities. Her long game was to get noticed. She would slingshot around him and eventually become manager in his place. She was consciously keeping notes on his absence. It had become her own private game.

She'd been organising a series of international projects that had been immediately handed over. There were requests from around the globe for pharmaceutical development liaison programmes in India, Japan, the USA and Switzerland. Julia dealt with them all professionally and with precise attention to detail. She was a consistently neat person, always triple checking documents. The programmes had been a huge success, thanks to Julia, but the international account managers at the BBP weren't even aware of her name.

She took another glug of coffee and waggled her toes to keep the blood flowing. A quick glance at Facebook. She popped a Zomec pill, company discounts applied. She noticed that Stu was staring at her from across the office again. She washed down the pill and closed the Facebook window. She'd been flirting with him over the past few weeks but never let him close enough for conversation. She smiled and checked her email for the thirtieth time in as many minutes.

The BBP operated a shared Outlook system, so colleagues could send an internal message and then literally stalk the recipient to see if it had been read. This also made it easier for Julia to manage Lars' inbox. He had gladly given her the authorisation. She managed a system of two inboxes; a first level that received the information meant for Lars, and forwarded it on to the second level which did all the work, and then sent back to the first level for sign off. The system worked perfectly. It suited Julia's control freak tendencies, and allowed Lars to get away with murder.

She looked at the screen and noticed that the first level was increasing in new messages. The numbers were already beyond (56).

'Ugh, what's going on with all this spam, Lars?'

"Remember your true self." "Beware the shadow animals." "Fulfil your life path." They appeared to be random self-help adverts.

'He's so bloody useless,' she mumbled, as she selected all and clicked to move them to the trash. As she did so, the messages closed themselves and then automatically opened the next one in the chain.

Return to Mt. Hōrai. Tengu is watching.

These messages also closed and re-opened. The PC had taken on a life of its own.

'Erm,' she shouted aloud to the open plan office, 'my computer's gone funny!'

More messages appeared, faster and faster, the screen mounting black lines of unread windows sent from an unknown address. She reached for her phone and hit the instant dial for IT. It was engaged. The keyboard wasn't responding as her PC rocked into meltdown; a cyber spasm of bit rot fitting unread messages at the inbox, hundreds every second (505).

'What the flipping heck is going on?'

'Problem, darling?' Stu was standing by her side.

She minimised her Facebook window. 'Oh, hello,' she smiled, pretending to be surprised to see him. 'You don't know anything about computers, do you?'

He pulled a chair over and sat slightly too close. 'What's up?'

Julia waved at the screen.

He stole the opportunity for a quick glance down her cleavage and then studied the messages intently. 'Have you signed up to some sort of horoscope thing?'

'It's Lars' account, actually.'

'Well, he certainly wouldn't use the company email for anything other than company business, right?'

Of course Stu would protect him. She knew that they were best friends who spent most of their time talking about Atari Shock. It was this fact that put her off pursuing any kind of relationship with him. She hoped that he hadn't seen her minimise the window, and wondered if she had signed up to a dodgy horoscope.

'It looks like spam,' he said, tapping at the keyboard. He hit control, alt, delete and escape. He hit delete several times. Then he realised that he looked like he didn't know what he was doing. 'Did you call IT?'

'Engaged.'

'I suggest you turn it off and turn it back on again.'

'I don't think I have the authority to do that,' she said.

'Allow me.' Stu flicked the off switch like he was James Bond. The screen went black. 'Never fails.' He smiled and thought about asking her for an instant coffee break to celebrate.

There was a hum and buzz as the screen booted to life. It whirred faster and began processing more incoming messages from an unknown sender (1,109). The messages contained the same text.

Return to Mt. Hōrai. Tengu is watching.

Another voice called out. 'Aw, it's so fucked.'

The Pill was on meltdown. All of the office computers were receiving the same random messages. The intensity of the emails was disturbing, hundreds of thousands of strange messages, popping up every few seconds. Everyone looked to each other for answers and for someone to blame.

Julia's desk phone rang. She gave Stu a fuck off or I won't fuck you later look.

'No. He's not here right now. I'm sorry, what?' She seemed more annoyed than usual. 'Well, yes. I'll tell him.' She hung up, seeming utterly defeated, and turned the computer off at the wall.

Stu stood beside her like a lost dog.

13

Las Vegas ached from the night before; feeling in its pockets for loose change, managing the cocaine comedown, hoping it wore a condom, trying to remember where it left its room keys, wondering why the car wasn't with the valet, hoping that the girl would just leave without asking any questions.

The spiritual science conference would start in an hour. Mike wasn't going to risk attending it sober. Hiding behind dark sunglasses, he was sipping a frozen margarita for breakfast; fresh lime, Cointreau, Tequila Gold and plenty of crushed ice.

'Are you ok?' asked a curious voice. 'You look terrible.'

Mike looked up and focused on the buffet hall. It was the newbie, Tadashi, holding a breakfast plate of tropical fruit.

'Looks can be deceiving. I feel great.'

Tadashi sat without being invited. 'Do you really think you should be drinking?'

'Do you really think you shouldn't?'

Tadashi ignored him and assessed his plate. He singled in on an individual piece of watermelon. 'What happened to you two last night?' he inquired, nonchalantly.

'Who?'

'You and Sarah Clarkson?'

Mike blinked away acrobatic, orgiastic flashbacks. 'We had some drinks.' He adjusted his sunglasses. 'Elvis is alive, right?'

Tadashi attempted a flat smile, but failed.

Mike sat back in his chair. 'I'm glad you came over,' he said. 'I want to talk to you about Lori.'

'Lotus Flower?'

He laughed. 'Sure, man, whatever you want. Look, I'm…' he chose his words carefully, 'I'm concerned that she's being over-stretched.'

Tadashi stared, mouth downturned, unimpressed.

'How about we just put on a show and get out of town, ok?'

Tadashi carefully placed his fork in the centre of his fruit plate. 'I am here to work with the great Malcolm Van Peterson for one reason, to usher in the age of enlightenment. He is on the verge of a new dawn, a new world. Does this not excite you, Michael?'

'It's Mike. Mike is fine.'

'We owe this achievement to the world, do we not? Provando e riprovando. Are you not a proud member of the Accademia del Cimento?'

'Yes, yes, all that, but seriously, look at the girl? She's lost it, man. She hasn't properly come back since New York. She's taken way too much.'

Tadashi began to divide the individual pieces of fruit into separate colours; red melon, blue berry and green kiwi. 'New York,' he said, 'was the greatest regression experiment ever documented. It was a defining moment for spiritual science. Professor Van Peterson's work was truly recognised on the international stage.'

'We crossed a line,' said Mike, sternly.

'I've studied the tapes. You did nothing wrong.'

'It's not about what happened on stage. It's what happened after that I'm worried about.'

Tadashi raised an eyebrow.

'I don't know how to describe it. Lori was, well, for want of a more scientific phrase, she was fucking possessed.'

Tadashi shook his head, disapprovingly. 'It was simply the darkness coming into the light.'

'Something spoke through her, and it spoke directly to us.'

'And what do you think that thing was, Michael?'

'Look, I'm as broadminded as they come. I don't get easily fazed, but what I saw that night, what happened to her after the regression was something that I've never seen before. I was monitoring the results. Her heart rate was normal. There was no evidence of heightened serotonin or adrenaline. Whatever Malcolm did resulted in a full on schizophrenic episode. She suffered a complete psychotropic breakdown. She said she was a god.'

Tadashi didn't blink. 'And this surprises you?'

'Look, I understand the point of regression therapy but why would she say a thing like that?'

'Because, Michael, maybe for that brief moment − she was?'

He took a moment and reset the conversation by raising his hand to order another margarita. 'Want one? Fresh limes?'

'No.'

'Aw, come on. They're good.'

Tadashi shook his head.

'Your loss.'

'Why are you here, Michael Jones?' asked the assistant, with a hint of condescension.

'It's Mike Vegas now. Dr Vegas to you.' The tequila was beginning to kick in.

'How did you come to join the Academy?' His tone was dominant. He was vying for authority.

'I answered an advert. Simple as that.'

'And what is your purpose?'

'My job is to make sure things don't get out of hand. Which is why I'm talking to you.'

'Your job, your responsibility,' he paused to exhale, commanding Mike's full attention, 'is to assist Professor Van Peterson in his search for enlightenment.'

The margarita arrived. Mike threw a twenty on the waiter's tray and thanked him. Were his credentials being questioned, or did Tadashi always behave this way, he wondered?

The advert had been suitably incongruous; a renowned spiritual scientist was seeking professional medical assistance for the presentation of a live stage show. It was a legal requirement. He saw the opportunity for easy money, and one where he wouldn't be forced to mix in the same academic and medical circles that he was used to. There would be no accidental bumping into old colleagues. That's all he wanted. He'd struck it lucky and found somewhere under the radar, where he could make a simple living and forget about the dark cloud hanging over his professional reputation.

On first impression he had concluded that Malcolm Van Peterson was a showman, an old Wild West alchemist pitching miracle cures and ointments. A little bit of showbiz couldn't hurt, he thought. The first few months were even enjoyable. Then, Van Peterson's daughter, Sarah Clarkson, joined the team; recent divorcee, hot headed young blonde with a power suit to match, and life got a hell of a lot more interesting.

They went on tour for a summer and their affair began right from the start. They slept their way through the Deep South and up to the ill-fated New York City. The tour was then designed to take in the West Coast, including a residency in Las Vegas, but when Tadashi appeared the atmosphere turned from showmanship to some kind of religious propaganda. They had been working together barely a few days but the young Japanese assistant was really beginning to cramp his style.

Mike had drunk half of his margarita before either of them spoke again. He decided not to take the bait.

'I'll help the old man search for whatever it is he wants to search for. Just so long as no one has a cardiac arrest in the process,' declared Mike. 'That is my one and only responsibility.'

Tadashi let out an audible grumble, clearly annoyed at Mike's lack of passion for the cause. 'Do you not understand what we are trying to achieve?'

He was a couple of drinks down and decided not to let himself be intimidated. 'Half a million dollars?' he asked.

Tadashi sniffed, offended. 'No, Michael,' he corrected. 'The Accademia del Cimento have studied the avoidance of speculation since sixteen fifty-seven. We are approaching a new dawn. It is with this spirit of learning that we find ourselves here today, ushering in the age of enlightenment. Provando e riprovando.'

'You already said that,' Mike interrupted, trying to undermine him.

'Do you know what it means?'

He slurped down his margarita. 'I have a feeling that you're about to tell me.' He smiled.

'Experiment and confirm. That is our mantra.'

'If at first you don't succeed,' nodded Mike.

'Try and try again, yes,' agreed Tadashi, excitedly. 'This is a re-evaluation of the properties that define humanity, a re-definition of our very existence. The Academy is the new authority, on the verge of a revolution of science, and it is of monumental importance.'

'Don't big yourself up now. That kind of talk is how wars start.'

'No, Michael! It is not how wars start.'

'I wasn't being literal. Calm the fuck down.' He adjusted his dark sunglasses.

'You will listen to me. I am explaining to you the importance of our mission.'

'Ok. Ok. I get it. It's important. Now relax. There are paying customers watching.' He raised his glass to a couple of tourists.

'You are about to witness a new dawn, a new age of awareness, and this is the aim and purpose of the Academy.' Tadashi spoke with a raised voice. 'The Academy will untangle the random. The Academy will try and try again. We will experiment and we will confirm, with unity and collaboration, until we chart the map between this world and the next.'

'The map of what?' spluttered Mike through his drink. 'I thought you were talking bullshit before, but now you're setting a new record.'

Tadashi was visibly annoyed, squirming uncomfortably on his chair. 'I am not talking bullshit.'

'Jesus, you take everything so literally. Chill the fuck out, man.'

'We are defining an existence beyond this mortal realm. Man has landed on the moon, but our experiments will take man to the next dimension, into the next life.'

'Are you sure you haven't been drinking?' interrupted Mike.

Tadashi stood up, kicking over his chair. 'You are an ignorant man, Michael. You have been judged. I have nothing more to say to you.' He walked out of the breakfast room.

Mike scratched his head, shocked by the tide of arrogance that he'd just witnessed. 'You have been judged,' he mimicked in a childish voice. He caught the bartender's eye and signalled for another margarita.

14

The image of a cerebral cortex, in all its grey glory, spanned a banner at the entrance to the Las Vegas auditorium that was about to host Malcolm Van Peterson's tenth spiritual science conference. It wasn't the most appropriate image but he hadn't seen it and no one was going to mention it.

The conference hall had a capacity for seven hundred. Only a couple of hundred seats were filled with the usual freaks and sceptics. They brought some funding in but Sarah knew that they were making a loss. This was her secret to carry, and a burden that she kept from her father.

Mike sat in the wings with Lori, or Lotus Flower, as she had insisted on being called since New York. He took her pulse and jotted down some notes. 'You're good to go.'

She beamed back at him, her eyes already showing signs of tripping out on the acid tab she'd taken forty-five minutes earlier.

The chime of a Tibetan gong rang out. The room hushed. Everyone waited. There was a cough. The rustle of a popcorn bag. The bell resonated. The lights dimmed. A Buddhist chant and a sub bass wafted in. A large avatar of Vishnu, the Hindu god of protection, was lowered onto the stage. The audience applauded and whooped as it settled. A spotlight shone on Vishnu's face. It appeared to both bless and judge the rowdy gathering.

Special Agent Carlton was taking notes at the centre of the auditorium. 'What the hell is that?' he laughed to himself when he saw the avatar. Tadashi was within earshot, just a few seats behind.

Professor Van Peterson walked slowly into view. The music changed to a synthesiser led arpeggiated loop; a deep and dramatic atmospheric drone. A spotlight followed him to reveal a red armchair at the centre of the stage. The light narrowed as he waited, saying nothing, staring into space. He looked through the audience like they weren't even there. He breathed, shallow and calm.

The professor eventually looked up and blinked in the glare of the spotlight. He composed himself and spoke. 'There have been many thinkers, many revolutionaries, contradictors who were deemed dangerous by the Holy Office. They transcended the obvious and asked questions, offering alternatives to the common ways of thinking. They fought for a system of beliefs that challenged the given doctrine. In the early renaissance of the fifteenth century, Copernicus allowed us to re-evaluate our understanding of the Universe by declaring that the Sun was at its centre, and not the Earth, as was commonly believed. His follower, Galileo, was labelled a heretic for supporting this theory. Together, they ushered in a new age of enlightenment.'

The musical drone continued.

'The Universe is forever expanding, uncharted, and awaiting a new generation of explorers to undertake a voyage into the unknown. We are those voyagers. We are a modern Galileo. We are Copernicus. We are a revolution.

We have a right. No. We have a responsibility, as creators of our own existence, to sit on the edge of that existence and to explore, to experiment, and to advance ourselves. But what is advancement? Is it change? Is it understanding? Is it becoming — like a god?'

Several uptight Republicans sat forward in their seats and got up to leave. Van Peterson noticed them being escorted to the exit by torch light. His lip quivered but he continued.

'Today we find ourselves with a similar challenge, to ask questions and to uncover the truth, to determine what control we have over our perceived reality, and to re-evaluate the natural laws of humanity. For the first time, we hold this power, right here and right now.' He took a moment to pull himself together and spotted Sarah standing in the wings.

She held her hand up to wave. He returned a sad smile that she found strangely alarming.

'Tonight, on this very stage, you will experience the New World.'

A man in the audience whooped and drank his extra-large Coca Cola. Popcorn bags rustled in anticipation of the main event.

'Quantum jumping,' said Van Peterson. His voice was somehow stronger and more confident. 'That is the name on which I have settled. It came to me last night, while discussing our incredible progress with my colleagues, both of whom I hope are in the audience alongside you tonight.'

Heads turned, trying to single out the clever ones. Carlton slid down in his seat.

'Quantum jumping,' he repeated, searching for hidden meaning in the words. He began to pace the stage.

'Fucking jump already!' shouted a man. Several people laughed.

Tadashi noted the guilty individual.

The professor ignored the heckler. 'This evening, you will witness a new dawn of past life regression. I ask our bold traveller to step forward, and to take the seat of sacrifice. Lotus Flower, please come forth.'

There was a ripple of laughter throughout the auditorium.

Mike walked Lori on stage. He held her arm to steady her. She was completely oblivious of the crowd.

'Please, sit.'

'Woo, Lotus Flower,' someone shouted.

She settled on the chair.

'Earlier this morning, I was talking with Lotus Flower…'

'She's not a flower,' came a drunken shout.

Van Peterson signalled for the music and his microphone to be made louder. 'We have started her journey into the next life. She has been taken to a new level of heightened consciousness. She is standing on the precipice; many lifetimes of history behind, many opportunities ahead. Shall we meet the real her?'

He no longer spoke to the audience. They were merely eavesdropping on the process. 'Hear my voice, Lotus Flower. Feel your soul expand. Become more than just the one, embrace the many. You are everyone you have ever been. You are complete. You are reaching out across the void, into the realm of formlessness. Feel yourself embrace the arms of the many. They catch you and they comfort you. They raise you up as your body lies dormant, the vessel that is no longer necessary. Their touch is warm to your skin. You are free.'

She sat, perfectly still, eyes closed, and then she spoke. 'We receive you.'

The room fell deathly quiet. This was exactly what they had come for. They were captivated.

'Tell me your wishes, ancient ones?' asked Van Peterson.

'We have been waiting for the one to lead us into the light.'

'What light?'

'The light that brightens the passage to your dimension.'

'Do you see the passage?' asked Van Peterson.

'We do.'

'How long have you lived this life?' he asked.

'Since the existence of existence itself.'

Van Peterson caught Mike's eye. He looked uncomfortable. 'And where are you now?'

'I am here, and I am now.'

'Woo!' shouted a lone heckler, only to feel Tadashi's firm grip on his shoulder.

'What do you see?'

'Yaoyorozu no Kami,' she replied in a voice that was beginning to sound unlike her own.

Agent Carlton stood up.

'Get down,' hissed an audience member. 'You're blocking the view.'

Carlton ignored him and moved forward a few seats, his eyes locked on Lori.

'The uncountable infinite gods,' she continued. 'The gods that reside in everything. They have been betrayed.'

Dust drifted across the spotlight beam; a microscopic particle in an infinite Universe.

'The eight immortals have no right to rule as they claim.'

'Tell me about the eight immortals? Who are they,' asked Van Peterson.

'Izanami and Izanagi; they have transcended the void. They do not belong in mortality. There will be a choice, a choice to repair the broken fragments of the afterlife, to return the immortals to their rightful place as slaves of the shadow wielder, or to witness the earth and sky tear each other apart, leaving the chaos of darkness.' Her voice became more aggressive. 'We send a warrior demon to return them to Hōrai, where they shall be judged by the great Oracle. We send a Tengu.'

'Woo, a Tengu!' shouted a voice in the auditorium.

'You are a drip of water in the cold pool that spreads underfoot. We are the guardians of your death.'

There was silence followed by a burst of uncomfortable laughter.

Van Peterson was assessing the situation. He quickly made his decision. 'You must return to us now, Lotus Flower,' he said. He looked to Mike, who was waiting in the wings.

'She stays,' said the voice.

'You will not keep her,' shouted Van Peterson.

The audience rustled, shocked by his outburst.

Mike took a step forward. Sarah stopped him. 'Wait,' she whispered. 'Not yet.'

'This is not acceptable, ancient ones,' demanded Van Peterson, appearing flustered.

Mike shook his head and pushed free. He rushed on stage, carrying a tray of implements. He took a syringe, tapped it and injected Lori's arm. 'Hey, little lady,' he whispered. 'That's enough fun for today. Come back to us now, ok?'

'Professor?' she called out, weak and frightened.

'Follow my voice.' Van Peterson held her hand.

Her body jolted in a spasm and her voice changed pitch. 'She stays.'

Lori fell unconscious. The professor let out a frustrated cry. He was losing her.

Mike felt the hairs on the back of his neck shiver and turn cold.

'We are the Protogenoi. We are the first-born. We are the primordial gods; Chaos, Chronos, Oceanus, Gaea, Hemera and Nyx. You have opened the passage. Soon, we will awaken and take back our ancient birth right.' The voice was no longer hers. 'You know how this ends, mortal?'

Van Peterson looked defeated, aware that the voice was now coming from no fixed position. He knew the answer. He could barely speak. 'With a sacrifice,' he replied.

The audience were stone cold, silent.

A shadow flickered off stage.

Mike felt a sensation curl deep in his stomach − the feeling of impending dread.

Carlton moved to the front of house and stood at the side of the stage, anticipating the first move of a skilful opponent.

Tadashi watched, fascinated.

'I am not afraid of you,' said Van Peterson, with a new found confidence.

The lights in the auditorium went out. There was total darkness.

The audience began to mutter. Then, spontaneously, they broke into rapturous applause. More people joined in until they were all cheering the showman and his magnificent Las Vegas spectacle.

The emergency lights flickered on. Mike and Van Peterson lifted Lori to her feet and carried her off stage.

There was whooping and shouting. Cries of bravo! Cowboy whistles. The stamping of excited feet. The crowd were shouting for more. Cheers and hooting. Excited squeals. A baying snarl. A terrified scream. The rip of bloody flesh and the pounding of otherworldly claws on mortal ground.

'Bring on the dancing girls!' shouted a man, as a creature loomed up in front of him. His smile turned to an anxious laugh just before his head was ripped clean from its torso.

Mike and Van Peterson stood in the wings. They watched the slaughter consume everything in its path as it washed over the auditorium. There was terrified screaming, pushing and scratching, and the trampling of feet. It was a desperate struggle in the darkness. People ran but were cut down in seconds.

Tadashi had climbed up on stage and was standing, transfixed, right in the middle of it all.

'Hey, you!' shouted Carlton. 'Get the hell out of here.' There was a growl from behind. The agent pushed a woman out of the way and threw himself to the floor, only to hear her scream as she was struck down.

There was an audible crack, the flurry of movement, and the auditorium suddenly filled with small, winged creatures that hovered in the air. They were insects – grey moths.

Mike and Carlton watched, amazed, as the moths created a faint blue aura around each human form. The auditorium filled with tall, blue, circular vortexes, each completely covering an audience member.

He felt a blow to the back of his head and Mike fell to the floor, unconscious.

Carlton scrambled out of the building, leaving them all for dead.

The flurry ceased as quickly as it had begun, and the threat vanished, along with the entire audience.

15

Berry checked the flight information and calculated the numbers. She was travelling at thirty-six thousand feet over Russia, at five hundred and forty-three miles an hour. It was minus eighty-three Fahrenheit outside. The cabin was pressurised to eight thousand feet. At this altitude, there would be twenty-five per cent less oxygen than at sea level. If the cabin lost pressure then there was a risk of hypoxia at around eleven thousand feet, reducing the alveolar oxygen tension in the lungs and subsequently the brain, causing slow thinking, loss of consciousness, and eventually death.

She sucked on a banana Jujyfruit. Her breathing was steady. The pressure had made her ears pop only once. She calculated that there was an acceptable zero point five percent chance of hypoxia.

Two cans of Hype energy drink and she was wide-awake, frantically explaining the rules of Atari Shock to Sarah, who hadn't actually asked to hear them. She sat quietly, staring at the small television screen in the back of the seat.

Berry felt like she hadn't spoken to a human being for a very long time, and apart from the phone call, she hadn't.

Her laptop was open on the small seat table. They were flying business class. There was in-flight Wi-Fi.

'Each player starts with 1000 kudos points. This is split by the player into five game-play categories; money, influence, drugs, guns, and random. Respect and status are earned by total hours of game play, and the more you have, the higher up the world leader board you climb.'

Sarah smiled and tried to indicate that she was more interested in the in-flight movie. George Peppard was kissing Holly Golightly. George was a fast mover. Berry wasn't getting the hint.

'Everyone's after the top spot. The top twenty positions are valuable real estate,' she continued between chugs of energy drink. 'The best players get extra points for the next game and can move on to become a super-pimp. Now, the super-pimp…'

'How often do you play this thing?' interrupted Sarah, realising that Berry was likely to keep talking all of the way to Japan.

'Well, always. I'm always playing,' she shrugged.

Sarah sat up. 'You're logged in now?'

'Course.'

'Go on then, what's happening?'

She calmly tapped a few keys. 'We've just lost a great player. One of the best. No one is in the mood for war.'

Sarah nodded, feeling like she was missing the point. 'Do a lot of people play then?'

'About seven million at any one time, but there's no guarantee they're actual people. Could be bots.'

'Bots?'

'You know, fake accounts. Little programmes that hoover up data like fruit flies.' Berry gave the conversation a slight pause and then continued undeterred. 'So, you can live out your fantasies...'

'As long as your fantasies involve drugs, guns and gambling, right?' interrupted Sarah.

'Yeah, but if Atari Shock's not your thing, there are other games out there that might float your boat? Mostly fantasy MMOs. I'm Splendour the trader in Silk Road. An Asmodian assassin called QueenFly in Aion. And a Night Elf called Melissa in Warcraft.'

'How do you find the time to play all these games?'

Berry rolled the Jujyfruit around her mouth. 'You make the time.'

'Couldn't you invent a game where you can be something nice, like a really good painter or a celebrity chef?'

Berry smiled with what was more of a grimace and lowered her head. Sarah thought she'd finally won a moment of peace and drifted back to the movie. Before she could relax there was an abrupt change of gear and Berry kept talking.

'Now, the super-pimp is all powerful. Everyone is out to do over the super-pimps, even people that you think are in your clan. So, to stay on top, you got to stay awake and stay online. Snooze you lose. When you're offline you can't respond. Sitting duck, mate. In player-safe mode, you're only as good as the co-ordinates you pre-programme. You really need to fend off attacks with bribes or have higher gun points if it comes to a shoot out. Or get the clan together and gank 'em. Gank 'em good.'

'Gank 'em good?' Sarah repeated the words, trying them out for herself.

Berry smiled. 'Now you're getting it.'

Sarah really wasn't getting it.

'I'm in player-safe mode right now, so I get updates on who's doing what. I'm not able to attack or trade. It's a bit like autopilot. I'm reading the thief forums about how this player called The Immortal got totally shafted. We're old sparring partners. He's been in my clan for the last forty-three games.'

'How do you know he's a he?'

'Huh?'

'The Immortal? Could be a woman?'

Berry sniffed. 'I just always thought of him as a he, with an avatar name like The Immortal. Only a guy would call himself that, don't you think?'

'Could be a bot?' suggested Sarah, trying to be helpful.

'He's definitely not a bot.' Berry took a gulp of Hype energy drink.

Sarah nodded with an uneasy smile. 'So you don't know who any of these people are?'

'No one knows who anyone is, but that just adds to the fun because you could be playing with anyone from anywhere in the world. The player could be any age, any sex or any tribe. That's the point of the game; even the condemned and the executioner can be on the same team, know what I'm saying?'

Sarah nodded, vacantly. She had no idea what Berry was saying.

'The Immortal must have fallen asleep because according to these stats he was saved by a player called Hotei, then he did nothing for about three hours. Everyone jumped on him while he was just floating around, being a dick, including me I'm not ashamed to say. When the weakest dog is down, the pack are quick to sacrifice one of their own. Now, there's a massive super clan after him. Biggest the game has ever seen.' She was surfing the sugar high, chatting at an air speed equivalent to the plane. 'After twenty-three hours of gaming he was totally zeroed, out of drug money points; influence, respect, guns, utterly pwned. Now, a good player would have hidden some of their inventory in a cash stash.'

'A cash stash?'

'This is risky because other players can find your stash and raid it, even trap bait it if they're good enough.' She popped another Jujy. Asparagus Bundle. 'You still with me?'

'I'm with you.' Sarah checked her watch. They had been in the air for barely three hours. She pulled a polite, uncomfortable face, unsure what else to say.

Berry didn't need to be asked twice. 'There are myths of shit hot inventory items hidden on the platform. These inventory items are the big prize. The most precious items that you can carry. No one has found them yet. We still don't even know what they are. Probably a sword. Cool, huh?'

Sarah was completely lost. The in-flight movie flickered. George Peppard was standing in the rain, looking pathetic. The soggy cat was hiding under a box. Holly Golightly was being passive aggressive again.

'What's going to happen to The Immortal?' asked Sarah.

Berry composed herself, curious as to whether Sarah was genuinely interested. She compared the risk factor against the alternatives and calculated that it was best just to keep talking. 'He's on the run. When he settles I'll have him killed.'

Sarah couldn't help herself from letting out a little shocked laugh. 'You can do that?' She was beginning to get the ruthlessness of the game and didn't think it sounded like a game at all. For the serious player, there was nothing fun about Atari Shock. If it was a game, then it was a game of life and death.

'Sure I can do that. Can't leave any weak links in the chain. We'll share the co-ordinates and set him up for a takedown. That's if the super clan don't get him first. I'm sure he'll be back though. He's too good not to be back. Probably has a cash stash somewhere in game time, or he'll borrow points from a loaner.'

The cabin lights dimmed. An alarm pinged in the distance. The safety belt sign illuminated. Berry hadn't unfastened hers since take off.

Sarah clicked her belt into place. 'You can get a loan?'

'If you're killed then you start again at the bottom of the leader board, which is basically like bankruptcy. Or you can re-set your wealth if you borrow points, but this is a bit dodge city, 'cos if you borrow from a loaner then they have a say over what you do with your points, who you give them to, what you buy or trade, and they can take stuff from you whenever they like.'

'You're their bitch?' smirked Sarah.

Berry laughed. 'Now you're getting it. You know, if you want to give it a go I can get you a buffed up avatar from a gold farmer on eBay? It'll be fucked and loaded?'

There was a commotion from the air stewards' bay; a raised voice, just enough panic to betray a sense of control. A steward walked swiftly down the aisle towards them.

'Miss Clarkson?' He was trembling. 'Miss Clarkson?' He checked the seat number next to Sarah.

'That's me,' she answered, still wondering what fucked and loaded meant.

'Your other passengers require immediate attention.'

She turned and spoke Mandarin to a man sitting behind them. It was the limousine driver. He immediately unbuckled and followed the air steward.

'I'll be right back.' She excused herself with a dutiful smile.

Other passengers? Berry thought she was the one? She realised that she'd been enjoying all of the attention and wasn't keen to share the limelight. She felt a conflicting sensation in her stomach as she wondered who the other gamers were.

16

Mist twisted around his ankles. The air was acrid and smoke-like. The ground was soft underfoot. He pushed a large palm leaf to one side and before him, towering and monumental, was the mountain island of Hōrai.

Rocks and debris fell from its jagged shoreline, dripping through a heavy cloud that seemed to hold the landmass in mid-air.

A branch snapped in the undergrowth. Smoke shifted in the trees. Low bushes rustled. Tadashi wasn't alone.

It was circling. He tried to find something to use as a weapon. The sound was moving closer. There was no time. He crawled on his hands and knees, trying to see what was causing the foliage to snap. The swirling mist was thicker the lower he got to the ground. His hands touched the soft soil, a mulch of leaves and twigs, then to his relief he felt something sharp. The root of a tree with a pointed end. It would have to do.

The sound was now coming from behind as well as in front. He followed it with his eyes, barely breathing, listening for movement. He could hear heavy breathing. An animalistic snorting. There was more than one of them. They were moving in synchronicity.

Tadashi held the tree root tighter in his hand. The sound was now directly behind him. He could feel hot breath on the back of his neck. He didn't dare look. Leaves swayed in front as something was approaching, coming straight at him. He was ready to lash out. Nothing appeared through the foliage. He closed his eyes for a brief second and a deep growl echoed in his ear. The animal was inches from his face. He could smell it. In the corner of his eye he could see the shape of a strange dog-like creature. It was looking directly at him.

Tadashi winced, preparing for the final attack of being pinned to the earth and sacrificed to slavering jaws. There was another hiss from behind and a rustle of leaves in front, but the advance didn't come. The creatures had him surrounded, but seemed hesitant. A hissing came from beside and again from behind. Then, he realised what they wanted. They were trying to force him in a particular direction. He was being herded.

He stood up and placed a foot forward. The rustling intensified and the hissing became fierce. He froze and stepped to the side. It stopped. He took another step and walked slowly in the direction that he thought it wanted him to go. He took a glance behind him and saw the arched back of a thin creature, black, without fur. It padded after him in the undergrowth.

He picked up his pace, trying to get a better lead. As he did so it moved faster. Leaves rustled. He looked behind to a wave of rippling foliage that was following in his tracks, moving in a curve that ushered him in a single direction. Either side of him now were wild animal growls. The creatures were coaxing each other. They moved closer, pushing him to the left, only for him to be shrieked at from the right and moved back in line. They were quickening, forcing him to break into a jog, then a run, and then the shrieking increased as something began snapping tight at his ankles. He felt a scratch each time he set down a foot. He turned and threw the tree root behind him. The creature leaped out of the way.

He was breathless, running frantically. He pulled on a large leaf and was confronted by a high, brick wall. There was nowhere to go.

The bushes rustled around him. The snap of jaws. The thuck of paws on mud.

'Get back!' shouted Tadashi, only to be screamed down by high-pitched squeals. He turned to the wall, his fingers clawing at the stone. He was cornered. The shrieks of the creatures pierced his ears. He spun back to face them, and expecting the worst, pushed himself up against the wall in submission.

The creature lunged. He lashed out, his hand making contact with the animal. He was surprised that it was hot blooded. There was another blow to his chest and this time the wall gave way behind him. Tadashi tumbled into darkness.

There was no sound, just the unexpected calm of falling. A spec of light where the wall had once been was now becoming smaller as he slid on his back down a stone shaft. He choked on dust, spinning in uncontrollable circles, gravity sucking him deeper into the unknown, until he landed on sand in a large chamber. The shadow animals howled in the far distance.

There was the strange scent of sandalwood and roast meat. Flames burned in tall, bamboo torches. Tadashi felt bruised and gasped as he tried to sit up. He blinked in the dim light. Shadows licked the walls, casting long, pointed shapes that were otherworldly and obscene. He heard rustles of movement in the shadows and could make out what looked like creatures with large dorsal spines, protruding beaks and fins.

The silence was broken by an inhuman voice. 'Be you a Deus?'

Tadashi corrected his posture and dusted himself down. He looked in the direction of the speaker. 'A what?' he asked. He was more curious than scared, wincing to see clearly in the darkness. 'I was chased. I fell,' he explained. His voice reverberated against the sandstone walls, echoing throughout the chamber.

The creatures were surprised that he had the authority to talk back without first answering their question. From another angle a second voice, this time soft and feminine, chirped up. 'Be you magical?'

'Entertain the court with your wizardry,' commanded the croak of a third.

'Yes! Entertain us,' squeaked a fourth, to the sound of approving chirps and tweets. 'If you displease us, you will be sent back to the shadow animals for their sport.'

The laughter of tiny voices squealed all around him.

Tadashi looked to where he thought the shaft had spat him out, and to where he presumed the dog-like animals were still waiting. He concluded that he had no option but to play along. 'I shall entertain you!' he shouted, over enthusiastically. 'I am an all-powerful and dangerous magician.' His voice bounced along the chamber walls and echoed into silence.

A creature scrambled over his feet, then another. There was a sudden desperate scurrying of claws and paws. Tiny objects hid in the shadows, bombarding over each other to get out of the way, squeezing themselves into the smallest of cracks as they scattered into dark corners.

Tadashi had the sensation that he was alone, until a black shadow reared up before him. It hovered, twice his size, allowing him to observe its exotic and otherworldly silhouette. It addressed him in a voice that was thin, sharp, and unused to speaking.

'You seek the sacred mushroom?'

17

The cargo section of the hold was pressurised to thirty thousand feet and had been sealed to quarantine items of a sensitive nature. A security guard could travel there and had all the comforts of business class, despite being surrounded by metal and rivets.

A cage, with bars like a prison cell, had been specially designed to house three lemurs in separate containment areas. One of them was screeching, tearing at its hair and swinging its arms around, smashing them against the metal bars. The other two sat quietly, staring at Sarah with sad, inquisitive eyes.

'It's been doing that for that last twenty minutes,' shouted the guard. 'It stops for a few seconds and then starts again.' He was incredibly stressed by what was obviously meant to be an easy gig. He didn't want to reach his destination with a dead precious cargo.

Sarah spoke calmly to the driver.

'Who's he?' asked the guard. 'Is he their keeper? Does he know what's going on?'

The driver took out a small, digital camera and started to take pictures. The lemurs didn't shy away from the camera flash. They didn't even seem to notice it.

The distressed lemur began jumping around the cage, trying to get away from something.

'What's it doing? Why's it running around like that?'

Sarah ignored him and indicated to the driver, who flicked the camera to film. He held it in the direction of the cage.

'He's going to film it?'

'There's nothing we can do now. Stand back, please.'

'What's wrong with it? Does it have a disease?'

'They've passed international quarantine. All the paperwork is in order. They're perfectly healthy.'

The lemur began to shake uncontrollably.

'It's bloody foaming at the mouth!' shouted the guard. He appeared to go into shock and covered his face with his hands. 'We need to land the plane.'

'Be quiet,' shouted Sarah. She looked at the driver. He acknowledged and focused his camera on the lemur that was now smashing its head against the metal bars.

'Use the tranquilliser,' cried the guard, becoming more distressed.

'Stay back. There's no danger to passengers.'

'The thing is in pain?'

She raised a hand and looked him square in the eye. 'There's nothing we can do,' she said, firmly.

The lemur let out a screech as it tore at its face, plunging its fingers deep into eye sockets, and ripping out both eyeballs.

'Jesus,' shouted the guard, staggering back.

It fell to the floor of the cage. It was dead. The other two didn't even blink.

Sarah checked her watch and turned to the camera. 'Lemur three. Six thirty-two AM, JST. The creature has had an attack. Self-mutilation to the face and eyes. Hysterical reaction.'

The guard stumbled against a chair and vomited.

The driver flicked a switch which sealed the metal bars to create a box with the dead lemur inside. 'To be safe,' he said.

18

An ambulance rolled up outside the spiritual science conference. The driver had already heard the incident report over the radio. The security images were conclusive – it was a body bag, clean up job. The siren wailed and slowed to a stop.

The building had been sealed off by private security, ready for a police investigation. Black and yellow tape spanned the doors and windows. The conference room was on lockdown.

Fuzzy black and white images were circulating, taken automatically during the event. Many were unclear. Some were completely blank. Enough displayed the aftermath of a horrific, animalistic takedown.

'Wolves,' said police Inspector Pulaski, as he reached out to steady himself on the car. 'A bloody pack of wolves, or lions. This town just gets sicker by the day. Have you checked the White Tiger habitat at The Mirage? And Southern Nevada Zoo?'

'No reported escapes or unusual animal activity,' replied a colleague.

He studied another picture and wasn't entirely sure what he was looking at. A petrified face was visible; hollow eye sockets and an open mouth. Several white streaks cut through the middle of the image in a blur, striking at speed. Perhaps they were claws or teeth, he wasn't sure? One side of the photo was over exposed, like a flashlight had been shone directly into the camera. Pulaski was relieved that the case had been taken seriously enough to be allocated someone from the FBI, even if that person was technically on their golf vacation, as Special Agent Carlton had explained when he intercepted the call.

Carlton flicked through the photos. 'How many victims were in the auditorium?'

'Over a hundred,' replied Pulaski. 'I haven't seen anything on this scale since the MGM Grand.'

He hesitated, offering the understanding that was clearly expected. Tragedy commanded the respect of hushed voices, especially in a city that wasn't used to being quiet. 'You were at the Grand?'

Pulaski nodded and averted his eyes. 'We bounce back,' he said. 'Vegas always does.'

When an electrical fire had broken out at the MGM Grand, a black mushroom cloud billowed over the desert for weeks. It was the worst disaster in the history of the state of Nevada, and all that the city could talk about for months. Seven hundred guests suffered toxic smoke inhalation, over eighty had lost their lives.

A priest had been sent from room to room, as high as the nineteenth floor, to bless the dead bodies.

Sin City survived but was deeply scarred. It brushed the ash from its shoulders, publicly mourned the victims, openly celebrated the fire department heroes and redecorated in paisley fire-resistant wallpaper. Within weeks, the tourists began to flood back through smoke stained doors.

'I'm sorry that you are confronted by such horror again, Inspector. I'll do everything in my power to help you and your team with this investigation,' said Carlton, with a firm nod.

That was all Pulaski had wanted to hear, confirmation that the agent was on his side, that he was one of them. 'Jesus bless you,' he said. 'I appreciate your words.'

Carlton knew how the department boys worked. He shuffled through the rest of the photo pack and came across an image of himself caught on camera. Tadashi was also clearly visible. 'Has anyone been inside yet?' he asked. Pulaski looked away. Carlton took the moment to fold the photo into his coat pocket.

'Forensic, paramedic, fire and animal control are all here. We'll send them in together in case anyone has survived, but judging by the security shots it was a bloodbath.'

Carlton could sense that Pulaski was planning to take Van Peterson down. Even if the incident couldn't be fully explained, the threat of death was clear from the photographic evidence. He would most likely be committed for first degree murder, which would mean life in prison, or if the state of Nevada were feeling particularly aggravated after the MGM trial, he could even face the needle.

'Where is he?'

'Back of the ambulance with his daughter and the medic.'

'And the woman who insists on being called a flower? What was it again?'

'Lotus Flower. We think she's an actress. Suspicious, if you ask me. She's been taken to UMC hospital.'

'Be sure to let me know if you find anyone alive in there. Tell me right away. I want to be the first to talk to them. The first, ok?' He tapped the FBI badge pinned to his jacket.

Pulaski nodded. 'We're lucky you were in town, Special Agent Carlton.'

'Can't see myself getting much time on the golf course now.'

'I appreciate you cutting your vacation short.'

'Well,' he sighed, 'when duty calls, we answer.' He sealed the security photos in a plastic bag and handed them back. 'Let's go talk to our mad professor.'

They had been checked for injuries and were declared fit, but weren't allowed to leave the police vehicle. Mike shifted on the hard seat. The incident had sobered him up pretty quickly.

Sarah was still trying to fathom what had happened. 'Did you see Tadashi?' She seemed anxious by his disappearance.

Mike was unsure what to say. 'He was on stage and then, seriously, they all just disappeared.'

'This is most interesting,' whispered Van Peterson. 'You saw him walk into the source of the disturbance?'

'He's dead, Malcolm.'

'Oh, no, Michael, far from it.' He seemed suddenly cheerful.

'You think he crossed?' asked Sarah. She was relieved by the news.

'He knew exactly what to look for. Lotus Flower opened the door and he walked straight through. Clever boy.'

'Incredible.' She held her father on the arm. 'Where did he go? Can he get back? Too many questions, papa?'

'I have my suspicions, dear,' he replied, 'but it is too soon to say for sure. We must return to the auditorium. If the entire audience crossed to the other side with him, then she must open the passage to enable their return. We must return with Lotus Flower.'

'Will you just stop calling her that?' shouted Mike, just as the door of the vehicle opened.

Agent Carlton and Inspector Pulaski surveyed the three of them. A couple of members of the Las Vegas metropolitan police stood behind, wearing full riot gear and carrying plastic shields.

'Malcolm Van Peterson?' asked Carlton. 'You must come with us for questioning. In private.'

'Anything you want to ask him, you can ask us too,' said Sarah.

'What's with all the heavy gear?' said Mike.

'Precautions,' explained the inspector. 'I don't know how you did it, but I'm sure as hell not going to let you get away with it.'

'Whatever do you mean?' asked Van Peterson.

'Where are the bodies?' Pulaski was ready for blood.

'This isn't the place to conduct an investigation, Inspector,' said Carlton. He took the professor by the arm and helped him down from the ambulance, speaking softly as they walked to the police car.

'Stall for time. I need to think this through. If it goes to court then you'll be convicted on the photographic evidence alone.'

'I can explain. In fact, it's quite simple.'

Carlton shook his head. 'Whatever happens, do not try and explain it. That's the worst thing you can do. Just state the facts.'

Van Peterson was placed in hand cuffs.

'I don't suppose that now is a good time to talk about funding is it, Jimmy?'

19

The space between life and death was tormented by an unfamiliar noise that wasn't quite music, and wasn't quite silence. The irritating sound was bleeding from tiny headphones that were stuffed into Hotei's ears. He was nodding rhythmically and performing a little dance. The ancient immortals realised that they were staring, and despite being exceptionally curious beings, thought they should probably be doing something more enlightened.

Bishamon was becoming increasingly annoyed. He dug his sword into the ground, causing jagged pot-holes to fill with mist.

Fokuro repositioned himself up on his short-haired deer, which trotted like a caged animal in a constant figure of eight.

Jurojin hobbled on his great iron crutch, stopping to cough up large globules of phlegm which he swallowed back down with a glug from his medicine gourd.

Benten hid beneath a large shawl, maintaining the ambiguity of being neither man, nor woman, but both.

The Imperial uncle, Daikoku, purified the air with his Jade crystal tablet, hoping that the essence would help to calm their immortal souls, and cease the horrible sound. The buzzing persisted, like the screech of a rasping insect.

The ancient guardians of the afterlife were being as patient as they could, but they had become tired of waiting. They kicked the clouds beneath their feet and cursed the birdman as it bathed in the sea of souls above. A dark mist had fallen on the mountain island of Hōrai, and in their absence, it was no longer protected against the evil that desired it.

ACHIEVEMENT UNLOCKED

LEVEL TWO

20

Stu offered Lars a cigarette as they sheltered from the rain in the entrance to The Pill. The weather had let up but it was still a miserable day.

'What's going on?' asked Lars.

'Julia Miller wants me,' replied Stu.

'What's really going on?'

'The servers are fucked.'

Lars wasn't in the mood for being played with. He felt irritable, uncomfortable in his own skin. He was beginning to get a headache and they were difficult to shift once they set in. 'You could have called me, mate?'

'Chill out, man. IT Bob ran an anti-virus across it and adjusted the firewall.'

'What does IT Bob know?'

'He knows everything. He works in IT.'

Lars was distracted by a row of black ravens sitting in a line on a nearby fence. He thought for a moment that they were looking directly at him.

'So, The Immortal's been crunked, right?' Stu was giddy with excitement.

Lars struck the lighter and smoked. 'Has he?'

'Absolutely knackered. Total wipe out. Bottom of the

leader board. The thief forums are talking about putting together another super clan to finish the job. Proper witch hunt. You joined?'

Lars coughed violently. 'Not yet,' he wheezed, trying to catch his breath. A wave of exhaustion hit him as he felt the spiralling sensation churn in his stomach. He closed his eyes.

'You alright, mate?'

He dropped the cigarette in a puddle, unsure why he'd accepted it in the first place. 'I'm fine. It was a late one, that's all.'

'Oh yeah? Something I should tell my sister about?'

'I was trying to beat you at Atari Shock, you know, like the rest of the fucking world,' smiled Lars.

Despite being a close friend and drinking buddy, Lars had managed to hide his Immortal identity. It was his superhero secret. The only people who knew were the guys at the comic book store, Zack and Wiki, and they understood the value of secrets. They were loaded with them.

He spent a lot of time with Stu but didn't trust him at all. Mostly because he was Claire's brother; a fact which enabled an over familiar intimacy that went way beyond a normal friendship. This status gave Stu a sense of privilege, and he always used it to maintain the upper hand.

'Keep trying, mate,' he laughed. 'Oh, message from Julia.'

'Your new girlfriend sending me messages through you now?'

'Perhaps she knew I'd be seeing you before she would?'

Lars couldn't deny that.

'So, the real news, Bishop's waiting to see you about an international project. She seemed pretty fucked off about that one.'

Lars nodded. Even when he wasn't playing, he was still on the virtual battlefield.

He approached his desk and saw a frantic Julia Miller punching her keyboard.

'What are you doing here?' She was surprised to see him.

'Erm, this is where I work.'

She flinched and smiled, remembering her professional etiquette. 'I think there's been a virus. I've no idea how it could have happened.' She glanced sheepishly at her screen. He noticed her minimise an Atari Shock game widget. 'He's waiting for you.'

They looked over to the desk where a smart suited, spectacled man was distracted by Lars' computer.

'I'd better…' mumbled Lars, as he prepared for the inevitable boss battle.

David Bishop was short; too short to command the authority that he had. What he lacked in height, he made up for by acute concentration. Despite the vertical challenge, he was incredibly intense up close. He forced a jagged smile as Lars casually waved an arm of greeting across the open plan office.

'I see that you're an Atari Shock player, Nilsson?'

The game window was maximised on his desktop. Lars immediately got the fear. He didn't remember leaving The Immortal logged on. The toolbar was red, indicating imminent attack. He'd never seen as much activity on his player-feed before. It was updating so fast that he could barely read it. The horde were ready to initiate their final takedown. The super clan had blocked all exits.

'Hello, sir. Who's been using my terminal? They clearly have no respect for the work place.' He tapped at the keyboard. 'Let me close this and we can catch up.'

Bishop smiled. 'We've all had a little dabble right, Lars? It's all the rage so my children tell me.'

'I'm far too busy for these immature procrastinations.' What had he just said? Immature procrastinations? It was hardly convincing. He smiled. There was a desperate silence. He felt the spiralling sensation swirl deep in his stomach, twisting in his guts. He couldn't be hungry. He'd raided an energy crate and shared the resources out across his life force spectrum. The raid would have guaranteed enough reserves for at least twenty-four hours. It dawned on him that he hadn't eaten, he'd powered up his avatar instead.

'I wanted to speak to you in person, Lars,' said Bishop, sitting opposite and getting comfortable. 'I haven't caught you at an inconvenient time, have I? I hear you're having some technical issues?'

'Not at all. IT Bob has it under complete control.'

'IT Bob?' Bishop cocked his head.

'Sorry, er, I mean, my technical team. Robert Brooks from IT. He's run an anti-virus and adjusted the firewall. He knows everything.' The ticker-tape feed had become a furnace of fresh information. He turned away. Sweat dripped down his back. 'How can I help you, sir?'

Bishop waved Lars to his seat. 'You're one of our best, Lars. Number one. You've been with us many years, yes, since college?'

'Indeed I have, sir. I'm very proud of the company.' The temptation was too much. His eyes involuntarily flicked back to the screen. He nudged the mouse, moving the tab higher to see what was happening in game space.

'And we are very proud of you, Mr Nilsson. Which is why we have agreed to offer you up for an exclusive opportunity.'

'Offer me up, sir?' Lars was surprised at his choice of words. He had no idea what his boss was talking about.

'It's a simple task. Call it a perk of the job, if you like. One that I think you may very well appreciate. An international assignment.'

The toolbar bar was flashing red – imminent game space attack.

He coughed and excused himself. 'One moment sir, I just need to check on the progress of the anti-virus.' He applied a hyperspace plug-in. The Immortal was sent teleporting around the Atari Shock servers. This would stall the attackers for a few more minutes.

'Lars Nilsson,' announced Bishop. 'We would like you to meet with our esteemed sponsor in Tokyo, Japan. Consider this a reward for your hard work at the BBP, and for your excellent management of the international liaison development projects.'

Julia let out a squeal from across the room. Bishop smiled, forcefully. A gleam in his eye had a hidden depth that Lars hadn't noticed before.

He was tempted to say that he couldn't leave the country. He had too many commitments. He was The Immortal. He was the super-pimp; the world famous gaming champion who was, right now, being fucked over by the rest of the online community, including most of the people in the office, and quite possibly his boss' children.

Despite being offered what was likely the opportunity of a lifetime, Lars simply wasn't interested. Perhaps he could send Julia Miller, he thought. She could go for him. He had more important things to deal with than an overrated work trip. How was he going to find time for Atari Shock doing whatever it was the BBP wanted, all the way on the other side of the world?

'This is a great honour. You will meet with our esteemed colleagues and witness a new product of theirs in the early stages of development. They like to do the face-to-face thing. You will be forging a very valuable business relationship.'

Lars realised that Bishop hadn't taken his gaze off him at any point during the conversation. The glint in his eye was penetrating, a nervous twitch becoming a rhythmic pattern.

'I should get back to my to-do-list.'

'That's ok, Lars. I can see that you're very busy. I'll get old Julia to relay all the information you need. Duty calls, right?'

Julia coughed from across the office.

'Indeed it does,' he smiled.

'Thank you for your continued professionalism, Mr Nilsson. You are a great asset to the company.'

Lars forced a smile, waiting for his boss to leave, but he was still staring, analysing him.

'Maybe I should enter the details in my calendar right now, sir? It is such an exciting opportunity, as you say.' He tapped at the keyboard, trying to appear calm, and raised his shields with all he had left. He'd sent The Immortal spinning through game space, teleporting so quickly that the horde had no chance of a direct hit. The method would only keep him temporarily safe however. There were no open portals. The impending doom of The Immortal had been suitably hyped and the numbers were higher than ever. The screen was flashing imminent attack, and GreySkull was back.

'I must tell you, Lars,' started Bishop with a nostalgic tone in his voice, 'I remember when I was first given an opportunity like this. It changed my life.' His voice faded into insignificance as Lars studied the screen.

'Player-feed: GreySkull launches Critical Suicide Game Space Attack. WARNING: Game space will be erased.'

Lars winced and smiled at the same time.

A critical suicide game space attack; it was essentially self-destruct, a move that the newbies would employ when they had nothing left to lose. It was a dirty trick, a vain hope that all players inhabiting the game space simply wouldn't notice or wouldn't care. GreySkull was planning to take out The Immortal, as well as the hundred thousand or so players currently blocking the exit. The co-ordinates would disappear into a black hole, erased forever, along with everything in them. Imminent eradication.

The Immortal flicked around game space, searching for a portal. Someone would crack. Someone had to value their Atari Shock profile more than the assassination of its top player. He would stare this one in the face and teleport out at the last second. GreySkull had shown his hand. All Lars had to do was wait for a portal to open and he would be free. He checked the co-ordinates. All blocked, with only a few minutes until execution. It was a last stand. A face-off. The end of a Western with fingers twitching on the trigger.

The player-feed ticker slowed, scrolling the message over and over.

'Player-feed: Critical Suicide Game Space Attack Initiated. WARNING: Game space will be erased. Game space will be erased.'

'Remember that when you leave next week,' said Bishop.

Lars looked up. 'I leave when?' A new game space became available. 'I'm sorry, sir, just a sec.' Lars activated the co-ordinates but rather than his avatar spinning into the safety of the vacant space – the profile completely reset to zero.

'The Immortal Inventory: Money 0; Drugs 0; Nukes 0; Shields 0; Kudos 0; Life force 0.'

'Fuck!' shouted Stu from across the office.

Several of the BBP office workers let out a frustrated cry, including Julia Miller.

A similar reaction occurred across the planet as tens of thousands of blood lusty players adjusted their glasses, opened Facebook, gave their pets the attention they craved, made a sandwich, and finally got on with what it was they were really meant to be doing. The Immortal had been eradicated from the Atari Shock servers. The hunt was over.

'Are you all right, Mr Nilsson? You look pale.'

Lars tried to acknowledge his boss but the spiralling sensation twisted deeper than before. 'I don't know what to say.'

'Yes. It is indeed an honour,' smiled Bishop, with a smug satisfaction. 'This isn't something that happens every day.'

'Of course, sir,' said Lars, unable to comprehend the incredible sense of loss.

21

A cup of cold coffee had been sitting on the desk for over half an hour. The professor was looking frail and exhausted. They had kept him waiting, locked away from Sarah and Mike, in a plain, white interview room.

Agent Carlton entered, followed by Pulaski. He placed a standard issue Texas Instruments cassette tape machine on the table and pressed record. 'State your name?'

'Really, Jim? Has it come to this?'

'State your name.'

He sighed loudly to show his disapproval. 'I am Professor Malcolm Van Peterson.'

'A professor of what, exactly?' quizzed the inspector.

'Well,' he cleared his throat, unsure how much he should say. 'I am a spiritual scientist.'

Pulaski looked offended.

Carlton pulled out an Old Gold and smoked. 'Please state, for the record, what that is?'

'I am endeavouring to discover the true nature of the human condition.'

'Now in fucking English?' interrupted Pulaski. Anger had already led him to his conclusion. The case was clear-cut. Van Peterson was guilty. They were all guilty, every individual associated with the spiritual science conference – clear up the mess, convict them all. Get them locked away for as long as possible and hope they died in the joint. The international press were going to have a field day.

Carlton tried to calm him down. 'Let me handle this, okay? Please go on, professor. But I ask you to keep the technical details to a minimum, for the sake of clarity.'

'I investigate what inspires us to live and die,' explained Van Peterson while studying the face of the increasingly frustrated inspector.

'Blow jobs and bowel cancer,' snapped Pulaski. 'How's that for an answer?'

'I'm sorry, I don't think I understand.' He looked to his old friend for help.

Carlton was maintaining a professional distance.

'You fuck with people, that's what you do,' continued the inspector.

'I hardly fuck with people.'

Carlton was going to have to let Pulaski get it out of his system. He was also intrigued what would happen if the professor was pushed a little harder.

'The people in the auditorium. You know what happened to them, don't you?'

'Indeed, I do.'

'Your entire conference, one hundred and twenty-six people were, I would say murdered, but it's probably more correct for me to say they were fucking slaughtered. Do you understand? Our team have been in. There's no one left. No trace. The bodies have vanished.'

Carlton could tell that the inspector was holding himself back. Had he not been in the room then he was sure that the interview would have become physical. 'Let's not jump to any irrational conclusions. Bodies don't just disappear.'

Van Peterson shifted, uncomfortably.

Pulaski was seething. 'I'm not going to ask you why, not now, but I am going to ask you how? I'm curious. I've never seen anything like it, and I've had Vegas in my life for so long, I can't remember what god-fearing folk are like anymore. Why do you people always bring your shit here? Seriously, what the fuck attracts you freaks to leave your mess in my back yard? It's pathetic. So, how did you do it? Mass hallucination? Mass suicide? I suspect dogs, or wolves. Was it dogs or wolves? Did you release a chemical weapon in the auditorium?'

'Do you have access to chemical weaponry?' asked Carlton.

Van Peterson spluttered, unsure what to say.

'One hundred and twenty-six people,' continued Pulaski. 'That makes you America's most wanted right now. You're going to the chair. There won't even be a trial.'

'You realise what he's saying?' asked Carlton. 'An incident on a scale such as this justifies the full force of the law.'

Carlton was doing what he could but his old friend was operating on an entirely different level. Van Peterson didn't seem to understand the implications or consequences.

'Explain what the heck happened in there, then at least the people who come to read this report in the future will have some idea of what's going on in that sick brain of yours,' growled Pulaski. 'You're going to be a case study for future generations of criminal psychologists and sociopaths. They're all going to want to know what the fuck you were thinking. How did you do it?'

Van Peterson tried to swallow. His throat was dry. 'I didn't do anything,' he whimpered.

Carlton wiped his forehead. Denial wasn't an option. It would only make the inspector angrier.

'Of course you didn't do it. How ridiculous of me to even consider that you might have conned over a hundred innocent people into signing up for your freak show, and then brutally slaughtered all of them, you sick fuck.' Pulaski was becoming more aggressive and leaning over the table.

Carlton sensed that his next move would be to turn the tape machine off. Then the professor would really be in trouble.

'I suspect a kami-kakushi,' spluttered Van Peterson.

'A what-the-fuck?' laughed the inspector.

Carlton interrupted. 'Professor, can you please keep your report as simple as possible. Just state the facts.'

'A divine kidnapping.'

'That's really not helping.'

The inspector guffawed and eyed Van Peterson, waiting for permission to fetch.

'Let me explain,' he said, repositioning himself on the cell chair. 'In ancient legend, the Tengu demon used to perform otherworldly pranks. It often took the form of a kidnapping, which always involved an ulterior motive, but generally the victim would become lost, disoriented, and be left alone to fend for themselves in an unknown place with no clue as to how they got there or how to get home. That is what I suspect has happened today – a classic kami-kakushi. It's actually quite exciting.'

'And who are you suggesting was kidnapped?' Pulaski asked, slowly.

'Well, all of them,' said Van Peterson, matter-of-factly. 'All of the people in the auditorium.'

The inspector was stunned to silence.

Carlton held his breath, anticipating what might happen.

'So, you're going to plead insanity. Is that your plan?'

'I'd like to stop now.' Van Peterson was trembling. He took a feeble slurp from his cup. 'My coffee, it's gone cold.'

'Fuck the coffee.' Pulaski slammed his fist on the desk. 'You are under suspicion of mass homicide, along with your colleagues, Dr Michael Jones, and your daughter, Sarah Clarkson. You might be wondering where they are?'

'I know precisely where Sarah and Michael are, at all times. It's Tadashi who can't be tracked.'

'I'm sorry, who the fuck is Tadashi?'

'He is a Shintoist,' said Van Peterson, trying to be helpful, but everything he said just made the inspector angrier.

Agent Carlton spoke with authority, in an attempt to diffuse the situation. 'He's a suspect. I've met him. We should bring him in.'

'You won't find him,' explained Van Peterson.

'And why is that?'

'Well,' he spluttered, 'as I just explained, I believe that he has been kidnapped.'

The inspector gave him a blunt stare.

'Has Lotus Flower been sedated?' asked Van Peterson, scared that the question might provoke a violent reaction. 'This is a very vulnerable time for her.'

'Ah yes, Lotus Flower,' Pulaski scratched his head, convinced that the old man was now just fucking with him. 'And what part does she have to play in this grand charade?'

'Lotus Flower was the subject of my conference. She was on stage during the incident. She participated in a very successful session of quantum jumping. You may be more familiar with it as trans-meditation or trans-regression? That's what provoked the kami-kakushi. It's very simple.'

'So, Lotus Flower murdered everyone in the auditorium?'

'No. I told you, she was simply the host through which the Kami were evoked. No one has been murdered. It's a trick. They are merely on the other side. You only perceive them to be dead, for they are no longer visible on this mortal plane.'

'Ah, of course. How simple.' Pulaski moved in close. 'If I thought I could get away with it,' he wheezed, 'I would punch you in the fucking face right now, professor.'

Carlton jumped in. 'Let me take it from here,' he interrupted. 'You've pushed him hard enough. He's an old man, after all. You're not making any headway. Let me go talk to the other two?'

Inspector Pulaski moved reluctantly towards the door. 'Enjoy your coffee,' he spat, allowing it to slam behind him.

22

Tadashi felt the presence of an obscure and violent force. A gust of wind blew and the torchlights extinguished, capturing him in a spotlight.

'You are here for the sacred mushroom?' insisted the croaking voice. A figure was hidden from view, swaying in the darkness. Shadows followed wherever it moved.

'What are you?' he whispered, astonished.

The shadow slid closer, creeping along the wall like a sundial. 'I am everything,' it cawed, close and menacing. Then, in a flurry of heavy shawl and feather, it was gone.

The chamber torches flickered to flame, revealing fresh scratches along the sandstone walls. A laugh drifted high in the cavernous chamber ceiling. It echoed in the rafters, swooping in spirals, plotting distant attack positions.

He squinted, curious to see what had approached, but the mysterious figure had slipped away.

Studying the walls, he was able to make out a variety of shapes and images; tall and long, animal-like but human. Brown and green etchings were cut into the yellow brickwork. Long lists and symbols stretched from floor to ceiling. He focused on a hieroglyph of a large pig or dog, or perhaps a donkey, the head of a crocodile, fine hair stretching to the floor. It was baying at the menacing figure of a man with the head of a bird, in subdued respect.

'Fascinating,' he muttered as he ran his finger down the etching. It was some kind of story. There were more characters. They held up their hands, protecting their faces, eyes closed, pained expressions, cowering at the threat of an altogether mightier being.

There was a violent rush of air and he was tripped to his knees. He reached out to break his fall but smacked his chin on the hard, stone floor. A figure moved forward and a strange pressure flipped him on his back. The impact was cold and inhuman. He was upside down and being dragged along the dusty stone by his legs.

'A closer look at the scrolls of Time?' the voice insisted, inches from his ear. It cackled, unable to form words with ease, coughing them out at him.

Tadashi could feel its ancient breath on his skin. Seconds later, he was flung into a dark corner. His head cracked against stone and all he could see was the blur of violent hieroglyphics scrawled up a wall; a beast was pulling apart the body of a man, tearing at limbs, tossing them in the air and catching them in a cruel and bloody game. Another etching of the birdman was next to it, carrying a staff that was part weapon and part sceptre.

He sat against the wall and touched his stinging chin. The pain had returned to his legs. He didn't know how far he'd fallen down the shaft. It felt like he was tumbling for minutes. His fingers were tacky and warm as he felt the sticky softness of blood. There was a fluttering of feathers and the smell of damp cloth. Tadashi tensed, sensing another attack. It came quickly and with purpose. He was lifted high in the air by an invisible force that twisted through the shadows and torch light.

'Behold, millennia,' coughed the voice.

The chamber was lit by flame, displaying the vast depth of scrawling sketches along its walls that carried on into an infinite distance.

He was forced by the neck to view the ancient hieroglyphic images; animals, birds, creatures unknown, ugly and beautiful, violent and at peace.

'These are the scrolls of Time – a record of all that will live and all that will die – and I am its keeper.'

A sharp shriek pierced his ears and he was dropped from a height.

'You bleed!' cawed the birdman in surprise.

The flutter of wings passed by his ear and powered high into the rafters. He turned, panicked, to see where it had gone.

'You bleed,' it sobbed from the depths of the catacomb.

The chamber torches snuffed out and Tadashi was left alone in darkness. He considered running but couldn't see his own hands. He blinked. Memories of the sandstone etchings were vivid, imprinted in white flashes in the intense dark.

'A mortal cannot pass into the realm of the dead,' choked the voice, 'and yet you have mortal blood?' The whispering words reflected a cautious uncertainty that dripped slowly down the chamber walls. 'How did you get here?'

Tadashi remembered the voice in the auditorium. 'The primordial gods opened a passage,' he replied.

A commotion sent a shivering pulse through the warm, stagnant air.

'You have free will?' The question echoed, reverberating throughout the dark chamber.

Tadashi didn't reply.

The birdman already knew the answer.

A distant torch flickered into flame, then another and another, until all the torches were lighting up slowly, one by one, restoring light and casting tall shadows. The chamber became a brightly lit room once more.

A single, solitary shadow remained in the middle of the room, darker than the others, deathly black, like a piece of the night itself. As the torchlight settled, he could make out the distinct shape of an egg-like form that the light couldn't penetrate. The shadow was smooth and perfectly composed. Slowly, it began to mutate, sharp spikes twisted, and from it stepped the physical form of Tengu.

The creature was impossible to comprehend, haunting and horrific — part man, part bird and part beast. It had the head of a huge black bird, shining silky in the torchlight. Its round eyes blinked as it cocked its head, showing no sign of humanity, just the lonely chill of a billion years of solitude in the blink of an eye. Its body was covered by a monk's red shawl, tied at the waist by a vibrant gold sash. It flapped tiny wings that looked insufficient to lift the bulky body. It wasn't clear where the head of the bird became the body of the beast. Tadashi could see muscles, defined and stocky under the shawl. Bare arms and legs appeared human but were black and purple and badly bruised.

The mischievous master of chaos stepped close, bowed, and went down on one knee. The claws on its toes scratched the dirt. 'You are dying,' it said, turning its head to observe him.

'What?'

'The end will be with you soon.'

'What do you mean?'

Tengu twitched. Tiny wings stretched on its back in a yawn and then settled. It held out a feathered hand as an indication to follow. 'Come. Observe your life path. I will show you your fate.'

He was lifted into the air, more carefully this time, by a hand and a claw.

'I am the keeper of the scrolls of Time, and these etchings represent every living thing. This is my responsibility. This is my curse.'

Tadashi was confronted by the image of himself, scratched roughly onto the sandstone wall.

'Behold — your destiny.'

The string of images repeated many times along the wall, and then split into another line.

'That is the lifeline of your daughter,' croaked Tengu.

'I don't have a daughter,' he said, confused.

'You will,' it croaked, bluntly. 'She will betray you.'

Tadashi was silent as he was shown the rest of his timeline, which ended, abruptly.

'Observe how the lifeline ceases. This is the moment of your mortal death. You listen. You decide. I will make you an offer,' said the birdman.

He didn't dare look it in the eyes.

'I seek two fallen guardians of the afterlife. They have been raised as mortal incarnations, boy and girl in spirit. You will bring them across the threshold and into my afterlife. My spirit animals will make them enter your path. You do this task for me and I will repay you with the gift of life.'

There was the sound of swirling swordplay. He felt a wisp of air as the invisible blade passed inches from his face.

'How do I bring them to you?' asked Tadashi, transfixed by the etching of his own timeline.

'The sacred mushroom,' said Tengu. 'My gift. It will be your passage.'

'There is one more task, traveller,' echoed a female voice.

He looked up to see Lotus Flower, hovering in mid-air. Her shawl flexed pure static electricity. She smiled.

'Bring me Van Peterson,' she said.

Beneath her stood all of the audience members from the spiritual science conference; an army of mortal souls, determined to fulfil the wishes of their powerful and ancient master.

'Do we have an accord?'

Tadashi shook his head, uncertain, and for a fleeting moment looked Tengu directly in the eye. He was shocked by what he saw. An intensely black, universally ancient, shark-like eye, stared right back at him. He felt a devastating loneliness in its gaze. There was no acknowledgment, no invitation, but he felt drawn to it, lost inside. It stared, reaching deep, sucking the humanity from his soul. It blinked and Tadashi was released from its grasp. He fell to the dirt where a flowering red fungus was emerging; bright white spots dotted on intense red flesh. It glowed in the flicker of flame.

He reached for the mushroom and plucked it from the sand, taking it in both hands. As he admired it, the fungus rotted in his hands, leaving deep red stains on his skin. The liquid elixir residue glistened.

Tengu snapped its beak to signify the end of the deal.

'It is done,' said Lotus Flower.

The birdman screeched with joy. A snaking tongue flecked along the sharpness of its beak. Blank eyes blinked with a turn of its head. It produced a bamboo reed instrument from thin air.

Tadashi cowered. 'Wait, Lotus Flower?' he pleaded, but her image had become translucent, evaporating into the sandstone wall.

'Now, we drink and dance.' Tengu breathed deeply, sucking in air and preparing to play his shō. A violent wind tumbled down the chamber and began to grow more intense as it inhaled. The flaming torches flickered in the breeze and extinguished one by one.

Tadashi felt increasingly dizzy. He tried to get its attention but the creature was lost in a swirling cloud of dust. 'What have I done?' he whispered, unable to breathe. He fell to the floor, too weak to stand.

A glass vial rolled towards him. The essence of the amanita muscaria flowed inside. Sand gathered around the spout and thickened to form a cork, which sealed the bottle shut.

Blue wisps of light began to circle his head. He tried to speak but didn't have the breath. He let out a gasp that went unnoticed in the increasingly dark chamber.

The birdman played the most beautiful and triumphant of melodies on the ancient instrument. The tune lilted, as though Izanami herself were playing. Tengu closed its eyes and danced, its tiny wings moving as slow as a butterfly as the music drifted around the chamber, restoring air, and light, and shadow. Tiny beasts emerged from the cracks in the walls and began to sway with the music, transfixed by the haunting melody.

Tadashi was curled on the floor. His suffocated skin had turned black and blue, aged in seconds as his spirit was transported back to the mortal world. In his hand, he clutched the ancient vial, which contained the essence of death itself. This was his gift, the sacred mushroom; the gateway to the afterlife.

23

'I don't believe that I have had the pleasure?' asked Carlton as he placed the cassette tape machine on the table.

Mike's eyes were bloodshot and tired. The hangover was kicking in. 'Dr Michael Jones.'

They shook hands, coldly.

'Let's have a little talk shall we, doctor? Anything I can get you?'

'How about a margarita?'

Carlton laughed. 'It has been quite a day. Perhaps you can tell me all about it, then we'll see if we can rustle you something up from the police station bar.'

'There's a bar?'

Carlton smiled and clicked a button on the tape machine. 'We're on the record. So, Dr Michael Jones, chief medical officer in Professor Van Peterson's Academy, as it is widely known on file. What, exactly, are your responsibilities with the group?'

'Well, I make sure that there are no accidents during the show.' It dawned on Mike where he was headed with his line of investigation. 'Hey, if you think I was responsible for any of this, then you should know I have no idea what the hell happened. It wasn't a publicity stunt, and it wasn't mass suicide or something crazy like that.'

'We're not accusing anyone right now, Michael. All we want to hear is your…' Carlton stumbled, 'your interpretation of what happened, ok?'

'Sure, look, you were in the audience too, right? I saw you leave.'

Carlton flinched and seemed uncomfortable.

Mike had the feeling that he'd just said the wrong thing and tried to correct it. 'I mean, I thought it was you. It was dark, you know. It was difficult to see anything.' He remembered seeing Carlton run for the door and a woman being dragged down by a shadow as he pushed her back into the auditorium to save himself. He could still hear her scream and picture the desperate panic on Carlton's face, lit by the swirling phosphorescence. 'Can I at least get a cigarette?'

Carlton reached into his top pocket and threw down a pack of Old Gold. He offered a light.

Mike took one and thanked him. Old Gold. Unfashionable. Past habit, maybe rations, he wondered. Carlton would be about the right age. He thought he'd take a risk and try to find some common ground. 'Army man, huh?' he asked.

'How did you guess?'

'Old Gold,' he said. 'A treat instead of a treatment.' He smoked, nervously, attempting a smile.

Carlton took a cigarette for himself.

Mike picked tobacco from his teeth. 'Look, it all happened so fast. I didn't see anything clearly.' He looked Carlton in the eye. 'I didn't see anything, ok?'

Carlton stopped the tape machine. 'I'm going to do you a favour.' He took a drag. 'I'm going to start the recording again, and this time, I'll expect you to be more co-operative.'

Carlton feigned a smile. 'You're the chief medical officer of this charade, which also makes you the prime suspect, do you understand me? Malcolm Van Peterson is just an old man. What motive does an old man have? Now you? A disgraced anaesthetist, angry with the world, alcoholic, depressed, detached, you have motivation written all over you, don't you think?'

Mike swallowed. Was Carlton trying to provoke a response, to make him slip up somehow?

'I know how you came to be here, Mike. You can't answer an ad in the back pages of a medical journal and expect to disappear from the world. The dead can't chase you but reputation can.' Carlton hit rewind until the cassette tape jammed. He crunched the stop button. 'So, let's go again, shall we? All I want to hear is your interpretation of what happened.' He paused to smoke. 'Are you ready, doctor?'

Mike took a drag and nodded.

Carlton pressed record. 'Dr Michael Jones, chief medical officer in Van Peterson's spiritual science team. What happened in the auditorium?'

He cleared his throat. 'The professor was mid-session when the lights went out, and then, there was screaming.'

'Did Van Peterson have something to do with those animals?'

'Those animals, whatever they were, they came from nowhere. I don't think Van Peterson was expecting them, or had anything to do with their release into the auditorium.'

'Did you get a good look at any of them?'

'It was too dark to see anything. I heard them.' He looked to Carlton for acknowledgement but his gaze was averted.

'You heard them? Go on.'

Mike smoked, nervously. 'Something was loose. Someone released a bear or dogs. I don't know. Whatever they were, they went through the audience like they were looking for something.'

'Looking for something? Are you sure?' Carlton seemed interested.

'It was systematic. The attack wasn't a slaughter. It was considered. That much I can be sure of. I have no idea what they were looking for.'

Carlton took a moment. He knew he didn't have long until Inspector Pulaski would insist on speaking with Mike himself. He also suspected that the creatures weren't looking for something – but for someone.

'Tell me about the other members of Van Peterson's team?'

'Well, Sarah Clarkson deals with anything organisational. I guess you could call her a kind of show producer, and then there's me. That's it.'

'That's it? No one else?' asked Carlton.

Mike took a drag of the cigarette. There was no reason to mention the Japanese guy, he thought. What would he say; the new assistant walked on stage and vanished? Disappeared into a giant circle of moths? It would just become another complication in an already inexplicable story.

'What about Tadashi Finjoto?' asked Carlton. He knew way more than he was letting on.

Mike smoked, thinking how best to reply. He was sure that if he wanted to the agent could easily have them all locked away, or worse, arrange for their sudden disappearance.

'The new guy? Right. I'd forgotten about him.' Mike smiled. 'He's not involved in the conference. He's just a spectator.'

'We need to talk to him too, Michael. Do you know where he is?'

'I don't.'

'Was he in the auditorium when the incident happened?'

They caught each other's eye and both knew the answer.

'I believe he was.'

'Was he injured during the incident?'

'I have no idea.'

'Do you know where Mr Finjoto is now?'

'You wouldn't believe me.'

'I'll believe anything right now.'

Mike regretted not being fully co-operative. The truth was going to come out, one way or another. He felt the need to try and salvage his reputation, and clean his already tarnished slate. He decided to change tack. He would tell them everything.

'Tadashi disappeared.'

'You mean he escaped the auditorium?'

'No. He disappeared, into a spinning circle of moths.'

Carlton glanced at the cassette machine. 'You realise that everything you say is on the record, Michael? You're a prime suspect in what could be the largest domestic homicide investigation in American history.'

'That's exactly what I saw.'

'And was this trick part of Van Peterson's stage show?'

'If it was, I wasn't informed.'

Carlton checked his watch. He was running out of time. 'I read an article about the spiritual science seminar in New York. An attendee described hearing a voice. Did you hear something similar today?'

Why was he asking, thought Mike, when he was in the room? They had all heard it. Carlton was going to deny that he was even there. That much was clear. 'The voice,' he paused, remembering the terrifying sound, 'was it really coming from Lori?' He exhaled smoke and regretted asking the question.

Both were silent, reflecting on the day.

'I think that whatever happened is just further evidence that Van Peterson is a psychopath and that we need to shut him down,' Carlton eventually said. He clicked the stop button on the cassette tape machine.

Mike finished his cigarette and crushed it underfoot.

24

'The needle. Lethal injection. Your papa is going to be sentenced to the death penalty, Miss Clarkson,' insisted Pulaski. 'It's considered humane. The guilty don't soil themselves at the moment of death.' He felt a little sick as he described the method but was clearly trying to provoke her. 'The government are actively searching for excuses to use it these days, and he's just handed the Supreme Court a case to be made an example of. If you don't co-operate,' he leaned in, attempting to hammer the final nail in the coffin, 'you will be responsible for the most lethal force of justice.'

Sarah was having none of it. 'You have no right to make accusations without an investigation.'

'And what do you think I'm doing now?'

'You're harassing me. I demand representation. I demand to see my colleagues, and I demand that the rest of this conversation takes place in a transparent and open environment where your behaviour can be monitored and regulated. That's what I call an investigation.' She sat back. She knew she was right. This wasn't a case for the Las Vegas Metropolitan Police Department. What had happened was way beyond the realms of a domestic investigation. These people weren't capable of even beginning to understand it.

'You aren't in a position to talk about rights, Miss Clarkson.'

She wasn't listening. She was lost in the memory of the auditorium event.

'People have been murdered,' he continued. 'We need to know what happened, for their families, for their children – for America.'

Sarah looked at him, blankly. She hadn't slept. She didn't feel tired. The adrenaline hit of the past twenty-four hours had been an injection directly into her soul. She had never felt so alive.

'I need to see Lori Carter. She will still be…' she chose her words carefully, 'unstable… at this time. We need to monitor her vitals. Dr Jones needs to be constantly at her side. Where is she? And where's Dr Jones?'

'She's in the hospital. He's in the room next door being interviewed by my colleague.'

'Is anyone with her?'

'She has medical professionals in attendance.'

'Do they know what she's been through?'

The inspector lost his patience. 'She's safe. Now please, I'll ask you again, stop wasting my time and tell me what the hell happened?'

'I need to speak to my father. We have to prepare her for any repercussions.'

'This event has resulted in the deaths of over a hundred people, Miss Clarkson.'

She knew that he was just another suit in the way of progress. He was out of his league. 'Then you haven't been listening,' she explained slowly, 'because they're not dead.'

The inspector sighed heavily. 'You are on very unstable ground here.'

'And your accusations are invalid without investigation.'

He was becoming increasingly annoyed by her defiance, convinced that she was suffering from some kind of emotional trauma, or worse, under the influence of one of Van Peterson's psychotropics, causing her to make wild and deluded judgements.

'There is a vital aspect that we rely on before any accusations can be made, and I have witnessed that to my satisfaction,' he explained. 'Evidence, Miss Clarkson.' He threw a series of black and white security photographs on the table. The scaled up images showed twisted limbs and torn bodies. 'Brutal, fucking, evidence. The unavoidable truth.' He threw down more pictures, piling them on top of each other, making a point of calculating the volume of the fatalities. He took one at random, checked that it was suitably horrific, and held it up to her. 'This is all I need. This is the proof that will take your little circus down. These images are undeniable. Security stills from the auditorium. The whole thing was captured, right there in black and white. This is what I call complete, unmitigated, and absolute evidence.' He threw down the last image.

Sarah looked at the picture. It was over exposed. A web of veins was caught up close to the camera. They curved in the shape of a fragile wing, delicate lines branching out, like the wings of a moth. He picked it up and studied it. In the background, heart-shaped wings were twisting across the stage. In the middle of the blurred picture was a man, standing in what seemed to be a cloud of swirling moths. It was Tadashi. She began sobbing, uncontrollably.

The cell door opened and Carlton walked in.

'What the hell are you doing, Inspector? Why is she crying? This is not the way to conduct an investigation.'

The inspector held up a picture, trying to justify Sarah's emotional state.

'I think you've done enough for today, don't you?' said Carlton, brushing away the photo.

He took a final glance at Sarah, before throwing the picture back with the others and walking out of the cell.

Carlton pressed the stop button on the cassette tape machine. 'That's him, isn't it?' he asked with a sense of intimacy in his voice. 'Finjoto?'

She composed herself and nodded.

He gathered the pictures together and flicked through a few. 'Why was he on stage?'

'He climbed up from the auditorium,' she answered, softly.

'Why wasn't he attacked like everyone else?'

She smiled through tears. 'I don't know, but it's a remarkable breakthrough.'

Carlton studied the photo one more time and then tore it into pieces.

'What are you doing?'

'There's nothing in that picture. The image is blurred.'

'What?'

'It's insubstantial. Invalid, right?' He smiled.

She blinked and wiped her eyes, unsure what he meant. Was he trying to help her?

'You have no idea how deep this goes, Sarah.' He waited for her to look at him. 'I'm not with the local PD. Look, I need to understand what happened in there, or there's no way I can protect you.'

'You're trying to protect me?'

'I'm trying to protect the best interests of the Academy, and the future of your father's work.'

'How do you know the Academy?' she asked, eyeing him suspiciously, unsure if this was a technique to get her to talk.

'Provando e riprovando,' he replied.

She caught her breath.

'New York, and now Las Vegas, they won't go unnoticed on the international stage. He's exposed,' said Carlton. 'He's broken the rules. The spotlight is on him, and now we have to work together to protect his achievements.'

'You're part of the Accademia del Cimento?'

'Let's just say that I have been working with your father for a very long time. In fact, you might even say that we never stopped working together. We can't let a little incident like this get in the way of progress now, can we, Sarah?'

She was confused but relieved. 'Where's papa? Can I speak to him?'

'I'm sorry. Not yet. Right now, we have to find a story that fits,' he indicated to the pictures. 'This won't be easy to explain. The Academy will do its best to protect you.'

The door buzzed open. Pulaski was stammering, on the verge of speech but unable to say anything.

'What now?' shouted Carlton.

'The people – everyone in the auditorium,' he gasped, 'they're alive.'

25

'If I could return for just one moment I would snatch the beak from its face,' boomed Bishamon, as he struck the skies with his sword. He was unable to reach the cackling shadow that tormented them from above.

'Patience, my brother,' said Fokuro, riding his deer into focus. It sneezed and made a snorting sound. 'Our brother and sister will return to us in time and all shall be re-balanced.' He drank from a hair-covered gourd and offered it to Bishamon who took a swig and spat it skywards. Fokuro cursed at the disrespectful waste.

Hotei looked up, having been caught enjoying way too much of a good thing. He smiled apologetically and pulled the headphones from his furry ears. 'Did you say something, my brothers?'

The deer tottered in a full circle and let out a questioning snort.

'For how much longer must we wait?' asked Bishamon.

'I have sent electronic messages,' Hotei announced. 'Both a warning and an invitation. They cannot be ignored. Fear not. Soon, the mortal fog will clear from their minds.'

'With respect,' grumbled Jurojin, 'even when the fog clears, the lost are not always facing in the right direction.' He waved his iron crutch in all directions to illustrate the point.

'Yes, yes, very clever,' mumbled Imperial uncle, Daikoku. He swung his Jade crystal tablet from side to side, calming a conversation that was unlikely to end well.

'I was simply making an observation,' coughed Jurojin, choking on the essence.

'And I thank you for it,' replied Daikoku, firmly.

Jurojin spat on the ground and took a swig from his medicine gourd.

'Patience, please, my immortal family,' begged Hotei. He twisted the headphone wires around his fingers. 'This century is very different to that of the Tang Dynasty. There are too many distractions. I simply require more time to study their mortal ways and to make the cosmic connection.'

'I'm sure you do,' mumbled Benten. 'I can smell it on you.'

Hotei sent a scolding look at the figure hidden underneath a shawl.

Despite harbouring an immortal concept of time, which meant that Time itself held absolutely no meaning at all, the ancient beings were beginning to give up hope that their lost brother and sister would ever return. They had suffered a terrible tragedy that neither of them really wanted to talk about. Idle hands led to harsh words, and they were getting on each other's nerves.

'Hotei?' asked Bishamon. 'Where did you get that magic music device?'

'From Izanagi, of course, with a little help from my spirit animal assistants.' He laughed to himself. 'With A Little Help From My Friends. I do like that one.'

The immortals were blank faced.

147

Bishamon stroked his beard with a sly grin. 'Will you permit a brother to sample the mortal toy that you have such love for?'

Hotei reluctantly passed over the iPod and showed him how to make it work.

Fokuro rode forward to command the attention of his colleagues. His deer made an authoritative coughing sound. 'Enough of these mortal distractions. I have a suggestion.' He spoke boldly and slowly. 'What if all of us were to traverse to the mortal plane in search of them?'

The immortals began to mumble and pretend to be distracted.

The deer trotted in a three-sixty degree circle. It was a routine that Fokuro performed to get the complete and undivided attention of his family. As he passed, he tried to catch the eye of each of them individually. All except Bishamon, who was dancing to The Beatles.

'You know full well that we will become trapped,' gurgled Jurojin, 'just as the reviver of the dead and our immortal sister?'

'Are we not already trapped here in the space between life and death?

'Perhaps you should offer yourself up for sacrifice if you feel so strongly about it, Fokuro?' accused Jurojin. He hacked up a green globule to display his outrage.

Fokuro's deer spun in a circle and raised its tail to show its anus. He coughed up phlegm and spat it at the deer's hooves. It brayed in disgust.

'Stop fighting you two,' Fokuro scolded. 'I am merely suggesting that this is a communal matter and that we should all do our best to help.'

'You've always thought that you're better than the rest of us, haven't you?' spluttered Jurojin. 'Up on your silly little deer.'

'Calm, please, my brothers,' interrupted Imperial uncle Daikoku. 'Our proximity to the mortal plane is affecting our judgement. Are we not clearly displaying mortal emotion right now? This is not the behaviour of an immortal being. I suggest a drink to calm our nerves while we consult with our brother, Hotei. He has spent more time in the proximity of their realm than any of us.' He waved his shawl like the entrance curtain to a theatre show. 'Brother, enlighten us, if you please?

The portly old man poured himself a whisky and affected a world-weary look. 'There are some mortal pleasures that are a joy to behold. Some of the things I have seen. The naked female form astride le petit cheval et Pigalle a' Paris.' He smiled, knowingly. 'The slashing jaw of the Carcharodon Carcharias Great White shark off the shores of the Gansaabi.' He shivered. 'The skilful twist of the maguro kiri bōchō into the bloody flesh of the Thunnus Albacares at the magnificent Tsukiji Fish Market.' He smacked his lips. 'Yes, the things I have seen — poverty, brutal violence, animal cruelty, avarice, vice, jealously, murder...' He held up his whisky glass to make a point. 'Addiction.' He took a mournful swallow. 'My dues are paid, my family,' he said, and then refilled his glass. 'I have been observing our fallen brother and sister since the birdman stole its way into Hōrai and we became displaced. On occasion it has been close, I can tell you, but I have always returned to the neutral safety of the space between life and death before the sacrifice had opportunity to take my immortal soul. For our brother and sister, I fear it is not so simple. They have already overstayed their time. Their suffering will have begun. You do not wish to remain in that place. None of you do.'

Jurojin stroked his beard in contemplation. 'I could not have put that better myself.' He bowed, respectfully. 'Thank you for your wisdom.'

Fokuro nudged his deer forward and invited Hotei to tell him more about the naked women on little horses.

'Can we not just leave them there and return home by ourselves? asked Benten, wrapping a shawl around her frail body.

Jurojin hacked a cough as gracefully as an immortal could. 'We cannot claim our mountain island as six and you know this. Only together are we strong enough to withstand the Protogenoi.'

Benten made a little cough. 'And what will become of them if they do not return?'

'Why so curious, sister, brother?' asked Hotei, swirling an ice cube in his crystal tumbler.

Benten noticed a touch of mortal arrogance in his gaze.

'You know what they say about curiosity and cats in the mortal world?' said Hotei.

'I am not a cat.'

'You may just reincarnate as one?'

Benten considered life as a cat. Perhaps the sacrifice wasn't so terrible after all?

'They will know when they have overstayed their time on mortal soil,' said Hotei as he crunched on the ice cube, 'because they will feel the pain of a thousand years of suffering. A mortal will die, and on their death they will swim peacefully in the sea of souls surrounding Mt. Hōrai. As an immortal that becomes mortal, upon death they will be born again, only to repeat the cycle of life and death for an eternity. With each new birth their soul will shrivel. Mortal life will become hollow. Nirvana will never be attainable.'

Benten pulled the shawl tighter and retreated.

Daikoku stopped swinging his tablet.

Jurojin hacked up a green globule of phlegm, as was his solution to almost everything. He drank from his medicine gourd and swilled the sweet wine in his cheeks.

The immortals were thoughtful, all except Bishamon, who hadn't heard anything. Headphones were still firmly placed in his ears as he performed a ramshackle dance around his sword to Twist and Shout.

Daikoku closed his eyes. 'Do not consider the matter any further. They will hear our call. We must wait.' He placed his palms together in prayer and within moments was sleeping as the seashore.

The immortals did the same and they all began levitating exactly two foot above the ground, meditating in a circle, trying to ignore the hiss of iPod headphones.

Benten opened an eye. 'For how long do we wait?'

Imperial uncle Daikoku twitched and his head jolted. He wiped drool from his chin. 'For as long as it takes,' he replied, majestically, legs folded in the lotus position.

Bishamon shouted enthusiastically over the rock and roll din, startling the immortals from their tranquil meditation. 'Izanagi must confront the hell hag Shozuka-no-baba, for only she can restore him to immortality.' He slammed his sword into the ground where it stuck fast. He grinned, shaking his hips, as he danced around it in a circle. They stared, grumpy, and chose to ignore him.

'I wish he would stop throwing that thing around,' spluttered Fokuro.

Bishamon turned off the iPod. He pulled the sword from the ground and held it aggressively. The immortals backed away. 'When the day comes, I will stare the water witch in the eye and tell her to stand back and allow Bishamon to pass,' he roared. 'I shall confront the Ōkami snake and slice its fat belly, draining it of all bodily fluids. I will squeeze its gall bladder until it is bone dry, and then we shall revive ourselves on snake blood wine.' He laughed, heartily. The music had gone to his head and he was reeling from the experience. He'd enjoyed way more than his fair share of The Beatles. 'Our immortal brother and sister must return to share with us the sweet taste of the mists of Hōrai; to stir their feet in the sea of souls and drink in the knowledge of the quintillions,' he announced. The headphone wires had become tangled around his sword. He flung it into the ground and the deer tottered to a petrified halt. It raised its tail to piss on the floor.

'Now look what you've done.' Fokuro patted it on the head. 'It's ok, dear.' It trembled, eyes fixed on the sword. 'She doesn't approve of violence.'

Benten pulled the shawl up to her face so that only her eyes were peeking through. 'What if they do not hear us?'

The immortals didn't want to consider the answer and rustled their robes, quaffing deeply from their wine gourds.

Imperial uncle Daikoku approached the deer and fed it mouldy fruit while stroking its nose. 'It would certainly be good to have some fresh fruit once more, that's for certain. They will answer our call. Do you not agree, Hotei?'

But Hotei was no longer in the space between life and death; he had picked up the iPod, gathered together the wires, and with a last look to his immortal family, placed headphones in bristling ears, pressed play, and prepared to traverse to the mortal plane and continue his efforts to bring back the fallen ones, and perhaps also top up on a little more of his favourite single malt.

He was long overdue a visit to his spirit animals; the Earth-bound helpers that he had tasked with the mission of finding the lost immortals.

26

If you withdrew the inconvenience of eating and sleeping, then Zack and Wiki had little else to ground them in what you might call – the real world.

They spent so much time online that they may as well have been avatars. They spent so much time together that talking to each other was just like talking out loud. They spent so much time staring at screens that they regularly forgot what each other looked like.

Their days consisted of internet trolling, blog scouring, eBay scavenging and battling through the Atari Shock Universe. Occasionally, a customer would find their way into the Amped Up Comic Book Store, but they would mostly be browsing and rarely buying. On the odd occasion when someone wanted to pay money for something that the store held on its precious shelves, the customer would be cold-shouldered into using the online shop. The atmosphere, therefore, was more like a chaotic library than a comic book store; a members' club for the self-detached.

Zack sat on the counter, throwing popcorn in the air and trying to catch it in his mouth. He was the kind of guy that would hi-five himself, more of a flatmate than a business partner. 'Frickin' game space attack. That was intense. Like a hostage situation.'

'It's a never ending battle against evil, dude,' said Wiki.

'A legend,' he grabbed the USB from Wiki's PC. 'That's what we have here. A legend in a box.'

'A simple trap bait programme,' replied Wiki, proudly. 'And don't drop that.'

He shifted the USB to his other hand and pretended to drop it. 'What's that then?' Popcorn bounced off his face as he threw it haphazardly in the air.

'A pugmark...'

Zack had never heard the word before but he didn't question it.

Wiki held his breath momentarily, waiting for some sort of reaction, and then continued in an exhale. 'A footprint, a paw print, the T-Rex stamp of approval in the thick mud of prehistoric glue. I presented The Immortal with an alternative to his desperate situation, and he took the bait, right into temporary storage on this USB. Thus, fulfilling our duty to the man upstairs, and buying us safe passage to higher plains.'

Zack nodded, impressed. He studied the USB like it had just levelled up in his hand to become doubly awesome. 'Don't look into the trap, Ray,' he stuttered, tossing a piece of popcorn that stuck to his +10 wisdom baseball cap, and he accidentally dropped the USB into the popcorn bag.

'Don't mess with immortal power, man,' scolded Wiki. 'Give it here.'

Zack shook the USB and licked off the sugar.

'Never lick a USB. You don't know where it's been.' Wiki wrestled it back, wiped it on his trouser leg, and put it safely in his pocket. He swigged the last dregs of Hype energy drink and threw it in the bin with the others.

Zack threw another piece of popcorn, which hit their only browsing customer. He uttered an apology and stuffed a handful straight into his mouth. The customer picked up a comic book, flicked through the pages, and then put it back in the wrong place. They made a mental note of exactly where the insult had just taken place, and stared at the customer until he nudged his way out the door.

'Get up to anything last night?' asked Zack.

Wiki shrugged. 'Modded my avatar to have hair like Goku, and a gun that fires giant Mario 'shrooms.'

'Seriously?'

'No, man. I was on Atari Shock like the rest of the fucking world.'

'Oh. I was looking forward to playing that mod.'

The customer eventually got the hint. 'Are you closing?' he asked, slightly confused.

Wiki smiled. 'Take your time,' he replied with an air of aggression, unintentionally exposing his teeth.

The customer put a magazine in the wrong place and immediately scuttled out.

'Don't forget to buy online,' shouted Zack after him, as he picked a piece of popcorn from his hair. The door slammed shut, signalling the conclusion to another busy day at the Amp.

Wiki double-checked that no one else was in the store, even though there had clearly been only one customer all afternoon. He flicked a bolt across the door and turned a little sign which showed a fist giving the middle finger and had the words "Nerd Cave Closed" on it.

They tidied up, putting comics back where they belonged, turning them to face the right way, and generally making sure that everything was exactly how they liked it.

'Evil top five?' challenged Wiki.

'At five. Coat hangers.'

'I hate coat hangers. Ok. Number four, hoovers.'

'Hoovers are pure evil. Number three. Saturated fat,' said Zack. 'And I love it.' He crumpled the empty popcorn bag.

'Still in at number two, any creature that moults, which makes cats cute and evil at the same time,' said Wiki.

'Sounds about right.'

'Ultimate evil, number one?' asked Wiki. They looked at each other. Neither of them wanted to say the name but they both knew exactly how this game had to end. 'After three,' they agreed.

'Three.'

Both said the name simultaneously — 'Tengu.'

The door swung open and slammed shut by itself. They looked to each other and winced.

'That was so frickin' Beetlejuice,' whispered Zack, as he felt the fear creep across his shoulders.

'Play it cool,' explained Wiki. 'No sudden moves and we'll be ok.' He nonchalantly checked the thief forums and tried to appear busy.

A customer IGM popped up.

'We got any more Green Lantern power rings in the inventory? Another bold member of the continuum's batteries have run out.'

"In brightest day. In blackest night," quoted Zack as he carefully stepped away from the desk, checking the walls around him as he did so. 'For the most powerful weapon in the Universe, they sure have a short shelf life these power rings.' He slid into the back room, quietly relieved that he'd been given an excuse to hide.

There was no one in the store but Wiki felt compelled to call out. 'Hello?'

The air felt warmer. The feed was spooling fresh information. The PC screen flickered. There was a fizz of electronics as the information jumbled and the programme quit and rebooted. Code spooled on screen at speed. He'd seen this before, the same night as Lars, and he knew exactly what it meant. He tapped at a sequence of keys. The PC wasn't responding. He closed a pop up and a pile of comic books fell to the floor.

'If you want to browse, that's fine,' he called out to the empty store. 'Just show yourself and browse, huh?'

Something scraped along a series of posters, causing them to tear on the wall where they hung. 'Zack? Is that you, dude?' No reply. 'I think we're going to need those power rings.'

The store was increasing in temperature. "Beware my power, Green Lantern's light!" shouted Zack as he bounced back into the room.

Wiki screamed and fell off his chair. 'You scared the shit out of me.'

A jugular animal roar filled the store. Posters burst into flames and peeled up the wall. In a moment of panic, Zack took off his baseball cap and threw it in the direction of the noise. It spun at the collection of comic books and posters but before it got even half way across the store it burst into flames. A pile of comics became ash. A table of collectables collapsed and burned.

'Whoa,' they shouted, jumping back, giving each other hand signals that they didn't really understand.

'Hit the fire alarm!' shouted Wiki.

Zack threw himself at the wall then realised that they didn't have a fire alarm. Beneath the churn of flames, a deep sound of breathing was becoming louder as it approached. Zack reached under the counter for a fire extinguisher. Black shadows lined the walls, casting jigsaw puzzle shapes on the floor.

'Did you get it?' shouted Wiki.

'The power ring?'

'No dick, the emergency box!'

'I got both.' Zack kicked a cardboard box over to him. The emergency box contained all manner of items that had been collected over the years. It was filled to the brim with the necessary weapons required to defeat a lost list of mystical threats; magic potions, trinkets and toys, snake skin, skulls and seeds.

Another pile of books fell, this time closer, and burst into flames. They screamed like schoolgirls as the shadow of a large figure reared up.

Zack tensed, raised the fire extinguisher, and stepped in line with the approaching chaos.

Wiki threw himself behind the counter. 'Stay back,' he shouted. He grabbed an item from the magic box and threw a handful of tiny yellow seeds across the floor. 'Pick them up, intruder,' he challenged.

The shadowy figure hesitated.

'Can't resist, huh?' taunted Wiki.

The figure emerged from the darkness, muttering obscenities, and bent down to pick up the seeds.

'See,' he cried, 'you have to pick up the mustard seed.'

There was a bump and another item rolled across the floor, grabbed quickly from the box.

'Is that garlic?' asked the shadow. 'Did you just throw a clove of garlic at me?'

'Stay back, daemon!' shouted Wiki.

'You're making me look silly, boys,' he said, eyes bloodshot and tired.

Zack panicked and fell to the floor. He crawled on his hands and knees, joining Wiki under the counter.

'Herushingu. Young King Ours. Ninety-seven. Be gone, vampyre.'

'What has this place done to you? Have you boys been imbibing of the gourd?' asked the portly old man, raising his palms in disbelief. His dark shadow was being cast through the flames. 'I'm sorry about all the fire and drama. It's an unfortunate effect of cosmic travel. Look, I've brought Izanagi's iPod back. I was wondering if you could fill it with Rage Against The Machine?' Hotei spotted the popcorn bag. 'Ooh, sweet mortal pleasure. Oh, you've finished the packet?' He smacked his lips as he spotted a single piece stuck to a Jaws poster and plucked it like a berry. 'Sugar. Glorious thing. Got any booze?'

Zack grabbed a wooden chair and smashed it hard onto the old man's head. 'Fuck you, Tengu.'

The old man crumpled to the floor.

'What the hell? You weren't meant to kill him,' shouted Wiki. He leaped out from behind the counter and started squirting a water bottle in a circle around the old man. 'Virgin holy water. I got my twelve-year-old niece to say a prayer into it.'

Zack held up his hand and they slapped a bold high five. He cautiously kicked the old man onto his back.

Hotei was conscious but his eyes were closed. 'I will never get used to this,' he groaned. 'Pain, blood, sweat and tears, such useless frailties.' This was the part of mortality that he hated.

Wiki grabbed the rest of the chair and slammed it against the wall, breaking it into pieces. He handed Zack a leg and they approached, holding the sharp spikes of wood. 'Wait. Is this chair made of aspen?' he asked.

'Huh?'

'It's meant to be aspen. You need an aspen stake to kill a vampire.'

Zack shrugged.

They were no Buffy, but the old man was no Christopher Lee. It would have to do.

Wiki decided to say something dramatic at the appropriate moment, right before ridding the world of the evil they had unleashed. He wondered if the old man would explode when he thrust the stake into his heart. 'Your vampyre hoard will not rise, Tengu!' he declared, as he plunged the broken chair leg downward, but it didn't strike. He felt an invisible force clasp tight around his wrist. He was paralysed. He looked over to Zack who was backing away from a group standing in the shadows. Another appeared next to him, taller, built like an ageing body builder.

'Our immortal brother is not Tengu,' said Bishamon, 'and he certainly isn't a vampyre.'

Fokuro tottered forward on his deer, knocking over a stand of comic books. He apologised and pulled out a small piece of rotten fruit and offered it to the animal. The deer made a snorting noise as it crunched.

Hotei looked up from the floor. 'You came? Are you not fearful of the sacrifice?'

The ancient immortals shuffled, coyly. It was a communal matter. They had all decided to help. The immortal group gathered in a circle; all shapes, all sizes, one sitting on a tiny deer, in the mortal space occupied by the Amped Up Comic Book Store.

'Hush,' whispered Daikoku, and Zack and Wiki stood peacefully in a dream-like trance. The panic melted away and they dropped the wooden spikes.

'They were expecting Tengu,' Benten said, softly. 'I fear we may be too late?'

'Do you have the immortal?' asked Bishamon.

Wiki held the USB above his head, just like he'd seen in a hostage video on YouTube.

Bishamon took it and gave it a sniff. It was sweet and sugary. He stuck out his tongue.

'Never put a USB in your mouth,' said Zack.

Wiki nudged him and raised his arms back in the air. They retreated and hid behind the counter.

Bishamon gave it a lick anyway.

'Release these spirit animals,' said Hotei. 'They have seen enough.'

Daikoku performed a ceremonious dance and waved his crystal tablet near Zack and Wiki, who were surrounded by a cloud of Jade essence. Moments later, the game playing, comic store owning, pop culture hoarding individuals, were transformed back to their original state, and two tiny lizards crawled up the table counter leg.

They sat on the edge of the PC screen and blinked, twitching their heads, intermittently lifting their legs, enjoying the heat of the computer monitor on their toes. They stuck out their tongues to clean their tiny, lime green faces. They were geckoes; spirit animals of the afterlife, servants of the immortal mountain island, Hōrai, and their work on the mortal plane was done.

'I will take care of these fellas,' said Hotei as he collected the creatures and dropped them into the pocket of his dirty shawl.

'So,' exclaimed Bishamon, 'this is mortality?' He shrugged, unimpressed. 'I thought it would be bigger.'

27

The eradication of The Immortal had sent shock waves through the online community. Someone had instigated a calculated attack on the seemingly unstoppable avatar. The thief forums were ecstatic.

Stu had immediately pinged Lars a text, demanding at least five pints to celebrate.

The Yorkshire Grey was an old school boozer, the kind of place that took pride in not having opened a window since the smoking ban. It strictly maintained the permanent scent of stale beer, body odour and the gents. It was a city pub, so it always had a strange sort of crowd; drifters and loners, single pint suppers, groups of overexcited women who would drink a large glass of white wine very quickly while checking their phones, and then all rush out at once into a waiting taxi. It was anti-Cheers; the place where no one wanted to know your name, and if they did get to know it, then you were in trouble.

As the official post-Pill debrief pub, Lars felt safe. This was home when he wasn't online in his cupboard room at the top of the stairs, or behind his desk at work. He checked his phone. His inventory was at zero. The last twelve hours had been crushing.

They were two pints down in forty-five minutes. Pretty soon it would be necessary to break out the crisps to soak up the booze.

'Is there more evil?' Lars asked, taking a thoughtful swig of beer.

'What kind of thing is that to say, mate?' laughed Stu.

He shrugged. He wasn't sure what he meant. He couldn't deny that if he really thought about it, it felt like the Universe was ganging up on him. 'More evil, just floating around picking on innocent people. One minute, they're perfectly happy, avoiding confrontation, keeping their heads down and the next it's all changed. Changed without a moment's notice.'

Stu was trying to hide a smirk.

'Why can't things just be left the way they are?' Lars scrunched his shoulders. He wasn't sure why he'd said it but he felt that it was something that he genuinely knew. 'There is more evil. Something has to be done.'

Stu stared at the fruit machine and wondered if he should get Prawn Cocktail or Cheese and Onion crisps first. 'Look, mate,' he sighed, 'I've been meaning to ask because, well, you've been acting a bit weird lately.'

Lars took a gulp of beer. So, this was how it was going to go down? Claire had sent in reinforcements. She was about to use the secret weapon – her brother.

'Is everything ok, mate?'

Boom. There it was. A direct hit.

Lars watched the lights on the Deal Or No Deal fruit machine flicker across Noel Edmonds' smug face.

'Claire's not happy.'

Boom. A second shot took out his failsafe shields.

'We're both worried about you.'

Slam. He was vulnerable, exposed, and with less than half a pint.

'She asked me to have a word about you staying up all night? You're not playing Atari Shock otherwise I'd see you logged in. So, what are you doing? If there's some shit going on that you need to tell me about, it's ok. I know you don't have anyone to talk to apart from Claire, and that's fine, sometimes you need to talk to someone else, right?'

He swallowed. His throat felt dry. 'You're her brother. Five seconds after I say anything to you, you'll have pinged off a text to her. She always knows exactly where I am because she knows that when I'm not with her, I'm with you.'

Stu was smiling, nodding slowly, listening with an air of judgement. 'Sure, mate,' he nodded. 'You tell me?'

'You think I'm hiding something?'

'I know you are.'

Lars laughed and felt strangely uncomfortable. He glanced around the pub, aware of a strange group of tourists at the bar. They ducked their heads when he looked in their direction. There was something different about them. They were wearing heavy raincoats and sprouting unconventional beards. A man shifted behind a raised newspaper. One knocked back his drink and ordered another, eyes obviously averted, like he'd just remembered something of great importance. The lights on the fruit machine spun in a hypnotic circular sequence.

Lars felt like he was being watched. 'We need more drinks,' he said and stood up.

The group flinched as he approached the bar; caught midway between going somewhere and trying to stay as still as possible to avoid being seen.

Perhaps it was time to confess, Lars thought. What was there to lose? Stu, in his usual confrontational way, was trying to get him to say something. He could be either honest and fight back with sincerity, or he could make a tactical diversion until he worked out his game plan. Both options seemed pointless. He at least had to choose one.

He ordered two more pints and noticed a pungent smell, unfamiliar to the usual sticky carpet residue of the Yorkshire Grey. Leaning at the bar, right next to him, was its origin. He had a long beard and a thick winter coat with strange patterns that looked like Japanese symbols. He smiled at the old man, holding his breath as he did so. 'Evening.' The old man moved away without saying anything.

Lars handed over a pint and braced himself for battle. 'Go on then, Stu. What am I hiding?'

'Don't try and deny it.' Stu smiled, smugly.

'Deny what?' Lars hesitated and then wished that he hadn't.

'I fucking knew it. I knew you were sleeping with her.'

What was he being accused of? He wasn't sleeping with anyone. In fact, he wasn't even sleeping. The realisation hit him. He couldn't remember the last time that he'd had a full night's sleep. Gaming insomnia had been an excuse to stay up late, and when he realised that he'd pushed it through until dawn, he just stayed up. It was a pattern that he'd found himself in on a regular basis, and it was one that worked. 'What the hell are you talking about, Stu?'

'You're shagging Julia Miller.'

'I am not!'

Stu was certain that he'd called it right. Lars had been acting strangely for weeks. Julia wasn't responding to his flirty advances, so the conclusion was obvious. 'She's been playing it cool with me, because she's sleeping with you.'

'Perhaps she just doesn't like you?' Lars scoffed.

'So you deny it?'

'Of course I bloody deny it.' He took a deep breath. 'Ok then. You want to know my secret?'

Stu smiled in anticipation.

'I am The Immortal.' Lars held his breath.

He didn't react immediately and instead took a gulp of his pint, mulling the taste over in his mouth before pulling the kind of face that said fuck you and tell me more, simultaneously.

There was a commotion at the bar. One of the old tourists seemed agitated. He was drunk, making a scene, unable to stand straight.

Jono, the landlord, was trying to calm him.

'Why the fuck didn't you tell me?' exploded Stu. 'We could have got sponsorship, endorsements. That's how these fuckers make money these days. Another pair of pints please, Jono,' he demanded. 'One for me, and one for my immortal friend here.'

Jono was struggling to get the tourist to sit still. Lars looked over, catching the old man's eye. The spiralling sensation lurched deep in the pit of his stomach as a wave of recognition shivered through him. He felt uncomfortably nauseous.

'Seeing as we're confessing, I'm GreySkull,' Stu said, with a matter-of-fact, shit-eating grin.

Wipeout. Total annihilation. Things had just gone nuclear. GreySkull; the cheap trick player with dirty tactics was sitting right next to him, and it was bloody Stuart. The betrayal hit him harder than the time Claire had reset their home broadband mid-game just to get his attention.

'You launched the critical suicide game space attack?'

Stu smiled, proudly.

'You cock. Your gameplay is sloppy and you cost me my fucking avatar!'

'I kicked your ass and you can't handle it. Here's to you, oh, immortal one.' Stu laughed. 'I was going to go for a cigarette but fuck it, I might smoke a tab right here just to keep seeing that stupid look on your face.' He placed a cigarette between his lips like he'd just got the upper hand in an impending Wild West shoot out.

'You formed the super clan? Why would you do that?'

'Don't get all grumpy. I didn't know it was you. It's just a game, mate. Let's get another drink.'

Lars stood up, shaking the table. 'I'm not drinking with you.'

'Calm down.'

'This is serious. You don't get it?'

Stu put his arm around him, trying to comfort him, but was pushed away.

'Don't touch me. You've fucked everything,' he said, still trying to fathom the extent to which his old friend had actually fucked everything.

'I'm not sure what you're trying to do tonight,' replied Stu, 'but it's getting on my tits and it's no fun at all. Ok. I'm going to have that cigarette after all, and when I get back, I want to talk to the old Lars again. The one that's grounded in this reality. Alright, mate?' He left the pub.

Lars was feeling increasingly unwell. He stared at the multi-coloured lights on the fruit machine as they spun in a circular motion. The drink had gone to his head. Digital bleeps from the game pinged around the room. He felt a flush of warm air, a breeze from somewhere tropical, carrying with it an unusual smell; the scent of earth and burning jasmine. He could see mist, vapour drifting in a perfect circle, orbiting a mountain. Through the clouds rose the towering spire of a magnificent, golden pagoda.

Eight figures sat, plump, in order of one through to eight. They wore flowing shawls that flapped like damp flags in a breeze. Their hair twitched pure white electricity.

He could see contorted faces hidden in the fog. They seemed to recognise him and reach out, deserted, abandoned. He heard a faint, terrified cry, and could see the desperate flailing of limbs.

A black bird flew high above in a circle, a tiny spec in the storm cloud sky. It spiralled, over and over, twisting in on itself, moving faster to form a vacuum that caught the clouds in a funnel. The wind pierced louder, screaming in a million voices, with hands reaching out, petrified faces, helpless in the storm. There was a streak of lightning and an eruption of insects. Tiny white moths, sudden and suffocating, spun in a vortex. He covered his face, brushing them from his eyes, flicking them from his ears. They flew in his mouth. He choked, unable to breathe, as a tropical cyclone crushed the air, and then Stu was standing next to him with a pint.

He looked at the pub clock. Ten minutes had passed in what seemed like seconds.

'What the hell is going on?' asked Stu.

Lars was shell shocked, unsure what to say.

'She's been waiting at the restaurant for over an hour, mate. She's really upset with you.'

Lars wiped his eyes. He was sweating. Had anyone seen anything? The towering pagoda? The cloud of moths? He stared at the fruit machine. Noel Edmonds grinned back.

'I think you'd better go,' suggested Stu, trying to jump-start his friend into action.

His silence said it all. She had entirely slipped his mind. Something had shifted and taken Claire with it. It was like she no longer existed. He caught the eye of the drunken old man, who sat up on a stool and raised a tumbler in his direction.

'Something just happened, Stu.'

'No shit?'

'I think I'm meant to be doing something about it?'

Stu blinked, unimpressed. 'If only you knew how pathetic that sounded, mate.'

Lars coughed and retched, right on cue.

'Aw, not here!' Stu shouted. 'Use the bogs for Christ's sake! What's Jono gonna think?'

He composed himself. 'I'm fine.' He closed his eyes, trying to stay calm. 'I gotta go.' Lars pushed on the table and his pint spilled to the floor as he projectile vomited on Stu.

'Oi,' shouted Jono. 'That's it.' He ran around the bar and grabbed them roughly by the arms. 'I've had enough of you two. Out!'

Stu was defensive and pushed back. 'We're having a family heart to heart.'

'You're drunk. Get out, or I'll make you get out.'

'You can't make us do anything,' shouted Stu. 'He's The Immortal.'

'Let's go,' said Lars, pulling Stu by the arm.

'One thing at a time, people. I haven't finished with you yet.' He staggered to the door.

Jono grabbed them both by the neck and pushed them violently outside. Stu fell through the pub doors and tripped a few paces forward, stumbling across the pavement and falling to his knees on the road, just as a passing car clipped him on the side of the head.

The thud was audible, heavy and hollow at the same time. Stu fell in a twisted heap and was motionless on the concrete.

The car screeched to a halt, then seconds later, sped away down the rain-smeared street.

28

M. V. P T R N'S 10ᵗʰ SP R T AL SC   CE CON   ENCE.

There was no power to the auditorium. The electricity box had fused during the event. Streaks of police flashlights buzzed the chairs. There was no sign of animal life or of a struggle of any kind. The room had been declared safe.

The audience members were back in their seats, talking amongst themselves, exchanging comments, expectantly waiting for the show to begin.

'What in Jesus' name do we do now?' cursed Pulaski. 'We've got a room full of people.'

His colleagues stared at each other.

'Well, they shouldn't be here. We've declared them all dead!' How was he going to explain this? He'd issued a statement of mass manslaughter. Now, here they were, laughing to each other and without a scratch on them. He lit a cigarette and considered the consolation in the piles of paperwork that had been saved. Maybe he could bury it? What happens in Vegas, stays. No one need mention it ever again.

Tadashi was standing on stage, dazed by the buzz of excited conversation. A light shone in his face and he waved it away, covering his eyes. The police officer lowered his torch, and then became suspicious and shone it in his face again.

The professor approached. 'What did I tell you? A classic kami-kakushi,' he laughed proudly, patting Pulaski on the back. The inspector grunted. He turned off his flashlight and smoked in darkness.

'We need to talk to each of them individually,' Van Peterson said to Sarah, 'document what they saw, where they've been? This is unprecedented. There's never been an event on this scale before. Isn't this exciting? Do you have the guest list, dear?'

'Of course,' she smiled.

'We need to verify the identity of every single one of them,' he demanded, taking control.

The police officers stood around like there was a bad smell in the room.

Sarah was feeling confident. They had done nothing wrong. Proof of that was right in front of them; living and breathing, shouting and laughing, trying to get someone's attention to place an order for a round of beers. Was it an elaborate hoax? A disappearing trick? She wasn't sure, but the accusations against them had just been nullified. The audience members seemed oblivious to what had happened.

'What an impressive spectacle,' laughed Carlton. He shone a large emergency lantern around the immediate area, trying not to appear overly cautious. He held it high in the air, like an ancient explorer. 'Las Vegas has never seen anything quite like it.' He shook the professor by the hand and touched Sarah on the shoulder, playing the congratulations out as best he could in front of the surrounding police officers. 'It's going to be a hit. Just give us some warning next time, so our police friends don't get carried away again, right guys?' He laughed. 'Can we please get some lights on? Surely you fellas are capable of that?' he mocked. He turned to the investigative team who were hovering around, wondering what the hell had just happened, and if someone had really wasted their day.

Moments later, the auditorium lights flickered on. The audience members cheered.

Mike was still handcuffed, presumed the most likely perpetrator of the event. The Vegas PD were determined to accuse someone of something, even if it was just making them miss their lunch. He caught Sarah's eye and winked. He seemed unshaken. She was relieved. The hours since the incident had flashed by. Their wedding bed and the room service club sandwiches, however, now seemed like a distant memory.

'Why is this man cuffed? The investigation is over,' Carlton said boldly. 'I recommend that we give them a warning. Issue some fines for wasting valuable police time. A stunt is a stunt. We live in a civilised society, gentlemen. Let's remember this wonderful event for what it was, just a fantastic and incredible illusion.' He indicated to the cuffs.

'So, this was all just some kind of crazy show then?' Pulaski asked, rubbing his eyes. 'We need to ask more questions.'

Carlton was evasive. 'Allow me, Inspector.' He turned to Van Peterson. 'Tell me, how many actors did you need to pull off the trick? Where did you hide everyone? Did you use trap doors?'

All eyes turned to the professor. 'A magician never gives away his secrets,' he answered.

There was a whistle from the stalls. One of the audience members raised their hands and made a cup-like gesture. He counted off the people around him and held up six fingers. Carlton acknowledged the order and smiled. The audience member went back to happily chatting away.

Pulaski was exasperated. 'This is ridiculous.'

'Here's the list,' said Sarah. 'Everyone is accounted for. They're all here. Safe and sound.'

'I want that verified by my people,' demanded the inspector. He signalled to a lieutenant who was unsure why he was still there. 'Get to it!' he ordered.

'Sir.' The lieutenant went around the audience, attempting to verify the list of names, and was promptly sent to the bar.

'Are we under investigation or not?' asked Mike, holding up his cuffs.

'You stand accused of putting on the most elaborate illusion that Las Vegas has ever seen,' declared Carlton.

'Well, that's that then. Now, if you'll excuse us, we need to brief our team of professionals before the next show. I apologise for taking up your valuable time, Inspector.' He smiled at Pulaski.

'Professor Van Peterson, I think it is the Las Vegas PD who should be apologising to you,' insisted Carlton.

'Oh, I wouldn't dare dream of it.'

Carlton turned to the inspector and waited.

Pulaski was stunned. 'You expect me to say sorry? After all that we've been through? This isn't over. You can't just write this off as a practical joke.'

'Oh, but we can, and we will,' said Carlton, firmly. 'Let me apologise on your behalf, Inspector. Professor Van

Peterson, you are no longer under investigation. Good luck with your future performances. I am sure that you'll be a huge success. I should remind you that all images from the security cameras are to be retained by my department. They will remain under my safe keeping. And can someone please release Dr Jones? There's really no need to keep him in those handcuffs.' Carlton ushered Pulaski towards the auditorium door. 'Allow me to speak with my colleagues at The Office,' he said, placing a firm hand on his shoulder, 'about a financial contribution to the LVPD.' Carlton smiled farewell to the group.

'I must speak with Tadashi,' announced the professor, and he immediately headed for the stage.

Tadashi was disorientated and sitting by himself. He felt an object in his pocket and uncovered a strange, glass vial. It glowed in the dim light of the auditorium. The bulb was sealed by a chunky cork, covered in what looked like green mould. A copper wire was tied around it in a mesh.

The contents were thick, organic; a combination of bright green water and heavy matter. He stared at the pulsing liquid and was drawn closer, mesmerised by what seemed to be a miniature tsunami folding over on itself.

The professor approached and Tadashi hid the vial deep in his pocket, feeling the cold glass on his palm with the radiance of the contents energising through his skin.

'My boy,' he said, holding out his arms.

Tadashi stepped back and greeted him with a bow.

Van Peterson hesitated and returned the bow. 'I have so many questions. There are many experiments that we must undertake.'

Tadashi seemed distracted.

'You did it. You performed the quantum jump.'

'It was remarkable,' he said, with a touch of sadness in his voice.

'We must re-create it, and you should take with you some kind of recording device, a cassette machine or Betamax. Is something wrong, my boy?'

Tadashi shook his head, struggling to explain what had happened. 'There were creatures, animals, shadows that followed me. I could smell them. They were not of this Earth.'

The audience members had begun trickling out of the auditorium, slowly realising that a show wasn't going to happen after all. They checked their watches, wondered how they'd lost half the day, and concluded that this was the best trip to Las Vegas, ever.

Mike and Sarah were finally alone.

'Some night, huh?' she said.

He nodded, stroking the abrasions on his wrists. 'What the hell happened?'

'The Accademia del Cimento will investigate.'

'Fuck the Academy. People died here last night, Sarah.'

'But they didn't die, did they?'

'You certainly share your old man's optimism.'

'What's that supposed to mean?'

'We've both been questioned under suspicion of mass homicide. Turns out it was all just a paranormal invisibility trick. So, everything's fine, right? Nothing to see here. Everyone back to your normal lives.'

'Are you ok?'

'No. I'm not ok. I don't know what I was thinking signing up for this mess.'

She waited for him to say more. He hesitated and looked away. 'It's fine, Mike,' she frowned. 'You know we can't get in the way of progress.'

He sighed. 'We really did just last one day?'

'I think Elvis might deserve an apology,' she smiled, as tears began to well in her eyes.

He wanted to hold her, to tell her that it was going to be ok – something was holding him back. 'Is this really the life you want?'

She looked over to her father and Tadashi. She wondered what they were talking about. 'I don't have a choice.'

'Carlton's got him marked. They know the old man's onto something.'

'That's exactly why I need to be there for him. To protect him.'

Mike shook his head. He knew that it was over. They embraced for slightly too long and then pulled themselves apart.

'See you in the next life,' he said.

She laughed, with sadness in her eyes, and walked away before he could see that she was crying.

29

The air hung thick and uncomfortable as rain filled the cold London air. There was the distant sound of a police siren. Stu was lying in a buckled heap.

The street lamps glowed brighter and appeared to dim.

Jono paced frantically up and down the pavement. He was beginning to go into shock. 'He fell, right?' he mumbled. 'Did you get the number plate?'

The more Lars looked at Stu's body, the more he swallowed back a rising sickness.

'Don't touch him. I'm calling an ambulance.' Jono ran inside.

Lars could see the shadowy silhouettes of people becoming more frantic through the frosted pub windows. The rain began to come down harder.

Time had slowed to a fraction of itself. One moment they were arguing, then they were outside. Now, Stu was dead on the dirty road.

'Stu?' he whispered. There was no acknowledgment. He didn't appear to be breathing. The spiralling sensation lurched and an idea came to him. It seemed utterly absurd but the more he thought about it, the more he realised that it was exactly what he had to do. His heart pounded. It couldn't be that simple. There was no way it would work. He took another glance at the pub windows, and now, six shadows were watching. An arm raised in cheers, holding the outline of a whisky tumbler.

Lars knelt. He felt that everything would be ok, so long as he tried. He held a hand over Stu's rigid body, and gently placed a palm on his forehead. His eyes were open, staring and lifeless. The skin was already cold.

Nothing happened.

Lars looked up to the shadows, feeling betrayed, unsure if he'd done it right. What was he thinking? Where was the ambulance?

Stu began to cough, and sat up.

'Holy fuck,' gasped Lars in relief. 'I thought you were dead.'

He looked confused, sad, haunted by a recent memory, or trying to recall the details of a fading dream. He stared at Lars, unsure who he was. Then a jolt of realisation seemed to hit him. 'I know you,' he said, blinking in the rain. 'I've seen you.'

'You hit your head pretty hard, mate.'

'I was on a tram.' Stu began to cry. 'I saw you through the window.'

'A tram?' Lars tried to help him up but he was terrified.

Stu scrambled to his feet and pushed himself away. 'Don't touch me,' he shouted, as he ran down the street.

The shadows had gone.

The pub lights were out.

How long had he been in the road? He wasn't sure. The pub door was locked. He felt weak and sat on a low wall, breathing slowly. He closed his eyes, drifting in and out of consciousness.

'Hello you,' said a low, husky voice. She was tall and thin, an unlikely woman to find alone on the empty streets so late. She didn't smile. She didn't need to. 'You look a little worse for wear,' she said as she sat next to him. She laughed softly, and moved closer. 'I'm Kitty.'

He held up his hand to shake. She ignored it.

'Lars Nilsson.' He swallowed back nausea, feeling her gentle touch on his shoulders.

She was brushing him down, lingering slightly too long. He could feel the warmth of her fingers through his jacket. It was comforting against the cold dampness of the night. The spiralling sensation faded and he felt an incredible sense of calm.

'There,' she smiled. She pulled out a cigarette and lit up. Her nose twitched slightly as she inhaled. 'You look like you need another drink,' she purred. 'I know just the place.'

They were sitting on high stools in an empty bar. He wasn't sure how he'd got there. They had walked a little way, and then, they were sitting. He didn't care though because he was warm, and the shivering had stopped. A jukebox played a nondescript tune that melted into the bar ambience.

'I think you're a little far gone for beer,' she explained. 'You need something more specific.' She ordered two whiskies by pointing at the bottle.

The bartender was unable to look Kitty in the eye as he delivered the drinks. He moved up the bar to give the strange couple some space.

Lars swirled the liquid and felt the vapours sting his eyes. He took a large gulp.

'Slowly,' she insisted. 'This is a Japanese sipping whisky.'

He looked her in the eye, holding the liquid in his mouth as it burned his tongue.

'This is a five hundred year old Hibiki. Matured in ancient plum liquor barrels. Can you taste the sacred fruit?' she asked.

He swallowed. 'I think so.' The flavour lingered in his mouth. 'I've never had Japanese whisky before.'

'There's a first time for everything, Lars,' she smiled. 'So, tell me why a guy like you is sitting all alone on the street?' She took a delicate sip.

He watched the tumbler touch her fleshy lips. Her nose twitched at the proximity to vapours.

'I've had a bad day,' he laughed.

She made a mournful, sympathetic sound, and stared at him through her glass.

The attention gave him confidence, exposing an ego that he wasn't used to. He wondered if it was the alcohol. 'What if I told you,' he said, 'that I used to be supremely powerful.'

'Oh, so sweet,' she smiled. 'And you aren't any more? That is a shame,' she said, almost in a whisper.

'I don't know what went wrong.' Lars was genuinely upset at the thought.

'Poor you,' hummed Kitty, staring without blinking.

'I think my wife is going to leave me.'

She pulled a sad face.

'And I just killed my brother-in-law.'

Her nose twitched. 'Bad day.'

'Well, I didn't actually kill him. In fact, I brought him back to life.'

She smiled, understanding his troubles.

'I have to go to Japan. It feels like it could be important.' He raised his hands pathetically, having performed his magic trick to the lack of an appreciative audience. 'How's that for fucked?' He reached for the whisky but she stopped him.

She slipped her hand onto his thigh and moved in closer. He felt an electric shiver down his spine as she touched him. She kissed him and he didn't resist. He closed his eyes. As she kissed him harder, he felt his breath steal away. Her tongue touched his. The spiralling sensation twisted deep inside. Kitty pulled away, stroking his face as she did so. He was captivated.

'I'm going to tell you a story,' she whispered. 'For many hundreds of millennia the ancient immortals of the afterlife sat in perfect harmony, commanding the passing of the seasons and the calming of the seas, raising the sun and lowering the moon. They tasted the shimmering mist on their tongues that surrounded the mountain island that they called Hōrai.'

He felt uncomfortable, suddenly anxious, but unable to move. He tried to breathe and inhaled a heavy air that went straight to his lungs. He felt weaker with every sensual second. The sensation of slow suffocation made him drift deeper.

Lars fell into a state of nothingness; nothing except for this woman, and her touch, freezing time and space in an instant, a snapshot of a reality that blurred the edge of his consciousness.

Kitty spoke with a dull, monotonous purr. She brushed her lips against his as she spoke, their energy combining as she stroked a soft hand across his cheek. 'The eight immortals breathed deeply, simultaneously, as one, inhaling the ancient sea of souls, and exhaling the winter snow. With every new breath, they inherited the knowledge of each individual that formed the dense sea of souls that flowed around their mountain island.

The eight swam in it, floated small boats in it, they made broth from it, and they got drunk on it. They were the eight immortals and this was their privilege. In return they brought peace, redemption, re-birth and release to the mortal dead who passed through Hōrai. But why should only eight wield so much power?'

Her story was intoxicating. His eyes focused on her shadow as she began to fade from view. He tried to reach out but she felt far away. Her image swirled in shades of colour; a broken jigsaw puzzle rearranging itself before him.

Pressure increased on his chest as she kissed him again, seductive and slow. The heavens imploded and became echoes of a world that rippled at the surface of another time and space.

'It was believed that the common collective purpose of the eight was divine rule over the afterlife. Their innocence was never questioned, their privileges never challenged, as they nestled between the legs of their immortal brothers and sisters like fat ducks on a spring pond. Far below, the shadow creatures scurried and snapped, baying for the darkness to overcome the light.'

Lars felt himself falling deeper into unconsciousness as her story continued. Her voice led him deeper into the darkness of his soul.

She spoke softly, careful not to wake him from his trance. 'Yaoyorozu no Kami; the uncountable, infinite gods of the underworld that reside in everything, and that are everywhere — they were the rightful rulers of life and death, and they were being ignored by the very individuals that they had entrusted with their power. The immortals claimed to know only peace and calm, and yet, they were always arguing. They drank wine and made too much noise on their disrespectful mountain island. They were worse than the humanity that they claimed to save. Something had to be done.

The Oni howled at the peak. Their keeper, a dark eyed Tengu, kept them well fed on the fallen souls that could not rise high enough to reach enlightenment. Taking the form of a winged Ōkami snake, Tengu was sent to appear to each of the eight immortals and to trick them into revealing their true nature, tempting them with tales of the mortal world, inviting them to declare their intentions as the un-rightful rulers of the afterlife.' She brushed her lips against his, kissing him before speaking again.

Lars fixed his eyes on her, staring into a reality that once was. He reached out but there was nothing to hold on to. He succumbed, allowing the weight deep into his lungs, swallowing down the thickness of Time itself. He gasped for a relief that didn't come – feeling only the warm suffocation of stillness — and stopped breathing.

All was black.

All was vacant.

His body was suspended in cosmic space.

'Enough!' boomed a voice that penetrated the room. Hotei stepped forward and approached Kitty. He held a small mirror up to her face. 'Enough of your lies. Leave him, Kitsune!'

She spun, cowering, scratching Lars across the face with three claws as she confronted the immortal and hissed, arching her back and bearing her teeth.

'Be gone, vixen. He is not yours to take.'

The mirror revealed an animal shadow that replaced her human reflection.

'Return to your natural form!' he commanded.

Kitty dropped to her knees and fell forward. Her dress became a pile of rags on the floor. The woman was gone.

Hotei lowered the mirror like a weapon and then turned it to face Lars. The reflection revealed him drifting motionless in space.

'This is not how you journey to the afterlife, my brother. Many will try to wrong foot you, many will try to tempt you, but your destiny has already been chosen. The course of your true path will become clear to you in time.'

He thrust his hand inside the mirror and grabbed Lars' helpless form. His limp body twirled like a leaf in water as it rose up to the surface. In a rush of white light he was pulled from the stillness and brought back to the surface of a reality that he had once inhabited.

He gasped, wheezing in a deep gulp of mortality, and opened his eyes. He didn't know where he was. He felt cold. There was a dampness on his cheek. It stung as he touched the bleeding scratches.

From underneath a pile of rags came the sound of panicked animal claws.

Hotei swung back and adopted a Kung Fu attack stance, right arm raised and mirror outstretched with knees bent, left arm retracted with his palm facing the movement.

A black nose appeared, then a short orange snout, until cautiously, two curious eyes stared around the room. The fox pushed out from under the clothes and stood fast, snarling. She shook her hind to reveal nine tails, which fanned out in a glorious display.

'Kitsune,' gasped Lars.

'You!' It looked at him and yelped, baring its teeth in a final attempt at intimidation.

Hotei held the mirror towards it and the nine tailed fox scurried for the door. She scratched her way under the wooden boards and disappeared in a flurry of fur.

'You have had a lucky escape, my brother. You would not have lasted a moment longer under her spell.' He shook his head. 'You succumbed to her seduction. You are weak.'

'I think,' Lars whispered, with a cold sincerity. 'I think, I just died.'

The old man smiled, shaking his head. 'No, Izanagi, you did not die, for you are the reviver of the dead.'

A white goatee beard twisted from his eyebrows to his ears and down to his chest. He was short, dressed in dirty clothes that looked like they had once been elegant silks. Embroidered images lined the faded material. The tail of the robe was particularly dirty as it dragged on the floor behind him. He reached deep into his pocket and unveiled a carved wooden flute. He smiled as he presented it to Lars, as though offering a business card. 'It is me − Hotei.' He trilled a burst of music and parted both hands wide, satisfied that this was enough to appeal to his long lost immortal brother. He offered a hand to lift Lars from the floor. 'You feel it, don't you? The sacrifice?' His eyes declared a shrewd world weariness.

Lars stared, exhausted. His head felt heavy with a dull pain. The name seemed familiar. Then, he remembered. 'Hotei? You saved me in Atari Shock?'

'I have been trying to save you for some time now,' he replied, 'but you barely look up from your screen. It took a while to work out how to reach you. Should I use Yahoo or Google, Hotmail or Hushmail? What's the difference? I still don't understand.' He looked to Lars and was disappointed to see a lack of acknowledgment. 'Although, it appears that you have been attempting to immortalise yourself in other ways, my brother?' He reached into his pocket and pulled out the sugar coated USB drive, on which two small lizards were cleaning themselves.

'What's on that drive?'

'Your spirit animals called it trap bait.'

Lars saw his opportunity. He pushed Hotei, snatched the USB and fell, terrified, through the door.

Hotei called out after him. 'You must stay with me for your own protection. This mortal world will consume you, Izanagi!'

Lars ran down the rain swept street and didn't look back.

'Well, my friends,' sighed the ancient immortal as he stroked his beard, 'he's certainly playing hard to get.' But the two tiny lizards had disappeared.

30

Lars tapped a key code and pushed the outer door to the offices of the BBP. He looked behind him one last time. To his relief, the streets were empty.

A light automatically flickered on in the lobby as he entered. He hit the call button and a lift groaned out of slumber in the near silence of the dawn chorus. The doors rumbled open and he was faced with his own image in the mirrored wall of the lift. He didn't recognise the man staring back; pale skin, vacant eyes, and a thick red slash from eyebrow to chin down the side of his face. His body ached. His face throbbed. The walking dead had taken the world, he thought. He looked beyond tired. He looked sad. He looked old. He felt like he'd just survived twelve rounds. He had no idea what time it was. The phone jabbed into his side. He pulled it out, expecting to see a hundred missed calls from Claire. The battery was dead. He would find a charger at his desk. That was the reason he had come here. He would call a cab and get home.

He shivered, pulling his jacket around him. As he put the phone back, he didn't notice two tiny lizards crawl up the length of his arm and stop to rest on his shoulders. He found the USB in his pocket, sticky with sugar, and before he knew it, the lift was open at the third floor.

The open plan office was in darkness. Shadows flickered behind every object. A table lamp was lit at the far side. Someone was sitting alone.

'Hello?' He scanned the room and headed straight for the light. There was movement. 'Someone there?' It was Julia Miller.

'Jesus, Julia! What the fuck are you doing here?'

'Where is everyone?' she sniffed, seeming scared, anxious in the empty room but reluctant to leave.

'Before you ask me the same question, this is why I am never in the office in the day time, right? I am a lone wolf. I operate alone. This is just how I roll. The night time is my prime time.'

She hadn't heard anything he'd said. 'There was shouting,' she mumbled. 'Noise, lightning, then everyone was gone. Shadows everywhere.' Her expression was blank and dream-like. She was staring into the dark corners of the office.

'Are you ok?' Lars approached.

She glared around the room and then stood. He could see her bloodshot eyes as she moved closer. Her face was stained with mascara. She handed him a piece of paper and vacantly walked to her desk, where she sat in darkness, staring at an empty computer screen. She had drawn something. A pencil sketch; a tall bird with a pointed beak and staff.

Lars screwed it up and threw it in a bin. 'I need to get out of here,' he said. 'I'll charge my phone. Then we can share a cab.'

In the far distance, he thought he heard the scream of a car alarm. He touched the side of his face. His fingers were sticky with blood.

'Erm, can I borrow some money?' he asked. 'For the cab?' She didn't reply.

'I can find an ATM, I guess.' His terminal was at the far end of the room. Some screens had been left on, sending shimmering shadows up the walls and across the floor. He reached his desk and looked back to Julia. She hadn't moved. His desktop was still logged in to Atari Shock. He scanned the information, blocking out the newbies. The Immortal was offline. Wiki had baited him.

'You've forgotten me?' Julia was standing beside him. The light from the monitor flickered across her face.

'What the fuck? You scared me.'

'You have forgotten who you are,' she said in a voice that was unlike her own.

A sharp pain gripped his right arm and ran along his shoulder.

'You have accepted this mortality?' She retreated into the shadows. There was a cackling laugh. Her voice was deeper, dry and coarse, like gravel and sand. A figure twitched in the half shadow, larger than Julia.

'You have made the sacrifice?' She laughed again, her voice booming. Something moved in his peripheral vision. It lingered and then disappeared.

'Julia?' he asked, but he knew it wasn't her.

'I will help you to remember,' whispered the voice as an object cracked him across the skull, throwing him to the floor. His vision of the office was blurred by a white light.

He was unable to breathe, lost in another space and time. He reached out and tried to get to his feet as a black shape approached fast and hovered before him. He felt a hand on his shoulder, preventing him from standing. His head began to sink. His mind and body were now two separate things. The shadow expanded in the blackness, shifting, hulk-like. He couldn't make out what he was seeing; spikes, wings, teeth. There was otherworldly breathing.

The office regained form but it was incomplete. Solid objects appeared translucent, a sketch of the place it had been just moments before.

He heard the flapping of wings and felt a gust of air across his face. He was desperate to catch his breath. Another blow hit him hard on the back of the neck, making him smack his head against the desk and fall to his knees. An object smashed against the wall above, raining cold fragments onto his face.

'How does it feel to suffer?' asked a voice in the darkness.

'Who are you?' mumbled Lars.

'Who are you?' it challenged.

'My name is Lars,' he spluttered.

'Phah,' hissed the birdman. 'Simple, childish name. Your real name was cast in the Zodiac, forged for you by the very masters of the Universe.'

He heard a sound; the click of something forced to breaking point, a snapping in the back of his skull. The sensation was physical. A dull, numbing punch.

Crack!

This time the force knocked his senses out cold, and he was displaced to a distant memory.

Lightning struck a mountain. A fork of heat rushed through the centre of a swirling typhoon. Through violent mists, Lars could see the black raven. The shape shifted as it thrust its wings into the air and flapped out a shawl to take a translucent human form. It stood in the clouds and cast a staff into the sea of souls. There were tortured cries in the mist as the creature jabbed at faces, gouged out eyes, and amputated limbs.

The birdman's head jerked abruptly. 'Kitsune's story is incomplete,' it croaked.

A bright green sky burned his eyes. He was sitting on the floor of what was once the office; at least he thought he was on a floor, it supported his body, but when he looked down there was nothing there. Instead, a richness of crop fields spanned like a patchwork, far below.

'I know this,' he whispered in recognition.

'Yes,' hissed the voice. 'You know this. Welcome to the high heavenly plain,' cackled the birdman. 'Your humble storyteller, Tengu; the shadow wielder, the commander of chaos, speaks with you from across the cosmic plain.'

He was sitting on some kind of platform. Wisps of cloud and a spray of bamboo treetops fluttered in a breeze. An occasional bird drifted beneath. The vast expanse of space and time was laid out far below.

'There is more to tell. Listen and choose,' explained a voice in the cosmos. 'I approached the infamous eight, and asked to join them atop their mountain island.

The Imperial uncle, Daikoku, purified the air with his pathetic Jade crystal tablet. How he loved to show off.

The insufferably rude, Jurojin, coughed up a globule of yellow and spat it at me. I was not impressed.

Benten, being neither man nor woman, and too vein to decide, fluttered his eyelids and pursed her lips, and with the flick of a castanet began to scribe the lyrics to a self-indulgent love song.

Hotei was too drunk to notice anyone other than himself.

The elder, Fokuro, was sitting, proudly, on his arrogant deer. He turned his head aside and denied my attention.

So, I took the form of a wondrous Ōkami snake. Venom dripped from my fangs as I licked away the anticipation of time itself. I hissed magical tales of mortality. The tiny deer just stared. Bishamon's temper reached a feverish state and he reached for his sword, threatening to hack the tip off my tail.

Izanagi, the master of the cloud-chamber, eyed me suspiciously but notably carried on with his duties, reviving the dead.'

Lars recognised the name.

'Yes,' croaked the voice. 'Remember your true self, Izanagi. I appeared before the beautiful woman, Izanami; the Mother Earth, the fertility priestess, your immortal wife, and she listened attentively while playing a mystical tune on her shō which lilted throughout the mountain island. I curled around her wrist, as a golden wedding band, and told her tales of mortal things; caffeine and television, gmail and instant messaging, pornography and credit cards, gaming consoles and recreational drugs, of kinky sex and sports cars, of emotion and euphoria. Should she wish to explore these mortal pleasures, then I would gladly exchange places until the day her thirst for mortality was quenched. If she agreed, she should break the perfect chain held by the eight, and throw herself from the mountain to the sea of souls below. From there, she would find her way to mortal Earth, and to a New World.'

'Have we ever?' she asked her family, halting the mystical tune that swirled from the reed pipes of her shō.

'We have never,' they answered, simultaneously.

'She returned to her melody, alternately inhaling and blowing into the shō in meditation of the things that she shouldn't really think of. Her music resumed and the immortals peacefully returned to their duties. There was life. There was death. Souls swirled around Hōrai.

I returned and made my offer once more. This time, I recounted stories of cats and dogs and sushi, of airplanes and MTV and dolphins, of women's magazines and cigarettes and DVDs, of eBay and Amazon and Atari Shock, of oranges and apples and porn star Cecilia Vega, of family, of children, and of mortal love and desire. Her shō abruptly ceased its melody.'

'Why never?' asked the immortal woman of her colleagues.

'It is not our place to be curious,' they insisted. 'Have some more wine.'

'She took the flask, and shortly her music was lilting once more. The eight drank and sung, and tended to the quintillions. The mists remained thick with saved souls. Millennia passed.

I appeared for a third time and attempted to coax Izanami with tales of Netflix and dinosaurs, skateboards and pigtails, French fries and latex, horror movies and The Beatles.

Her shō ceased its resonance. She could resist temptation no longer. She broke the embrace of the immortals, bringing unbalance to the perfect alignment, and causing them to tumble down the mountain and into the sea of lost souls. They fell in order of one through to eight. They had shown their true nature and were unworthy of the task entrusted to them.

The shadow animals screamed with joy as the immortals scattered in the darkness. My Oni herded them to the space in-between, teeth gnashing, screaming up at the mountain. A bright river of fire filled the valley floor. Mists rose up the mountain side.'

The heat became more intense as Lars listened. He could taste it. He was trapped, sweating, and unable to move. His throat was becoming choked by the heat. The air hung like a desert plain, the scent of an empty wasteland of death.

'The shadow animals chased the immortals between the cracks,' continued the birdman, 'deep down to mortal Earth. They ran, blindly, every second drifting further away from themselves, stuck in the loop, trapped in the perfect circle of isolation between life and death. They hid, they cowered, and they screamed for their lives.

Only two chose to continue further, beyond the space between life and death, deep into the cracks of mortality. One of them, Izanagi, was you.'

Another blow slammed against Lars' temple. Crack! His head absorbed the full force.

'How does it feel to suffer?' screeched the voice.

Lars raised his arms in protection.

'You have tasted much mortal fruit. The suffering will continue for as long as you desire to exist on this plane. You cannot live here. You are not one of them. You are displaced. You are being consumed. Give up your tedious mortal pleasures and return with me. Sit astride the mountain island once more. Stir the soup of souls with your toes. Feast on the quintillions of the lost. Sanctify my authority as master of the cloud-chamber. Become an immortal once more and kneel before Tengu. I offer you redemption, I offer you a choice, to live alongside me in immortality.'

Lars braced himself for further blows but they didn't come. The presence gradually became distant.

'Is that it?' he called out. 'I'm just supposed to choose? Between a crazy old man, and whatever the hell you're meant to be?' He felt exhausted and weak, dizzy with wild images of the story. He tried to calm his breathing. The room was strangely cold. Julia had gone. The stranger had gone. There was silence in the night.

'Choose,' it repeated.

'I want...' He paused. He knew exactly what he wanted but realised that he'd never taken the time to tell her. 'I want her to be happy. I want to have a family. I want...'

A hideous, high-pitched scream interrupted and the dark shadow of Tengu hovered above. A single eye, perfectly round and piercing, stared directly at him. The infinite depths of Time reflected back.

'You dare to abandon the land of the polluted dead?'

The room rose in temperature. Computer monitors began to splinter and buckle in the heat. Papers burst into flame. Curtains and chairs burned. Lars pushed himself under a table.

'You choose to not return by my side, then you will never return,' screeched the voice. 'I will make you understand the meaning of the choice that you have made. All that you love – will be taken.'

A rising river of flame licked the office walls. Lars bolted for the door. He heard a scream and turned back to see Julia, trapped, surrounded by flames.

'Lars!' She was desperately searching for a way out but was blocked by office furniture. She reached out to him, terrified, like the fire had woken her from a deep trance. Heat stung his eyes as he tried to find a route through the debris. The flames were overwhelming. The floor began to splinter and crack beneath them. Julia plummeted into the furnace below.

The offices of the **BBP** disintegrated in a blaze as the shadow of the birdman flickered in flame.

31

Tadashi and Malcolm were bedside in a small room that Carlton had arranged for Lori's recuperation. The walls were painted the kind of hospital colour that wasn't quite yellow and wasn't quite white. There were no windows. A small television set was mounted on the wall. It was turned off.

'Don't be worried if she doesn't speak. She's quite heavily sedated,' said the duty nurse as she pulled the door closed.

The professor watched her struggle with fitful dreams. 'Where are you, my dear? Come back to us.'

Tadashi held the glass vial tighter, deep in his pocket. The liquid essence began to glow.

'You are both so unique. You have seen the New World, the new dawn of existence beyond the threshold of our dimension. Someday, may we all be as lucky as you and journey to the space in-between, to determine its origins, perhaps even find a new existence?'

Lori shifted under the covers and opened her eyes. She looked around the room.

'My dear, Lotus Flower, you're awake.' He held her hand.

'The sun is beautiful,' she said as she studied Van Peterson's ageing features. 'I love to watch the mist rise from the leaves and drift into the open sky.'

She seemed in shock, her pupils dilated.

'Return to us,' said the professor, but she wasn't listening.

'Sometimes we sing. All of us together,' she said. 'We sing songs of love. It bonds us and bring us together as one true being.' She looked straight into his eyes. 'There were too many of them. I couldn't fight it.'

'My dear,' he held her hand tighter. 'I am so sorry. I have put you through so much.'

'I couldn't move at first. Then, I accepted my fate and joined with them,' she said. She closed her eyes and began humming. 'I see through ten thousand eyes. I have the strength of a hundred limbs. I spring high into the air. I float over any obstacle. I crawl through the undergrowth like a cat.' She breathed slowly to the rhythm of the melody, her head in the clouds, as she felt a comforting warmth surround her like the first sunshine of spring. 'I leap into trees. I scan the ground like a hawk. I am no longer the one. I am many.'

Van Peterson was becoming scared. 'She's speaking gibberish.'

'No,' whispered Tadashi. 'I know exactly what she means.'

'I am the seeker. I am the hunter,' continued Lori, in a dream. 'I am the desperate yearning of eight million souls. Together we have purpose.' She began to writhe under the sheets. 'Professor, I don't know what they want me to do. Help me, please?'

He could feel the heat of her skin radiate through his. He felt her forehead. She was burning up. He had lost control. 'What do we do, Tadashi?'

He felt in his pocket and revealed the ancient vial. The old man was drawn to the strange essence inside.

'What's that, my boy?'

'You were meant to find the amanita muscaria. It is a gift from the gods themselves,' smiled Tadashi. He held it up to the light and it sparkled, luminescent. 'And now, it is my gift to you.'

They were silent as he pulled the cork from the bottle. His hand shook as the liquid emanated a radiant green glow. 'I am to have a daughter one day.' Tears began to well in his eyes. 'I was shown my own death.'

'Come now, I think you should rest. I have put you both through so much.'

Lori's eyes snapped open. 'No. They are waiting for you. He must show you the true path to enlightenment.' She smiled, reassuringly, and turned his palm in hers.

'What are you doing?'

'You will follow me to the other world,' she said.

A single drip of essence fell from the vial and sunk into the old man's skin.

It disappeared instantly.

For a fleeting moment, Malcolm Van Peterson realised that he couldn't remember his name. Soon the thought was gone, washed away like a wave crashing on the shore. He forgot fear, desire, emotion, objects, all living people and all living things. Nothing existed, except for Lotus Flower, and her beautiful melody. His mind drifted. His soul energised. He forgot the reason for anything. Everything just was.

'This is peace,' whispered Lori. 'Follow me to Hōrai. Yaoyorozu no Kami welcome you.'

The old professor closed his eyes, feeling the sun on his face as a tear of contentment rolled down his cheek. He nodded his head gently and smiled. His breathing slowed.

'Come to us,' she called.

His head began to drop on his shoulders, falling like a sleeper. He couldn't fight it. He was barely drawing air, floating up to a distant mountain. Trees scattered at its base, surrounded by twisting rivers and fragrant waterfalls. High up, Lotus Flower was waiting. She wore a floral shawl that flickered and snapped in the mountain air. She called to him.

'Follow,' she beckoned, her voice falling on him as a tender kiss.

He reached out, desperate to hold her, to stroke her hair, to bring her lips to his. The clouds swirled at his feet.

'We love you,' she sung, as she drifted higher into the clouds, leading him further from the mortal plane.

He kept his gaze on her, pulling himself higher, yearning to be with her. Nowhere mattered. Nowhere existed.

He reached her body and kissed her deeply, and as he did so, he felt his body fade. He was at peace, listening to the gentle vibrations of space and time. He evaporated with the touch of her soft skin on his own. His soul became one with the mountain island.

Malcolm gasped a final breath and his body relaxed. His hand hung lifeless in the hospital room.

Lori opened her eyes. The professor was slumped in a bedside chair. She smiled and looked up to see two people watching. She closed her eyes again, and Lotus Flower breathed the last of her mortal life.

Tadashi replaced the cork. 'There are no doors, no

walls, and no borders that contain you now,' he said. 'You are free.'

Sarah stood in the doorway, having witnessed the final moments of her father's life.

Agent Carlton checked his watch and took a note of the time.

32

Lars ran home without stopping. Was he experiencing some kind of violent breakdown? Since he'd first heard the call of the fox, reality had shattered like a mirror to expose otherworldly events beyond. His face stung to the touch. Had he really been scratched? The bleeding had stopped. He was sure it looked bad.

He managed to get his keys into the lock and hesitated. Was Claire home? It was mid-morning. She must have already gone to work. He would call in sick, clean himself up, and wait for her to get back. Then he would show her how much she meant to him. He would tell her everything that had happened.

He was about to turn the key when he heard a clatter in the dustbins. He spun around, leaving the keys hanging. 'Show yourself,' he screamed, turning the bins to the ground. He lifted a lid and a small, fluffy animal raced up his arm. It leaped across his shoulders and yelped as he caught it by the tail.

'Stop it you two,' croaked a voice. 'That's no way to greet each other.'

A squirrel bounded to the floor and sprung up onto the head of the ancient immortal. It cursed in tiny squeaks, and made itself comfortable in the weaves of his hair.

'You again?'

'You must allow me to speak with you, Izanagi,' said Hotei. His eyes sparkled generations of wisdom. His hair twitched pure white electricity.

'Stop calling me that.'

'What would you rather I call you?'

'Lars. My name is Lars.'

The old man spat on the floor. 'I refuse to call you Lars. The hell river, Shozukawa, overflows. Shozuka-no-baba runs wild and free. The afterlife fills with lost souls seeking redemption, and you wish to be called, Lars? Pathetic name.'

'Just leave me alone.'

Hotei was taken aback. He snorted, deeply offended. He stroked the squirrel on his head, and composed himself with a gulp from his gourd. He closed his eyes, breathing the cheap bourbon scent deep into his lungs. 'Simple pleasures. It is no wonder you forget. How many reincarnations must you witness before you realise the truth, Izanagi? I should have insisted that you return much sooner,' he took a drink, 'but perhaps I too have become accustomed to a little mortal pleasure, every now and then.'

Lars took a glance at the front door. He wanted to go inside. He wanted to go home. He felt like he should try to sleep. Had there really been a fire? Had he started it somehow? Did Julia fall? The old man must have followed him, he thought. Was he the dark figure in the office? He was feeling increasingly unsafe in the street. He took a step closer to the door.

'You know where that leads, don't you?' asked Hotei. 'Only to suffering.'

Lars hesitated. He felt a stab of pain as the spiralling sickness lurched in his stomach.

'The sacrifice. It is with you already,' said Hotei. 'Your soul is being consumed, Izanagi. The pain will become unbearable in time. Soon, you will die another mortal death, and the sacrifice will take you. You will be reborn into constant suffering. You will remain forever fallen, unable to function on mortal Earth.' He laughed to himself, despondent. 'How can I expect you to understand? You are so much like them now – so distracted.'

The old man's sincerity was haunting, somehow preventing Lars from turning the key. He felt a connection but was unsure to what.

'You cannot survive here, for you do not belong here.'

The squirrel opened an eye and watched through hair and fur.

'You really don't remember me, brother? We drank together. We played together. We swirled our toes in the sea of souls.' Hotei performed a traditional folk dance, a Yangge of remembrance. He indicated for Lars to join him but soon became flushed and stopped.

The squirrel spun several times in a circle, twisting its tail into the old man's hair.

'We are lost without you, trapped in a space where we do not belong. You must choose to follow your true path,' explained Hotei. 'That is all this has ever been about, your responsibility to make a choice, and to live by it.' He stood on the pavement, expecting his answer, taking regular slugs from his gourd.

Lars recognised a deep sorrow in the old man's eyes. The lines on his face suggested many years of loneliness. Deep wrinkles betrayed the innocence of a man who had seen too much in many life times. Hotei continued his slow dance. It seemed to Lars that he too was suffering.

'You are not going to turn that key,' said Hotei, 'because you know that what I say is true – your life is a lie, Izanagi. I am sorry if this is difficult for you to fathom, my brother, but you are not of this world.'

Lars stood on the steps with his back against the door. He eyed Hotei suspiciously. 'If I went home, right now, would you leave me alone?'

The old man laughed. 'That is all I have ever wanted for you, but that door will not lead you home. Your home is far away, and your journey begins in the Orient.'

'Japan?'

Hotei shrugged.

'You're here to take me?'

The old man took a gulp of whisky and laughed. 'You think I should click my fingers and you'll fly there? I might be immortal but I am not a magician. Follow the signs, Izanagi.' The old man patted the squirrel snoozing calmly on his head. 'This is a spirit animal. They are all around us. Sometimes, all you have to do is listen to them.'

'Like the fox?'

His mood changed abruptly. 'Kitsune is a scavenger for Tengu. She will search for you again, and continue to do so until she delivers you to him.'

Tengu is watching, thought Lars. 'Old man?' He swallowed. 'I think it already knows where I am.'

Hotei was panicked. He summoned the squirrel and it sped off, performing a full circle investigation of the immediate area, checking the trees and shadowy corners. 'Tengu? Are you sure?'

'It kicked the shit out me,' laughed Lars, with tired reflection.

'Did it ask you to make a choice?'

'It was pretty angry.'

'What did you choose, Izanagi?'

Lars took a breath. 'I chose Claire.'

'You chose destruction. The birdman will never leave you at peace, so long as it knows your intention to stay. We are your true family, Izanagi, you must realise that before it is too late.'

Leaves spun to the ground as the squirrel leaped from branch to branch above them.

Lars shook his head in apology. 'No, old man – you're not.' He reached for the keys and the door swung open.

Claire was waiting for him. She looked exhausted. She'd been crying. He looked back at the pavement. Hotei was gone. The squirrel rustled in the trees above. The door keys hung in the lock. Clouds began to darken the sky.

He stood on the step as rain began to fall and grinned, pathetically. 'You're alive!' he gasped, moving towards her.

She took a step back and used the door as a shield. 'Of course I'm bloody well alive. I'd say the same thing about you, if I gave a shit, which I don't.'

'We have to get inside. It's not safe on the streets.'

'If it isn't safe on the streets then why didn't you come home last night?' Her voice was cold and determined.

'We need to talk.'

'You had that chance and you blew it. Why are the bins on the floor?'

He ignored the question and held up his hands, pleading with her. 'Look, I've got so much to tell you.'

'Then you can tell me from there, where you belong, in the gutter with the rats.'

The squirrel twitched in the trees. Drops of rain began to fall. He realised that Claire had every intention of leaving him on the doorstep. She'd not tried the unwelcome at home tactic before but she had clearly reached her last resort.

'Claire, I love you,' he pleaded. He reached out a hand, and to his surprise, she took it. 'I'll tell you everything. It all started when I saw a fox.'

'You saw a fox?' she asked, confused.

'In the bins, yeah. I was playing Atari Shock and it called to me.'

'I'm sorry, what?' Her hand loosened.

'Seventeen hours and twelve minutes into game time.'

'You can remember that,' she stumbled, 'but you can't remember to meet me in a restaurant?'

'Please, I don't want to argue. I just want to tell you what's been going on. I can't believe that I've not been including you. In fact, it's important that you know everything. I need to start at the beginning.'

'Ok. So where have you been all night?'

'I went to a bar. There was a fire. I think you're in danger.'

She let go of his hand. 'What happened to your face? Is that blood?' She was losing interest, becoming suspicious.

'From the beginning, please?'

She nodded, reluctantly.

'I was scratched, by a woman, who was actually a fox.'

'By a woman?'

'In the bar, yes. We had a Japanese sipping whisky and she told me a story.'

'You're having an affair?'

'No,' blurted Lars. 'Of course not.'

'Bloody well sounds like it!'

'I was seduced by a kitsune.'

Claire shivered. She had seen it coming, something that she couldn't quite put her finger on. She considered herself to be an easy-going person but was feeling more provoked and uncomfortable with him than ever before. Things had been difficult. They had been drifting. She'd never felt it as strongly as this. Since their marriage, it was as though he had been increasingly reluctant to spend time with her. He had a lack of focus for anything that wasn't to do with the game, like an entirely different personality was challenging to take over. She had tried not to worry about it, thought it was all a phase, but it was clear to her now. A sensation flowed through her, calling from the dark corners of her mind – she didn't know who her husband was any more.

'A kitsune?' she winced, unimpressed.

'It's a minion of Tengu,' he explained, unsure if she was really following.

'I feel sick.' Claire decided that the most logical reaction was to totally lose her shit. 'You stay up all night. You never have time to talk. When you do, all you say is this bullshit. Why can't you just stop obsessing about these bloody computer games.'

'This isn't a game.'

'Well, it certainly sounds like one. When are you going to spend some time with me, Lars?'

He looked blank.

'You say you love me but you really don't act like it.' She sighed in desperation. 'Ah, what's the point?' She wiped her eyes. 'How did we get like this? It's like you've disappeared,' she sniffed. She thought he'd said everything there was to say – he hadn't.

'Claire, I need you to listen to me.'

'I'm right here.'

'I'm feeling...'

'What, Lars? What are you feeling?'

He blinked, unsure how to phrase it. 'I'm feeling – lost. I need to go to away for a while.'

She was stunned. She didn't know whether to laugh or cry. How could he say such a thing? She stared at him, deeply hurt. This wasn't the Lars that she knew. He looked terrible. Tired. A scratch across his face from who knows what. He was a stranger in her own home. Where had he been? She couldn't trust him. He seemed more pathetic to her than ever. She felt a sudden anger rise inside her, and retaliated. 'Zelda the warrior princess need a new helmet, or something?'

'You're in danger.'

'You're threatening me now?' Her lip started to tremble. He tried to take her hand and she pushed him away. 'No, Lars. Not anymore.'

'But Tengu is watching.'

'Fuck you. Show some responsibility for once in your life, and that doesn't mean being so bloody selfish.'

'I'm not being selfish. I'm doing this for you.'

'Oh, come on, Lars. For me? You're doing this for me?'

'I'm doing this to protect you.'

'Because I'm in danger?'

'I need to go to Japan.'

The words hung in the air.

'Oh, that's just fucking incredible. So, you're going to go

away and have a little think about how lost you're feeling are you? Don't be so bloody pathetic.'

'I have to go,' he replied, determined that he was doing the right thing.

'Then I won't be here when you get back.' She wasn't looking through him as she so often did. She was staring directly into his eyes.

Lars knew that this was the moment. He knew exactly what he was supposed to say – I'm sorry, and that of course he would stop playing games all night, and that of course he wasn't going away. It was as simple as that.

His head spun. He began to sweat. The nauseous feeling twisted deep in his stomach. He could feel the sensation becoming stronger by the minute. Something was happening, something bigger than them. The pieces of a much larger puzzle were falling into place.

Claire waited for him to speak. She pulled the door tighter to encourage him.

He made his decision. 'If I don't go, Tengu will take everything I love. That's you, Claire.'

She swallowed back a shiver. 'I flushed Mr Chips down the toilet.'

The door slammed in his face.

Lars put his hand up to the wood. A dizzying, concussive sensation overwhelmed him as he felt the life he once knew – evaporate.

On the other side of the door, Claire was pressed up against the wall. At her feet, a pair of hollow eyes stared up. The whisp of an animal face swirled around her waist. It smiled with dog teeth. She could feel its hot breath on her body.

A tall shadow hovered above her, oppressive and claustrophobic. She felt it slide over her shoulders, lingering like a draught. She turned her head to confront it and caught her breath at the demonic sight of Tengu.

Lars was shaking from the overwhelming series of events. He reached for the keys that were still hanging in the lock, and lowered his hand. His decision had been made. The door would stay shut.

Hotei appeared on the pavement, surrounded by a gathering of spirit animals. The squirrel twitched next to a couple of black cats. They licked their fur, keeping an eye on Lars as they did so. A line of small birds sat on the fence above the bins. A rotund and heavy badger paced up to him and sniffed his feet. It turned its head with a look of sad understanding.

Lars wiped his eyes but there were no tears. 'Have I lost her?' he asked.

The ancient immortal offered him a mournful smile. 'She was never yours to have,' he replied.

33

The police officer stood in the drizzle. His colleague hovered behind. Claire was holding the front door open, just enough to make eye contact. She kept the security chain latched.

The officer presumed that he had caught her at a bad time and began to apologise, until he noticed a set of keys hanging in the lock. 'Had a forgetful night, have we?' he smiled.

She wanted to close the door but they showed no sign of leaving. 'Thanks for returning them.'

'Is this the address of Mr Lars Nilsson?' The officer looked at her with a sideways glance.

'He's not here. Come back later?' She looked over her shoulder and forced a smile.

'What's your relationship to Mr Nilsson?'

'He's my husband.'

The officer could see that she was shaking. 'Is someone with you, Mrs Nilsson?'

'No. There's no one here. Would you like his mobile number?' she replied, nervously, closing the door a little.

'When did you last see him?'

'This morning.'

'At what time exactly?'

She tried to give the officer a helpful look but appeared distracted. 'Erm, around nine, I think.' She pulled the door tighter. 'I have to go. I'm late for work. Perhaps you could visit him in his office?'

'So, he hasn't heard?'

'Heard what?'

'The offices of Bishop, Banes and Price were destroyed in a domestic fire last night.'

'Maybe he's there right now, dealing with the situation?'

'We understand that he's the registered Health and Safety Officer. He's not on site. We were given this address by a company director, Mr Bishop.'

'I'm afraid I can't help you. He's not here. I have to go.' She closed the door. She could still hear them talking outside. The police radio bleeped and squelched. There was a distorted voice. A muffled conversation. Then, silence. She breathed a sigh of relief and then jumped as the door bell sounded. She cautiously opened the door.

Both policemen were now wet from the rain. 'Sorry to disturb you again, Mrs Nilsson. May we come in and ask you a few more questions?'

'I don't have time,' she said.

'Mrs Nilsson, I must insist.' The officer smiled as he placed a boot firmly in the doorway. His colleague began speaking into his lapel radio.

Claire realised that she wasn't getting rid of them. She pulled the door open and immediately pressed her back up against the wall.

They smiled and thanked her as they stepped into the hall.

Claire was standing in the kitchen with her arms folded. She was uncomfortable, fidgeting, still wearing her baggy nightclothes.

'Is everything alright, Mrs Nilsson, if you don't mind me asking?' The officer studied her with a smile.

She flicked on the kettle instead of answering. The front door slammed shut and she screamed, balancing herself against the kitchen counter.

The officer's colleague walked in. 'Bit of a draught,' he said. 'Blew the door right out of my hands.'

She wiped her eyes and nodded with a nervous smile. They stood, listening to the sound of the kettle boil. Steam began to rise from the spout, and as it did so, a grey shape materialised behind the police officers. Hollow eyes and black teeth hung in the air, as a creature paced back and forth across the kitchen floor. It was taunting her. Playing with her. She was petrified as she watched it loom larger, becoming darker, and then just as the police officer turned to glance over his shoulder it vanished in an instant. The kettle boiled feverishly.

'Mind if I put the light on?' he asked. 'So I can take some notes.' She nodded. The officer pressed the switch. The shadow had gone. 'You seem unsettled, Mrs Nilsson?'

'I could answer your questions at the police station,' she sniffed, wiping away fresh tears. 'We could go there now.'

'That really won't be necessary, but if you don't mind, my colleague might take a quick look around the house?'

She shivered at the thought.

'We won't keep you for long. I appreciate that you've got work to get to.'

'I think it's important that I tell you everything down at the police station. I don't have to change. I can go just like this.'

'Really, Mrs Nilsson, that won't be necessary,' smiled the officer, intrigued by her persistence.

'He's gone,' she said through tears.

'Who has? Your husband?'

Her eyes flicked from the policeman to the wall behind him, expecting the shadow to re-materialise at any moment.

'Where has he gone, exactly, Mrs Nilsson?'

'Japan.' She tried to smile and held her hand across her mouth, as if having said something that she shouldn't have.

The officer looked at his colleague. 'Did he tell you that he'd gone to work this morning?'

She was trying to hold it together but becoming increasingly hysterical. 'I lied. We had a fight.' She stared around the kitchen. Steam rose to the ceiling.

'It's ok, Mrs Nilsson.' His colleague nodded that he was going to take a look around. 'Do you have reason to believe that he's left the country?'

'I think so.'

'Has he taken his passport?'

'I haven't checked.'

'Do you know where he might keep his passport please, Mrs Nilsson?'

She blinked and nodded but seemed reluctant to leave the kitchen.

'I should inform you that your husband is currently being investigated for a domestic fire at the offices of the BBP. He might also have information on a missing person, a colleague of his, Julia Miller. It does seem unusual that your husband told you he was going to Japan. Rather a last minute trip? You're not going with him?'

'We never go anywhere.'

'I want to rule out any possibilities that your husband might be withholding information that could be vital to this investigation.' The officer paused. 'Would you happen to know exactly where in Japan he's intending to go?'

She was transfixed by steam rising from the kettle. Mist drifted in the air. 'He saw a fox.' She held her arms tight around her body.

The officer raised an eyebrow, encouraging her to continue.

'He came home with a scratch on his face. He said a fox did it to him. It tried to fuck him,' she blurted.

The officer spoke calmly. 'Let's make that cup of tea, eh?'

'I can do it,' she insisted. She wiped her face and struggled to hold the kettle.

'Mrs Nilsson, does your husband have any…' the officer hesitated, 'any problems that you know of?'

'Problems?'

'At work? At home?'

'Of course not. He's a bloody geek. He doesn't have problems. Apart from what tomb to raid.' She laughed, feebly.

'Something you should see,' shouted the colleague from upstairs.

Claire screamed and dropped both mugs of hot tea on the floor.

The officer breathed a heavy sigh when he saw the state of the cupboard room. Files and boxes had been turned over. Papers were scattered everywhere. Someone had been looking for something. An old PC was still on. It had an Atari Shock screensaver.

'What in Christ is that smell?'

His colleague pointed to a half empty fish tank with a crack in the glass. 'What do you make of all this, Paul? Don't look normal to me, that's for sure.' He pushed the chair aside and tapped on the keyboard. The screensaver flashed the words 'Access Denied.'

Claire hovered on the landing, staring down the stairs behind her.

'He's a gamer then is he, Mrs Nilsson?'

She didn't reply.

'Any sign of a passport?' whispered the officer. 'Check those drawers.'

They pulled open a small filing cabinet.

'Bingo.'

A passport was on top of a pile of bank statements and bills. 'At least we know he hasn't skipped the country.'

'Either way, she's acting very strange.'

'Think he's violent? Domestic? Drugs? She didn't seem to have any bruising. Nothing obvious anyway.'

'Let's take her in. Have a chat with social services, yeah? Go from there.' The officers agreed, leaving the rotting smell of a mouldy goldfish tank, and muttering to themselves about Atari Shock, and if they were both in the super clan at the time The Immortal vanished. They agreed that the game hadn't been as good since.

Claire nursed a cup of tea. She was unable to drink it, visibly shaking, staring at the smallest of shadows.

'Mrs Nilsson,' said the officer with an overly calm tone, 'you've said some things that are quite concerning...'

'It came in the night,' she interrupted. 'It was still here

in the morning. Staring at me from the end of the bed. Those eyes were just staring.' She crumpled to her knees and collapsed on the kitchen floor.

'Radio for an ambulance. She's lost it. Let's take her in.'

The officer touched her shoulder and she screamed.

'It's ok, Mrs Nilsson.'

They reached down to lift her to her feet. She fought back, kicking wildly.

'If you don't calm down I will be forced to detain you.'

She lashed out, scratching him across the face.

'This isn't working.' He unclipped handcuffs and secured her hands behind her back.

'No!' she screamed, trying to scramble away on her knees.

'Calm down, please, Mrs Nilsson.'

'No. No. You don't understand.'

The officer radioed for an ambulance. 'Female. Mid-twenties. Sudden attack of hysteria. She is being detained...' He stopped, distracted. 'Hey, Paul. What's that?'

'What?'

'That shadow. Right there.'

They stared at a black shape that had materialised on the kitchen floor. It reared up to form a physical object, low to the ground, like a large dog. The shadow animal bared black teeth and locked them in its sights through hollow eyes as it clawed purposefully towards them.

34

Lars walked the streets for what seemed like hours, trying to retrace his steps and find the bar where Kitsune had seduced him. He wasn't sure what he was looking for. Evidence? Proof? Meaning? He checked every possible alley for familiar doorways but couldn't find the steps down to a bar.

He passed the Yorkshire Grey, trying to determine the direction in which they had walked. The pub door was bolted shut. He stared through the window and could make out the shapes of half-finished pint glasses on tables, like the pub had been evacuated in a hurry. There was no sign of movement.

He stepped back and found himself standing in the exact spot where Stu had been struck down. He moved onto the pavement. Reaching in his pocket, he checked his phone, and remembered that the battery was dead.

An ambulance sped by. The morning felt apocalyptic.

The sign on the door of the Amped Up Comic Book Store said "Nerd Cave Closed." The boys must have had a long night, he thought. He knocked. He knew it was useless to try and rouse them.

Eventually he found himself back at the flat. He picked up the bin lids that were still lying on the floor. There were no animals in the trees, no badgers, squirrels or birds. Claire had taken the keys from the lock. He knocked and the door swung open.

'Claire?'

She didn't reply. The corridor was dark. All lights were off. He let the front door click shut behind him.

There was a broken coffee mug on the kitchen floor.

'Claire?'

Strange that she would go out and leave the door unlocked. His keys were on the counter. He ran upstairs and checked the bedroom. She was definitely out. A bag was on the floor with her mobile inside. This was a bad sign. She must have gone to see Stu and she must have left in a hurry.

When Lars saw the empty fish tank he realised that shit had really gotten serious. She had flushed him. How could she take all of this out on an innocent fish? 'Sorry, Mr Chips, old friend.'

He began looting essential items, grabbed some cash and his passport from an open drawer, and stuffed them in his pocket.

He hadn't checked Atari Shock for what must have been over eight hours. It was time to confront the worst. He woke the screensaver and entered his password. The brutal truth flashed up on screen.

Inventory: Money 0; Drugs 0; Nukes 0; Shields 0; Kudos 0; Life force 0.

His Immortal legacy was officially offline.

Exhaustion hit him like a sonic boom. He stumbled to the bedroom, resources entirely sapped. With the last of his energy he managed to plug in his phone, and collapsed on the bed in his clothes. Within seconds, he had closed his eyes and was unconscious.

As Lars slept, the walls thickened with a spiky residue that spread across the ceiling like a cluster of insects. It covered the floor and crawled up the bedside, eventually forming a clump of black mass that hung directly above his face. Carefully, it dribbled down, accreting layers of an unknown substance to become a shark tooth stalactite that paused inches from him. It shimmered like a sail in a gentle breeze, swinging to the rhythm of his breathing, awaiting further instructions. An unreal mist formed at the end of the bed – a physical entity that was neither in this world or the next. The eyes of an otherworldly creature observed him from across the void.

He stretched out to check his phone and felt a shivering shock when he saw the date. Two days had passed.

He fell out of bed and ran downstairs. 'Claire?' he shouted, to no reply. The broken mug was still on the kitchen floor. He dialled her number, and as it connected he felt a sudden relief, until the phone rang in the handbag upstairs. He listened to her voice message and felt, for some reason, that she was already very far away. He tried Stu but it wouldn't connect. His number had been blocked. A voice inside was urging him, convincing him that the next thing he had to do, was call a cab.

Rain fell harder as the car stopped outside Heathrow, Terminal Five. Lars had been sick out of the window. The driver threatened two hundred pounds in damages.

He immediately felt sick again as he caught a whiff of the smokers huddled by the entrance. He paid with a credit card and stumbled to the check-in. The sickness was stronger than he'd felt before, as though sleep had made it worse. He felt a hollow feeling inside.

At the check-in desk, the clerk took his passport, looked him up and down, and began typing.

Was something following him? He felt exposed in the open airport terminal. He was shivering, dehydrated, and beginning to feel scared. The past twenty-four hours felt increasingly unreal. Lars was staggering towards an unknown destination like his life depended on it, but he had absolutely no idea where he was going.

The clerk printed out a set of tickets and handed them over. 'Head straight to gate thirty-two. They're waiting for you.'

'Who's waiting?'

'Next, please.'

He was ushered on. He walked through security, and just as he held his arms up to be patted down, something caught the security guard's eye.

'What's up, Steve?'

'Lizards.'

'Wot?'

'I just seen two lizards,' announced the security guard.

'Where?'

'On that young gentleman's arm, just as he raised 'em.'

'Are you sure?'

'Been doing this job twenty years, mate. I know lizards when I see 'em. Excuse me, sir?'

Lars tried to smile. It came out as more of a frown.

'Are you carrying lizards?'

He emptied his pockets, embarrassed. Travellers stared, unsure if they'd eavesdropped correctly. He took off his jacket, shook it, and held up his shoes for inspection. They were put through the x-ray machine. There were no lizards.

'Leave him alone, Steve. Lizards, indeed! You can go, sir.'

He was waved through, with security man, Steve, left to live with the troubled uncertainty that he had definitely seen two tiny lizards.

'Final call for passenger, Lars Nilsson. Please head straight to gate thirty-two.'

A wave of sickness overwhelmed him. He felt the nausea swirl inside and ducked into the public toilets where he retched into the sink. Travellers kept their distance. People were staring.

A janitor was sloshing a mop and bucket around the floor. He stopped to shake his head, reaching conclusions, wondering why so many people thought it was fine to drink heavily at airports, like the usual drinking hours just didn't apply in this no-man's-land oasis.

'You need help, son?'

Lars shivered and waved him away.

'I'll have to come back and clean this mess up, you know,' he grumbled.

Lars knew that the janitor had gone to alert security. He splashed water on his face and looked at himself in the mirror for the first time since the BBP lift. The one staring back was gaunt, black puffy bags under wide eyes. He looked weak but wired. He splashed more water and rubbed his neck. Lars ran his fingers through his hair, and as he did so a large fistful fell away. He stared again in the mirror and tried to focus on the image before him as it began to fragment into strange, digital quadrants – blocks and shapes, not unlike the raindrops on the bus window. The image was reforming, reshaping, reorganising the pieces that made up the man he once recognised. He blinked and washed his face again, hoping it would bring clarity but the image in the mirror no longer looked like his own.

The next time he looked up, an entirely different person confronted him. An older version of himself was staring back. He touched his cheek and the reflection did the same. He blinked, unsure what he was seeing.

The image was now of a bald, old man. He looked into sparkling, inquisitive eyes, and felt a deep connection.

'Izanagi?' he asked, with a whisper.

The face in the mirror nodded affirmation and smiled.

Lars felt the delirium of sickness. A white light began to emanate from the mirror, flooding the room, cleansing it. As the energy increased, the sickness began to subside. He was instantly more awake and unusually stronger. He touched his face and Kitsune's scar melted away, leaving instead, a thick tuft of spiky white beard. He rubbed his eyes and the old man copied him exactly, but with a slightly delayed reaction.

'Who am I?' he asked, unsure if the image in the mirror had the ability to speak, or if this was just another in a series of acute hallucinogenic episodes.

The reflection of the old man became animated and stroked its goatee beard. After a contemplative pause, it said, 'I am he, and you are he, as you are me, and we are all together.' It grinned, knowingly.

'That's a Beatles lyric,' said Lars, glumly. 'You just quoted I Am The Walrus.'

'One of our favourites,' said the reflection. 'It felt appropriate given the circumstances.'

Lars wondered if he should really be encouraging whatever it was.

'You haven't allowed yourself the time to think this through,' said the reflection.

The old man had deep, engaging eyes that were exactly like his own. The image was in fact identical to Lars; an exact representation, but with the additional lines formed by old age and acute wisdom. He wondered if the man looked like him, or if he in fact, looked like the old man.

'Time,' said the reflection, 'that most precious of constructs. If you have too much time, you waste it. If you have too little time, you are crushed by it. Time is on your side.'

'That's the Rolling Stones.'

'I like that one too,' replied the reflection, stroking its bald forehead.

Lars felt compelled to do the same, with a slightly delayed reaction. 'Is this real?'

The image of the old man shook its head. 'I don't think I know that one? Radiohead? Maybe The Smiths?'

'It's not a lyric.'

'Well, that's no fun.'

'Can you tell me what's happening?' asked Lars.

'Can you tell *me* what's happening?' repeated the reflection.

Lars winced. As did the old man.

'You already know the answer,' said Lars.

The old man smiled. 'Yes, we do.'

'Hey!' shouted a voice. The janitor was standing at the entrance with his mop.

Lars turned back to the mirror and the image was of himself once again, but there was a distinct change. He no longer had any hair. He was bald, with the beginnings of a fine, white, goatee beard.

'This ain't no place to have a haircut. Don't leave your mess in my sink, son.' The janitor pushed his bucket into the crowded airport, muttering as he went. 'What is this world coming to?'

'Urgent call for passenger, Lars Nilsson. Please head straight to gate thirty-two.'

Walking through the airport, Lars felt strangely disengaged from the people that surrounded him. The terminal became a symphony of internalised monologues and he could hear every single one of them; hopes, dreams, desires, fears, longing so deep that it was even unknown by the person that yearned for it.

An alternative angle had presented itself. He could focus on each individual with such accuracy that he felt he could read their very soul. He would never have imagined how simple it was to allow himself to read it all so clearly. Slow down. Time is on your side. The isolation brought with it a new found clarity, a confidence to see everything for what it truly was.

The spiralling sensation was a calling. Something was trying to reach him from far beyond the limits of this world. That someone − was himself.

'I'm Lars Nilsson,' he said, breathless and sweating as he handed over his boarding pass at gate thirty-two.

'You sure about that?' asked the stewardess with a laugh. She touched him on the arm. 'My little joke. Should have seen your face.' She smiled. 'This way.'

Lars looked through the terminal window. On the tarmac was a silver and white passenger jet displaying a spiralling yin and yang symbol on its tail; the logo of The Foundation of New World Technologies.

35

A flicker of naked flame battled with shadows that stretched like a heavy cloak along the sandstone wall.

'I accept the gift,' croaked a voice in delight. It reverberated around the chamber.

The dark shadows spread and with a sound like a flurry of feathers it shifted in shape to reveal further protrusions; spikes and spears, casting an image that was unlike anything the professor had seen before. It contorted to display a tall, pointed sceptre, which swirled and rested on the floor in an elegant show of power.

Laughter filled the void. The creature was taunting him. 'Do you know what I am?' coughed the voice. 'I will show you.'

Van Peterson reached out to protect himself as the substance spread like an army of zombie insects. He pushed against it and his body became trapped in a sticky, thread-like substance, as he stumbled into the eternal abyss of the cosmic web.

ACHIEVEMENT UNLOCKED

LEVEL THREE

36

Chieko had respect for tradition. It dictated every aspect of her life. She lived by a series of ancient rules that had been treasured for centuries. As a young Buddhist, she was proudly understanding and yet firmly stoic. She followed a strict routine every day, as she prepared a dish of medicinal cooking, a tonic brewed for generations; the recipe for Samgyetang, Ginseng Chicken Soup.

First, she would wash away the blood. The carcass would then be placed breast side up in a large pot. She would let it simmer for precisely fifteen minutes while performing breathing exercises, inhaling with the rhythm of the boiling water as it permeated the flesh. She would then turn off the flame and allow the chicken to rest in the hot water while she performed her Foundation duties for exactly ninety minutes. Once they were complete she would add the final ingredients; ginseng, wine, salt, and bring the soup back to the boil for a further forty minutes. During this time she would sit quietly beside the pot and meditate.

Chieko knew that the simplicity of time itself, made this ancient recipe absolutely divine.

37

Neon lights twinkled through a glass wall, casting rainbow coloured shards across the room. High backed chairs were in shadow around the table, lit only by a light bulb. The filament glowed, hovering in the air like a golden moth, illuminating the immediate circle of wood beneath. His guests were shrouded in silhouette.

'We are committed architects of the New World,' said Dr Tadashi Finjoto, as he reached for an ashtray and tapped confidently on the Gurkha Black Dragon cigar. He paused to taste the scent of the room; rich leather and the deep peat of smoke.

The dark wood of the table top glistened, revealing etchings of an ancient grain. A slender bottle of Johnnie Walker Black Label was unopened at the centre. Next to it, a silver dish was filled with perfectly spherical ice cubes. This was the deal marker, to be laboriously opened, slowly served, and only toasted at the point of acceptable agreement. Until such time, it remained the token of a promise waiting to be fulfilled.

Dr Finjoto had been talking in a relaxed manner, taking time to allow his guests to settle before the real business. A tension had fallen on the boardroom, appearing to force the cigar smoke to take on a life of its own and spiral around the light bulb.

'We have a unique opportunity,' he said, emphasising his point with a twirl of the Black Dragon, 'to realise the life's work of a great man.' He took a deep drag of the cigar and continued. 'I sincerely believe that Professor Van Peterson was close to discovering humankind's hidden levels by unlocking the true expansion capabilities of consciousness.' He spoke softly, focusing his attention on the guests. 'The time has come for a New World; for your world, my friends. By joining together, at the very pinnacle of our success, we will make this world a reality.' He brought the cigar to his lips and allowed himself a moment of indulgent self-reflection while holding the taste in his mouth. As he exhaled, the thick smoke caught the light, forming a series of intricate shapes like a Rorschach test. They hung in the air, twisting slowly, gradually revealing the physical form of a figure at the opposite end of the table.

It hunched, looming large over the room. Dark spikes feathered out to form broad shoulders. It lowered its head and turned to expose silhouetted facial features that were not human. There was the clack of affirmation and a rustle as the creature shivered and repositioned itself. The smoke lingered.

Dr Finjoto leaned in with caution, as if trying not to provoke a startled snake to strike. 'I have what you want,' he whispered into darkness. 'They are yours, if we have an accord?' He took a moment to enjoy the feeling of power achieved by having the complete attention of the beast.

The bottle of Johnnie Walker Black Label vanished. Finjoto smiled in acknowledgment.

'Now, if you will forgive me, I must welcome our esteemed guests.'

38

The scale of the city was overwhelming; home to over thirteen million people, most of who appeared to be on the congested streets. Islands of bright light shone through pools of darkness; traffic lights, street lights, starkly lit restaurant windows with a complete disregard for mood lighting.

Berry didn't feel tired. There was too much to take in. She watched the movement of traffic as the car cut through the crowds with authority. Her mind buzzed. The world outside was in constant motion.

As they swept past a street market she caught a glimpse of strange fruit of all types and sizes, raw meat piled up in bloody slabs, large white eggs, tanks of fish, frogs and prawns clinging to the last dregs of life next to deep bags of spices, brown and red and yellow; the street side stench of putrefaction twisted with the beauty of vibrant colour.

A large snake was curled in a wicker basket. She felt an instant déjà vu and slunk back in the seat, shivering at the sensation. 'How long?' she asked.

Sarah was staring ahead. She caught Berry's eye in the mirror. 'Not long,' she replied, seeming distracted. Their gaze lingered for a fraction of a second. Sarah had more to say, until the ringtone of an unfamiliar phone disturbed the moment. Berry lost herself in the streaks on the car window and then realised that the sound was coming from her own bag. It was the company iPhone. The contact details flashed on screen – Dr Finjoto.

'Miss Butler, welcome,' announced the well-spoken voice; deep, rich, like the fine cigar that he had been smoking just moments before. The voice felt close somehow, as though he were sitting right next to her. 'I trust your journey was acceptable?'

'The flight was fine. Thank you,' she mumbled.

'You have taken the opportunity to read our welcome pack?'

It was pure puff and had made no sense at all; high-end commercial speak on a scale that she'd never read before, not even on the most pretentious blogs and designer websites. The propaganda brochure featured posed photographs of young Japanese professionals wearing thick-rimmed spectacles, holding test tubes up to a subtle blue light.

"We are a virtual think tank dedicated to realising new technologies. World leaders in advanced studies of neuro-anatomy, techno-physiology and neuro-sampling. These are the tools of creation."

With an elaborate name like The Foundation of New World Technologies, and a brochure filled with convoluted tech speak statements, it was still unclear to Berry what the company did. The pack was straight out of a futuristic self-projection of who this company aspired to be, she thought. It was a pep talk for the non-believer. Smoke and mirrors. Pure and simple.

"The Foundation fundamentally believe that a new dawn of learning and memory will be achieved through the studies of advanced neural network programming, integrating the principles of neuro-chemistry, neuro-endocrinology and molecular biology, with superior technological innovation. We have a responsibility to the world, and will maintain our extensive research for the benefit of future generations."

For a welcome pack, it wasn't very welcoming. She had flicked through the pictures and quickly forgotten about it.

'I read it, Dr Finjoto,' she replied, like the good student she felt contractually obliged to become.

'I wanted to greet you personally.'

Berry caught Sarah's eye in the mirror. She was watching, listening in on the conversation. It seemed like she knew every word that he would be saying. Sarah was the first to look away.

'I will see you soon, Berry Butler,' said Finjoto. 'You have arrived.'

The call cut off as the car pulled into a driveway and a wide gate swung open. She heard the crunch of metal as they bumped into a courtyard and slid from the busy street like they had never even been there. A corrugated door lifted and they drove into a brightly lit car park. They stopped next to a door which opened to reveal a lift. The car doors opened automatically. The synchronicity was perfect.

Berry checked that she had her things, and realised that she'd given most of it to the driver at the airport. All that she had was a small bag with the iPhone, her laptop, the welcome pack, and her Jujyfruits. As she stepped out of the car, the humid atmosphere of exhaust fumes and the smell of the city immediately hit her. She felt a wave of nausea and was suddenly light headed. She recognised the sensation. The sugar crash had caught up with her. She reached into the bag and popped a Green Apple Juju.

Stepping into the lift brought temporary relief. The wall was mirrored and the girl that looked back seemed exhausted and scared, not at all how she imagined herself. Black, frizzy hair bristled under trendy specs. She lifted her glasses to clean them and saw that her eyes were bloodshot. Her pupils were like pins. She licked her lips to hide the cracks in her skin.

'The bags will be taken to your room,' said Sarah, as she typed a key code and the doors closed.

Berry couldn't tell if the lift was moving up or down. It could have even been moving sideways. She was feeling increasingly disorientated by the second.

The doors opened to reveal a vast hall decorated in executive orange and brown, tasteful and bland at the same time. There were no windows. Large oil paintings of traditional Japanese design hung along the wall, delicately lit to show off the detail. The buzz of conversation hummed at a constant level beneath the distant piano muzac coming from somewhere high above. A large water fountain spouted at the centre of the reception area, showing off the vast ceiling height.

Berry felt as if she was breathing a different kind of air. It smelled thick. It clung to her like it could suffocate her in a second if it chose to.

Groups of people moved through the space, busy to be somewhere else. Everyone was moving. No one looked at her. No one made eye contact.

A young girl was waiting at the reception. She was dressed immaculately in a grey suit, with sharp corners and curves. Sarah spoke Japanese with authority and stepped aside to allow Berry to be processed.

'Welcome to The Foundation of New World Technologies, Miss Butler,' said the receptionist. 'Sign here, please.'

She felt her eyes closing. A fatigue had hit her like she'd never felt before.

'Miss Butler?'

She looked blankly at the receptionist. 'Sorry, I feel dizzy. The air…'

'The air is triple filtered,' explained the receptionist. 'It is the most purely conditioned air in the world. Sign, please.'

'Yes. Sure.' She looked at the guest book and couldn't remember the last time she'd used a pen.

Sarah's mobile vibrated and she excused herself. Berry watched her walk across the foyer. Her hand covered her mouth as she spoke. She didn't look at all like she'd just travelled halfway across the world. She stood, perfectly straight, and nodded like the person on the other end of the phone were standing directly in front of her. She seemed anxious.

Berry turned back to the receptionist who seemed concerned that her presence was causing the reception feng shui to become misaligned. She scribbled on the document without reading it. The receptionist smiled and placed the paperwork in a black padded folder. 'You are welcome,' she said, before disappearing through a discreetly hidden door.

Sarah's manner had shifted on arrival. The conversation was now strictly business. She finished the call. 'You have a meeting in the boardroom facility.'

Berry reached out, holding on to her jacket, stopping her from turning away. 'We're not going to the hotel room? I'm really tired.'

'Miss Butler, you have a contract meeting with Dr Finjoto himself.' She smiled, sharply. 'This way, please.' The intimacy of the long haul flight had faded. She was now cold and abruptly formal.

Berry popped a Jujyfruit. Perhaps she was just tired, she thought. She would be ok after a rest.

They walked through the lobby. Photographs of staff hung along the walls; clean cut and perfectly framed. They were studying screens, x-ray machines and papers. The poses reminded her of the welcome pack.

'The Foundation currently have two hundred staff, all working on specialist areas of the project,' explained Sarah, 'but these facilities are capable of a thousand. We're now leaving the accommodation area.'

'We're not in a hotel?'

'This is a unique facility run privately for, and by, The Foundation of New World Technologies. Everything you need is just a phone call away. You have the iPhone I gave you? The Foundation runs on its own private network. Normal phones won't work here.'

They passed through a doorway and entered a long corridor. It was brightly lit, like a hospital. Berry began to notice small security cameras hanging intermittently along the perfectly white ceiling. Some of the marketing pictures now featured smiling faces next to thoughtful, scientific looks.

'You are one of a carefully considered collective of professionals who have been selected to input directly into the development of the project. You will work as a team, a collective effort for the greater good, you are architects of a New World generation.' Sarah was reciting the speech like it was from a textbook. Eye contact had stopped entirely.

She was self-conscious, like she knew that she was being listened to.

'When can I see the city?' asked Berry, hoping to shift the conversation back to a level of familiarity.

'There are vouchers in your welcome pack, should you wish to apply for an excursion. Fill in the required details and your request will be processed.'

Berry wondered if the welcome pack was either very expensive to produce, or just totally over rated.

At the end of the corridor, the low ceiling disappeared to expose a vast, open space, like an airport terminal. Soft seating areas were placed about but no one sat. More employees were busy, holding clipboards, pushing thin carts that looked like filing cabinets on wheels. They were all immaculately dressed in perfectly crisp, grey suits. Escalators led in all directions. Palm plants looked far too healthy to grow where there was no natural light.

A futuristic truck was hauling a row of cargo crates on trailers. It hummed, high pitched, as it buzzed effortlessly across the floor. Yellow plastic and silver chrome gleamed in the light. The yin and yang symbol of The Foundation was proudly emblazoned on the side.

Berry felt exposed, overwhelmed by the shift in scale. 'What is this place?'

'This is Central Holding,' explained Sarah. 'From here you can reach any area of The Foundation in the shortest possible time. You'll see that each area is clearly sign posted. You can't get lost.' She waved her hand over a security block and the door automatically opened. 'Wait inside,' she ordered.

39

The Tokyo skyline shimmered in a heat haze beyond a wall of floor to ceiling glass. Skyscrapers and glass towers were twisting in the bright window. The contours were jagged, shifting abruptly, as spires and buildings hung at oblique angles. A long table spanned the middle of the boardroom.

Berry had counted the number of chairs several times. There were definitely twenty.

A man entered and stood at the far end. He raised his nose and tasted the air. 'The perfect reflection of a city two kilometres above,' he announced, proudly. 'An achievement of New World engineering.'

She was momentarily caught in the detail, distracted by the slow movement of vast shapes. 'It doesn't look real,' she said.

'The light is refracted.'

She was too far away to read the expression on his face. He too seemed lost in the wonder of the neon glass. 'The bending of light can cause some beautiful illusions. See how it moves like the stars?' He made a distinct show of finishing his admiration of the view and then waved a hand. 'You may sit.'

She pulled out a chair, then changed her mind and pulled out another. She changed her mind again and sat on the first one.

'I see that you are very chaos itself,' said Dr Finjoto.

She smiled, unsure if he meant it as a compliment or criticism, and reached into her bag for a Raspberry Ripple Jujyfruit.

Finjoto didn't sit. He stood at the end of the table, peering at Berry through thin glasses that made his gaze seem even more intense.

'You said that the city is above us? So, we're below ground?' she asked, trying to find a suitable ice breaker.

'Space, required by The Foundation, would not be possible in a city such as Tokyo above ground. It would be less…' he paused to consider the word, 'suitable.'

'You need a lot of space?'

He smiled. 'It is perhaps more of a question of privacy, of professional security. There are many projects in development that are not ready to be shared with the world above.'

'I still don't understand what you do here, Dr Finjoto,' Berry said, matter-of-factly.

He took his time, glancing at the skyline and then back to the room, like he was addressing a much larger audience. 'It is my honour to discuss your contract and to initiate you into The Foundation of New World Technologies,' he eventually said.

She looked at the floor, sucking on her sweet.

'You will be working at our head office for the next four weeks, or until such time that the project is complete. You have met Sarah. She has been assigned to you as your personal assistant.'

Berry raised an eyebrow. Sarah was working for her? It seemed the other way around.

'At this juncture,' Dr Finjoto continued, 'I must inform you that all work you create, think, or devise, while under the employment of The Foundation may be used for further research and exploitation by the company at a later date, should you no longer be under contract.'

'I'm sorry, what?'

'Your contract contains further detail. I am merely offering you the headlines.'

Next to him, in a perfect pile, was a stack of papers and a single pen.

'We have already established your guide price, and this has been paid into your UK bank account. A further five hundred thousand pounds GBP will be transferred on signature of a month's development work.' Finjoto tapped on the thick body of paperwork, at which point a young girl, much like the receptionist, appeared with a separate copy and stood next to Berry.

Finjoto nodded and the girl placed the paperwork and a single pen on the table. She stood back, bowing deeply at her waist, holding this pose for a few seconds before moving away, her eyes fixed firmly on the opposite side of the room.

Berry wasn't sure what to do, so she sat, patiently, and sucked on the Jujyfruit.

'I will leave you for one hour to read and to sign,' said Finjoto. He nodded with a slight bow and began to walk away.

'Wait. I have questions,' she called after him.

Dr Finjoto stopped and turned. He looked at her and angled his head slightly without making a sound.

'What am I going to be doing?'

He was closer now and looked much older than she'd first imagined. His skin showed deep signs of ageing. His hands were delicate and small. He wore a black suit and tie and had neatly greased hair. He appeared less confrontational up close. Dr Finjoto was clearly a master of using his surroundings to project an exaggerated and authoritative self-image.

'There will be a time for questions, Berry Butler. Now is not that time. Please read the document and sign.' He turned his back to her but didn't move. It was a show of dominance rather than an indication of leaving. He stood perfectly still. Waiting.

Berry realised that she was taller than her host. It gave her a modest confidence boost. She wasn't going to let his power play intimidate her. 'You want me to sign a shit load of papers but I still don't know what I'm doing here? What's the scam, a new game, yeah? A game about heaven and earth, gods and demons, light and dark, Superman and Spiderman? Ok, whatever, that's fine, but what platforms are we working on? What's our ESRB rating? We got some adver-gaming considerations? Who's this all for, a clothing manufacturer, your fucking government?'

Finjoto was silent. He spun around and stared at her with a down turned mouth and piercing eyes. His nostrils flared aggressively. 'Miss Butler, should you wish to leave the project then you will be deported and legal action will be taken against you for loss of income. I would advise you not to contemplate the matter any further and to be respectful and compliant.' He stood firm. 'Read and sign,' he said, challenging her from the opposite end of the table.

'This just isn't how I do things,' she said. 'I know my rights.' She didn't have a clue. She wasn't even sure if she'd verbally agreed to the contract already. The fact that they had wired her money was possibly complicit, but she was feeling bullied and uncomfortable with the arrogant attitude of the man who claimed to be her employer. She could always send it all back, she thought. She hadn't even checked her account. Who were these people? Everything was happening so fast. There was no time to think things through and this scared her. The Foundation wasn't like any gaming development office that she'd been in. 'So what is it about me that you can't get from anyone else?' she asked, defiantly.

Dr Finjoto gave the impression of calm authority but he was beginning to lose his temper. He twitched as he stood, composed and determined.

'Is there even a game at all?' The question made Berry feel immediately vulnerable.

He took a deep breath, bringing his palms together in prayer, then placing them carefully and firmly on the boardroom table. He hunched slightly, his posture becoming animalistic, like a panther ready to pounce. He leaned in, pursing his lips. 'Have you ever felt that you are not quite yourself, Berry Butler?'

She tried to swallow. Her mouth was dry.

'Have you ever dreamed that you are someone else entirely? That you have always been someone else, and will continue to be, recurrently, over and over.' He smiled with a slight leer.

'I don't know what you're talking about,' she said, catching his gaze.

Dr Finjoto walked to a small bar where he poured out a fresh glass of water. He held it out before him and allowed her shape to fill the space. He seemed captivated, studying how her image became translucent in the water refraction. 'You will be immersed in an experience unlike any other,' he said. 'You will live the game, feel the game, interact with the game in a way that has never before been achieved. You will play emotionally and intelligently. You will discover new depths and reach the very gates of Nirvana itself.' He looked her in the eye. 'This glass of water represents you, Berry Butler. It encapsulates everything that you are on this mortal Earth.'

In a single gulp, he swallowed the glass of water whole, and placed it upside down on the table.

'You belong to me,' he said, before leaving her alone with the thick and overwhelming contract.

40

Dr Finjoto paced confidently down the auditorium stage. Key words flashed on screen as he spoke, photo printing themselves into the minds of the audience with each bold statement.

'Famine, disease, entertainment culture, instability in our communities, civil violence and global conflict – this is not the future that was planned by our elders. We head not to enlightenment, but to the putrefaction of the soul. Our world is in crisis, my friends. It is not too late to change.'

The Academy murmured in anticipation.

'We must examine where this cancer has come from; this so-called modernity that threatens to rot the soul. There is a corruption at the core. The impact has been horrific and it has hung over us for many generations. The selfish actions of the few have affected the many. Something must be done, and we at The Foundation of New World Technologies have the solution.'

The Academy applauded.

He stood, proud, taking a moment to gauge the reaction. 'There is fear inherent in a new generation of indifferent youth, a terrified struggle for approval and acceptance. Imagine a world free of this terror, a world of vast and beautiful opportunity, a palette of creativity that allows for the freedom of experimentation with no consequence other than the rich stasis of learning and the gift of enlightenment?'

The Academy applauded.

'I offer you a new existence; the ability to live, grow and experience a life free from fatalistic consequence. For what is there to take from our world in its current state? Birth, growth, enforced conformity, useless learning, stress, the desperate plea for acceptance, the hollow desire to be remembered, to outlive our shallow, painful, pathetic social existence on this Earth, only to watch loved ones grow old, friends and family pass away, our faces in the mirror reveal the signs of an imminent and unavoidable death.'

Chieko was watching from the back of the room. Somehow his words seemed more potent in front of the influential gathering. She felt a shiver down her spine as he spoke.

'What if it were possible to elevate above the chaos, beyond the self-destruction? There has never been a greater need for a sanctioned retreat such as the one that we have harnessed; a safe haven for those of us who are ready to move beyond this mortal plane and on to a higher level. We are offering each and every one of you a chance for release, for escape, and for self-validation. We are offering you a new dawn. We are offering you the chance to die and to live again, to re-spawn many millions of times, to create your own worlds. This is what our platform will provide; technology with a soul.'

The Academy applauded.

Dr Finjoto stared at the floor. The room fell silent. There was barely a breath. Eventually, he looked up and saw Chieko watching. She smiled back at him. He didn't flinch but the next time he spoke his voice was softer. He adopted a tone that was more intimate and engaging. 'It is widely believed that Professor Van Peterson's research was a fantasy that verged on recklessness. His subjects were no more than animals, and his research, a form of mental abuse. The spiritual scientific community believes that it is better off without him. It is in the light of this dishonour that The Foundation propose to save the name of Van Peterson. His death was a shock to his peers, especially to myself.'

There was an uncomfortable shifting in the audience.

'I was with him the night he came up with the phrase. Quantum jumping.' Finjoto paused for effect. 'As his former assistant, I will continue his research under new regulations issued by the Medical Institute of Neuro-Science. I will deliver the freedom that he promised. His research will be continued and a new dawn of human consciousness will break. Provando e riprovando,' he declared.

The audience chanted back the phrase out loud.

'Esteemed colleagues of the Accademia del Cimento. I give you your future. I give you – Project Tetris.'

The auditorium burst into rapturous applause and congratulated themselves as the words were displayed on screen. A spotlight struck the stage, illuminating a metal object; a cage meshed in copper wires. Inside was a single wooden chair. To Chieko, the cage appeared haunting and surreal, even though she'd seen it many times before in the laboratories on Sub Level Six. This was a New World object, a platform to another space and time, the awakening into the descent.

Finjoto hushed the auditorium. They obeyed immediately.

'Following new partnerships that have come into effect since Van Peterson's death, the project and its associated assets have now become legal property of The Foundation of New World Technologies. The Academy will complete his work. The platform will be harnessed and you shall all take your rightful place in the next life.'

There was a burst of applause in acceptance.

'It is time to present you with our latest achievements direct from the London laboratories. We have induced three Strepsirrhini primates with a significant dose of NST, and they have made the successful journey between this world and the next. Our test subjects have been transported overnight from the United Kingdom, and we will have the honour of observing them in a typical state of total immersion.'

A phone vibrated in Finjoto's pocket. He checked the message and brought the meeting to an abrupt halt, leaving the Academy in an excited, but bewildered, vacuum.

41

The clinical lighting of The Foundation holding facility made Sarah appear paler than she was. A group of staff were standing around the cage that contained the dead bodies of three lemurs. They had all suffered extreme reactions to the administered dose of NST.

Dr Finjoto was visibly angry. 'You are sure that they were healthy when they left London?'

'They were.'

'How long between each outbreak?'

'Three minutes, exactly,' explained Sarah.

'Who reported the first incident?'

'Security.'

'Is he one of us?'

'Works for the airline.'

Finjoto glanced over to the car driver who bowed and left the room.

'Does anyone at the BBP know?'

She shook her head. 'Not yet.'

'Report back that the live-stock were received in good health. Show me the images.'

She passed over a tablet. He swiped through the pictures without a hint of emotion.

'It was a complete psychotropic breakdown. They were terrified. Something was threatening them.'

Finjoto nodded. 'Dosage?'

'3/4 ml.'

He stroked his chin, double tapped a QuickTime and the scene played. Sarah's voice could be heard in the back ground.

'Lemur three. Six thirty-two AM, JST. The creature has had an attack. Self-mutilation to the face and eyes. Hysterical reaction.'

Finjoto watched the lemur tear holes in its eye sockets and fall to the floor. He handed the tablet back without saying anything.

The incident was catching up with her. Sarah was trying hard not to get upset. 'They committed hara-kiri,' she said, through the beginnings of tears.

He stopped her from saying anything else and indicated for all of the staff to leave. When they were alone, he turned and touched her intimately on the cheek.

She immediately started crying. 'I'm terrified, Tadashi.'

'I understand, my Sarah, but you have nothing to fear.'

'We've been micro-dosing the animals for months now. The kick was nothing new. Something's wrong. Something's changed.'

'Nothing has changed, Sarah. This is just a small set back.'

'It pushed them over the edge. You saw the results. We can't progress with the NST without sufficient time to regulate the effects.'

'The Academy have gathered. We will not let this matter prevent us from achieving our timeline,' he explained.

She laid her head on his chest and sighed deeply. She felt safe in his arms. It had been such a long time since they'd held each other. The Foundation restrictions offered them little opportunity to be alone together.

'You have suffered a great shock,' he said in a hushed whisper as he held her close. 'Don't worry. There will always be challenges. It is in the very nature of what we do and in all that we are trying to achieve.'

'Have you ever thought that what we're trying to do is wrong?'

He brushed the hair behind her ear. 'Isn't the fact that you're asking the question enough to validate the need to find an answer?' he replied. 'The world needs us. The world needs you, Sarah, to keep trying.'

She looked at the metal cage. She could picture the lemur frantically clawing itself in the eyes. 'I'm not sure how long I can keep doing this,' she said, softly.

'The mortal world is crumbling, Sarah, tearing itself apart, and why? Because people are afraid, fearful of their own existence, desperate to prove themselves in the small amount of time they have on this Earth. Fear makes us so desperate to kick each other to the ground. Is this not why there is so much conflict in the world?' He held his hands either side of her face. 'If we are afraid, then we are nothing more than these animals in a cage, tearing out our eyes rather than confronting the mysteries of the Universe. Do not fear change, darling.'

She moved in close to kiss him. Tadashi allowed the intimacy. She closed her eyes and rested her head on his chest again.

'Perpetual clinical reincarnation is a gift from the gods themselves. Together we will unlock the passage to a world more beautiful than life itself.'

She smiled and sniffed away tears.

'Your father would have been so proud.'

Sarah allowed herself to relax. 'Sometimes I wonder if we should have let the Academy die with him.'

Finjoto flinched and tightened his arms around her, clasping her so close that her breathing became restricted.

'Tadashi, you're hurting me,' she gasped. She was trapped in his embrace, unable to break free. 'Tadashi, stop. I can't breathe.'

He seemed lost in a trance, unaware of what he was doing, until his grip weakened and he was stroking her hair again like nothing had happened.

'Do not be concerned, darling. We will continue with the next stage of the project, on schedule and as planned.'

She shivered and wiped away tears, deeply confused about what had just happened, and now more fearful than ever of the man that she had given herself to.

42

The first sensation that Lars acknowledged was the perfumed smell of bed sheets. He felt the crisp warmth of the duvet; feathery light and neatly pressed. He opened his eyes. He was in a hotel room.

A space-aged propeller fan spun slowly on the ceiling. Mounted on the wall was an oversized television. A cookery programme was on screen. The sound was turned down low, showing the preparation of spicy king prawn noodle soup. He watched, thinking nothing, until the door buzzed. He leaped out of bed and realised that he was already wearing a white bathrobe. As he approached the door, it automatically clicked open.

A young woman stood, looking immaculate, in the doorway. 'I am to welcome you to The Foundation of New World Technologies,' said Chieko. 'I am pleased to inform you that Dr Finjoto will see you soon. Please dress suitably. I will return in forty minutes.'

Lars had vague memories of the flight. He remembered sleeping most of the way, a car from the airport, climbing into bed, but he couldn't remember exactly when he had arrived. How long had he been asleep?

'Please, also this,' smiled Chieko. She presented an envelope in both hands. 'Instructions for your meeting.'

She bowed deeply and stepped back. The door clicked closed.

The envelope contained a business card with his name on it, and a series of instructions.

1: Introduce yourself using business card in both hands. State English name and company. With firm handshake.

2: Speak when addressed first by the doctor.

3: Never speak to any member of staff, unless first introduced.

4: Be punctual.

5: Never look the doctor directly in the eye.

6: Remember ...

He threw the letter on the table and opened the wardrobe. There was a pressed suit, a shirt and tie, and polished black shoes.

There was no phone or Wi-Fi signal. He wondered if he needed a different sim card. The room had its own phone, however, and he considered calling reception to ask them to connect a call. What was the time difference? Perhaps he could get them to call her for him?

The sickness had subsided and been replaced by a sensation that he didn't recognise at first. Then his stomach rumbled and he realised that he was hungry. An English menu by the television displayed a list of meals with code numbers but no prices. He hit zero and the call was immediately answered.

'Mr Nilsson? How can I help you today?' asked an overtly cheerful voice.

He placed an order for a club sandwich and fries; the international executive anytime meal. He was about to ask to be connected to an outside line but the receptionist cut the call. He would try later, he thought.

There was a stone wet-room with a huge shower. He turned on the tap. Steaming water rained down just as he caught sight of himself in the mirror. He was bald. He remembered that he had lost all of his hair at the airport. His white beard was thicker now. He was pale, thinner than he remembered. He looked fragile, and had black bags under red eyes.

He found himself thinking about Claire and paranoia gripped him deep in the stomach. He pictured her alone in their London flat. Had he really abandoned her? The gaming, The Immortal avatar, all seemed an absurd distraction. Just a shallow waste of time. What had it brought him other than the end of their relationship? Why had he even agreed to come here? What had he expected to find, a mysterious mountain island? She was right. He hadn't taken any responsibility. All he had done was run away to pursue another fantasy, just as he had done all of his life.

There was a buzzing sound and the door opened. A young woman stood in the entrance with a beautifully prepared tray. He took the platter in one hand like a dumb waiter and thanked her with an overstated nod. He felt an urge to ask if she had any more information about his itinerary. She looked at him with a confused and apologetic smile. He shrugged. She smiled again, and before he could take a glance down the corridor she closed the door. He carried the tray to the bed.

His mind wandered as he munched on fries. How long had it been? Days had passed since the game had sent him the curve ball of Hotei, Tengu is watching, and the nine tailed fox? He stared at a long strip of frosted glass along the wall. It was difficult to tell if there was daylight beyond. The light seemed natural. It flickered with shadows behind it. The effect made the room feel less isolated. He wasn't sure if it was a window or just decoration. Perhaps the frosting was for his own privacy and the world was just a few inches behind? Could someone see him? Was Tengu watching? Was this luxury room some kind of observation centre? The paranoia sunk deep to the pit of his stomach, triggering the familiar spiralling nausea. He took a bite of the club sandwich and ran to the bathroom to be sick.

Two tiny lizards climbed the wall and drank droplets of shower dew as they watched over him.

43

Chieko walked confidently into the boardroom with a tray of steaming green tea. Berry had passed out on the pile of papers. A drool mark smudged the ink. Her face twitched. 'Miss Butler?'

She woke with a jump and sat upright. The clinging embrace of sleep was new. The awakening wasn't welcome. 'Where am I?'

'You are at The Foundation of New World Technologies. Some tea, please?'

Berry checked her pockets and was relieved to find a pack of Jujyfruits. She selected a Red Rose and stared around the room as she sucked on the sugar sweet. A terrific nightmare clung to her like a damp shawl; the vivid image of an island floating on thick, swirling cloud. She remembered the sensation of being trapped between earth and sky, the clouds below moving like a black, threatening sea. Waves crashed, spiking in the air. With every clash, she could make out the stretching limb and moaning face of an otherworldly figure, grotesque arms reaching out, desperate to pull her down into the twisted sickness of the sea of abandoned souls.

A shrouded figure was circling at height. It slowed and

stopped and turned its head. 'Yomi-no-kuni,' it said. She had awoken with a violent spasm.

The tea was reviving. The document was signed with a smeared signature.

Chieko gathered the papers. 'I will take you to your room.'

Berry sat cross-legged on the bed. She felt hollow, unlike herself, like she'd been asleep for a month. She was unused to the abrupt shift of consciousness from sleep to being awake without the hit of sugar and caffeine.

A small speaker hidden in the ceiling repeated a message in broken English: 'Miss Butler, your presence is requested in fifteen minutes. Please make your way to the reception area… Miss Butler, your presence is requested in fifteen minutes.'

She opened the wardrobe. Her bags were unpacked and clothes were hanging, neatly pressed and zipped in protective covers. She looked for her travel bag and found it on a counter next to half a pack of Jujyfruits. She popped a couple of sweets and stumbled to the bathroom.

44

Lars was perspiring, despite the air conditioning. The suit made up for his lack of professional experience by presenting him as the perfect international pharmaceuticals representative. He hastily presented the business card, holding it in front of him with both hands, eyes averted, as instructed in the letter. 'I am Mr Lars Nilsson from Bishop, Banes and Price in the United Kingdom. We are grateful for The Foundation's generous contributions, Dr Finjoto.'

Finjoto made a point of taking his time. He was skilled in the art of revealing very little about his emotional state. He waved the card away. 'We are pleased with the BBP's desire to form a genuine working relationship, Mr Lars Nilsson.' He said the name in a way that sounded forced, as though trying it out for the first time.

The stony expression seemed courteous, yet dissatisfied. It was difficult for Lars to tell.

'Mr Nilsson will be preparing a presentation to take back to London,' explained Chieko.

He felt a flutter of panic as she said this. He'd been so caught up in the events of the last few days that he hadn't considered what might happen when he went back. He felt further away from home than he'd ever been.

'Very well, Mr Nilsson,' said Finjoto, his mood now noticeably brighter, 'we will make sure that you have enough stimulation to make a most impressive presentation.'

Lars smiled, shoulders back, chest out, as instructed.

Dr Finjoto inhaled a long breath of air, staring him in the eye with a slight look of repulsion in his gaze. He then smiled and placed his hand professionally on Lars' shoulder. At this proximity, Lars could smell his expensive suit. He could literally taste the authority in the air.

'We will proceed with your presentation notes in due course, but tonight my new friend, my brother, we relax and get to know each other.'

Lars nodded. He hadn't been instructed on this part. Go with the flow, he thought. 'I like the way you guys do business,' he laughed, averting his gaze, and then smiling a wide grin to balance it out.

Finjoto tightened his grip and pushed him forward as they followed Chieko down a corridor. The strip lighting was brilliant white and had the atmosphere of a private hospital, clean crisp walls displaying inoffensive pictures of business practice and corporate achievement. They walked down several corridors and took an escalator to a level where the décor changed from bright white to soft brown and yellow. The pictures lining the walls were no longer of Foundation employees fixed in contemplative poses; white coats and dark glasses holding vials and vessels to microscopes. They were now scenes of beaches, sunsets and palm trees. Waves were crashing on the shoreline. Pretty young girls danced in super small bikinis. The industrial flooring had become soft, purple carpet.

'This way, Mr Nilsson,' ushered Chieko.

They passed through a wooden doorway. She flicked a switch and waved a hand to welcome them both inside.

'Mr Nilsson,' coughed Finjoto. 'Let us celebrate the future success of your presentation in a manner to which I am sure you will become accustomed.'

Lars smiled a nervous grin.

The room was small, boxy, and felt used. It was a stark contrast to the clean perfection just a few corridors away. A large sofa lined three of the walls. A glass table in the middle was prepared with a tall bottle of Smirnoff vodka, a couple of mixers, a bucket of ice and two tumblers. An enormous flat screen television filled a wall. Several remote controls were lined up symmetrically in the middle of the table.

'Sit, please.'

Lars chose his position. 'Are we watching a movie?'

Dr Finjoto didn't respond. Instead, he picked up the Smirnoff bottle and studied the label, then tapped it with his finger and nodded to Chieko who promptly left the room.

Lars sat upright, expectant, slightly giddy at the sudden change in mood of his host.

Dr Finjoto took off his suit jacket and flung it on the seat. He sat back and sighed loudly. 'This is when we relax, Mr Lars Nilsson,' he announced, pulling out a packet of cigarettes. He tapped them in the unnecessary way only seen in Sixties movies and offered one. They lit up and smoked quietly.

There was a knock at the door. A queue of eight girls walked in and began to parade in a line. Chieko was standing at the entrance. She closed the door and left them to it.

'Please, you may choose,' offered Finjoto, pointing his lit cigarette and scratching his head nonchalantly. 'You are my guest.'

Lars raised his eyebrows in a confused grin. He laughed, unsure of the nature of the comment. He reached for a glass, keeping his eyes fixed firmly on the group before him. 'I think I need a drink.'

'No,' commanded Finjoto. 'Choose first. Then we drink.'

He sat back. One of the girls broke the line and helped him remove his jacket. 'Uh, thanks miss.'

'They are all excellent singers.'

'I'm sorry, singers?'

'For the karaoke. You will require a harmonising partner who will offer the perfect balance to your vocal capabilities. They are all extremely competent, Mr Nilsson.'

He took a relieved drag of his cigarette.

45

Her grey business suit was a little tight but she thought it looked okay. The formality of it even made Berry feel important. She studied herself in the mirrored lift as it travelled down to reception. She counted the floor numbers as she passed.

The doors opened to an elegant lobby where the five star hotel atmosphere persisted. It seemed even more so that she was its only guest.

'Miss Butler?' Chieko smiled and bowed gracefully, averting her eyes.

'Where's Sarah?' Berry asked.

'She is busy, Miss Butler. You will follow me, please.'

'What's she doing?'

Chieko didn't reply. They were wearing the exact same grey suit. Chieko carried it off impeccably.

'Is this right?' Berry indicated to her outfit. Chieko nodded, expressionless.

They continued through the lobby of Central Holding, passing doors and lifts that seemed to lead to a honeycomb of possibilities, until they reached a glass frosted door labelled Laboratory Eight. Next to the lettering was a clock-like symbol, like nothing that Berry had seen before. Chieko pressed an intercom and spoke in Japanese. A light flashed and the door became transparent to reveal a white room with clean, reflective walls and a space that seemed much larger than it was. The door evacuated a hiss as she pushed on it. She indicated for Berry to go inside.

The lights dimmed. Through a window to an adjoining space, Berry could make out the image of a man, lying flat on what looked like an operating table. Above him hung a large copper cage, bound in thick wire and green strips of metal. It was swinging, like it had only recently been elevated.

She reached into her pocket and pulled out a Cherry Red Jujyfruit. She sucked on it as the man sat up and rubbed his eyes. He was wearing a white hospital gown and Dr Martin boots. Small pads connected a string of thin wires across his forehead and chest. They trailed to the floor and disappeared under the laboratory desk. He removed them with a vacant expression as he watched Berry through the glass.

'I will leave you now,' said Chieko. She backed away with a slight bow.

The man was now sitting, facing the window.

She waved.

He didn't respond.

She wasn't sure if he could see her.

He sat, seeming preoccupied by thought.

She sucked on the sweet.

'So, you're our whizz kid?' crackled a voice, loud and distorted over an intercom.

She looked at the speaker in the wall and then back to the man. 'Can he hear me?' she asked, out loud.

'He can hear you.' The man reached for a beaker and a pack of pills in a silver box. He casually flipped the lid, necked a single capsule, and took a swig of water. 'The first thing you do is take the pills. This will stabilise you. Stop you from getting the bends. Ok? The pack will be labelled with your name and metadata.' He looked at her with tired eyes. 'I guess we should start at the beginning, right?'

She blinked in the bright laboratory lighting.

He didn't pause to let her reply. 'In the eighties, the Institute of Educational Sciences undertook a study to test how the repeat play of that cute little game called Tetris, effected learning and memory.' He laughed to himself. 'Fucking Tetris. I know, right?' He popped another pill and slugged back some water. 'Twelve sessions for thirty minutes, followed by cognitive skill tests. Guess what? Short bursts of gameplay had a positive effect on learning ability. Spatial perception, visualisation and mental rotation, all improved. Learning and memory improved. They gave it a name. They called it − the Tetris effect. How about that? Playing computer games gives you powers. You heard it first right here, folks.' He laughed and checked his pulse, going through the motions like a pilot undertaking post-flight checks. 'Next, enter your blood pressure. We've had sixty seconds, right? One of the side effects. The complete inability to keep track of time. It's a real bitch, like jet lag on steroids'

'It's been one minute and fifty-eight seconds,' Berry replied without thinking. 'Since I first saw you.'

He nodded, trying not to seem impressed. 'So, we can argue all night long about how the casual brain training of Tetris can improve us as people; our ability to learn, to perceive, to perhaps even deal better with life's little challenges?'

'Like a level up?'

He laughed. 'Sure, kid, just like a level up.'

'Is this what you're doing here? Trying to improve?'

'I'm hungry. Are you hungry?' he asked, diverting her from the question.

She shook her head and crunched on the Jujyfruit.

'Ok, let's get the formalities out of the way. Dr Michael Jones. Pleased to meet you whizz kid.' He held his hand in the air, trying to make a connection through the window. 'Lumberjack shake through a glass wall?' He raised his eyebrows and waited.

She caught his eye for the first time. He seemed instantly older but not feeble. He had the heavy weight of experience. She made a guess at how old he was, maybe late forties. He suffered from a look of intense fatigue; unshaven, scruffy morning-after, desperate drinking to stop thinking. His pale skin looked like it hadn't seen daylight in a very long time. She cautiously approached the wall and held her hand in the air. They moved their arms together, shaking hands from either side of the glass. They didn't need to touch. She felt the cosmic connection.

'Ok. Back to business. They call it game transfer phenomena, right?' Mike spoke as though he were standing right next to her. His distorted voice boomed over the intercom. 'Imagine a gaming infrastructure where the player is completely in control of not only the game play but also the nature and environment of the game itself. The player has already determined the scenario; the challenges, the conflict and the means of resolution, and can alter this state of play mid-session. Through the cognitive processes of learning and memory, and a little chemical stimulation of our own creation, information is released as if recalled for the first time – like a dream state influenced by cause and effect. Detail that is typically hidden beyond the realm of consciousness is unlocked like a pure dose of muscle memory.'

She gave him a dubious stare.

'Let me finish, young grasshopper,' he said. 'When we're in this unconscious state, our brains go through some housekeeping. We put everything back into the filing cabinets, defrag, re-order and make sense of the influences and impressions made upon us during our waking hours. The process that enable game transfer phenomena are apparent during this state, when we're asleep, for example. But it's not sleeping, and it's not waking – it's somewhere in-between. It's hypnogogic. Cool word, huh? When you hit exactly the right level of consciousness, you can maintain it, you can control it, and you can play it, just like a game. Like surfing a wave at Big Sur. See what I'm saying?'

She was blank faced.

'By the way, if you're trying to impress me right now then you're doing an excellent job. Man, you've got a poker face on you.'

She squirmed with a mixture of embarrassment and concern.

'Tell me when we're at seven minutes. At seven minutes we take the next pill pack. In-between, we rehydrate, rebalance the electrolytes, and grab some chow.'

She noticed the IV connected to his hand.

'Saline and fifteen percent glucose,' he explained. 'In your case, we'll up that dose to twenty-five, right? I heard you like the sweet stuff.'

She swallowed the Jujyfruit.

'It also contains seven-fifty levofloxacin, five g's of ibuprofen, and a little extra something from the Beta Boys.'

'The Beastie Boys?'

'Beta Boys,' he smiled. 'Hah, you'll meet those dudes soon. They're our cooks. Genius twins of the outer chem labs. They interpret Professor Peterson's psychotropic recipes. The dosage is dependent on the host. Unique to every individual. I'm on a permanent ten percent right now. I guess we'll start you on two.'

Berry let out an impatient sigh and looked for somewhere to sit. The room was full of objects that looked like they shouldn't be touched; test tubes and screens, clean polished surfaces and spotless glass. It was the antithesis of her London flat, with its retro pornographic magazines, sweet wrappers and stacks of hard drives and DVDs. How long had she been away? She was beginning to lose track of time. She realised that she hadn't seen a clock since she'd arrived, only the strange symbol on the laboratory door. She remembered that no one knew where she was and wondered if she should be feeling lonely.

Mike was tapping notes into a computer while performing physiotherapy stretches. He was groggy and half asleep. This was routine to him. He continued to speak with a confident clarity of thought. 'The player is engaging in self-censorship all the time that they're under. The experience is recalled as new but the subject is essentially re-playing material that has already been vetted by themselves. So, the player is both the cause and the effect. They decide how little or how much they want to participate. They control the action, the characters, the situations, as if writing their very own live action screenplay, starring themselves. The platform is an adventure into the subconscious.'

'Platform? Like a run and jump?'

'Working title, bit of a hangover from the old man that one. We use words to describe it like platform, levels, and game, but only so that our mind will accept what's happening and not get lost in its own random expansions. The human consciousness is a vast and unchartered territory, Berry. It's easy to get a little lost in there. Do you like Chinese food?' He pointed to a large floor to ceiling door and indicated for her to open it. She pulled the handle to reveal a fridge loaded with cardboard cartons of noodles and rice.

'Grab me one. I like it cold.'

She pulled out a carton and took a pair of chopsticks that were sanitising in a test tube.

'Help yourself?'

'I'm ok,' she stuttered, and popped another Juju.

Mike rubbed his eyes and hit buttons on a keypad. The laboratory door opened and the air felt suddenly lighter. 'You don't need a white coat and a PHD to come in, you know,' he said.

Her heart pounded. She stepped cautiously over the threshold and into the bright surgical whiteness of the lab. They stood, staring at each other, and she held out her hand to shake.

'We've already done that, Berry Butler.'

She blinked, struggling for the right words. The moment was immediately diffused by his wrinkled smile. He didn't look anything like the kind of man who would work in a high tech laboratory. He wore an old t-shirt under a heavy hospital gown. The artwork design was hand drawn, Asian art; the image of a flying elephant. He took the noodles and began to eat as if on a casual canteen lunch break.

She wondered if she had been brought to the wrong room. Perhaps there had been a mistake? Why were they in a laboratory? With the speed he was sucking down the noodles, she wasn't sure if she could take him seriously.

'That's the thing with being under, you really miss the food. So, enough about me, let's talk about you. Why are you here?' he asked, inhaling soba.

46

Half a bottle of Smirnoff and a pack of cigarettes had been consumed. Distorted pop music blasted from karaoke speakers too large for the room; Sweet Caroline by Neil Diamond. Three of the girls danced in front of the flat screen. They didn't know the words but sang along anyway.

Dr Finjoto was stroking the thighs of two bikini-thonged assistants who sat either side of him. 'We are about to change the world, my brother,' he shouted over the music.

'That's a pretty bold thing to say, doctor,' laughed Lars, distracted by a girl sat on his knee who was flicking through the pages of a karaoke song book almost twice her size. He was dizzy with the intensity of the party. The vodka had kicked in and he was lost to the unexpected atmosphere that had come out of nowhere.

'This is a new dawn,' Finjoto continued. 'Nirvana approaches − the day when everything will be reset. There will be no past, no future, only the now.' He raised a glass.

'To the now, Dr Finjoto. To the here and the fucking now.' Lars reached for his tumbler and knocked it onto the carpet. The girls giggled and screamed. He changed his focus and grabbed the packet of cigarettes.

Finjoto leaned over and offered him one, and then shouted angrily at the dancing girls. They immediately left the room.

'Hey, come on, man. What's with breaking up the party?'

Finjoto smiled. The girls reappeared, carrying a silver tray with fresh ice, mixer and another bottle of vodka. He signalled for the girls to continue dancing. They picked up microphones and were back in the party like they hadn't left the room.

Lars laughed, drunkenly enjoying the charade of business hospitality.

'Tell me about yourself,' asked Finjoto. 'Who is Lars Nilsson?'

'Oh, er, dunno. Guess I'm just a guy.' The nausea had completely gone, blasted by jet lag and alcohol. He took a deep breath and smoked to compose himself.

The girls giggled and toyed with the microphone. New York, New York came on and they began kicking a can-can like dance. They knew this one.

Lars was distracted by the dancing, enjoying the show, until he felt the firm grasp of Finjoto's hand on his shoulder.

'Please, do not stop. I would like to know all about you,' he demanded. 'Then I have a gift for my most esteemed guest.'

'Thank you. Very kind.'

Finjoto smiled.

Lars was beginning to feel light headed. 'OK. Well, I'm married to Claire, she's my wife. I have a job at the BBP. Julia Miller is sort of my wife there too, but we don't sleep together, nothing like that. Stu is just jealous. I saw a fox, and had some crazy dreams, and my avatar got stolen but I've got it back now on a USB, so that's good. I'm still totally crunked though. So, that's me. How about you?'

Dr Finjoto smiled. 'Fascinating,' he said, as he placed a silver flight case on the seat beside him and unlocked it. He pulled out a thin tube of blue liquid, encased in a moulded rubber cavity. It was an underwhelming reveal but Finjoto seemed pleased. The tube was unbranded, apart from a white label with black printed writing:

AMANITA MUSCARIA NST 8 ML.

Finjoto smirked like a child when he read it. 'Here,' he said, offering the vial to Lars.

He was hesitant but realised that this was how business was going to proceed. He accepted it gratefully and studied the tube, unsure if he was meant to say anything specific about it.

Music blared from the speakers. The girls sang along to a song that they didn't understand.

'Do you know what is in this vial?' asked Finjoto.

Lars studied it against the light. 'Well, erm, it's a chemical,' he replied, matter-of-factly.

'This tube contains the elixir of the gods,' said Finjoto, transfixed.

Lars glanced at the dancing girls, who were now swaying together, all eyes fixed on him. He sat forward, uncomfortable.

Finjoto smiled and began to laugh. The girls also began giggling.

'This is a joke, right?' he smirked. 'You do this to all the guys I bet? Take a few pictures; embarrass them at the next international office seminar? Hey, I can take it. I'm a sport.

Whatever you want, and whatever you think is funny. It's fine by me.' He reached for a fresh glass and nervously filled it with ice. 'You sure are a crazy character, Dr Finjoto. I tell you, I've met quite a few crazy characters these last few days. Just wait until I tell Stu about this. The Wickster will be impressed too.' He poured himself a large vodka. 'You sure are a character, Dr Finjoto. That's what you are – a character.'

Finjoto leaned in. 'Who will be the lucky one tonight, my brother?' he asked, his mood becoming overly friendly once more.

'Lucky?' Lars laughed. 'What do you mean? Karaoke?'

'No. Not karaoke,' said Finjoto, with a lewd smile.

Lars awkwardly took a long drink. 'I'm a married man,' he spluttered.

'I do not mean a simplistic sexual encounter, Mr Nilsson. I am referring to the New World. Which of our party will you choose to enlighten?' Finjoto waved his hand before the group of girls.

He reached for his jacket. 'Well, I think that's enough entertainment for me. I'm pretty tired. It was a long flight. So, thank you for your kind hospitality, Dr Finjoto. I'll head back to my room now.'

Finjoto was staring at the test tube. 'I think you know to what I am referring, Izanagi?'

The name sent a shockwave of terror though him. They looked at each other, and the moment of realisation clicked. Finjoto interrupted it with a shout and the girls all rushed onto Lars, holding him by the arms and legs.

'What the fuck? Hey!' They were smaller but he was outnumbered. He struggled to push them away. Their combined strength was enough to hold him down.

'I know exactly who you are, Mr Lars Nilsson,' smirked Finjoto. 'Let me help you to discover the true nature of your identity.' He grabbed Lars by the throat and jammed his head back. 'Do not struggle. You have been heading towards this moment every second of your mortal existence, Izanagi.'

The girls held him tighter.

'Return to the space beyond death and open the doorway to the afterlife.' He removed the cap to reveal a pipette. The glass instrument hovered above his face as a single blue droplet fell into Lars' terrified, blinking eye.

'The darkness will consume the light, Izanagi,' said Finjoto. 'Yomi will no longer be locked out of reach. Together, we will guide the quintillions across the threshold and into the mortal realm of the living. You will show me how. It is Tengu's will.'

The girls broke away. Finjoto replaced the pipette and instructed them to leave. The music ended.

Lars rubbed his eyes, blinking furiously, desperate to wipe away the liquid but he could already feel it take hold.

'Do not fear. There is nothing more beautiful than what you are about to experience. I give you mortal emancipation. I give you − your death.'

He began to convulse, rolling frantically on the floor. His skin was on fire. He coughed up a white froth. His face twisted and he let out a soft cry; a whimper that sounded like a thousand years of sorrow in a single sound, as the intense psychotropic explosion clawed deep into his consciousness.

47

Mike invited her to sit. She clambered up awkwardly next to him. 'Back in the Fifties, during old man Peterson's era, they were constantly chasing the dream of psychotropic enlightenment. They called it quantum jumping. He had the backing of some pretty influential people, but there were too many issues, too many casualties, so those people have changed their minds.'

'Who are they?' She tried not to swing her legs from the table top.

'The people who are always there in the background. The unavoidable truth seekers.'

'Oh,' she nodded, slightly disappointed at the answer.

'So, our brains have organisation,' he explained, 'a running order for the hundred billion neurons; cells and synapses that connect and transmit data, electrical pulses of energy that we decipher into information that is learned or created. It's this system that can be manipulated. We can literally change the order. It's essentially brain training on a massive scale − erasing and expanding memories, ideas, thoughts, passion, desire, emotion, personality; we can rewire the whole fucking thing to create a new language, an instant character shift. How about that?'

'I'm afraid I still don't get it. Is there actually a game?'

He wiped his face. 'Ok. Crude example, if a player can convince themselves that they can jump over a building, become a super-being, even fly like a bird,' he said, 'then on the platform — they will fly.'

Was this some kind of virtual reality project or mind control game? She popped another Jujyfruit. Grape Bundle.

He seemed like a good person, enthusiastic to share whatever it was they were trying to do at The Foundation. Despite the crazy talk, there was something about Mike that she felt she could relate to. He seemed sincere, and inspired in her an empathy for a haunting and unspoken sadness. The sensation that they both shared this feeling made her feel calm. She felt that she could trust him.

'Have you flown?' she joked.

'Fuck yeah. Many, many times.' He laughed.

She was surprised by his answer.

'You have to be in the correct state of mind to allow the process to occur. In our waking hours we're on red alert, over-stimulated by everything around us for our own protection. Take it back a few levels and you reach somewhere else entirely. That's when consciousness can literally be played, and you, Berry, will become a grand master.'

She smiled. She liked him. 'This really doesn't sound like a game to me.'

'Think of it as a level playing field for your imagination to run wild and yet stick to the rules governed by our waking state. But this isn't a dream. You won't suddenly realise that you're naked and the toast is burning.' He hesitated. 'Not had that one? Used to have that on loop.' He finished the carton and wiped his mouth on his lab coat sleeve.

She looked around the room, unsure what to make of it all. 'So, I'm going to fly?'

'Who knows what you'll be capable of, Berry. Can you get me another?'

She slid off the table.

Mike stretched. He looked more awake and excited by the conversation. 'You will surf the platform of conscious unconsciousness. Consider the emotional impact; how the player will feel like they're witnessing a scene, created by themselves, for the very first time.'

'So, this is like a virtual reality experience?' she asked, pulling a carton of noodles from the fridge.

'Yes, but no, no, not at all. The thing is, it's not virtual at all. It's very real. It's actually happening.'

She sucked on the Juju in defeat, becoming more exasperated at his explanation. 'We're at seven minutes,' she said without thinking any more of it.

He laughed. 'I wasn't sure when Finjoto first mentioned you, but I get a good feeling about us working together.' He cracked a tube and swallowed a pill. 'There's a little more time, so how about I try and make that brow of yours frown a bit more, eh?' He stared at the wall, lost in thought, and then continued to talk without warning. 'What you're going to experience is a conceptual reality, Berry. Whatever occurs will seem familiar to you as you're the originator of the story. It's a story that will constantly surprise and engage you. You're drawing on life experience, on things that have already happened, material that will constantly adjust to the limits of your anticipation to achieve a thrilling experience. Some events may be more, shall we say, extreme than others but you will never go beyond the limits of personal control;

never scare beyond the perception of fright, never push the boundaries beyond what you have already determined as acceptable. The player has already decided the outcome of the scenario, and they're merely participating in the memory of game-play. Still with me?'

She pulled a fake smile.

He paused to wipe his face and continued to speak with his mouth full. 'You'll experience constant problem solving, challenges influenced by your ability to learn and repeat. This should all be pretty familiar after Atari Shock, right?'

'You know Atari Shock?'

'Of course I do.' He swallowed soba noodles. 'RPG games aren't enough for me anymore, and when you experience this thing, they won't be enough for you either. Nothing has existed like this before. You're at ground zero; front line shit. You've been given the opportunity to create something special. We have the DNA to a complete neural gaming infrastructure where imagination is reality. The player will feel a connection between themselves and a fictional creation of their own imagining. This is emotional gaming for the soul. It's like a Stargate to another dimension. Do you understand? All you need is the correct chemical stimulus to help you on your way. So, Berry Butler, are you ready to experience the New World?'

She smiled a crooked smile, unsettled by whatever expectations he had of her.

48

Lars swept aside a sunburned branch. The brightness forced him to cover his eyes. As the sunspots cleared, he realised that he was looking at a patchy piece of grass in the middle of a burned out jungle. He blinked. The sky was hyper-real, almost translucent. The air was bright blue with a hint of pink sunset. This was like nothing that he'd ever seen before, and yet the place seemed strangely familiar.

Dr Finjoto was gone. The girls were gone. There was no music. No vodka. No cigarettes. Just the foul, lingering taste of confusion. He pressed up against a tree, breathing heavily, trying desperately to remember the circumstances that had brought him here.

There were brick buildings at either end of the field. An armed guard was standing in full military leaf pattern camouflage; Vietnam War Boonie Suit fatigues, tiger stripe streaks of black, green and tan, type 3 AK-47, locked, loaded and hanging from a strap around his shoulders. The guard turned and Lars hid in the undergrowth, holding his breath. Sweat dripped from his forehead. He wiped his hand across his face.

There was the sound of raised voices and the guard looked sleepily over as the door of the brick building flew open. Two men dressed in camouflage gear stomped out. They were chatting like old friends. One of them confidently loaded a weapon and spun the barrel. Lars couldn't hear what they were saying but thought he made out the words 'no thumb up.' His heart pounded in his chest. He pushed his back against the tree and looked up into the strange, fluctuating sky.

The dealer pointed to a paper target of a moustachioed man pinned to a post at the other end of the pitch. The customer fired a single shot. It was surprisingly loud. The paper was torn in two. There was a laugh and the sound of congratulations.

'Again, my friend, again,' came the words across the field. 'You must train, if you are to be number one.'

Lars could make out a sign on the brick wall. "Do not Touch Gun." The building was a mounted library of old-fashioned firearms. Small labels were written underneath each vintage weapon; 'K50,' 'M60,' 'UZI,' 'AK-47,' 'Dragonov Russian Sniper,' 'London Scorpion .32,' 'RPG-7.'

The customer was picking up a gun, feeling the weight and then comparing it with another. He wore dark sunglasses and a floppy green hat. He was constantly chain smoking. He applied straps and attachments. He looked like he knew what he was doing. The dealer was encouraging him with each well-selected decision.

Lars turned to a rustling sound in the undergrowth. There was heavy breathing and the cracking of twigs as the snout of a large black creature revealed itself just feet from where he was cowering. The shadow animal looked straight at him.

'You know, firing a gun is one of the biggest thrills you can have. Better than sex. Better than drugs,' drifted the arrogant voice from across the pitch. 'We're drawn to it. It's human nature.' He fired again and the paper split and fell.

The animal reacted to the noise and found a new target across the pitch. It stalked in the undergrowth and paused to focus on the two men.

Lars could feel the heat emanating from its spiny body as it breathed, heavy and low, with a slight growl each time it exhaled. If he was dreaming, then he'd never dreamed as vividly before. His senses were acutely tuned to everything around him; in particular, the creature, and whatever it was, it smelled bad.

'You are very good,' said the dealer.

'Number one,' said the man, puffing on his smoke.

The animal had the monstrous head of a bat, with the hind haunches of a tiger, and the long thin slashing demon tail of a dragon. It was hovering on the spot, eyes locked on its victims, hesitating as a cat might stalk its prey. Lars pushed himself up against the tree as the creature passed. It didn't seem to notice him now that it had shifted its attentions. He breathed as softly as he could and took a step away. He crunched on dry twigs and winced. The creature didn't move. It held its head perfectly straight, locked in the direction of the two men. It began twitching, preparing to pounce.

Lars took one more glance at the wall of guns that glistened in the afternoon heat. This was his chance, he thought. Even if they weren't loaded, he could use a bayonet to protect himself. The creature let out a snarl and began to run. Lars ran in the direction of the brick building as fast as he could.

'Firing a gun is a trip,' continued the self-appointed number one, 'a simultaneous high and come-down. The shoot-em-ups have been trying to perfect this thrill, this adrenaline rush for like, ever, but they never quite got there.' He was re-loading as he spoke, puffing on his rolled up cigarette. '3D and VR, just too tacky man, too much like a cartoon. Suspension of disbelief, it's a hard thing to perfect. The brain doesn't want to believe.' He threw his roll up on the floor. 'But shooting a living, breathing thing,' continued the customer, 'man, that's way better than any computer game.'

Lars was almost at the brick building when he saw the customer point the Magnum .44 in the dealer's face. A shot rang out and the man's head came clean off. There was a second shot and the guard was grounded. The customer stood, arm extended, with his thumb down.

A hideous, high-pitched screech shook the roots of the jungle. Black ravens lurched from surrounding trees and spun in circles, turning the sky black, as the shadow animal landed on the customer with claws slashing.

More shots were fired.

There was silence.

Lars looked up through long grass. The creature was on its side, tail flicking, until gradually its body became vapour-like and it evaporated into a dark smoke that drifted away in the breeze.

The man dusted his shoulders off, casually checked his gun, and strolled aggressively at Lars. 'Hey! Yes, you. Found it too, huh?' he shouted. 'This is my cash stash. Get up, asshole.'

Lars struggled to his feet but was too exhausted to move. Instead, he sat, as the man got closer, waving his hands in disgust.

'You are not taking these co-ordinates. They are reserved for the professionals,' he shouted. He was visibly trying to calm himself, going through a series of deep breathing exercises. He then pulled out a pre-rolled joint from his glasses case and lit up. The stranger took a moment to smoke while contemplating the situation. 'How long have you been playing?'

Lars looked at him. 'Was that a tiger with the head of a bat?'

'Level three shadow animals are more ghost. They've got a few glitches. Keep thinking they're hidden even when they're out in the open. Kind of easy to pick off right now but I'm sure they'll fix that. Then we're fucked, right?' His smile was one of assured experience. The man picked pieces of strange coloured leaf from between his teeth and reached his arm out to Lars. 'Need a loaner? I can be your loaner if you're out of power-ups? You look pretty ganked, man. Lumberjack shake?' He grabbed Lars around the arm and pulled him to his feet while simultaneously shaking his hand. 'What's your handle, dude? Your name? Who the fuck are you and what are you doing on my patch?' He waited, impatiently.

'I'm...' Lars hesitated. A name was looping in his head, one that he recognised but was unsure what it meant to him. 'I'm Izanagi.'

'So, Izanagi, I'm going to call you Izzy. Don't mind if I call you Izzy, do you?'

Lars shrugged, unsure if he should mind. He looked at the bodies. 'Did you just kill them?'

The man glanced over and then back at the shivering newbie. 'You wanted the loot? Sorry, I got here first. I told you, this stash is mine. You rather I put a flag in the ground and mark my territory? We're not on the fucking moon. You were in the bushes, playing with that big cat. I got that too. Was that yours? It's free-for-all, you know.' He puffed on the smoke and handed it to Lars. 'If that was your animal then I'm sorry. Everything's fair game on the platform.'

Lars accepted the cigarette. He took a deep toke and closed his eyes. He wished that everything would return to normal. He breathed slowly, then spluttered and choked the smoke back up. The man was still waiting for him when he opened his eyes.

'The name's Dr Vegas,' he said. 'So, how many power-ups you got? I got some cool ass power-ups. Level one? Fuck that. Level one is just piss ant, right? It's no fun taking out the shadow animals with basic melee. You need to level up to the cool shit as fast as possible.'

Lars' eyes began to water. He rubbed them furiously. 'What is that stuff?'

'The smoke? That's pure mandrake, my friend,' said Vegas, becoming suspicious of why Lars was asking so many questions.

He took another quick toke. 'Am I dreaming?' he asked with a tropane alkaloid cough.

Dr Vegas lost his temper. 'I fucking knew it! So you found a back door? You come here pre-buffed? That's not a cool way to beta test, man. This thing is gonna end up vapourware if they make it too easy. Jesus.' He stomped in circles on the spot, thrashing his hands in anger, unsure what he should do with them. 'Give me that back,' he demanded.

Lars handed over the mandrake cigarette. Smoking seemed to calm Dr Vegas down.

'You met the witch? Did you even know there was a witch?' Vegas asked, smarmily. 'Have you finished level three?'

Lars shrugged, unsure what to say.

'I'm judging by your knowledgeable reaction that you haven't, you didn't, and you haven't. I bet you still have a bicycle. You do, don't you? This loser still has a bicycle,' he screamed at the sky. 'I totally buffed mine up, man. Upgraded to a moto. I got an engine and everything, so fuck you.' He smoked, furiously. 'Look, it's snivelling little cheats like you that spoil this thing for the rest of us. You know that, don't you? Where's your animal?' He stomped and looked into the sky, raising his arms in question. 'Call your animal. I wanna see it right now.'

Lars shook his head. 'I don't have an animal.'

'Did you even get the map?'

'I don't think so.' Lars winced, unsure if he was saying the right thing.

Dr Vegas took a toke and threw the stub on the floor. 'Look. I don't know how you got here, but let's face the facts, you're in. Congratulations, newbie.' He took off his sunglasses and seemed more intense. 'Have you seen her?'

'Seen who?'

'Don't fuck with me, man. Of course you know who. Where is she?'

'I don't know who you mean.'

'Sarah, damn you. Where's Sarah?'

Lars saw the twisted glare of someone who had lost all touch with reality. 'I haven't seen anyone. I promise. I don't even know how I got here,' he cowered.

'Let me give you a few words of advice, compadre.' Vegas spoke slowly, trying to make it easier for the newbie to understand. 'This place will be your living hell unless you wise up and get with it. Stick to town. Don't go near the shadows. Let the moths guide you. Shit, why am I telling you all of this? It took me months, maybe years to work it out. I don't fucking know.' He was clearly angry with himself.

'Where am I?' pleaded Lars.

Vegas blinked in the hyper-real sunshine. 'Welcome to the afterlife. Now fuck off back to level one, newbie.' He raised his gun and fired.

Lars disintegrated in a cloud of grey smoke, which dissipated in the warm breeze.

A black raven lurched into the air and circled several times before disappearing over the horizon.

High up in the eaves of a tall palm tree, two old men were struggling to keep balance. The ancient immortals, Bishamon and Jurojin, had watched the entire event unfold. Their mission to receive their immortal brother, to welcome him to the space in-between, had been rudely interrupted by the violent stranger with the magic cigarettes.

Jurojin swiped at a fly buzzing around his face. He used his iron crutch to prevent himself from falling.

'What right does this stranger have to walk our lands with such arrogant authority?' mumbled Bishamon. 'He is not one of us.'

'Agreed,' declared Jurojin, blowing hot air out of his nose in an attempt to stop the fly from landing on it.

'He is a minion of Tengu, sent to distract Izanagi from fulfilling his destiny,' observed Bishamon.

'As much as I enjoy doubting you, my brother, I fear that

you are correct,' muttered Jurojin. He swiped, missing the fly, and fell to the jungle floor with a thud.

'I will tear the head from his shoulders,' vowed Bishamon, as he watched Dr Vegas kick start his moto and rattle across the hyper green field.

49

He had taken her pulse, height, weight and bloods; a single syringe of dark red sugars, haemoglobin, red blood count, white blood count, differential count, platelet count.

She was on a moving treadmill. A digital camera was directed at her as she fell forward. Wires stretched from her arms, forehead and chest.

'Keep going,' he said, encouragingly.

She felt like she was about to collapse and stumbled, tripping over herself, reaching out for balance, but she couldn't stop. She wanted to impress him.

'Break through the pain barrier,' he said. 'Beyond what you imagine possible.'

She began to struggle, feeling faint, her arms and legs becoming weak.

'Keep trying, Berry. You mustn't give up.'

She acknowledged with a final burst. Her mouth was dry and her chest burned. The treadmill slowed.

'Have a drink. Here. That concludes the physical stuff. You've done well. Are you going to be sick again?'

'No,' she said, smiling through the exertion, satisfied that she'd given it her all.

'Take a rest. We'll go through some questions and

then play a little game.' He gave her a reassuring wink. 'Don't look so worried.'

She tried to smile.

'Now, there's one vital conflict that we need to iron out, so pay attention. When on the platform any sense of identity will become confused. It will literally fade away, like the drives are being wiped clean. This presents a risk to the working memory. Your mind will try and make sense of where you are so it will feel challenged. That's when an advanced state of traumatic encephalopathy can occur called chronic chaos displacement. It's essentially massive brain trauma. Then we're into all kinds of shit; depression, aggression, impaired judgement, memory loss, so that's why we take the pills from the Beta Boys. Got it?' He smiled cheerily.

The Rorschach test had been going on for over forty minutes; a series of questions ranging from family medical history to her first pet. He seemed interested in documenting everything.

The room was cold and empty apart from a plastic desk and plastic plant. Berry had the face of someone who'd just worked out a puzzle and then instantly forgotten the answer. Jet lag, and an increasing sickness, were distracting her. She was finding it difficult to concentrate.

'A fox.'

'And now?' He held up another image. Blue butterfly patterns were smudged onto white paper.

'The sea.'

'And this?'

'A tree.'

She stared at the plant. It was too beautiful, too green for the windowless room. She decided that it was a fake and found herself thinking about the lotus flower on her shelf back home. How many days without topping up the vase? It would surely be dead. She imagined the beautiful pink leaves wilting to a shrivelled brown fist of dried shreds.

'Are you ok?'

'Tired. That's all.'

'Just a few more questions. Tell me about your diet. What do you normally eat for lunch?' He was slowly flicking through the pages of a document, waiting for an answer. After a short while, he looked up to encourage a response.

'Cereal,' she replied.

He didn't write anything. 'Cereal?'

She nodded, nonchalantly. 'Just cereal.'

He turned several pages. 'Do you sleep well?'

She blinked. 'Sometimes.'

'How many hours do you sleep on average?'

'On average?' She chewed the inside of her cheek. 'Four?' She shrugged.

'Four hours?' He seemed impressed and made a note.

'No. Seven or eight,' she interrupted. 'The usual amount of sleep needed. Put that down.'

He seemed suddenly less interested and wrote something. She was looking increasingly pale.

'Do you feel sick?'

'I'm fine.'

'Need some water?'

'It's jet-lag, that's all.'

'Do you exercise?'

'I walk around the flat.'

'Able to perform regular bowel movements?'

She smirked. 'Guess so.'

'Smoke?'

'Sometimes.'

'Drink?'

'Not really.'

'So, onto the interesting stuff. Tell me about your experiences. What's your perfect recipe?' He read from a list: DMT, MDMA, MDEA, MCPP, LSD, Cannabis Sativa, Cannabis Indica, Mescaline, Peyote, Angel Dust or Shrooms?' He took a short breath. 'There's also an option for OTHER.'

She swallowed, thought for a split second, and popped a Banana Jujyfruit. 'I don't really go in for that kind of stuff.'

Mike was confused. He checked his notes and re-checked them. 'So you chem lab your own high then? You've got a chemputer?'

'No. What's a chemputer?' She was unsure what he was getting at, worried that she was saying all the wrong things. She wasn't used to failing tests, no matter how bizarre.

Mike had prepared for the moment when he would first meet the whizz kid. On the announcement of her arrival, he was convinced that everything would change. She would provide him with the answers that he'd been seeking, to mounting questions every time he took a pure dose of the NST. Each trip was a leap of faith from which he was never sure that he'd return. She would reveal to him the earth shattering truth of what happened when he found himself lost in the otherworld founded on extreme adrenaline shock and the vast, terrifying, expansion capabilities of human consciousness.

He had tried to picture her face. What was a pill popping computer whizz kid with an exceptional CV in recreational drugs supposed to look like? He had mulled over all possible outcomes based on the information that The Foundation had given him. The scene would always play out the same way. She would enter the room; a supreme-being, hovering god-like, several feet above the ground, white light surrounding her physical form while a human shape, typically feminine, strikingly beautiful, compelling and commanding, would reach out and touch his soul.

But when he met her, she was just an innocent looking young woman who seemed more confused than he could ever have imagined. He hadn't expected her to be so fragile. She was pale, unhealthy, tired and weak, bright as a spark, but certainly not hovering inexplicably above the ground in an otherworldly state.

'Do you trust me?'

She wanted to please him. 'Sure,' she said. 'Put down a bit of everything. I've tried a bit of everything.'

'Don't worry. We'll work this out.' He was clearly frustrated. Mike ticked several boxes, turned some pages, signed the corner of a page, sniffed and raised his head slightly before he spoke again. This time he seemed more distant.

'Let's move on. How's home? Anyone else in your life who would miss you?' He scanned the document. His voice was steadier and more monotone.

She was hesitant.

He nodded. She had already answered his question.

'I live with my husband. My husband,' she said. 'He's waiting for me. At home. I miss him. He'll be expecting me to contact him soon.' She looked Mike in the eye and held a perfect poker face.

He smiled but didn't say anything. He knew that she was lying. 'Do you have children?'

She scratched her cheek and held her breath. This was her embarrassment mechanism. The desperation for air was a perfect distraction to whatever was really going on. Whenever she did this, it felt like a valve was being shut off deep inside. She found the uncomfortable sensation comforting. She held her breath for as long as she could, and her mind started to wander.

Mike waited for an answer.

'No,' she eventually replied, exhaling slightly. She couldn't remember the last time that she'd had any kind of physical relationship. Maybe college, she thought, nothing serious. Nothing that wasn't any more than just a curious replication of something that she'd seen in a porno clip online. The desire for any meaningful relationship had been filled by something else entirely – by her virtual life online. It was both her partner and her child. She'd never considered that she might crave anything else. She looked at the floor and waited for the next question.

He finished the notes and cleared his throat, turning a page and filling in small boxes, checking his watch and writing some more. 'Now,' he spoke slow and calm, flicking though the thick document. 'Why are you here, Berry?' He looked at her, reassuringly, and waited.

'I was invited,' she replied.

He coughed and looked directly at her. He held his pen, preparing to write down her answer. 'Go on.'

'I'm pursuing my ambitions.' She watched carefully, hoping to encourage a positive response. 'And I'm looking for…' She shook her head, unsure how to answer.

He seemed disappointed and became distracted by his notes. Everything was going so well. Then she'd lost his attention.

'Have I failed the test?' she asked. 'I've failed the test, haven't I?' She was upset. 'Can we start again? I can do better.' She fidgeted on her chair.

'You did fine.'

'Really, I can.'

'No, Berry,' he snapped.

She was startled by his abrupt change of mood. 'Have I done something wrong?' She looked to him for reassurance.

'What we're trying to do here needs you to be one hundred per cent committed. You can't doubt yourself.'

She nodded.

'From this moment on, you are to do everything you're told. It's for your own safety. Ok?'

She blinked, confused.

Mike swallowed, struggling slightly with the words that he knew he had to say. 'Change into those clothes.' He got up to leave.

On the laboratory bed was a white hospital gown and a pair of black Dr Martin boots.

'Dr Jones?' she shivered, unsure what had just happened. She felt exposed, threatened, almost violated by his change of attitude. It felt as if there had been some kind of betrayal. He was treating her like a test subject; a lab rat for his experimentation.

'Just change, Berry,' he said, giving her a sad glance of reassurance. 'It'll be much easier if you co-operate.'

50

The room was empty apart from two wooden chairs set at a rough table. A light bulb hung from the ceiling. The walls were dirty. There were no windows.

Lars was dazed, trying to remember what had happened, and how he had come to be in this strange room. A series of distant memories haunted his memory. There had been an aeroplane. A hotel room. Club sandwiches. Dancing. He had the vague recollection of a man patting him on the back, offering him cigarettes, smiling and welcoming him.

The door opened and Sarah entered, carrying a tray with a sandwich and a glass of water. She was wearing a white lab coat. She sat on the chair opposite and smiled sympathetically. She seemed intrigued, almost fascinated to see him.

There was a strange familiarity, as though they had passed by each other before, but never had a reason to stop.

'Are you hungry? Do you have a headache?' she asked. Her tone was caring, almost maternal, showing the confident intimacy of family members looking after one of their own.

He couldn't tell if he was hungry. He had no concept of time. Had he been sitting in this room for hours, perhaps even days?

His head hurt but it wasn't a headache. Instead, his brain felt electric — burned out from a static shock of misfiring synapses. His mind wasn't processing any normal information. It was a sensation that he'd never felt before; not exactly painful but not pleasant either, like an adrenaline rush, totally vivid yet fuzzy, impossible to recall even the simplest of recent memories.

'Have some water.'

'Has there been an accident?' he asked, shaking his head, groggy.

'Your memories will return soon.'

'Is this a hospital?' He blinked in the shadowy room.

'Are you in pain?'

'Not really.'

'Do you feel anxious?'

'If you keep asking me questions then I will.' He smiled.

'Good to see that you have a sense of humour,' she said. 'Now, do you remember your name?'

That was a strange question to ask, he thought.

She noticed an etching on the table, clawed many times over, and turned her head to see it more clearly. The shape scratched into the table top was some kind of hieroglyphic; the image of a tall man with the head of a bird, a pointed beak, and a staff. 'Can I see your hands, please?' she asked, softly.

He raised his hands and was shocked. His fingernails were cracked and broken. The tips of his fingers were bloody.

'Does it hurt?'

He shook his head.

'Do you remember your name?'

'You already asked me that.'

'So, what is it?'

'It's…' he had to think, struggling to remember. He wanted to say a name that he didn't recognise. Every element of his body was urging him to say it. 'It's Lars.' He laughed, nervously. 'My name is Lars.'

She watched him intently, observing every reaction.

'There was a party, right?' He looked to her for reassurance.

She was unsure what to say. 'Do you know what this is? On the table? These markings?'

He didn't recognise them. 'I'd like to go home now,' he said.

She smiled, humbled. 'I'm sure you would.' Her voice was sincere.

A memory was coming back to him. His forehead was wrinkled in thought. 'If I can get my level up, work at getting another couple of thousand power-ups on my status, then I'll be ok,' he explained.

She let him talk. His brain was clearly working out the situation for itself.

'I've watched my friends die on the battlefield and risked my life to revive them,' he explained. 'I've worked hard to build up my cash stash. I've made more enemies than followers. I have an army. I am an Immortal.' The thought struck him hard. He began to cry.

A thin shadow flexed in the corner of the room. It slid across the ceiling, catching his eye.

'She's dead, isn't she?' he wept. 'It was my fault. I didn't save her. I didn't save Julia.' The memory of the incident in the offices of the BBP was pushed to the front of his mind. 'Stu? He was hit by a car. It wasn't my fault.' He looked to Sarah for the answer. 'Where's Claire? What have you done with her?'

Sarah observed him like he was a puzzle waiting to be solved.

'Everything needs to be re-set,' he mumbled. 'It's the only way to return to Hōrai.' Further clarity was coming back to him as he was struggling to understand a flood of distant memories. Then, an image came to him, as clear as anything that he'd ever seen or imagined. He remembered a man pointing a gun in his face and pulling the trigger. 'He shot me.'

Sarah watched him, curiously. 'Who shot you?'

'Dr Vegas.'

She smiled. It was unmistakable. Like a code word. He had made contact. All the time that he'd spent in the lab, dead to the world, subdued by the psychotropic effects of the NST – had just been validated. 'You're jumping,' she said.

Little did they know, that in a cheap Las Vegas hotel room over twenty years ago, their short-lived, spontaneous marriage would result in a keyword that would cut across cosmic dimensions – Dr Vegas. It wasn't possible for Lars to know the name any other way.

'He was looking for someone,' said Lars, still dazed by the vivid images replaying in his mind. 'He was looking for Sarah.'

She shivered at the sound of her own name and seemed suddenly mournful.

The shadow pulsed, spreading across the ceiling behind her. Lars blinked as it flexed, and watched a leg stretch out from a bulk of blackness that clung to the ceiling, testing the floor before resting.

A second leg reached down, scratching the wall as it went. The movement distracted him as he watched the shadow unfold, captivated by the slow and mesmerising dance. He started to panic when he realised what was taking shape before him.

'You're hyperventilating,' she said. 'Take a breath.'

The shadow flexed again and four distinct lines stretched from ceiling to floor. The image was becoming clear. Tiny spikes jutted from each of the shadow legs. They flexed in his direction. He became wide-eyed and desperate, his face white with terror, as Lars realised that the creature was a huge spider.

She checked her watch and took out a small Dictaphone. She spoke calmly. 'Four thirty-two PM, JST. Subject number eight, Lars Nilsson. NST administration, approximately 3 to 6 ml.'

'It's moving,' he said, as another four black legs positioned themselves on the wall, and a black mass lowered itself into their mortal dimension.

Then came the click, click, click; a sound like twisted spokes on a slow moving wheel.

'I can hear it,' he whispered.

'Did it speak?' She was excited and observant. 'What did it say? Was it Dr Vegas?'

'It's not a voice,' he replied, becoming more terrified. 'It's clicking.'

'It's what? Where is it?'

He looked her in the eye as the creature rose up, eight legs protruding from the massive hulk of the shadow spider.

It made the sound as it moved; click, click, click.

'It's right behind you,' he whispered.

There was a flash of light and a perfect circle of white moths appeared. They spiralled in the corner of the room, awaiting further instructions. The light shone brighter, protecting Lars and Sarah from the spider's dark advances, causing the shadow to retreat, until suddenly it lunged, stomping the insects into the walls and ground. The circle evaporated and the room was filled with black shadow once more.

There was a blur of movement as the spider drove down to attack Lars.

He panicked and screamed, falling to the floor, pushing himself under the table.

'There's nothing here, Lars. Just you and me. Whatever you think you're seeing is an illusion. It's a physical manifestation of your subconscious. It can't hurt you.'

He fixed his eyes on the shadow spider as the legs shook above him. He heard a rasping sound, like the splitting of car tires as it leapt across the room and bounded in attack again. This time the leg landed inches from his face.

'It's making holes in the wall,' he shrieked.

'Your subconscious is conflicting with the psychotropic dose. If you panic you could hurt yourself. Do you understand, Lars?' reassured Sarah.

The spider was pulsating on the wall, shifting its position from one leg to the other.

'Stay calm, remember; whatever you think you're seeing, it's not real. It doesn't exist.'

'Black shadow spider' were the only words he could say.

A leg smashed into the floor, sending fractured splinters into the air.

'Did you feel that?' He was petrified and cowering, as the spider began to flex chaotically around the room.

The shadow spider was breaking across dimensions, clawing its way from the land of the dead, shredding the cosmic web that masked this mortal word from the next, as it smashed its legs against the wall. Shards flew.

'What was that?' Sarah suddenly remembered the Las Vegas spiritual science conference, the night when Lori had opened the door to another world and the auditorium flooded with violent shadows. She checked the corners of the room. They had turned black with a web-like substance that seemed to be growing from somewhere beyond.

'The shadows,' she said, feeling a shiver take hold of her body. 'They're back.' She punched the panic button. The security alarm flashed red. She climbed under the table and held him. 'Don't worry,' she said. 'They will be here soon.'

The spider lunged, legs ripping the table from above them, throwing it effortlessly against the wall.

'Woah.' She fell back, shocked. 'How did you do that?' She spoke, breathless, into the Dictaphone. 'There has just been a massive psychokinetic incident. The table moved. No, it flew against the wall. The subject is terrified.'

'Don't call me that,' moaned Lars, through tears.

'There are splinters from somewhere. The walls seem to be oozing some kind of web-like substance.'

He screamed as another leg slammed down beside them, cutting into the floor.

Sarah heard the sound of tiny shards scattering all around them. 'There was a noise. Just now. Like rain. Like falling glass.'

Lars pushed himself against the wall as the shadow scuttled and reared itself up, ready to pounce.

She watched him, astounded, studying his reaction. Her hand shook as she spoke into the Dictaphone. 'I don't know how he's doing this. The table has been completely broken.

The subject is causing huge damage to the walls and floor. Splinters − from nowhere. He's looking at something. I can't see what he's looking at. He's terrified. He's performing some kind of involuntary telekinesis.'

'Don't move,' shouted Lars. 'Stop talking.'

The creature repositioned itself on the wall behind her. She shook her head in disbelief and continued documenting the incident. 'There was a light. I saw insects. Moths. In a circle. They disappeared.'

Lars ducked to the ground, hiding his face in his hands.

'Listen to my voice. It will pass. The vision will pass. Try to calm yourself. You're in control, Lars. You're making all of this happen,' she tried to reassure him.

The spider began to flex.

'The subject is extremely agitated. This is manifesting in a powerful psychokinetic energy.' She crouched before him as he cowered on the floor and pulled his hands away to hold them. She stared into his eyes and saw the image of a creature reflected back. A large, hulking spider was rising up behind her.

'Tengu is watching,' he whispered, as the spider shot across the room and stabbed a leg straight through her stomach.

Her eyes widened as she felt the object burst through her chest. Her back stiffened from the impact. She coughed up blood and felt her body being lifted into the air. She looked down to see Lars smiling up at her.

Her body slammed violently against the wall, cracking her head on the hard surface, leaving a deep red stain on the white brick. She fell to the floor and the creature attacked. It stabbed her over and over, pummelling at her.

Lars backed into a corner; wide-eyed, petrified, as the door opened and a group wearing HazMat suits rushed in. He could feel himself being held in a tight head lock. He didn't struggle as they administered the injection. A wave of fatigue rushed through him. His eyes fell heavy as he watched the black shadow spin Sarah's helpless body in a dark thread. Her head was visible above the cocoon, vacant eyes staring at him, as he fell to the floor in the foetal position.

'Don't let him go into apoplectic shock,' said Dr Finjoto. 'Document everything. Update the files. The Academy want hourly reports. Capture any further incidents.' He picked up the Dictaphone, spun it back and clicked play. 'Tengu is watching' said Lars. He clicked the machine off and put it in his pocket.

'What about her?' asked a voice. It was Chieko.

Sarah was lying on the floor. Her blood-stained suit was crumpled. She was bleeding from her eyes and nose. There were no sharp objects in the room but she had clearly been repeatedly stabbed.

The table was turned over on its side. Finjoto saw the image of Tengu scratched into the wood. 'Have her body incinerated,' he said.

The shadow spider recoiled each leg one by one; the click, click, click becoming more distant as it crawled back across the threshold of the living and retreated to the land of the dead.

51

What Mike had gained in experience, he lacked in presentation. A spread of colourful wires were crudely bound together and trailing along the floor. They disappeared into the wall of Laboratory Eight, through some kind of homemade circuit board.

Berry watched the procedure being prepared. She stood, awkwardly, her hands by her side, as she rolled a Cherry Red Jujyfruit around in her mouth. His attitude had changed in the click of a finger; a schizophrenic personality twist and he was someone else entirely. He was distant, talking to himself − still friendly, but totally detached. She wondered if it was a side-effect of whatever it was the Beta Boys had been cooking up.

What were they attempting to do − play consciousness, exploit a hypnogogic state, open a Stargate to another dimension? She was feeling increasingly uncomfortable with his intentions and beginning to get the fear. She shivered, realising that she was sweating, despite the triple air-conditioned room. She noticed the security lanyard around Chieko's neck. She had clocked it before, while changing into the white gown and DMs.

She realised what her subconscious was trying to tell her. She had to get out. She had to run.

Mike seemed lost in a world of his own, at ease preparing the final checks of his strange invention. 'When we pieced together Van Peterson's notes and recreated the platform,' he explained, 'we improved the process of total immersion. The ride was bumpier back in eighty-two. Lotus Flower sure had a heck of a tolerance, I can tell you. The good old Beta Boys have refined the formula since.'

Berry had no idea what he was talking about.

He tapped a keypad on the neural processing equipment. 'Just think of it as like having a few too many strong cups of coffee. It's as simple as that.'

The laboratory bed rattled as it dropped and locked into place.

Chieko was measuring out a syringe of blue liquid. She smiled sympathetically and removed a plastic sheet covering the bed, revealing black leather straps at the arms and legs.

'What's that for?' Berry asked, a panic rising in her chest.

'Trust me,' he replied. 'I've been doing this for years.'

'You will feel a scratch,' said Chieko, as she nicked Berry's arm with a tiny needle.

'What the..?' She felt a deep, calming sensation.

'To prepare you for the procedure.'

'I'm not having any fucking procedure.' She stumbled and Chieko guided her to the laboratory bed.

Berry felt herself detach from everything around her. She was delirious. Her eyes began to roll back. The air tasted of a foul chemical, like it was discreetly poisoning her. She took short breaths, trying not to let it into her lungs. Palpitations began to thump in her chest.

There was something about her reticence that wasn't sitting well with Mike. The character profile supplied by The

Foundation didn't seem to match the scared young woman before him. 'This kid knows what she's doing, right?' he asked, almost mulling the question over to himself. He had expected her to be more engaged in the process, more outgoing, and not so anxious. She seemed excited by the concept of deep gaming but was uncomfortable by the initiation of the NST.

'All of the documentation is in order, Dr Jones.'

'It's just that, she's not like the others. She doesn't claim to have any knowledge of recreational psychotics. She didn't know any of the kicks on her application form.'

'I can assure you that Dr Finjoto himself has personally selected her, Dr Jones.'

Mike nodded. There was nothing more that he could do apart from begin the procedure. 'Set the faraday cage,' he said.

Chieko reached for the controls and pressed a green button. A heavy metal cage swung across the room and hung above the laboratory bed where Berry was now lying unconscious.

Mike hit a series of keys and then spoke aloud. 'Ok. NST test number one, with lucky contestant number nine, Miss Berry Butler.' He looked to Chieko. 'Do it.'

The lights went off with a thud.

She was in darkness. Her breathing was shallow. She opened her eyes and saw a group of people gathered around her. She couldn't make out any faces. They were in shadow, silhouetted against the bright light of the laboratory. Her forehead was being caressed with a soft, damp cloth.

'I'm not doing this. Fuck it,' she heard herself moan. 'Call Finjoto. Tell him I'm out.' She found herself on her feet and cleared the contents of the laboratory shelf onto the floor. Glass smashed. Papers flew in the air. The group screamed and jumped back.

She bolted at Chieko and pulled hard on the lanyard. It slipped from her shoulders. Berry fell for the laboratory door. She held it up to the sensor and to her relief the door slid open. She calculated her options, weighing up the odds, problem-solving the most likely outcome of this increasingly absurd situation.

White lighting starkly lit the corridor. She was completely disoriented. She remembered to turn back and use the lanyard to seal the door. No one was following. She had made it out.

She looked both ways. The corridors were identical. Which way? She had to make a choice. Falling against the wall she stumbled forwards, her DM boots pounding on the floor. There was no time to take them off, no time to look behind. Sealed doors ran parallel along both sides of the corridor. Each one displayed an infinity symbol; small, black, spiralling, with hands that increased by one pointed arm with each new door that she passed. Small frosted windows prevented her from seeing inside. A series of tiny security cameras ran along the ceiling. For a split second, she was convinced that one followed her as she ran by. She didn't know where she was going, she just needed to get out, and get out now. There must be a way back to Central Holding, she thought, a way back to Sarah. She would help.

Berry remembered the company iPhone. It was in her room. She had to get to the lift and get back to her room. She ran down a maze of corridors in the underground labyrinth of The Foundation and came to a junction where she could turn either left or right. There were no signs to indicate the way to Central Holding. She chose to go left, reached the end of the corridor, and then headed right. As she ran past a small window − she stopped. She could see inside.

A group were gathered around a table, wearing white coats and holding digital tablets. She recognised Chieko, Dr Jones, and Dr Finjoto with another man that she'd never seen before. She blinked and stared in shock as she saw her own body lying on the laboratory bed inside the room. She slapped her palms against the glass and screamed, trying to wake herself. The faraday cage was manoeuvred over the bed and lowered on top of her unconscious body. She hit the glass as she watched herself being hidden by the cage.

Berry screamed and fell back against the wall, sliding to the cold, hard floor. She recognised the circular symbol on the door of Laboratory Eight. She had run in a circle, and ended up right back where she started.

What had she done? Put her complete trust in a group of people that she'd never met? The fearful realisation hit her again; even if she found a way out, she had no idea who she would contact for help. She was alone. She always had been.

Berry climbed to her knees and began to crawl away. As she did so, her right arm lurched forward into the floor. She could feel the hard surface liquefy beneath her as she flexed her fingers. The more she struggled, the more the floor became fluid. She pulled her hand out of the strange mass but the surface seemed to disperse under pressure. Her left knee disappeared as though into jelly. She dug her elbows in and managed to pull her knee out as she toppled face first into the oozing mass which engulfed her entirely.

Chieko finished injecting the NST. The heart monitor was barely registering a response. 'She has passed.'

'My friends,' said Dr Finjoto, calmly. 'We have made exceptional progress. The Academy will be most pleased.' He turned to his colleagues. 'When you are ready, Michael, the next level of enlightenment is in your capable hands.'

Mike gave them a weary smile. 'I'll prep the session myself.'

Chieko bowed in acknowledgment.

Dr Finjoto waited for the door to close and then turned to her. 'You know what to do now, my daughter?'

She bowed again.

52

Mike's resistance to the NST had built up over the years. He now needed a complete transfusion every time he embarked on an inter-dimensional trip. He casually inserted the hypodermic needle into his vein and started the pump on its cycle. He sipped a small coffee and waited.

The process was temporarily cleansing. He checked the monitor and caught himself counting the minutes until the solution flushed through his system. He had no choice but to sit and wait for the drip, drip, drip to purify his bloodstream and allow him to access the New World. When he was under there were no days, no nights, only the struggle for survival and the heart pounding turn at every corner. Time ceased to exist.

Waiting for the infusion to run its course, however, was an unavoidable necessity. It felt endless compared to the pure adrenaline rush of the quantum jump. In the laboratory, time would always pass the same way – slowly.

He had been swept along in the after-shock following Van Peterson's death, towards the no-mans-land of The Foundation and the New World, as Finjoto so fondly called it.

During these solitary moments of intravenous introspection he would drift back to Las Vegas, to Sarah and the honeymoon suite at The El Rancho. Elvis Presley tunes would swirl in his mind as the infusion pump whirred; the Glory Glory Hallelujah of fuck-it celebration and tie-the-knot desperation. They had been dating for barely six weeks before the Vegas run of the spiritual science conference, and as things played out, they lasted barely six hours more. Thinking of Sarah was a temporary tourniquet, a quick fix, but it too would always lead to the same train of thought. He would be back in the operating theatre, the patient's heart monitor racing as he frantically double-checked the dosage. The cold sweat of horrific realisation would break over him when he confirmed his miscalculation; panic, guilt, denial, gut-wrenching fear, as he hid the evidence and allowed the surgeons to come to their own confused conclusions, presuming the attack to be an allergic reaction. His heart would pound when he realised that there would be an enquiry, and that he had to clear his bloodstream for any evidence of alcohol. The cold sting of the needle as he tried not to bruise the skin. The yellow vacancy of the patient that lay motionless on the operating table. He couldn't remember her name but her face was as clear as it had been all those years ago. There wasn't a day that went by when he didn't think about her and how her death had spun him in a direction that he could never have anticipated.

He checked the IV solution and felt the cold, clean plasma in his bloodstream, followed by the pure rush of the NST. The infusion pump registered fifteen minutes left on its cycle.

What had he expected? A miracle cure for the mistakes that he'd made, validation, even forgiveness? Was that why he'd spent so much time lost in an NST-induced coma? He was an impostor, a fraud, and a professional failure; as much of a doctor as Gonzo or Venkman.

Trying to hide from his professional mistake, he had answered a wanted ad for an anaesthetist on Van Peterson's tour, and unexpectedly found himself in the arms of Sarah.

He would attempt to nullify the sadness by indulgently tracking her iPhone on The Foundation servers. He would watch her signal drift in and out of rooms, and pause, before passing back the way it had come. Circling up and down nearby corridors. Never travelling in his direction. He never left the lab so their paths never crossed. She had no idea how close they continued to live their lives. Somehow, eight years had passed. Why didn't she visit him? Did she even know where he was? She had become a GPS ghost to him. She had become just an avatar. They both may as well have suffered the same fate as her father.

He reached for the laptop, punched in his security details, and checked her status on the company intranet. She had returned from a forty-eight hour assignment to London. Two clicks and he was at the map. A blue dot was moving fast along the main route through Central Holding. She must be on a buggy, he thought. She was travelling into the Environmental and Clinical Waste Disposal Zone. He'd never seen her in this part of The Foundation before. Something compelled him to pull up a CCTV video. He felt the need to see her, to reassure himself that she wasn't far away. He clicked on cams and verified her co-ordinates.

The Foundation buggy was zipping through a bustle of people. He double-tapped to zoom in. It was an open-top waste disposal truck. There was a single driver. It wasn't her. The rear of the truck was loaded with sealed plastic bags. He double-checked the co-ordinates and watched the GPS move in synchronicity with the CCTV image. The truck moved beyond camera range. Mike cancelled the feed. He watched as the dot continued into the Waste Disposal Zone and stopped. Seconds later, the signal disappeared. He refreshed the page. The blue dot had gone. He searched The Foundation contacts list and her listing was greyed out.

[Declassified]

He reached for his phone. Even after all this time, her number was still on his speed dial. The call flat-lined. He redialled to the same effect. He hit zero for a central operator who answered him by name.

'Dr Jones? How can I help you today?' she said, cheerily.

'Put me through to Sarah Clarkson.'

'You know I'm not allowed to do that, Dr Jones.'

'Just put me through.'

'This call has been documented on The Foundation intranet.'

'I don't give a fuck,' he interrupted. 'I want to speak to her. Right now.'

The receptionist was silent.

'Well?' he commanded. 'Can you do that for me?'

'I've just checked, Dr Jones. Her comms have been declassified.'

'Is her cell phone broken?'

The receptionist was becoming flustered. 'I don't know. I've not seen this before; maybe once. There's no more information.'

The NST was beginning to flow through his system. Mike wondered if he was already under. Was he having this conversation? 'Don't leave me guessing, when did you see it before?'

'Erm, after the chemical accident. Two years ago.'

He was outraged at the receptionist's incompetence. 'What are you telling me? There's been an accident?'

The receptionist hung up. He hit zero and got through to a different operator.

'Dr Jones? How can I help you today?' asked an overtly cheerful voice.

'I need to speak to the person I was just talking to,' he ordered.

There was a pause and the tapping of a keyboard. 'I'm sorry, Dr Jones, we have no record of another call today.'

'I was just speaking to a receptionist on this line.'

'One moment − I'm sorry, Dr Jones, we have no record of another call from you today. How can I help you?' she asked, cheerfully.

Mike slammed the phone down and pulled the intravenous drip from his arm with the NST now active in his bloodstream.

53

Sarah held her knees tight to her body as she cowered in the doorway of a stone shrine. Piercing eyes. Mournful shrieks. Desperate tears. She felt fear like she'd never known.

The world was transparent. There was movement all around. Swirling ghosts in the night, blue spirits drifting in the stale air. A flicker of smoke drew images that faded away into nothing. She recognised some of the outlines; a tree, a bicycle, people walking, bodies moving, all leaving thin, vapour-like trails behind them.

She heard the chime of a heavy bell in the distance. A love song to loneliness. It rung, slow and steady, announcing her arrival. Despite the movement there was no other noise, no sound to accompany the visions, just the distant hum of submerged action – the flutter of a presence seeping in from an unestablished space.

A ghostly human form passed by. As it did so, it seemed to evaporate and was pulled up into the air. She watched it disappear into a translucent vacuum of swirling mist that floated up to a huge mountain island in the sky.

The abandoned congregation had lost faith. They shared a collective lack of motivation, shuffling aimlessly in a pilgrimage with no purpose. Shadows reflected on the dark cobblestones. Storm clouds swirled above. Unidentifiable streaks of white and blue flecked the sky like rain. Raised voices buzzed in a vibrantly wired synchronicity.

The unknown world was in a state of sacrifice, chewing itself up and spitting itself out. This was a place torn apart – a place that shouldn't exist.

Something bumped her in the back and she was pushed forward to walk slowly amongst the crowd of solemn figures that moved silently, heading nowhere. A tall building loomed gothic behind her, twin spires in the air, lanterns swirling like a lighthouse. This was Central Station; the entrance to the afterlife.

Two large clocks were mounted on the face of the building. The metal hands of one clock rotated chaotically forward, speeding up and slowing down. The hands of the other timepiece spun backwards, counting down the remaining minutes to the end of Time itself.

Hour by hour, minute by minute, second by second, the station flooded with shadows as they were granted access to the afterlife in the event of their mortal death. A continuous stream of souls emerged across the threshold of a dream.

On arrival, they would be issued with a travel ticket, and allowed access to the trams. Once they had embarked a tram of their choosing, the lost souls would circle the afterlife in a loop. Every path led back to Central Station. As they rode, their memories would fade, their eyes would become tired, and they would drift aimlessly in a figure of eight on the tracks until they were offered a chance to join the sea of souls that surrounded Mt. Hōrai. A new keeper of the afterlife wasn't offering enlightenment, and the reviver of the dead had been long since missing.

Sarah took a ticket and stepped forward. She noticed railings at her feet, metal grooves in the cobbled pavement. She stopped to study them but was being pushed onto them. She elbowed back. The pressure of the growing crowd was too great. There was no space to move. She felt her feet vibrate. There was movement in the earth, on the tracks, and she looked up to see the bright lights of a tram churning towards her. A bell rang and the crowd around her eased, just enough for her to push back into the group as the heavy metal tram hurtled to a stop.

She was caught in the movement of people as they shoved their way on-board. She took a reluctant step inside and found herself sitting on a window seat opposite a thin, blonde woman.

Claire Nilsson had also been dragged across the threshold and into the land of the living dead. She stared out of the window with a vacant expression; sad, lost and alone, waiting for someone. She had given up hope, become resigned to her fate, just like the hundreds of thousands of forlorn faces that surrounded her.

Sarah could see the shadows more clearly from her seat. White ghosts were passing in all directions, zigzagging across her path. Dark shapes conflicted on a collision course, sweeping through each other, as though neither of them were even there. The pathways of the afterlife were packed with congested trams and speeding bicycles, pushing down narrow cobblestone paths. It was a violent chaos; the jostling for position, persistent movement that went absolutely nowhere.

The tram bell rang and the ghostly vehicle moved on, taking its passengers on a journey of forgetfulness.

54

His memories were blurred – bright lights, groggy confusion, the sting of the cold needle, the rush of burning pain. His eyes were red and stung whenever he blinked. An oxygen mask was fixed so tightly to his face that every time he took a desperate breath, it tightened even further.

Two anonymous figures were forcing him down a brightly lit corridor. His hands were tied behind his back, wrists bound with plastic ties. Heavy boots dragged behind him. He was too weak to struggle, too strung out to speak. The dirty medical gown clung to his body as he was pushed through a doorway. Lars noticed the sign. Faraday Eleven. Sub Level Six.

The lights were dimmed. The corners dark. Figures stood in silhouette in the shadows. He couldn't see their faces. Damp air battled against dehumidifiers. There was a continuous drone, the hum of constant noise, perhaps a fan or air conditioning unit in another room? Two words hung at an angle on the brick wall; "Unity" and "Collaboration." Beneath them were a series of Japanese characters.

In the centre of the room was a metal, box-like structure with a large riveted door. A bright strip light flickered on, revealing that the entire room was encased in a brown, copper coloured cage. A series of thin blue and red wires led along the floor, tracing out of sight.

Dr Finjoto and Chieko were waiting, dressed in white surgical gowns with blue plastic boots and facemasks around their necks.

Lars struggled, trying to see his captors, but all he could see were shadows.

'Malcolm Van Peterson was ahead of his time.' Finjoto's voice rebounded around the room, indicating that the space was much larger that it appeared. 'He was a pioneer, until time caught up with him, and he lost everything to the crumbling walls of old age.

Perhaps that's why he treated me as he did? Like a son. He was as eager to involve me in his plans as I was to learn them. For a while, I was his salvation, keen on the preservation of his soul, then he became just a peasant who thought too much.'

Dr Finjoto paced around the cage and out of sight. 'He was a hand to mouth thinker, always searching for the next project and the next dollar, but it wasn't a simple matter of funding that held Van Peterson back. He believed that he had discovered riches of a different kind. He believed that knowledge brought him enlightenment, and that suffering brought him validation. Pain and sacrifice were all a part of the process.' He shook his head in disagreement. 'He believed that he was better than everyone else, for he had contemplated the mysteries of the Universe and achieved what? A theory? That was enough to motivate him to his death. He lived poor, and he died forgotten. So what did he really achieve?'

Dr Finjoto approached Lars who was breathing heavily through the mask. 'He achieved — absolutely nothing.' He slammed his fist onto the metal cage. The sound reverberated around the room. 'Van Peterson was a micro-dot in the infinite abyss. He had so much potential but his ideas lacked scale.' He nodded to Chieko. 'My esteemed guests, I offer you the final phase of Project Tetris. The combined energy of our two subjects will literally tear open a passage between this life and the next. You are about to witness the shifting of one plane to reveal another – the breakdown of the building blocks of reality itself.'

The wall behind them became transparent, revealing it to be a huge, reverse mirror. A vast lobby spread far into the distance. Long tables were lined up in a row. There was a hive of activity. The atmosphere was intense. Hundreds of people were shouting at each other, throwing cigarettes, drinking Hype energy cans, slapping each other on the back, sitting crouched up in their chairs, some lying face down on their desks, asleep amongst the din of camaraderie and play. There were wires everywhere. A rack of impressive computer fans whirred along the walls behind a framework of shining chrome metal.

Lars managed to lift his head enough to see the adjoining room and could make out the familiar flashes of images on computer screens. Gradually, the sound filtered into the caged room, like a volume control being increased. Sonic bleeps and bit-crushed crashes filled the air; the sound from a computer game. He heard shouting in a language that he didn't recognise and shuddered when he understood a series of key phrases.

'Inventory; Money, Drugs, Nukes, Kudos, Life Force, Game Time, Cash Stash, Raid.'

There was the chant of an IP address.

'Employ!'

A thousand fingers tapped at computer keyboards. Voices shouted in perfectly practiced unity and collaboration.

'Behold the physical incarnation of your virtual world,' said Finjoto, as he presented the room to Lars. 'What you see before you are the human mechanics behind what you call, Atari Shock. My gold farmers have worked ceaselessly, day and night, and whenever you have been playing they have been right by your side; each individual dedicated to a single task — to guide you here, Izanagi.'

Lars vomited into his oxygen mask. He choked, inhaling the liquid into his lungs.

Chieko looked concerned. She pleaded with her father, and after a prolonged moment of thought, he allowed her to remove the mask. Lars retched and gasped as he fell to his knees. He heaved on the floor, spitting bile and breathing in panicked gulps of air.

'Now, it is time for you to enter the cage and bring about the dawn of my New World,' said Finjoto. He observed the space around him; the ominous faraday cage, the watching shadows in the darkness, the frantic typing of the gold famers, the multitude of screens and wires and mayhem. He opened the cage door and it swung wide to reveal two high-backed, wooden chairs. A body twitched inside, held fast by thick leather body straps. It was Berry.

She was falling in and out of consciousness, her eyes were staring and hollow, rolling back in their sockets, flickering behind closed lids. Her face was gaunt, bone stretching over skin. She jolted, fingers twitching in an active state of REM. Tangled wires trailed in a crude clump of multi-coloured plastic. They disappeared through the wall and continued into the hive of activity next door. Smaller wires crawled like a creeper up her legs and arms and neck. They twisted with clumps of hair clipped to her roughly shaven head. Two drips were attached to her left arm, held secure by blood-dried bandages. One drip was clear liquid and one blue; the colour of the NST. A portable infusion pump was registering her vital statistics.

Dr Finjoto waved a hand and Lars was pushed, screaming, inside the faraday cage. 'Strap him down. Prepare for total immersion.'

A Tibetan bell rang out to symbolise the cleansing of a tranquil passage to the afterlife. The atmosphere of violence was thick and threatening. There was a soft buzz of chatter from the room next door and the hiss of ambient noise. The wall connecting the gold farmers sealed to darkness, causing the faraday room to fall into shadow.

Lars could hear the murmuring conversation between Finjoto and the mysterious group. He closed his eyes, longing that the past twenty-four hours were just some kind of wild, fantastical dream, and that he was at home with Claire. He would wake up at any moment and she would be waiting to shout at him, telling him to take a shower and stop staying up so late. That was all he wanted, to be back where he started, for everything to re-set to the beginning – just like in the game.

He tried to move but his arms and legs were paralysed. He felt the sting of the needle and the cold rush of intravenous flow.

'Are they sedated? He's struggling,' observed a deep, southern American drawl. Agent Carlton was surrounded by his team as they prepared to watch the next stages of enlightenment. 'She doesn't look too hot either.'

'I can assure you that she is in perfect health,' replied Dr Finjoto. 'All vital signs are being constantly monitored. And his reactions are purely involuntary. They are already deep under, and will have no knowledge of this event once they cross.'

The group crowded around the cage were taking notes, as if Lars and Berry were the subjects of a warped experiment, and that this was just another seminar.

'Berry has responded perfectly to the NST. She is committed to the discovery of the New World and has embraced her true identity,' echoed Finjoto's voice in the darkness. 'Lars, I fear, has more to learn before he will be ready. His quantum jump is somewhat...' he stuttered, searching for the correct words, 'somewhat erratic.'

'Why are they wearing the black boots and gown?'

'Our research has shown that on the other side, while their sense of present identity will fade, the subject can retain a residual memory of this existence. The white gown simply presents an alpha state for the transferential experience; a plain canvas if you will, to enable them to truly embrace their previous incarnation.

The boots perform a basic function; grounding the subject in the faraday cage in which you see they are contained. They will insulate the subject against any potentially harmful spikes or electrical pulses, while the body takes root in both this life and the next.

The cage acts as an anchor, ensuring that the subject will reset and start again, should they fall victim to an unpredictable tragedy.'

Carlton was impressed. He'd never seen anything like it. If Finjoto had indeed completed Van Peterson's work, then the impact would be immense. The necessary sacrifices would not have been in vain. A lifetime's work would be justified. 'If only Malcolm were alive to see this.'

'We have Professor Van Peterson to thank for coming this far,' said Finjoto. 'We will never forget.'

Carlton tapped the metal work. 'So, this cage — it's some kind of conductor?'

'Imagine, if you will, the coil of a spring being constantly pulled. If you keep stretching it, then with prolonged use, it will never return to its original state. The faraday cage prevents the ping between this world and the next from corrupting their mortal soul. Without the cage, there is a danger of losing the subject on the other side.'

The group took notes.

'Show me how it works,' asked Carlton, a flutter of morbid excitement in his chest as the absurd experiment played out before him.

Finjoto signalled for total immersion to commence. 'I give you passage to my New World,' he said.

Berry and Lars jolted simultaneously, causing the group to let out a distressed gasp as the increased NST dosage took hold.

'Please, be silent,' scolded Finjoto. 'This is why they are strapped down.'

Lars began grinning; insane, yellow teeth, blood dripping from the deep scratches that had reappeared on his cheek.

'Administering the NST' said Chieko, as she activated the intravenous flow.

Lars managed to keep his eyes open long enough to see the group watching, holding clipboards, chewing on pencils, all staring at him as he began to hyperventilate.

The convulsion began in his left arm but swiftly took his whole body by surprise. Some of the group began to laugh, disturbed by the strange events. His forced grin twisted into a leer, an ugly grimace that caused his body to shift in shape. He appeared to be fighting the transformation as a war between impulse and self-control raged in his body and mind. His fingers twitched. A hundred volts were charging through his system.

'What do you see, Izanagi?' demanded Finjoto.

A camera was trained on the cage, catching every moment. The sight was haunting. No one turned away. They were studying the reactions, fascinated by the terrifying state. It was freakish and yet utterly captivating. His eyes were flitting, his senses peaking. The camera turned to show the reaction of the watching group.

Finjoto's muffled voice could be heard shouting. 'We have yet to achieve an advanced state in controlled conditions. Remember, the simian sessions only reached level three, and they did not survive.'

Berry was also lost in a confined chemical lockdown. Too strange to switch off, too disturbing not to keep watching, the camera zoomed in tight to her dilated yellow pupils which were locked in a helpless fear.

There was pin drop silence. Mouth open. Eyes wide. Terror.

'Embrace it,' commanded Finjoto. 'Guide me to Hōrai.' He knelt before the cage. 'Oh, glorious Tengu, I sanctify your authority as master of the cloud-chamber. I return these mortals as a sacrifice so that they may show us the way to the darkness of your polluted land, and we will travel into the New World unhindered.'

A large, black shadow dropped to the floor with a thud. The group turned in the direction of the sound. Nothing registered on camera. They all acknowledged hearing something fall. There was a click, click, click as it tapped at the void between the realm of the living and the dead.

'You see it, don't you? Testing the walls between this life and the next?'

Lars and Berry watched as the gigantic spider approached. It passed straight through Finjoto and continued crawling towards the cage. Black shadows began to leak down the walls of Faraday Eleven.

The shadow spider loomed, hissing and clicking. It raised its front legs in the air, flexing hairs like spines. Eight eyes watched from the darkness of the space between life and death. Lars and Berry were trapped, powerless against the otherworldly creature, as it prepared for the final strike between realms.

Lars closed his eyes as the spider reared up and lurched two legs into his chest. He stared, petrified, as he coughed a sharp and final breath. Berry screamed as the spider lunged again, shredding guts from his stomach, casting his internal organs into the air. The Tibetan bell resonated.

Agent Carlton and his team saw nothing other than Lars locked in a frantic fit, his body rippling in shock inside the cage.

Then came the spike, the abrupt peak of distress, sudden and sharp, as if a light had been switched on to reveal things that should have been left invisible in the dark. Berry was screaming, biting her lip as she visibly drew blood which she spat at the camera lens. 'Fuck you, Finjoto!'

A hand wiped the camera, smudging the image.

'They are in control. Observe and learn,' shouted Finjoto.

Agent Carlton turned his head away, clearly disturbed.

Chieko took a step back, confusion and fear welling inside her. She had never seen her father behave in this way. She slipped out of the room, unnoticed.

Berry's mouth was moving but no words were audible. Her face was overtaken by a wave of convulsion. She began to retch, heaving violently.

The video camera zoomed in.

'This is normal,' reassured Finjoto.

Sitting bolt upright, fingers twisting, held by the straps in the faraday cage, Berry began to laugh which slowly twisted into a scream that left her in tears.

'This is all part of the process,' Finjoto could be heard shouting. He knew that the moment had arrived. He sat in the metal chair that adjoined the faraday cage and calmly rolled up his sleeve. He applied the tourniquet. The syringe was prepped and ready at his side. He didn't flinch as he injected the NST. He tightened his arms into the chair straps and sat back, closing his eyes. He felt his arms and legs tense. His muscles convulsed in the intravenous rush. 'Guide me across the threshold,' he said.

A bright light glowed like a furnace as a ball of white electricity began to emanate from inside the faraday cage.

55

Chieko had expected to find Mike in his laboratory. The room was in blackout. The lights automatically flickered on.

The bed was in the upright position. The infusion pump was paused. An intravenous line hung, dripping to the floor. The office phone was off the hook. He had tried to make a call and then paused the IV cycle. She listened to the dead dial tone and considered hitting redial but knew that it would be traceable and logged.

She checked the infusion settings. He had prepared a new NST trip and the process had been primed for an increased dosage – two bags of plasma. He had never gone that deep. He would be under for weeks, maybe months.

She opened the GPS on her phone and searched for his signal. He had been in Central Holding, passed by the security offices and double backed on himself several times before moving on. He had chosen a complicated route. He was trying to cover his tracks. Now he was heading to the outer chem labs. She realised that he was going to see the Beta Boys.

The laboratory window was glass frosted. Mike couldn't make out anyone inside but he knew they were there. They were always there.

He scanned his phone on the terminal. The door slid open and loud eighties music blared out: Tears for Fears - Everybody Wants To Rule The World.

Two guys were sat on laboratory chairs with their backs to the door. A row of PC monitors spooled player-feed information, but the boys were distracted by something quite different to Atari Shock. They crunched on tortilla chips, swinging their legs to the music, laughing hysterically.

A couple of naked Japanese girls were gyrating along to the song behind a meshed wire wall, swinging themselves around like something they'd seen in a RedTube video. White lab coats hung off their shoulders. One of the dancers spotted Mike and she screamed. The boys spun around and scrambled for the old skool cassette tape machine. It smashed to the floor as they crunched the stop button.

'Ooh, damn,' said one. 'That's gonna to cost a mint.'

'They don't make 'em like that anymore, bro,' said the other.

You might have been convinced that you were seeing double – instead you would be looking at the Beta Boys; twin brothers and genius chem lab cooks at The Foundation of New World Technologies.

They were identical and they played up to that. Both had retro spectacles. Both had designer tennis shoes. Both were wearing baseball caps and colourful hoodies under their lab coats. One hoodie was green, and one was red. As these were the only clothes that they ever wore, this had become the most obvious way to distinguish between them.

'Mike Jones, alive and in person,' they sung in unison, with the same mischievous glint in their eyes.

The girls covered themselves and started edging for the door.

'What the hell are you doing?' scolded Mike. He spoke as if talking to a single person, giving the boys equal attention. It was a method that usually got him what he wanted.

'Whatever the hell we want, man,' replied Green hoodie.

Red hoodie nodded and repeated back half the sentence. '...the hell we want, man? We're on our screen break.'

Mike shrugged. 'Are they on a screen break too?'

The embarrassed girls hid.

'They're interns,' said Green, with a slow drawl. 'Studying advanced neuro-anatomy, techno-physiology and neuro-sampling.' It was straight out of the welcome pack.

'No shit?'

'And all you're qualified to know is that their names have been carefully chosen to protect their identity,' said Red. He made introductions. 'Ladies, meet the legendary, Dr Jones.' The girls bowed their heads sharply while covering their modesty. 'Dr Jones, meet Debbie Does Dallas and Burt Reynolds. And before you ask, yes, we were educating them in popular movie culture when they chose their English names.' The Beta Boys laughed and slapped a high five.

'Fine, boys. What you get up to down here is your own business. I don't need to know any more, but I do need your help.'

The Beta Boys sensed the urgency in his voice and asked the girls to leave, mumbling about meeting up later to role-play. Both were suddenly serious.

'Stats, please?' asked Green.

He hesitated, then handed over his phone. They scanned it and passed it back. He watched them study the monitors, occasionally touching the rims of their glasses.

'You've just come back from a trip? A real long one too.' Green seemed just like a pharmacy advisor behind a counter.

'Fuck, three weeks under?' said Red. 'Damn, bro. Are you pure yet?'

The Boys took off their glasses and looked Mike in the eye, but as they did so, they glanced up at a security camera in the ceiling.

He followed their glare and noticed a blinking red light. This was unusual. They always re-routed their CCTV during breaks. Perhaps this had become more difficult? The cameras would have registered him in the corridor already. Now he would have to head back to the security offices and erase the laboratory logs as well. He raised both hands innocently and stood back. 'I'm pure, okay?'

The Beta Boys winced.

Something was up.

Green went back to checking the monitor. He frowned and tapped Red's arm, indicating the screen.

'One moment, caller,' said Red.

Mike leaned against the wall. 'Take your time, boys.' He forced a smile and found himself considering his options. They were trying to warn him. Perhaps the pick-up wasn't going to be possible and he would have to find another way?

The Beta Boys huddled together in close conversation, occasionally looking up. 'Houston, we have a problem,' said Red. 'Your access has been revoked.'

'There's an orange flag from your lab assistant,' said Green.

'A what?'

'You're not to be given any further dosage.'

'She doesn't have the authority to do that.'

'She does, man. She's top level. Higher than you,' said Green.

'I think I know why you've been shut down,' said Red.

Were they talking about Sarah? Did they know where she was?

'Something's telling me that he's a little behind on the latest news,' mumbled Green.

'The NST fried the brains of three Strepsirrhini primates yesterday,' explained Red. 'They suffered a complete psychotropic breakdown.'

He suddenly felt more scared. Did this have something to do with her disappearance? 'Who was monitoring them?'

'London Labs,' they said together, knowing full well that he'd know what that meant.

'You know where she is, don't you?'

They looked nervous.

'They don't, but I do,' stated a voice from the entrance. Chieko held out her hand. 'Your phone please, Dr Jones,' she demanded.

He could get past her, he thought. He could get back to the lab and run the course as planned. 'This has nothing to do with you.'

'I'm afraid it does. You have to let me help you or you will never see Sarah again. Your phone,' she repeated.

He reluctantly handed over the phone and to his surprise she pulled off the protective cover and smashed it against the wall, cracking the screen. She then removed the sim, snapped it, and put it in her pocket. 'Turn around.'

'What?'

'Turn around, Dr Jones.' She placed her palm on his lower back. 'This would normally hurt,' she said, 'but I think you have so much in your system right now that you won't feel a thing.' She pulled a surgical scalpel from a belt at her waist, uncapped the blade, and felt along the base of his spine with her thumb. 'Your phone is not the only way that the Academy have been monitoring you. The phone is just a formality. The real data is transmitted from this device.'

He felt a slight pressure as she located the gradual shift in scar tissue. She cut a skilful nick into the skin and with her thumb she massaged out a small, circular piece of plastic. She showed him the tracking chip.

'Fuck. How long has that been there?'

It had the initials CIADST imprinted on the side. 'This is an original. Professor Van Peterson would have fitted you during the spiritual science tour. Your every movement has been recorded by the Academy since. Wait. I need to stop the bleeding.' She tore open a padded bandage and covered the wound. 'Please, we don't have much time.' She turned to the Beta Boys who were running their thumbs along the base of each other's spines. 'I need you to give him all of the NST plasma that you have.'

'Wait, what? You just revoked his access?'

'I restricted his access as soon as I knew that he was going to do it by himself,' she said. 'You need me by your side, Mike, to monitor you, or you will never make it back. You will be trapped on the platform indefinitely.'

He laughed. The faces of the Beta Boys were deadly serious.

'My father has lost his way. He will never be able to control them.'

'Your father?'

'I am the daughter of Tadashi Finjoto.' Her eyes were suddenly scared. 'And it is my responsibility to stop my father from achieving his sacred mission.'

Mike realised why she'd been assigned to his lab; she was Tadashi's daughter. She'd been at his side for longer than he could remember. She was highly trained and had observed every advancement of the platform with keen interest. She was his permanent shadow, watching all, filing reports, nursing him back from the edge of consciousness. She was a spy in his own ranks.

'What were your orders?'

She looked to the ground. 'I feel so ashamed.'

'What did he tell you to do?' shouted Mike.

'I was told to replace the NST with a lethal dose of morphine. You were not coming back from your next trip.' She held his gaze. 'I'm sorry, Dr Jones, he has collected all of the data that he needs from you.'

Was this why Finjoto had asked him to remain part of the Academy? To be an expendable part of an experiment? 'You're his daughter. How do I know that I can trust you?'

'Ask me anything, and I will answer truthfully,' she offered.

'Is Sarah still alive?'

Chieko bowed her head. 'She is no longer on this cosmic plane, but I believe there is a way to bring her back.'

'What are you saying? Where is she?'

'We must hurry. The subjects have already begun the quantum jump.'

'They're jumping?' exclaimed Green. 'What dosage?'

'Total immersion. They will be permanently under the influence of the NST.'

'That'll kill them,' said Red.

'For sure,' confirmed Green.

'It will not kill them,' she whispered, 'for they are not of this world. My father has been using you to explore the process of total immersion, but he no longer needs you because he has found them. The NST contains the essence of the sacred mushroom, amanita muscaria. It is a gift from the land of the dead, from the primordial gods themselves. You have not been engaging in psychotropic enlightenment, Dr Jones. You have been dying and living in death.'

Mike rubbed his eyes. He wasn't sure if he'd heard her correctly. The NST flowing through his bloodstream made him wonder if the conversation was even happening.

'He has been lying to you, Dr Jones. He has been plotting with the Academy ever since the kami-kakushi incident in Las Vegas. He intends to gain passage to Yomi-no-kuni, the underworld, and to bargain with the ancients who command it. He does not understand the impact of his actions. He is lost in the pursuit of an unattainable goal. The Academy cannot take the afterlife like it were a prize. This world will be unlocked for the control of the primordial gods. They will awaken and there will be nothing to stop them. All will be destroyed. All will be death.

'How do you know all this?' he asked.

'The sacrifice,' she replied, solemnly. 'I feared that this day would come and so I too have been preparing — I have been preparing you, Dr Vegas.'

A flash of recognition washed over him as she said the name. Chieko knew about his unsanctioned trips for NST plasma. She had been increasing his dosage to a level where he could survive on the platform for longer. She had been initiating it all along.

'You have the ability to confront the dark forces of the otherworld for you have done so many times before. You have spent so much time alongside them that you know exactly how to defeat them. The time has come for you to use your powers.'

Chieko had been training him. She had enabled him with the ability to play the afterlife like a game.

'You must go deeper than ever before. You must help them all, and prevent my father from initiating his misguided plan.' She bowed in respectful confidence. 'I trust you, Dr Vegas.'

He felt that Sarah was nearby, she was just invisible in the darkness, waiting to be shown the way. If she was lost somewhere on the platform, then it was up to him to find her. Mike was determined to defy the divine cause and effect. He had been doing so for many years.

'You sure about this?' asked Red, as he handed over the bags of plasma.

'I'll see you in the next life,' smiled Mike, with a crazed look in his eye.

56

A blinding light was emanating from inside the cage, blasting the silhouettes of a mysterious group against the wall. They had stopped taking notes and were staring, captured by its glare, like animals trapped in oncoming headlights. Mike pushed his way through them and was confronted by Special Agent Carlton.

His eyes were narrowed, his pupils like pins, his face transfixed in a concentrated stare. He had aged significantly since they last saw each other in the police cell in Las Vegas. Seeing Carlton again after all these years sent a terrifying shiver down Mike's spine. The instant he recognised him the pieces of a puzzle became clear; Van Peterson, Lori, Sarah, Berry, Lars, Dr Finjoto and even himself, they were all part of a grand plan, necessary to achieve what the Academy had called progress. With every twist and turn towards completion, the shapes had been destroyed to make way for the next vital piece to fall into place. It was the repeat play of a game that would never end, no matter how many lives had to be sacrificed. Provando e riprovando; try and try again, this was the spirit of the Academy and it came at any cost.

Chieko fell into the room. 'Father, no,' she screamed as she witnessed the terrible experiment. 'We're too late.'

He was unconscious and bleeding from his mouth, eyes rolling in a frantic REM state. His breathing was beginning to slow. She pulled at the straps and unfastened the tourniquet. His arms fell limp by his side. She inspected his body. An invisible force made him too heavy to lift.

Mike opened the faraday cage and the light intensified as he disappeared inside. It was growing brighter, swallowing him, as it absorbed the life force that surrounded it.

Finjoto and Chieko were hidden by the glare as the light flooded the room. She rushed to the Tibetan bell and rang it as hard as she could. The deep sound of the gong resonated, causing the light to dissipate, and Lars, Berry and Mike to become visible inside the cage.

The gong also seemed to force Carlton to snap out of his trance. The group came to their senses and fled the room, leaving their clipboards on the floor. The video camera was kicked over in the struggle, with the red light still recording.

The Tibetan gong vibrated, its deep reverberations cleansing the passage between worlds; sonic shock waves keeping the white light at bay, draining its power, as it was reduced to a candle light flicker inside the faraday cage.

The room fell into a darkened lull.

All was quiet.

Carlton reached down to turn the camera up on its tripod and checked that it was still recording. The hairs bristled on the back of his neck in the anticipation of what was to come.

'The procedure has begun,' whispered Chieko. 'We must leave everyone exactly as they are.' She knew what she had to do. With methodical technique she hooked the NST plasma bags up to the active intravenous infusion pump, and went through a series of checks on each of the subjects.

Berry was stable and registering a constant heart rate. Her father's vital signs were weaker, his breathing slowing to occasional gasps of air. She felt for Lars' pulse and lifted his eyelids. His body was unresponsive. He had stopped breathing. The machine registered a flat-line. The hospital gown was covered with blood. She checked for impact wounds but found nothing. 'This is wrong. This shouldn't have happened.'

Berry groaned and let out a soft whisper, trying to speak. Mike leaned in, taking her hand in his.

'Find me,' she whispered, before drawing a sharp intake of air and exhaling her last breath.

The room was silent.

A voice spoke in a whisper. 'Just because you cannot see me, you believe that I am not watching?' The words echoed away into the dark corners of the room.

'Tengu is watching,' whispered Chieko.

'The daughter of Tadashi is right,' echoed the voice. 'And I know who you are, Michael Jones. I have seen your destiny carved on the sandstone walls of Time itself. Follow us into the afterlife, and I will gladly show you the desperate truth of your mortality.'

Mike cautiously stepped out of the cage. Carlton crouched lower, hoping that his presence wouldn't interfere with the process.

'The bargain has been well met. The accord has been settled. It is the end of your world,' crackled the voice. 'I bring eternal darkness to your mortal plane. Humanity will be released. I take your dimension as my own.'

'Never,' shouted Chieko.

'Ah, young daughter. Quite unlike her father. Finjoto was able to see far beyond the professor's short sight. You, however, lack your father's vision. Your world must die in order to be reborn. I bring you freedom. Yomi-no-kuni, the underworld, is here. Your world ends now,' boomed the voice.

With all of her might, Chieko pulled on the thick rope tied around the Tibetan gong. The bell sounded and the white light extinguished entirely.

The room fell dark.

Tengu was gone.

Mike reached out to steady himself. 'Are you there?' he whispered in the darkness.

'I'm here,' she replied.

'It's gone.'

'No. It hasn't.'

There was a flicker from Finjoto's heart rate monitor. It moved again, inconsistent, but registering life. The LED display drew fast lifelines across the screen, lighting up the room in green streaks as Finjoto jolted upright in his chair. A terrifying transformation was occurring. He was changing.

His face was shifting into some kind of creature. His arms extended to form long, black feathers. His head fell back and chin pointed out to become a sharp, black beak.

Chieko fell to her knees, terrified by the horrific metamorphosis. She cried as she kneeled by his side.

Finjoto's head turned sharply at an angle.

'Don't touch him,' shouted Mike, but it was too late.

Tengu jumped, twisting in the air and landing on Chieko, holding her in a headlock and crushing her windpipe. She struggled to breathe, trapped fast.

'Come, daughter!' it shrieked. 'Embrace the next life.' The light began to emanate from inside the faraday cage once more.

Mike used all of his weight to kick the creature away. 'Leave her, Finjoto.'

The birdman spun around the cage, disappearing into the shadows. 'Finjoto is no longer on this mortal plane.' There was a flurry of feathers from the corner of the chamber. Shadows began to creep up the walls.

'You ok?' asked Mike, as he helped her to her feet.

'The gong,' she wheezed, breathless, 'we must keep the resonation stable. We must prevent the passage from being opened both ways.' She reached out to strike it again. An object flew through the air and knocked her to the ground.

Mike watched the shadows spread. The door of the faraday cage flew open and he was sucked inside. The door slammed shut. The noise of metal on metal reverberated around the chamber. He grabbed at the walls of the cage. Something was inside with him.

The creature loomed large and powerful, flying onto his back. It pinned him to the floor and clawed at his neck. He gasped, struggling for air, pushing away the body that was no longer Finjoto. A faintness overcame him. He was desperate to release its grip from his throat. Blue ghosts swarmed the chamber as he struggled to breathe. He was going to die, thought Mike.

His mind drifted. He wondered where Sarah was and if he would ever see her again. He thought of the missed opportunities, of the times in New York and Las Vegas, the lure of The Foundation and the years under sedation while he explored the platform. He thought about Van Peterson, the man who had lead him on his strange journey, and who had ultimately brought him to the moment of his death.

The creature was now fully formed. Its arms were covered with large, black feathers. Its legs were red and blue, bruised with the rigours of human transformation. Tengu, the shadow wielder, the master of chaos, had fulfilled its desire and taken Finjoto's mortal body. It clawed at his throat, intensifying its grip.

The last thing that Mike saw before falling unconscious was Chieko standing over them. She gripped the surgical scalpel and slashed out, and her blade sliced Tengu's neck.

The birdman gasped, wide-eyed and desperate. With wing-like hands it clutched at its windpipe. Mortal blood gushed. It screeched, unable to stop the bleeding, the life force rushing from its veins. Its eyes expressed terror and sadness in the moments of its death, as it felt mortal emotion for the very first time.

The transformation reverted and Finjoto was now splayed in a pool of dark blood on the floor of the faraday cage. Mike was unconscious beside him.

The white light re-ignited and engulfed the room.

Chieko reached out for the Tibetan gong. Before she could sound it the light became so intense that it burned her eyes. She turned away, shielding herself from the glare. The chamber became translucent, exposed by the explosion of white light as the passage between life and death was opened. In an instant, it pulled its passengers from one plane to the next. The light subsided and the cage was empty.

Chieko approached the gong and struck it one last time, allowing it to resonate throughout the room, feeling the vibrations penetrate her soul. 'I wish you safe passage on the other side, my father, my colleagues, and my immortal family,' she said, as she closed her eyes in silent prayer.

On opening them, she was no longer Chieko Finjoto. A ghostly white face was richly painted with makeup; blue eyebrows and red cheeks, lips as purple as fruit. Long black hair tumbled down strong cheekbones. Beautifully intricate nails were painted on large, firm hands.

Carlton approached and offered a shawl of flowing red silk, spotted with green butterflies. 'I welcome you to your mortality, oh immortal one, Benten,' he said, with a humble bow. 'You have performed such a great sacrifice.'

Benten smiled, and turning her back to Carlton she unbuttoned the grey suit, allowing it to slip to the floor. She held the shawl against her skin revealing the curve of a naked breast. 'You wonder if I am man or woman?' she asked, turning her head. 'I am both and I am neither. I am one, and then the other. It is my will and my way.'

Benten pulled the shawl tighter, feeling an overwhelming sense of peace and protection from the soft silk, as a cold chill swept through the room. 'There is much work to do on the other side. The land of the afterlife grows dark. The fertile blessing of my lotus sister is absent. Nothing grows. Nothing blooms. All dies.' She pulled the shawl high over her face. 'As do I.'

Benten had made the sacrifice to enable the return of their immortal brother and sister. The bridge that spanned dimensions was now broken, and Benten would suffer a mortal death.

Agent Carlton noted the time and recorded the data into the camera. Benten was already breathless and becoming weaker with each new step. He helped her through the door of Faraday Eleven, and to die in her new world.

The fate of the afterlife was in the hands of the reincarnated guardians once more. Their quest was about to begin. Luckily, they had expert help, from the psychotropic-addled anaesthetist known as Dr Vegas.

ACHIEVEMENT UNLOCKED

LEVEL FOUR

57

The bath water was lukewarm in the afternoon heat. The shadow animals couldn't trace him if he stayed submerged and semi-conscious. It was a theory that had yet to be proved wrong.

His memories were inconsistent, like they'd been suggested rather than lived. Sometimes he wasn't sure if he was remembering parts of his own life or someone else's, or if in fact the snatches of information that he could recall had been totally imagined. He allowed his mind to drift to a white room that seemed like a distant memory.

'They're not how I imagined them to be,' he heard himself say.

'The special ones never are,' replied a familiar voice. 'They've undergone the full NST therapy?'

'They have,' he heard himself reply.

'Any side-effects? Sickness or memory loss?'

'Lars has been sick several times. He also complained about sickness over the past few weeks.'

'Before the treatment began?'

'Yes.'

'That is unusual,' murmured the voice.

'He had a name for it. That's right, he called it spiralling.'

'I see.'

'Berry is holding up.'

'Of course she is. Any hallucinations?'

'Not that I'm aware of.'

'Do they appear to be displaying any signs of anxiety?'

'He seems distant, detached. She is curious, but calm.'

'They are ready,' said Dr Finjoto. 'Professor Van Peterson would be proud of your work, Michael. Tonight we honour his memory. Proceed with total immersion.'

Dr Vegas had been productive enough to build a shack made of tin and bamboo. It nestled secretly in a clump of trees near a shrine, and was so well hidden that he kept forgetting where it was. He'd found the roof of an old cattle shed, and over weeks, or months, or years, or perhaps it was just two minutes, transported it through the undergrowth on the back of a sacred cow. He'd precariously balanced the roof on a handmade bamboo structure that spanned a rusting tin bath. Sometimes the sacred cows stuck their noses in and jostled for space. He felt that they had as much right to live there as him, and the cattle smell added to his invisibility.

This was his entry point. His save point.

When Dr Vegas had first arrived in the afterlife, a time that he couldn't recall, he'd levelled up from tram passenger to independent bicycle thief pretty quickly. Soon, the bicycle wasn't enough to bypass the animals that skulked in the shadows, so he undertook some mechanical engineering and built his trusty moto using spare parts that he'd stolen from a broken down tram. He'd paid extra attention to crafting a set of weight-loaded panniers, using some seat covers and a large coiled spring. He decided that he needed to be able to sort anything he collected by weight. This was somehow essential to long-term survival. He couldn't risk being weighed down. He had to be able to sort through his inventory and get rid of the heavy stuff fast. Every time he discovered a new item, he would carefully weigh it in the pannier and assess whether he should save it by dumping something else in its favour. He pretty soon established that progress wasn't calculated by distance, but by inventory and power-ups.

Was it possible to make friends in this place? Dr Vegas didn't think so; everyone was too preoccupied with their own shit, always staring off into the distance. He did try talking to a girl once, and they hung out for a few days while he spun stories of midtown life and his apartment with the roof top garden and a view of the Empire State building. He made most of it up. He couldn't even remember if he had an apartment.

He had occasional daydream-like images of a flat on the Upper East Side, where he dealt cocaine to the rich kids while keeping an eye on the big screen sports. He was going through medical school. Working late nights and long days.

He also had a vague recollection that he'd arrived in this otherworld with the intention of setting up a mail order hash delivery service. He'd calculated the perfect plan to make dollars utilising his client base in Manhattan, and a box of four hundred and twenty-thousand books of Cambodian stamps that he'd found under a bin, each featuring a tiny picture of a dinosaur. The idea was to mail the herb in handwritten letters directly to the client. It was fool proof, apart from the fact that he couldn't remember any of his client's addresses, or find a post box.

He'd also tried to export lizards; fifty dollars each, free money under every stone. Then he discovered the land mines and changed his mind. Dr Vegas lost face. His shadowy assistant lost an arm. He stopped speaking to the ghosts after that.

Perhaps the IRS had reclaimed all of his possessions? He didn't know, and he had no way of re-tracing his steps. Was there a raid, were there beatings, was he deported? He tried not to think about it. He had no real recollection of anything. This strange land, with its purple skies and blue clouds, was his here and now. He'd gotten used to it. He quite liked his life. It was a good place to maintain a commitment to his addiction.

He would spend his evenings in mass production; rolling a crop of local weed into thin spliffs that he chain-smoked every waking minute. He even attempted to train his right brain to stay awake and operate the basic motor functions required to roll and smoke in his sleep, but he kept setting fire to his hair. He cooked up his own concoctions, blending plant extracts, trying to lose as many days as possible in a single psychotropic overdose. He had no idea what the plants were. He rolled them anyway. It passed the time. He felt the same buzz even when he didn't smoke them. The hallucinogenic tropane alkaloid called a Mandrake, somehow kept the demons in the shadows, and the satellites behind the clouds.

When he wasn't smoking, he spent his efforts trying to document his travels with as much accuracy as possible. He tried to commit everything he saw to memory, but soon found himself stuck in a loop, repeatedly remembering the same things over and over again, like tracing the worn groove on a favourite vinyl album.

He wasn't afraid of death, because he knew that death was a fake. He had seen it often and waved to it cheerfully as he passed it by on his beaten up moto. Death followed him, determined to do its job, intent on his destruction, but it rarely caught him.

On the odd occasion that he was snatched by death's cold hand, however, he'd been transported across dimensions to wake up on the laboratory bed with Chieko standing right next to him, handing him a carton of cold soba noodles. She was the championship manager; training her rookie for the greatest fight of his career.

The moment he reverted to this mortal state, his memories of the afterlife were locked out of reach.

Dr Vegas was a chaos wrangler. He was a scientist of random. Lying up to his ears in the tin bath, his thin joint like a periscope above the waterline, he was stuck in an afterlife loop, spinning in circles, utterly destitute and yet strangely content.

Another traveller had appeared, and Vegas knew that he had to get to him before the dark creatures of the otherworld.

He lunged out of the bath, his head almost breaking through the shack ceiling. He pulled on his khaki jacket and stomper boots and headed out into the vaguely familiar unknown.

58

His thoughts were a scrambled blur of eight-bit crunches and repetitive white noise as the sound of arcade computer games competed for dominance; Tetris clashed with Donkey Kong, Frogger with Galaga, Street Fighter with Double Dragon.

His head burned from the static shock. He felt utterly exhausted. His memory was shot with holes, like a jigsaw puzzle with all the wrong pieces; an intricate portrait waiting to be painted, problems to be solved before being able to move on − the gameplay of the human condition.

Lars had no recollection of his journey. He held no possessions, just a white hospital gown and a pair of black Dr Martin boots. He hitched up the gown and ran across the dusty street towards some kind of twisted shrine.

Degradation and decay was on every street corner and down every alleyway. Rubble was everywhere; piles of dead sand, stacks of dirty bricks and dust.

A chain gang of shadows stood back from the path. They formed a queue, a waiting line of solemn faces and sad eyes, tired of trying to recall a life that was no longer available.

The sun was burning hotter with bright white and intense streaks of sharp colour; pink, red and orange. There was no breeze, not a cloud in the sky. Flags were perfectly still.

He headed for a large golden building. The shrine sparkled in the sunlight. He noticed the detail, the fine curves and swirls that made a statement above the dirty road it was built on. Objects were strangely familiar, but otherworldly. Ornamental faces looked down on him from the rooftops. Leering gargoyles twisted as he passed.

A heavy tram rolled out of nowhere, and he saw it just in time to avoid going under its wheels. It stopped just a few metres away. He scanned the faces of passengers, who stared out of the window in blank, soul-searching suffering. He caught the eye of a woman and they looked at each other with a faint flicker of recognition.

Lars raised his hand in silent greeting, and his wife, Claire, stared back. She allowed the flicker of a smile to form across her face.

He struggled to remember why this person would have anything to do with him. She looked lost, tearful at the increasing realisation that she too might know him, and that maybe they had once meant something to each other. They both felt the sensation of missed opportunity – of a life together that had now been denied.

'Ticket?' asked a voice. She turned. The bell tolled, and the tram moved on, grinding up the street to continue its circular journey through the afterlife.

'Claire?' he shouted, remembering her name, but she was lost in the frenetic energy of a carnival to the end. Lars stood alone in the road. Had he really just seen her? He walked quicker, tugging at the shoulders of shadows that stared back with melancholy eyes.

He felt utterly alone. He was shaking. Sweat streaked his chest; a cold turkey comedown caused by the sudden realisation that he was somewhere totally unfamiliar. A rising nausea made him shiver as the fear kicked in. Blood flecked the whites of his eyes. A nervous tick began to claim his body. He picked unseen things from his arms.

The afterlife spun in a whirlwind of alien voices and high-pitched screaming, the march of lights and metal and heat and noise.

Then came the frantic fit of adrenaline shock and he vomited in the dirty gutter. The relentlessly motion was too much, never stopping, never at peace. Shadows crept beside him like a Warcraft pet; a Mechanical Yeti or Guardian Felhunter. They sloped in the dirty guttering, flickering in the sky like bats, and crawling through cracks in the stonework ground. He could feel the darkness forming shapes that watched him as he stumbled through the crowds. He was drawing too much attention to himself.

A massive animal appeared before him. Across its back was a delicate shawl, a weave of red and gold patterns, swirling with wing-like shapes. The sacred elephant cut through the afterlife like a titanic. It was the only slow thing on these frantic streets. Further up the path, where the tram had stopped, a woman was standing alone.

'Claire?' He ran up to her, forcing his way through a group of shadows, and pulled her by the shoulder.

Julia Miller spun around and stared, blankly.

'Oh, it's you,' he said, disappointed. 'Don't you recognise me? It's…' He tried to say his own name but couldn't remember it, as though the memory slot that contained this information had become corrupted.

She looked at him with sad eyes.

He felt an intense déjà vu, ignited by a memory deep inside, one that he didn't want to recall. Flames and falling, the drip, drip, drip of the BBP. Julia, trapped and terrified, blocked by flames. 'Lars, help me!' The heat stinging his eyes.

'Where does that tram go?' she asked.

'Huh?' He fidgeted on the spot and scratched the sweat from his scalp.

'Where does the tram go?'

'I, uh, I don't know.'

She shook her head and turned away as a wave of forgetfulness broke over her, and Julia Miller was lost to the afterlife.

A small flock of ravens landed on the roof of a neighbouring building. The elephant appeared again out of nowhere, and was suddenly beside them. It extended its trunk, snakelike and slow, wrapping it around Julia's waist. He was petrified as it lifted her into the air. She didn't struggle. She was caught in a trance. The elephant slammed Julia's body into the ground and then released her limp body.

Lars crumpled to his knees in shock. The elephant snaked its trunk towards him. He scrambled to his hands and feet, narrowly avoiding its grasp. It sent a jet of water to wash its face and a pool of shadowy blood trickled into the gutter.

The twisted body of Julia Miller lay violated in a heap.

There was a soft fluttering of tiny wings, and a circle of moths began to form around her body. The insects spun as they covered her completely, capturing her soul, and casting it into the air to swim in the sea of souls above.

Lars watched them disappear.

The elephant lumbered off, disappearing down a side street in search of its next victim.

As the day grew older, the sun began to draw shapes of long limbs and arching backs across the brick walls. Shadows stretched out on the broken ground, appearing from nowhere, crawling through cracks in the dry earth. The shadows animated to become creatures that began to move, increasing in size, turning their heads.

He had to get out of there, he thought, and hurtled down a path, stumbling to a stop in front of two piercing eyes. A deep, guttural snarl scattered a cloud of brooding ravens. The hulking creature padded a translucent claw forward, its muscular back aimed in his direction.

The shadow animals had found Izanagi.

59

Berry was confronted by a fairground of swirling movement. A gust of wind brushed her ear, playing static in her hair. Storm clouds surrounded distant, snow-capped mountains. Trees sparkled with pure, white crystal. A palace shone, platinum, in the mist.

As she looked more intently the clouds were moving, drifting in vast circles, blending together as though in an embrace. The images separated and she could make out distinct faces – too many to count. The pure white crystals weren't crystal at all, but eyes, welcoming her, relieved at her eventual arrival.

She felt intense love. She recognised every individual, instantly, and all at once. 'The quintillions,' she said in a whisper of realisation.

'Welcome, Izanami, oh, immortal sister. I am Imperial uncle, Daikoku.' He swung his Jade crystal tablet, purifying the air around her.

The wind increased and a swirl of dust began to loop on the ground. In a flash of intense light, a circle of tiny white moths appeared. The perfect circle began to spin around her legs, swirling in a vortex that moved up her body. She closed her eyes, feeling the soft fluttering of wings and the comfort of home – but something was wrong.

She caught the scent, an intense smell of blood-clotted fur, the putrid taste of death.

The air became bitterly cold. The breath was stolen from her as a claw scratched down her back and she was pushed to the dirt. A dark shadow lunged above. The haunches of a large animal pounded on the ground as it singled out an individual in the crowd. The creature lunged and landed on him, tearing at his body.

Slam! Lars was spun over in the dust.

Berry stood in the swirling circle, energised by her vision of the quintillions, the strength of a thousand souls flowing through her, and she watched as Lars wrestled with talons that snapped close to his face with drooling breath and snarling teeth. With the flick of a wrist, she tossed the creature onto its back, and with the slightest of breath she blew the shadow animal into the estuary waters.

She wasn't sure how she'd just done it. The action had come naturally, like an attack combo long since forgotten. It was pure instinct. She held out a hand and helped uncle Daikoku to his feet.

'I am impressed by your newly acquired skills, my immortal sister,' he mumbled. 'Imagine what knowledge you bring on your return to Mt. Hōrai?'

Through the swirling dust she could see Lars on his back in the middle of the road. He was wearing a long hospital gown that clung to his malnourished body, and a worn pair of black boots too large for his flat feet. He sat up, anxiously scratching his rough and unshaven scalp. Wisps of a white beard covered his face. He seemed too young for such heavy facial hair.

Daikoku jumped in excitement when he realised who was lying on the road. 'You have travelled together? How wonderful,' he laughed.

Lars was exhausted. Dirty sweat dripped from his forehead. He used the tattered gown to wipe his brow, and squinted in her direction.

She left the magic circle and the spiralling moths fell away from her body. They hovered, lazily, trying to keep up with her as she walked over to him.

Daikoku felt proud that he had recovered them both together, and with such ease. The immortals had waited an age — they could spare another few minutes, he thought. His immortal brother and sister had chosen to appear to him. Songs would be written about this moment. Tapestries would be woven in his honour. Perhaps they would even name a wine after him? "Imperial Uncle, the saviour wine." He looked forward to tasting it. There would be a celebration on their mountain island tonight, and he would make a speech. He would tell stories of how he had fought off the shadow animals, summoned the spiralling moth vortex, and rescued his immortal brother and sister from the clutches of Tengu. It was his destiny, he would say. One day, they shall all have the opportunity to be as great as him. Daikoku stroked his beard triumphantly, and watched Lars and Berry speak, wishing that they would just hurry up.

The sun was bright behind her head, causing her silhouette to outline against the neon sky.

'Want a Jujyfruit?' she asked, and realised that she didn't have any pockets. 'That's strange. I must have left them somewhere.' She laughed, confused. She studied Lars as he lay on his back on the dusty ground, arms beside him, boots directed skyward. 'I know you, don't I?' She couldn't place where or when they had met.

He blinked. His neck twitched. He concentrated harder on the cloud formations. They watched the sky together. There was a connection from another place and time. Neither of them could place it.

In a flash of recognition, he remembered a young woman typing details into a digital tablet. A man in a suit had made introductions.

'Lars Nilsson and Berry Butler, it thrills me so deeply to see you together at long last. Do you remember anything of the last few hours? − Nothing? Good. Then we will continue.'

The dust was beginning to settle.

The circle of moths had caught up with her and were beginning to spin around her feet.

Lars was distracted by a dragonfly that passed overhead, hovered for a second and then buzzed away. He sat up in the road, feeling stronger.

Daikoku was becoming agitated. 'We must go now,' he beckoned from across the street. 'Tengu is watching.'

Lars heard the name and another flash of recollection hit him. He remembered where he'd seen her before. She was wearing the same clothing; a white hospital gown, in a white laboratory, empty apart from a table and four wooden chairs. Eight large cards were face down, four on either side of the table.

He heard the distant sound of his own voice.

'Is this the game?'

'Take a seat. No footsie, and please don't touch the cards yet.'

'There aren't any screens or controllers?'

'Ah, but there are both screens and controllers. Closer than you think. Ok, so we're going to try this three times, grounded, elevated, and in separate cages.'

'Cages, Dr Jones?' Berry frowned.

'Would you prefer I use the term, faraday shield, Berry? Does that sound more technical?'

'Technical works,' she smiled.

'Well, technically,' he glanced around the cage, 'the cooking chamber of a microwave is very similar to this.'

She frowned again. 'Don't start calling it a microwave, please.'

Lars felt an overwhelming sensation of anxiety, and wondered when he could go back to his luxury hotel room and order more room service.

'Lars?' asked Mike, checking a document and flicking a switch on the wall panel.

'Hm?'

'You're going to be the sender. Pick any card. Don't show her the image. Show your camera only. Then, you...' Mike touched Berry on the shoulder, 'simply receive by picking up any card in front of you. Show it to the camera over your shoulder. When you hear the buzzer, move on to the next card. I'm going to have to shut you both in, but don't worry, I can hear you and I'm watching everything.' He pointed to a small camera housed in the ceiling. 'If you hear a noise, a shudder or vibration, it's perfectly normal and just the mechanics of the room. If you feel uncomfortable, I'm right outside. We're going to run it three times. Ok?'

Mike began to close the door and stopped. Berry looked up expectantly. 'No cheating!' he smiled.

The door hissed shut.

They remembered the exact moment when they had first met in the white laboratory room at The Foundation, and just as their eyes locked in recognition, a heavy tram swerved around the corner at speed and collided with them both, crushing them under its wheels.

Daikoku watched in horror as the bodies of Lars and Berry imploded into a cloud of dust, and the tram passed straight through them. The perfect circle of moths evaporated.

The old immortal was left alone on the street. He purified the air with his Jade crystal tablet, checked that no one saw what had just happened, and skulked off, kicking the ground and cursing Tengu under his breath. He hoped that songs wouldn't be written about this particular disaster.

60

Lars materialised on the riverside and was immediately spotted by three tiny shadow creatures. Their size, however, didn't temper their aggressiveness.

One had bloody sockets where its eyes should have been but it didn't seem to navigate by sight. They leaped on him, grabbing at his legs and arms.

'SkullMonkeys!' he screamed, as he fell face first through a hedge.

The shadows were expert hunters, only visible when it was too late. They floated in the tropical air, they were around every corner and always behind you. There was no escape. The lemurs followed, intent on ripping him limb from limb.

Dr Vegas heard the scream. He had been waiting for the timely re-appearance of Izanagi. He wearily focussed on the commotion and double took a well-rehearsed De Niro 'you talking to me?' before going back to puffing on his joint. 'Heal and run,' he shouted. 'Dodge and build. This is basic stuff.' He knew that to prevent attack you had to keep moving, never stay in the same place for too long, and always maintain your health from falling below a third. The new guy, Izzy, it seemed, still had a lot to learn.

After some consideration, he casually stubbed out his joint, brushed back his long, curly hair and took another glance at the approaching mayhem. This was pretty pathetic game play, he thought. He raised a hand, nonchalantly, to acknowledge the existence of Izzy who was kicking back the three lemur shaped shadows that were clawing at his face. His moto popped and puttered to a start. He reached for his glasses case and pulled out a fresh mandrake joint.

Lars landed on the back of the bike. 'Go, go, go!' he screamed.

The moto began to wobble up the road, Vegas' bandy legs pushing the bike up to an acceptable getaway speed.

'I thought for a moment that I'd lost you at the cash stash, dude,' he said. 'But I had a feeling that you'd turn up again eventually.'

A larger shadow appeared around the corner, talons ripping the ground, long tail whipping the gritty road.

'Get your head down. We need to stream,' said Vegas.

They ducked and moved faster as they swerved onto the pavement, playing chicken with the oncoming trams, avoiding trees, candlelit lamps and shadows of the walking dead. The moto hurtled between two trams, and they skidded, barely inches from it.

The sabre tooth shadow followed close behind, drool puffing in the air.

Dr Vegas had observed how the lost people of the afterlife seemed to stand together. Perhaps it gave them the familiar comfort of a life they once knew? He searched for a group and pulled up to use them for cover. Lars looked behind. There was no sign of the shadow creature.

'Dominated! Double points for comrade assist,' laughed Vegas as he lit up his smoke.

'What were those things?'

'That, Izzy, was a Sabre, and a bunch of crazy assed Streps. Nasty fuckers. They know how to work as a team. They'll try and take you out at any opportunity.'

'Why are they all after me?'

'I don't know, but you sure are drawing a lot of attention.'

Slam! A tram landed on its roof next to them. There was no time to talk. Vegas revved the moto and pulled away. Lars lost his grip and fell backwards onto the dirt. He was immediately crushed underneath the falling tram.

Vegas steered straight over a mound of grass and swerved to miss an ornamental statue. The shadow animal smashed through the figurine, sending its concrete head flying into a group of ghostly street-walkers. The moto buzzed as fast as it could, swerving either side of the approaching trams.

A creature appeared to his left; dog-like, with huge talons for claws. It blinked, head down, maintaining speed. He had given the creatures avatar names; this was an Ogg. To his right was another creature; long neck and beak, with powerful legs like an ostrich. This type he had called Ozz.

Vegas tried to streamline but they were gaining. The sky turned black as a mass flew inches above, landing on a tram up ahead. It swerved from its tracks, turning on its side and blocking the road. Vegas slammed on the breaks. The scooter spun out beneath him.

He sat on the dirt, reached for a fresh joint, and lit up. After a drag he brushed down his shoulders and whistled. A wild, rasping shriek replied, and a golden gryphon pierced the sky. It dived straight at the larger of the shadow animals and flapped its almighty wings at the snout of the Sabre, causing it to tumble under the Ozz but just as the gryphon seemed to have the upper hand it was smacked to the floor.

'Dammit,' smoked Vegas.

The shadow animals formed an attack triangle; two either side and one behind, as they homed in for the kill.

In a flash of bright light, Lars materialised on the opposite side of the tram-line. The creatures hesitated and changed their strategy.

'About time!' shouted Vegas. He kick-started the moto and Lars leaped on the back. They spun down a side street and hurtled through a narrow alleyway.

'We got ourselves an Ozz and Ogg, and our friend the Sabre is back. It just took out my fucking gryphon.'

'They're creepy enough without the crazy names,' shouted Lars, holding on tight as they sped along the quayside, with three shadow animals snapping jaws barely inches behind. 'You've got a gryphon?'

He swerved to avoid impact, and the Ogg ran straight into a lamppost with a cold, hard smack. 'So, you re-spawned?' shouted Vegas with a laugh.

'That's been happening a lot.'

They steered onto tram-lines. Vegas knew exactly where he was headed. He'd previously spotted a broken bridge that spanned the estuary, just on the edge of Central. It was now a permanent fixture on his Map of Everything. He'd never seen anyone cross it before. It looked weak and dangerous, and completely unable to hold a speeding moto and its passengers. It was perfect.

The Ozz and Ogg had regained their footing and were focusing in for a fatal strike.

'Bridge!' shouted Lars.

'That's the plan.'

'What if they follow us across?'

'We're not going across.'

The wood splintered the moment they were inches onto the bridge. Zombie ants crawled between planks. Wheels spun. Rope split. Vegas and Lars sat tight as the engine revved and they dropped.

The Ozz tried to stop itself but was hit by the pursuing creatures. It snapped in the sky, wings flapping, unable to take flight, and all three shadow animals plunged uncontrollably into the muddy depths.

Dr Vegas managed to get a final toke of mandrake cigarette before the moto slapped into the water.

Lars was flung head first in the air. As he fell in what seemed like slow motion, a strange sensation overcame him. He wasn't scared. He felt somehow stronger, focused, and more confident. I think I've just levelled up, he thought, as he took a face full of dirty water.

61

The sun burned crimson in the neon purple sky. She felt groggy. Her short-term memory was shot through. She stood before a shrine with no recollection of how she got there. The giant stone statue of a serpent curled up the steps. Eight snake heads were frozen, hissing to attention at the top. Berry cautiously climbed the steps and tripped over the top stone, landing on her knees next to a cage filled with small birds.

The vendor asked her something in a language that she didn't understand. He held the cage like a lantern, showing her how it was full of sparrows, struggling for space, and then pointed to a dragonfly that was now hovering above her head. She heard the hum and flicker and looked up to see the beautiful clash of colourful wings against the vibrant sky. The shadow of a lemur dropped husks of dry fruit on the dirt.

The vendor snapped open the cage and took out a bird. He offered it to her. She smiled, awkwardly, and carefully received the bird between closed palms. He bowed and stepped back, keeping his head low.

It didn't struggle, instead, it pitched its head and looked at her, then fixed its stare on the dragonfly. She released the bird into the open sky. It flashed straight up and disappeared into the brightness of the sun.

Moments later, the sparrow was overhead. It buzzed them both, looping and diving back down to the shrine. The dragonfly spun in tight spirals, becoming agitated, unsure which direction to move. The bird seemed to grow larger with each pass, the sun giving it the energy to transform, stretching out on the breeze. In a single movement it swooped down and swallowed the dragonfly whole before shooting back into the sun.

Berry tried to follow and was blinded by sunspots. Blotches of white blurred her vision. The glare made her dizzy. The flash of the sun became the shine of a laboratory lamp, and she was projected to the memory of another time and space.

'Let's get to know each other better, huh?' suggested a friendly voice.

'More questions,' she sighed.

'How often do you play some kind of game?'

'Series or RPG?'

'Immersive,' smiled Dr Finjoto.

'Every day.'

'And for how long, would you normally play?'

'Seventeen, eighteen hours,' replied Berry. 'It gets better the longer you play.'

Chieko was entering notes into a digital tablet. 'When do you sleep?' she asked. 'If you are playing for eighteen hours?'

'Well, that's part of the game,' Berry replied. 'Snooze, you lose. And you don't want to lose. Not when you've got leader board stats and a cash stash to play for. You have to stay on it. It's hard work.'

'Work?' asked Finjoto.

'Yeah,' Berry shrugged. 'It's an achievement.'

Lars laughed. Whoever this girl was, he was in good company, he thought.

'There's game-play like Atari Shock, where you're always on and responding to threats, so you'll play a session for longer.'

'You play Atari Shock?' he asked, suddenly interested in the conversation.

'Doesn't everyone?'

'I'm in the league,' he nodded.

'Are you now?' she smiled.

'Who's your avatar?'

'I can't tell you that,' Berry scolded.

Dr Finjoto watched the interplay between them. There was an instant bond, despite them having never met. He enjoyed the relationship that was forming and wondered how long it would take before they completely trusted each other.

'When were you last on?' he asked.

'They're a bit tight with Wi-Fi here.' She stared accusingly at the camera. 'You?'

Lars seemed distressed. 'I think I was playing, just now.'

She heard a shriek and saw a flash of silver talons as a small, red gryphon appeared over the trees. The sparrow had shapeshifted.

The vendor dropped to his knees and began mumbling incoherently.

She watched the gryphon loop in the sky. Seconds later, it dropped and landed on one of the snake heads. The creature was elegant, more unique than anything she had created in her games. It had the head of a lion and the body of an eagle. It clawed at the stone and watched her. She turned to the vendor. He had disappeared.

Berry had just gained her first power-up; a red gryphon, level one. It flashed skywards.

The shrine had an ancient door that was weather beaten and scratched. Ornamental carvings spanned the shutters. A rusting metal bolt locked the intricately embossed entrance.

The left shutter featured carvings of strange guardian creatures, claws and teeth raised in defence; a long tailed lion, a dragon, and a large bird were etched perfectly into the wood. Their tails curled along the panel, holding the bolt that sealed the doorway closed, giving it magical strength.

They were defending their position from another creature. It had sharp pointed ears, thin piercing eyes, a slender backbone and nine tails. It was Kitsune; twisting in mid-air, leaping high in an attempt to vault across to the other side.

The right shutter portrayed a layer of swirling clouds, out of which jutted the spire of a palace. Eight figures stood in a row with flowing robes and twisting hair; one sat on a deer, one held a large sword, one a fan, and one a tablet. They were all drinking from gourds.

Berry pushed the door and it rattled. It was bolted shut. There were no windows. There was no doorbell. It looked like it hadn't been opened in years. She found herself staring at the carvings, concentrating deep into the clouds, and as she did so they began to move. The more intensely she looked, the more the clouds animated to reveal detail beyond. She watched, captivated, as the mists took on the shape of a walled castle.

Kitsune became defensive, spreading her nine tails in a wide peacock fan. The guardians jostled to protect the space, raising their claws and tails, curling tighter to block the entrance.

The bolt shook.

As the mists began to fade, Berry could see more detail; spires and tiles, stone carvings and steps. Mt. Hōrai was exposed.

The fox seemed more determined by the temptation of a fortress that was no longer hidden from view. Her nine tails swung. The creatures lashed out but Kitsune dodged them elegantly, undeterred, waiting for the moment to leap across to the opposite panel. The bird struck out and caught her by the leg. A tail broke her fall and she scrambled under the lion's legs, tripping up the dragon to spring over the metal bolt and fall, flailing, down to the fortress deep within the wood carving.

The three guardians leaped after her and down into the mountain valley below. Berry watched them shrink smaller, twisting towards the fortress until they had all disappeared.

The bolt rattled and the door creaked open.

Berry squinted to look through the cracks. There was no movement, no light, just the invitation of an open door. She moved inside to the smell of dust and decay. Fragrant candles hung in the atmosphere. Hundreds of Buddha statues cluttered up the room; gold and bronze and concrete, upturned palms and docile smiles. On the walls hung painted friezes that depicted ancient immortal tales. Her eyes landed on one particular panel of a large winged elephant, and next to it, she saw the outline of herself.

She touched the fabric, feeling the weave of the thread that perfectly resembled her own image. It was identical, almost photographic in reproduction, apart from having hair tied back high on her head. She was wearing a long, flowing robe, and carrying a strange musical instrument with many bamboo reeds surrounding a mouthpiece.

A Buddha was watching at prayer, calm and happy. It smiled, holding its toes, as though in mid-conversation. Several figures moved in the shadows and she realised that some of the Buddhas weren't statues.

'Welcome, Izanami, oh, Mother Earth,' exclaimed an old man from up on his tiny deer.

They had called out, and she had finally been drawn home. Berry had climbed the peak, to the realm of formlessness, and was now alongside her ancient immortal family once more. She breathed a silent sigh, feeling the rush of a past life flow through her, until Bishamon ruined the moment.

'Been enjoying yourself, have you?' his voice boomed.

Her sense of Nirvana was short lived.

62

The container ship, Oracle, had been condemned since it grounded on a bank off Australia's notorious Coral Triangle. To the locals, it was a cursed ghost ship that had claimed the lives of its fifteen crew during the accident, trapping them in the lower decks, doors slamming shut and locking by themselves, the sinking stern and rising tide drowning them all.

Every full moon the families of those that perished would throw rings of flowers and create small floating vessels of incense to float either side of her. It was believed that this would keep the ghosts of its crew at peace. She remained stranded on the coral, until the East India seas took its sacrifice, and the ship was claimed. Eventually, it disappeared without trace, and found permanent docking in the afterlife.

Cold water hit him hard. He was spun upside down as the current pulled him deeper. The more he struggled, the more the pressure increased and the further from the surface he seemed to get. He was drifting, unsure which way was up and which down.

There was a flash of movement in the murky brown water as an object approached. A small tail flexed behind a plump, orange body, its head pushing forward, streamlining through the darkness.

Mr Chips appeared and swam up to Lars. It spun around him several times in greeting. The fish began to suck in the algae and silt, clearing a direct path to a row of equidistant portholes that spanned the side of the huge, submerged ship.

It sped through a porthole, leaving a trail of tiny bubbles. Lars swam after it. The ship creaked an ominous warning.

The temperature inside was colder. He could barely make out the glowing orange dot of Mr Chips as it guided him between the ship's metal walls. He couldn't see his own hands as he swam past mysterious objects in the dark, feeling his way into an underwater room. The floor was now wall, the wall now the ceiling. He followed Mr Chips deeper through an angular doorway, down a narrow corridor, and into what felt like a much larger space. He searched for a glimmer of colour. The fish had disappeared into the hull. He closed his eyes and listened to the vessel's haunting moan. He kicked his feet, treading water, floating weightless.

It occurred to Lars that he had no desire to breathe. There was no rush of panic. No terrifying need to inhale. No desperate lack of oxygen. In fact, he had completely forgotten that he was underwater.

There was a swirl of water at his neck. Something brushed his leg. Another tug at his arm. He struggled as he was suddenly pulled feet first through a doorway and into the unknown guts of the vessel.

The thud of a heavy door reverberated up ahead. He was pulled past glass portholes and could see his own image twisting through the water. He also made out the slender tentacles and sharp beak of an octopus, moving inches

behind his head. Its eye blinked as it propelled him forward.
Lars wished that he hadn't looked.

The creature stopped and he was suspended in the
water. Before them, the dark green, brass handles of an
ornate chest glowed in the depths. The clasp began to move
and fell open to reveal a bright crystal dagger on a bed of
silver pearls. At his side in the murky gloom, hovering inches
from his face, appeared the toothy sneer of the water witch.

The hell hag blinked an alien eye as she studied him,
penetrating his soul, eyes as black as a shark. She moved
closer. Her scowling face glowed green. Dark hair swirled
around her ancient form.

The only light came from the glow of the water witch
herself. It was enough to catch the sparkling fractals on the
dagger's hilt. The decoration was of a swirling dragon. It
breathed fire which thinned to the end of the sharp blade.

He felt his right hand being pulled back at the wrist as
each of his fingers were splayed out by the grip of tiny, lasso-
like tentacles. Lars watched the crystal dagger lift and turn
towards him in the water. He felt pressure around his waist
as the dagger moved. He tried to scream but there was no
sound. He was totally at her mercy. He felt burning pain as
the knife began to jab into his palm. The slicing movement
cut with quickening stabs, carving detailed holes into his skin.
It showed no sign of stopping. Blood began to linger with the
water, swirling in spiralling figures of eight.

Mr Chips watched from the shadows.

He felt tension in his left wrist and tried to scream again
when he realised that the dagger was moving to his other
hand. It began to carve more shapes, blood evaporating
into the water as it plotted holes in his skin. Eventually the

stabbing stopped and the pain subsided, leaving a dull, numbing ache.

Shozuka-no-baba moved in close. She placed the tip of her finger on his temple and slowly traced lines around his cheek and chin, moving down to his throat. She clasped his neck in her hand, their faces almost touching. He felt the glow of her body on his skin. Her eyes were penetrating. Her gaze captivated him as he found himself lost in a forgotten memory.

The intercom crackled. 'Let's go again. Lars, when you're ready?'

A low throbbing sound was increasing like the sound of a distant thunderstorm.

'This is freaking me out,' sniffed Berry. 'I can't do this anymore.'

'It's ok,' he whispered. 'We can do this. We're in it together.'

A buzzer signalled to start.

He reached for a card, changed his mind and picked a different one. He held it up to his camera with both hands. Berry nodded and picked her card. She held it up to the camera. Lars tried to read her expression. They waited. There was a buzz. Both cards were placed face down.

Lars reached for his second card. She didn't look at him this time. She nodded, reached for hers, and held it up to the camera. A buzz. The cards were replaced.

As Lars reached for his third card, Berry began to cry. Her hand was already hovering over her choice. They both showed their cards to the camera.

'Again, please,' scratched Dr Finjoto's distorted voice over the intercom.

The vibration stopped. There was a clicking from all corners. The room was being raised and locked into place. The vibration hummed again.

The buzzer sounded to begin.

Lars shuffled the order and picked up a random sequence of four cards. He placed them face down on the table. Berry watched the metal door, her head turned away from him, not even looking at the cards in front of her. As soon as he'd finished, she stood up and threw her choice of cards face up next to his.

She turned to the security camera. 'There. Can I go now?'

There was a thud and a clicking sound. The heavy metal door swung open. Berry left the cage in tears.

'Hey?' Lars called after her.

Finjoto's voice boomed through the speaker. 'Let her go. You will stay for one more session, please.'

The door sealed shut and a strip light buzzed. The harsh light reminded Lars of a useless internet fact; when an insect is electrocuted, its body parts can scatter up to seven feet. The insect literally explodes.

He felt the urge to turn the cards over. The four symbols were exactly the same – a butterfly, a snake, a monkey and a dagger.

'The decision that you now make will determine the fate of the afterlife,' buzzed the distorted voice. 'Choose, Izanagi, fight to reclaim your immortal right as the reviver of the dead, or stay on your pathetic mortal path and force the quintillions to suffer an eternity in limbo?'

The sneer of the water witch was now inches from his face. 'I give you the strength to fight, if you so choose,' she hissed.

A glimmer of light reflected on the hilt as the crystal dagger began to move again. He felt his arms and legs being pulled tight as the blade sliced into his back, cutting intricate, spiralling patterns into his skin.

63

'For how many years have you avoided us, Izanami?' scolded Bishamon.

'Long enough to count the hairs on my deer,' scowled an unusually angry Fokuro.

'And where is your husband, the master of the cloud chamber?' asked an increasingly suspicious Jurojin. His face was smudged with dust and phlegm. He cleared his throat, gobbed on the floor, and then cleared his throat again. 'You can also explain to us where Benten and Hotei have gone as well, while you're at it?'

Berry took a step back and looked for the door that she was sure she had just come through. There was no longer a door, just another mural along the wall; eight figures in long robes, striking poses and carrying strange, ornamental objects.

Jurojin tapped his iron crutch on the ground. 'Too much time on mortal soil. She knows not who she is.' He sprayed her with spittle, before swallowing it back down like a cat that got the cream. 'She is the one who displaced us,' he gurgled. 'She must be punished.'

Bishamon leaned on his sword and adopted a threatening pose. 'Immortals never forget.'

Fokuro kicked the side of his deer and turned its back on Berry. 'She cannot be trusted.'

The ancient immortals muttered in agreement.

'Stop this foolish talk. You're scaring her,' said Imperial uncle Daikoku.

Berry was unsure what to say. They were treating her like she was meant to know them, like a child who had stayed out beyond curfew.

'Why did you ignore us for so long, my sister?' bellowed Bishamon, dragging the sword at his heels. The air wafted, paper thin, as he flung it around him.

'Don't be concerned,' said Daikoku. 'He likes to wave that thing around.'

Berry shuffled on the spot. 'I'm sorry. I don't know what you mean.' She was unsure if the group were taunting her for their own amusement.

Fokuro made a gesture as though recalling the bleeding obvious. 'Our ancient brother sent you messages, did he not? Remember your true self. Return to Mt. Hōrai.'

They all searched her face for any sign of recognition.

'Tengu is watching? Surely you got that one? I mean, who ignores a message that says Tengu is watching?'

The immortals muttered to themselves in agreement.

'You really know none of this?' asked Fokuro. 'The electronic messages were sent to you in the most intimate form of digital communication, as direct messages on Atari Shock? Hotei assured us that it's the shit, right now.'

The other immortals raised their noses, disapprovingly.

'His expression, brothers, not mine,' explained Fokuro.

Berry looked at the four immortals.

Bishamon stared straight back.

The others felt slightly self-conscious and bowed their heads.

'Am I dead?'

'Dead?' sniggered Jurojin, disguising it with a cough.

'Dead?' bellowed Bishamon. His lip started to quiver. 'You are dead many times over, lotus sister,' he smirked, trying to stop himself, before bursting into hysterics.

Laughter boomed. The immortals patted themselves on the back as they fell about. Jurojin spluttered and heartily coughed up green phlegm. Even Fokuro cracked a smile.

Imperial uncle Daikoku, however, was not smiling. He purified the room with his Jade crystal tablet. 'That's enough.' The laughter subsided and the immortals were serious again.

'Where is Izanagi?' asked Daikoku, with a sympathetic smile.

'Who?'

'Your immortal husband? You travelled together, did you not? I greeted you both,' he hesitated, 'until you were stolen away from me by the horde. Do you not remember?'

She vaguely remembered a man lying on the ground, wearing a white gown and DM boots, a dark creature that flew through the air, and then a tram, and then, nothing. 'I'm not married,' she said, confused.

Bishamon balanced on the hilt of his sword. He wasn't laughing anymore. 'This is far worse than we could ever have imagined. She has truly become a mortal. Tengu will tear the soul from her pathetic frame.' He turned away, disinterested.

The immortals began to disappear into the shadows.

Only Daikoku remained. He stopped swinging his crystal tablet. The stress of trying to recover Izanami and Izanagi had caused his ancient beard to grow so long that his face had become a mass of hair, sunken eyes and wrinkles. He revealed a shrivelled peach from under his shawl. The skin was old. White fungus peppered the outside. He forced down a disgusting bite.

'Do you recall the moment when we first met, when I introduced you to the quintillions?' he asked through a mouthful of mould.

Berry remembered arms stretching out, desperate faces expressing fear and anger. 'People, I saw lots of people,' she replied. 'They were terrified.'

'We are immortal alchemists, caretakers of the souls that pass beyond life and into death,' he whispered. 'And you were once just like us.' He took her by the hand and offered her the peach. 'Take a bite. It will help you to remember.'

She sniffed the mouldy peach and took a nibble.

'It is time for you to accept who you truly are, Izanami.' He began to swing his Jade crystal tablet and incense filled the air. The scent was reassuring and soporific. 'Close your eyes. Think back. Where is Izanagi?'

The taste of the peach was strange, like damp soil. She felt her head drop as she inhaled the Jade essence. Berry wasn't sure what she had just said. 'Sorry. Was I speaking? What was the question again?'

'Your answer was perfect, Berry. Well done.' Dr Finjoto was satisfied.

Her memory appeared to be intact after the stresses of the immersion trip. The elements that had rooted themselves in her consciousness were fascinating. Just like Lars, she was obsessed with the core functionality of role-play; collect items, unlock quests, battle creatures and evolve.

Lars appeared to be much more disorientated. His mental state was fraught. Finjoto had expected that. He had been given a much higher dose, after all. He was aware that the subjects might forget how to perform basic bodily functions. He would leave Lars under Sarah's supervision while they proceeded with Berry. 'You may relax for a few minutes until you are called again,' he said, before leaving the room.

Chieko stood quietly, observing them, but saying nothing.

'Can I get a coffee?' asked Berry. 'And my Juju's?'

Chieko used the intercom.

They sat in silence, waiting for the coffee to be delivered. Minutes later, the door slid open and a tray arrived.

'You know, seven cups of instant coffee contain a total of three hundred and fifteen milligrams of caffeine,' Berry said. 'That's six cups of strong tea, nine full fat Colas, four Red Bulls, or half a can of Hype.' She took a cup from the tray. 'What do you weigh, Lars?'

'Huh?' He was groggy. He seemed half asleep.

'Roughly?'

'Erm, twelve stone something, I guess.'

'You could drink one hundred and thirty-seven espressos before death by toxication.' She looked at the swirls in the black liquid.

He started yawning. 'I might put your theory to the test.'

'Takes a few days for the jet lag to pass.'

'What was all that about? All those questions?'

'I guess that's how they do things? They're taking all this pretty seriously.'

'I…' Lars laughed, 'I can't really believe this. I'm having some trouble remembering why I'm here.'

'Man,' said Berry. 'I'll have what he's having?' She turned to Chieko, who remained expressionless.

Lars smiled. There was something about Berry that made him feel comfortable. She had an attitude that he instantly related to. Berry also sensed the connection. He already felt like a very old friend.

'Did you have to sign a contract?' she asked. 'I think they're stealing my ideas. They're paying me for stealing them, so I guess that's not theft, right?'

'I think that's called employment,' smiled Lars.

Chieko seemed unimpressed.

'We're developing a new platform, right?' said Berry. 'That's all I've been told. Some new format of epoch system gaming. I haven't really worked it out yet.'

Lars looked blank. His eyes were tired. A shadow cast itself up the wall and he shivered. 'Wow. That flight really took it out of me,' he said. 'I think I'm seeing things.'

'You are having a hallucination?' asked Chieko. She moved to the intercom and hovered over the emergency button.

'I'm just tired.'

Chieko made a note of the comment on her digital tablet.

'Had a good welcome party did you, Lars?' sniggered Berry.

'Seriously, I can't remember.'

'We must have that in common. We don't travel well.' Berry drank her coffee. 'You a developer?'

He shook his head. 'I work for a pharmaceutical company.'

'Wow. Big guns,' she smiled. 'Are you working on the game?'

'I guess so. I'm not sure. Hey, can we get out of here. I'm feeling a little claustrophobic. Is there a window?'

'We're sitting in an underground laboratory in Tokyo. There are no windows,' said Berry.

'We're underground?'

'You've still got a lot of catching up to do, haven't you?'

He felt that there was something about her that he could trust. 'I think I'm running away,' he said.

'Really? From what?'

Lars shrugged. 'Life? Failure? Something frightening, like an evil spirit.'

Chieko shivered, involuntarily.

Berry was straight faced. 'I'm sorry to hear that, Lars. I'm sure it's not as bad as you think. It never is.'

'Thanks for the advice.'

'Hey, now that we're sharing, how about we trade avatar names? I'll tell you mine if you tell me yours? How about it?'

Lars laughed. 'You changed your mind?'

'I like you,' smiled Berry.

He nodded. 'OK, hot shot. So I was The Immortal.'

'Greetings programme, I'm Primordial. You're The Immortal? That's hilarious. You really screwed up, didn't you?'

'I just told you, I got hacked.'

'You're back to level one, newbie,' she sniggered.

There was something familiar about the phrase. Lars struggled with the memory. He remembered the sugar-coated USB and tried to find it, but the hospital gown didn't have any pockets. 'Where are my clothes?'

The intercom buzzed and Chieko answered. 'Lars, Miss Clarkson would like to see you now.'

'Sarah? Can I speak to her?' asked Berry. 'I haven't seen her since we got here.'

'Miss Butler, you are to follow me. Dr Jones is ready for you.'

'OK. Hey, watch out for those evil spirits, Izanagi.'

'Who?'

'Izanagi? Where is Izanagi?'

Berry opened her eyes. Uncle Daikoku was next to her. He touched her on the side of the face in reassurance. 'Welcome back. I see that you have been through so much during your mortal incarnation. For that, I am sorry.' He examined his Jade tablet, brushing away a little imaginary dust.

'It is time to tell you of your former life for you clearly do not recall. You were responsible for breaking the magic circle of eight. You brought the underworld, Yomi-no-kuni, on this land. You enabled the pollution of the afterlife with the undead souls of the quintillions. We have been trapped in the space between life and death ever since our fall from Hōrai.

You have a responsibility to put back all that you have done wrong and to restore life to our abandoned existence. Our land has changed, my immortal lotus sister. The fruit grows mouldy on the trees. Every day is a challenge. There are new rules that we do not understand. Where we once rode bicycles in the sunshine through lush green meadows, eating fresh fruit and watching beautiful birds in the skies, shadows now wreak chaos. Instead of the lilting beauty of your shō, mechanical sounds now fill the air; high-pitched tweets and chirps. Strange creatures spin along the dry dirt ground, consuming every living thing in their path. I think

I now fully understand the origin of this curse.' Daikoku's eyes widened as a red gryphon screeched and appeared through the sunlight. It landed on the branch of a cherry blossom tree and flapped its majestic wings. 'The Universe continues to weave wonders, my dear Izanami, and you command it to reveal the terror of your wildest imaginings.'

64

The hyper-real sun was setting on the river as rows of lanterns were self-igniting alongside it. A single bubble broke the water, followed by several more, until Lars appeared, gasping for air at the surface. He swam to the bank and retched, pulling himself out of the river and rolling on his side. He blinked in the fading sunlight. The horizon was a conflicting sequence of neon.

Haunting images of the water witch stared back. She had given him a choice – and a gift.

The scrawling inscriptions had healed, forming complex scars on his skin like a Rorschach test. He studied the lines on his arms, running his finger along the spiralling scar tissue, tracing patterns that reminded him of the wings of a butterfly. As he did so, the outlines began to glow bright pink. The scars burned. He blew on the wounds, trying to cool them, and a flurry of moths appeared as if having peeled away from the shapes in his skin. They flew in a circle above, hovering in a shambolic cloud.

'You don't stay still for very long, do you, Izanagi?' said Hotei, as he trudged along the muddy riverbank. He pulled a gourd from his belt, took a swig, and offered it. He panted, as if to show that he'd been searching everywhere for him.

Lars took the gourd and swallowed. The liquid burned his throat and lips. He coughed. 'That's not water.'

'I didn't say it was. Twenty-one year old Ardbeg, single Islay malt. A little mortal pleasure that I've acquired on my travels.' Hotei nodded to the circle of moths fluttering around his head in an insect halo. 'Quite an impressive gathering you've acquired.'

Lars swatted a moth out of the sky.

'Stop that!' cursed Hotei. 'These creatures are sacred. See how they have become attracted to you as you've grown stronger. They are the very essence of life itself.'

Lars shrugged an apology and took another gulp from the gourd. He let the whisky burn his lips. He was desperate to feel something normal, something recognisable, something human.

'I also see that Shozuka-no-baba has bestowed her gift upon you?' smiled Hotei, as he admired the scars.

'The water witch?'

He coughed. 'Well, I doubt that she would appreciate you calling her that. You might like to call her, Oracle. She's a fan of formalities.'

He held up his palms to show the old man. The scar tissue markings had disappeared. He passed back the gourd. 'I saw Claire. She's here,' he said, despondent.

'I was afraid that you might come across each other.' Hotei sighed. 'I think it is time that we discussed your options with the rest of our immortal colleagues. Don't worry about the moths; they will follow wherever you go. They are a part of you now.'

Something flicked and jumped in the distance. A small black cloud was shifting shape as it propelled itself down the riverbank.

'Oh dear, this is not good,' stuttered Hotei. 'Come. Time to go.'

Lars watched the morphing mass approach, and realised that it was a ball of spinning spiders. 'Super clan!' he shouted, as he leaped to his feet. The moths followed, channelling in his slipstream as he ran.

'Find your immortal family, Izanagi,' shouted Hotei, 'or you will never stop running!'

The hurtling insects flew by in pursuit of Lars and his sacred circle of moths.

In the cool evening of the afterlife, a zombie ant was crawling over a mountain of dirt, carrying a twig four times its size. It struggled, determined, making moderate ant-like progress, until the sound of a shabby DM boot thumped closer and crushed it underfoot. A second zombie ant prized the twig from the crushed remains of its family member, and carried on like nothing had happened.

Dr Vegas was hunched on his moto, picking off detritus, getting the best he could from a damp mandrake joint. He studied his large, yellow map. It was still incomplete. He smoked and pondered, turning it three-sixty degrees and tilting his head. He'd made a huge leap in his evolution after discovering the Map of Everything, as he called it. He had levelled up to become the afterlife's Darwin, just not a very productive one.

He hadn't seen Lars since they'd plummeted into the river. He was beginning to suspect that the quest was over, and that Izzy hadn't re-spawned, but his concentration was shattered by a familiar scream.

A rustling, itching, clawing sound was also getting louder. The super clan of spinning spiders spun along the riverbank.

Vegas spotted them just in time to lift his feet as the swarm catapulted itself underneath. 'Can't leave you alone for one second,' he said, as he kick started the moto and sped after them.

Lars was terrified, running as fast as he could, tripping over his feet, landing face first and then scrambling to run again.

Dr Vegas caught up with the swarm and ducked around them. He scooted up alongside. 'I thought you'd proved my theory wrong there, Izzy?' he shouted over the buzzing engine.

Lars was too breathless to respond.

'You've got lizards on you?' said Vegas, spotting two tiny lizards hitching a ride on Lars' shoulder. The moths caught up with them and fluttered directly above their heads. 'Oh, and moths.'

He glanced behind him. The spiders were gaining. Dr Vegas took his hands from the throttle and lit up. He scratched his beard and shivered at a sudden change of temperature. There was a flash of light and a miniature swirling typhoon appeared ahead. The grey moths, seeming drawn to the light, began to form a circling vortex. It increased in size and spun faster on the pavement, shining brighter in the dusky evening.

The spider swarm was gaining. A few lead spiders were landing on Lars' neck. The lizards ran along his shoulders to pick them off, crunching them down and wiping their eyes with their tongues in satisfaction.

Lars leaped over the vortex and landed awkwardly on the other side.

Dr Vegas shot past on his moto.

The spider swarm ran directly into it and was sucked up in the swirl. The vortex vanished, taking the cloud with it, leaving a couple of rogue moths fluttering inches above the ground.

Lars was flat on his face, breathing heavily into the dirt.

Vegas doubled back and pulled up alongside.

The last of the white moths struggled in the breeze and fell to the floor. One of the lizards clambered down to it, taking the moth in its mouth and crunching heartily. At which point it pulled a strange face that lizards really shouldn't make, and started to roll around on the dirt. Moments later, it had sprouted two web-like wings. It confidently took to the air, buzzing above Lars, having levelled up into a dragonfly.

65

Dr Vegas sat on his moto and flapped out a large piece of paper which expanded to twice its size. 'It's all about eliminating the options,' he said. 'That's how you navigate through this thing successfully.' Worry lines creased his forehead. 'I've been plotting the moth circles,' he explained. 'If I see one, I draw a circle. If they re-occur, I put an X in that circle. See? Thing is, I can't work out any connection between them. There's no pattern. No symmetry.'

The map rustled in the breeze. Lars could see lines and crosses scribbled haphazardly on it. There was a cigarette burn on one corner. It looked fairly detailed and well worn.

'I've constructed a grid across the entire region. I've hand drawn all the buildings, fields and outhouses, ready for further investigation.'

'Can I see?'

Vegas folded the map back into his pocket. 'Get your own fucking map,' he said. He flicked an arm spasmodically in the air to relieve the tension, and smoked.

Lars realised that he was dealing with a professional.

'Your path will become clear in time, Izzy,' Vegas said with a wise exhale of mandrake.

'Like in Tomb Raider?'

'Sure,' he nodded. 'Just like in Tomb Raider. Let me give you a few cheats though so you make it through the night, because the way you're behaving you're going to be vapourware by morning. Ok, first things first, the shadow animals are evil bastards. They're going to do everything they can to crunk the fuck out of you. You're basically food to them. They'll get you looking in one direction, and then sneak up on you from the other. Those things chasing you, even the tiny spider ones, they were shadow animals.'

Lars listened.

'So, if you see or feel the presence of a shadow animal, in whatever form, then you run. Jurassic Park, man. That's bread and butter right there.'

'Got it.'

Dr Vegas laughed to himself and shook his head, as though reluctantly congratulating someone for making him the punchline of their pathetic practical joke. He took a puff of mandrake.

The skies churned purple. The clouds spun in slow circles. The sound of tiny wings fluttered above as the dragonfly was exploring its newfound abilities. It flicked at speed, buzzing overhead, glimmering colours hovering like an angel.

Vegas glanced up. 'Ok,' he said. 'I see that you've got yourself a dragonfly. That's level two shit, right there. Silver blue; at least shows some progression to your gameplay.' He took several puffs and came to his conclusion. 'There's something about you, Izzy. Something that I don't see in any of these other shadowy assholes. You're different.'

Lars was trying not to look at the dragonfly, pretending like he'd seen it all before.

'How about I show you through the next few levels, huh?' He whistled. In a flash, a small lion-headed bird, the size of a parrot, streaked down from above and landed on Vegas' shoulder.

Lars screamed.

'It's ok, man,' reassured Vegas. 'These things are on our side.'

The gryphon rolled its piercing eyes. It shrieked an otherworldly cry that caused the trees to tremble and the purple clouds to crack into fragmented pieces. It flicked out its forked tongue and stared at Lars with snake-like curiosity. Its head twitched from side to side, uncertain which eye to watch him through. It clawed on Vegas' shoulder just as a dog would settle by the fireside. Eventually it closed its eyes and was calm.

Vegas puffed, contentedly. 'This is a supreme golden gryphon. Level forty. Titanium claw attachments and night vision pro – a work of fucking art.' He smoked like it meant nothing.

'It's a tiny lion bird.' Lars reached up to stroke the creature's mane but the gryphon opened its eyes and growled in a way that a bird really shouldn't. He took a few steps back.

Dr Vegas felt that he was doing the right thing by helping Izzy on his quest. Had an increased confidence in his gaming partner. For some reason, they kept being brought back together, like there was something anchoring them to the same location. This was a good sign, he thought. There was something nagging him though. 'I have a theory. I want you to help me prove it. Let's head to the shack.'

Lars looked at his tiny dragonfly and felt inadequate. The golden gryphon squawked.

The path was riddled with potholes. Dr Vegas swerved constantly and without notice. The bike bumped but they didn't slow down. Lars was balanced on the back of the speeding moto. They were far from Central Station, and began to pitch higher as they climbed into the hills. Vegas wore driving goggles that were smeared with dead insects. Lars had inhaled more than he could count.

'You levelled up,' shouted Vegas over the engine noise. 'It's going to get more difficult from now on, you know that, right?'

They drove through a broken metal fence and down a dry mud pathway. The dense jungle foliage stood tall either side. Palm trees jutted into the perfectly purple sky. Lars had no idea where they were going. He wasn't sure if he would be able to find his way back if Vegas left him. The speeding bike bumped down a track, as fast as the suspension would allow. He held tight. The dragonfly buzzed overhead, followed by the supreme golden gryphon. They reached a rocky peak and stopped.

'There she blows.'

'There what blows?'

'The shack.'

A corrugated sheet of metal was thrown on top of a tree.

'I can't see a shack.'

'Exactly,' nodded Vegas, proudly. 'Sometimes the clearest solution is often right in front of you. You just have to stop overthinking things.'

He hid the moto beneath a stack of palms and disappeared inside.

Lars hovered by the doorway, and after plucking up courage, he entered.

The floor was covered with dry leaves and wood. There were a couple of old wooden crates. The space was mostly taken up by a tin bath. It looked like a cow had used it since Vegas had last been there. Palm tree leaves disguised the roof.

'That's a design innovation,' explained Vegas. 'More people should do it. If it gets too hot, you can rip a few leaves off and let some air in, and it makes a nice noise in the wind, you know, like a tree noise. Very therapeutic.'

'Is this where you live?' It hadn't occurred to Lars that he might be in this strange place long enough to have to find somewhere to stay. It was dawning on him that maybe he was stuck here.

Vegas pointed at the crate. 'Take a seat. I want to try something,' he said. 'You are not re-spawning back to level one. You are getting vapourised and coming right back where you left off.'

'So?'

'Do you trust me?'

Lars shrugged. 'Not really.'

'Trust, Izzy. It's the most powerful inventory item you can carry.' Dr Vegas placed a silver dagger on the crate in front of them. It looked exactly like the one that had cut him in the depths of the sunken ship.

'Where did you get that?'

The dagger sparkled, catching the occasional beam of light through the shack walls. 'There are ghosts in this city, man,' said Vegas. He indicated to the knife. 'I want you to stab yourself.'

Lars hesitated and then burst out laughing.

'I am not joking,' Vegas snapped. 'Take the knife and stab yourself.'

Lars waited, his eyes darting between the knife and Dr Vegas. He stood up and backed away.

'Where you going? Take the fucking knife.'

A raven drifted over to poke its head through the palm leaves and watch the commotion from above.

'Do it,' shouted Vegas. 'Do it! Cut yourself, man. Stab yourself in the face.'

Lars reached for the blade and held the knife in the air. At that precise moment, there was a rustle in the leaves and a moth crawled into the shack. More moths appeared and a soft breeze began to increase.

Vegas smiled and winked. 'I knew it. Look.'

Above the tin bath swirled a spiralling cloud of white moths.

Lars blinked, suddenly aware of his actions, and dropped the knife.

'You've passed the test.'

'That was a test?'

'The moths. They come when you're in danger. They're protecting you. You have great power, my friend.' Dr Vegas smoked with a knowing shrug. 'And with great power comes...'

'Great responsibility?'

'No, dude. Moths. Obviously.'

The cloud had now become a vortex. It twisted in the air and started to drift away, carried along by a breeze.

'Follow those insects,' shouted Vegas. 'This is exactly what we've been waiting for. We need to find out where they go.'

The moth cloud shapeshifted as it hovered in the sky, a physical Rorschach test of strange shapes; spiders and birds,

twisted faces and alien insects. They followed as the cloud
crossed back the way they had come towards Central Station.
It spun straight onto approaching tram-lines, breaking into
fragments and reforming on the other side of the tracks.

Dr Vegas waited for a break in the approaching trams.
He took two steps forward and disappeared from sight as
a heavy tram churned up the dusty road. Lars spotted him
again in the middle of the road. He watched Vegas take two
steps forward, then one step back to avoid being crushed,
then two more steps up the road, one across, three right, one
back, and two forward again. He waved from the other side.
'You coming or what?'

Lars hopped up and down, waiting for a gap in the
speeding vehicles. 'Frogger, right? I can do this. It's a classic.'

A shrill, repetitive theme tune began to play in his head
as he heard the eight-bit jumping sound each time he moved.
Bells churned as trams sped inches from him. He looked left
and right, and tried another step forward as a bicycle spun
behind, followed by another tram. He was in the middle of
it all now; two forward, one back, three to the left and right
into a tram.

There was a jarring thud as Lars was vapourised, leaving
behind him a cloud in the shape of a skull and crossbones.

On the other side of the road, Dr Vegas was smoking,
and beginning to look impatient.

Lars appeared right back where he left off, flashing
three times and then stepping into the road again. The
vehicles were approaching from both sides and appeared to
be speeding up. Three steps left, one forward, the eight-bit
sound effects pinging in his mind as he moved. Lars hesitated
and then ran without looking, straight across the road. He

threw himself onto the ground and rolled over to narrowly avoid being crushed.

'You're a natural,' said Vegas, totally unimpressed. 'Now, come on.'

The moths were landing by a stone shrine with a vast, wooden door, where they were crawling through the cracks and disappearing inside.

'First things first.' Vegas puffed. He added the building to his map, using the ash from his cigarette to mark the spot.

Another moth landed, followed by five, six, seven more. There was a flash of cold air which rushed out from under the door with a white light.

'Imminent vortex,' said Vegas. He took a contemplative drag.

Lars had an increasing feeling that his new friend had completely lost it. 'We're so going to get fucked by an end of level boss with infinitely superior powers to us, aren't we?'

Vegas smiled and thrust open the door. All was cold and silent inside. The heavy door closed behind them. Shafts of light glimmered through cracks in the walls. They looked around, barely able to see their hands before their faces. There was a draught from somewhere below.

Lars scratched around on the floor. 'This goes down.' He ran his hands along cracks.

'Man, this is so fucking Indiana,' said Vegas.

Lars found a frayed rope that was practically invisible, hidden against the wall. He pulled it and metal clattered in the darkness. A dull noise vibrated, increasing in volume, as a large vent appeared in the floor. They felt cold air rushing upwards as a tall, metal box elevated from a shaft. It was a lift.

Dr Vegas handed Lars the joint. He patted him on the back and smiled a crow's feet grin. 'Whatever you find down there,' he said, 'I think it's what you've been searching for.'

'You're not coming?'

'This one is a solo mission, Izzy. The next part is up to you. Trust me.' Vegas turned and pushed on the door. He headed outside, leaving Lars alone in the cold, damp shaft.

He stepped into the lift and cautiously pulled the rope. The crate shuddered and dropped into darkness. As he went deeper, it grew colder, and a musty smell increased. He braced himself against the sides. Eventually, the lift slowed to a stop and he stepped out. The cage rattled back up the vent. A light was visible down a long passageway, where a series of shadows were being cast up the wall.

'Hisashiburi, Izanagi,' said a deep, rasping voice with a hacked cough. 'Long time, eh?'

Lars was surrounded by a strange group with flowing robes and hunched backs. The ancient beings held hands to form a circle, as they closed in on their immortal brother.

66

'Stand back all of you,' boomed Jurojin. 'Do not go near him. We must hold this investigation thoroughly and with extreme caution.' He wobbled, balancing on his ornate walking crutch. He had grown increasingly older and more fragile in recent hours. The effects of the changing afterlife were beginning to take their toll.

He struggled to uncover a large gourd that hung around his neck and approached Lars with a crippled shuffle. 'If ever there were a time for the metaphysical healing properties of your Jade crystal, Imperial uncle, then that time is now.'

Daikoku bowed gracefully and conducted a slow and mesmerising purification ceremony, stepping beyond time and space in a dance that allowed the essence to calm everyone within its reach.

Jurojin moved so close that he and Lars were almost touching noses. In a single movement, he tore the gown at his chest and seemed instantly dissatisfied.

'Where is your belly? Have you not been imbibing in the mortal splendour? Should he not be fat with imperfect fruit?'

Lars patted his stomach and shrugged in an, intend to get down the gym more often, kind of way. His own image was reflected back in Bishamon's broadsword. The beard was now bristling and ginger beneath a completely bald head. He looked like a pale imitation of the surrounding immortals with their bulging bellies and flowing sequinned robes. They harrumphed, disapprovingly.

'Where are the marks?' declared Jurojin. 'He does not display the scars of the master of the cloud chamber.'

Lars knew what they were looking for. The scars created by the water witch. He offered his hands for inspection, but the deep cut lines were gone.

'It is not him,' concluded Jurojin. 'This is not Izanagi. Sacrifice him to the Oni.'

Bishamon raised his sword to Lars' neck.

'Wait,' slurred Hotei. 'I can vouch for him. I have followed his journey through mortality. I have witnessed all that he has had to endure. My spirit animals have been at his side, and they remain with him. Show them?'

Lars was confused. 'Show them what? The markings? They've gone.'

'No, Izanagi, where are your spirit animals?'

'I don't have any. Do I?'

'Raise your arms.' Hotei patted him down like an airport security guard. 'Where are your lizards? Ah, here's one.' He pulled a tiny lizard from his beard. The dragonfly buzzed overhead and landed on Lars' head. 'I see. Unconventional, but not without effort.' Hotei indicated for Lars to stay calm. He would sort everything out.

Lars was relieved to see the familiar face, even if it was the shadow that had been stalking his every move — the drunken master of the afterlife, and also he was beginning to suspect, his very old friend.

'This is Izanagi. I can assure you.' He took a dramatic gulp of whisky to emphasise the point. 'He knows this as well as you.'

The immortals mumbled to each other.

'Do you know this to be true?' asked Bishamon. 'Do you know who you are?'

Lars hesitated, unsure.

'Drink with us,' coughed Jurojin. A wisp of cloudy haze emanated from the animal hair gourd as he flipped the cork. 'Drink.' He splashed it in Lars' face, who gagged at the stench of sweat and bile. 'Drink!'

Hotei gave Lars an encouraging look to suggest that drinking the horrible liquid would be a good idea. He gulped as much as he could and immediately retched up bile.

The immortals laughed, holding their bellies. 'More!'

He took another drink and tried to hold it down. The smell was repulsive. 'What sort of wine is this?'

'That is not wine,' laughed Jurojin. They fell about laughing, wiping away tears.

'What do you want?' shouted Lars. 'I haven't done anything to you.'

'Oh, my dear brother, but you have,' explained Daikoku, 'and you continue to do so, over and over.'

Fokuro rode up on his tiny deer. 'Hotei has appeared to you so many times...' The deer made a noise of affirmation. 'In the repetition of the electronic games that you so adore, as a suited figure of authority in your pathetic place of work, even as rain water on a bus window, and what did you do? You ignored all of his humble advances.' He raised his shoulders like the statement were obvious.

'I didn't ignore anyone.'

'What would your wife have to say about that, Izanagi?' asked Hotei.

Lars remembered standing on the doorstep in the rain. Would things have been any different if he'd turned the key? Would he even be here now? 'Where is she?'

'She is right here,' replied Hotei.

'Claire?'

'Claire Nilsson is not your wife.'

Berry stepped out of the shadows. She was wearing a long, embroidered robe that stretched down to cover her bare feet. Her hair was tied up high on her head. Swirling make up covered her white, painted face.

'Behold, the goddess of creation, and your true wife, Izanami.'

'Hey,' she said.

Bishamon dug his sword into the ground. 'Dress him. Remind him.'

The immortals knelt and put their hands together in prayer as the goddess, Izanami, approached her husband, offering him a robe of his own. She helped his arms inside each sleeve and handed him a small, patterned, paper fan. She smirked and bowed, as instructed, and took several steps back.

'Now,' exclaimed Bishamon, 'that is more like the master of the cloud-chamber that we all know.'

Lars pushed his shoulders back and considered waving it. He held the little paper fan, feeling very much unlike the master of anything.

The immortals were deeply unimpressed.

As he unfolded the fan, a flicker of realisation hit him. 'You were sending me the Atari Shock IGM?'

414

Daikoku looked to Hotei with a smile. 'He begins to remember.'

'I got a load of junk mail about how to change my life and how I was on the wrong path and stuff. Become your real self. Beware the shadow animals.' He realised what he was saying as he spoke. 'Return to Mt. Hōrai? That was you?'

Hotei nodded. 'Did you not always know this, deep down?'

'I thought it was spam.'

'What is spam?' asked Daikoku.

'It is food,' explained Hotei, in his wisdom of all things mortal.

Daikoku muttered that he'd never had the pleasure and would be curious to taste it.

'He was seduced by Kitsune,' said Hotei.

The immortals mumbled to each other, concerned.

'The minions of Tengu will continue to hunt you while it torments us from the stolen throne of Hōrai,' explained Bishamon. 'They will try to distract you from your true calling.'

'The cracks have formed,' said Fokuro. 'Hōrai has become overwhelmed by Yomi-no-Kuni. The afterlife is doomed unless you choose to return to us as the reviver of the dead. Do you not see this, Izanagi? Reclaim your land. Seek forgiveness from the quintillions and choose to become immortal once more. You must heal the sickness before the darkness consumes the light.'

'He must accept this truth for himself or it will mean nothing at all,' declared Bishamon. There was a commotion as he suddenly adopted an aggressive attack stance. He raised his sword and prepared to strike.

'Hey, easy,' cried Lars. 'I thought we were on the same side?'

But Bishamon wasn't threatening him. Dr Vegas had climbed down into the chamber.

'Stand back. I see a minion of Tengu.' Bishamon sliced the air with his broadsword. The immortals retreated into the shadows.

'Whoah!' Vegas ducked as the sword barely missed his hat. 'Who the fuck are these creeps?'

'Beware, he may transform at any instant,' cried Daikoku.

Bishamon jumped and started to pound Vegas in the face with his fists. He spat out his joint to avoid swallowing it.

'Stop!' shouted Lars. 'Let him go. He's one of us.'

Bishamon held his broadsword across Vegas' chest.

'He has warped your mind, Izanagi. This creature cannot be trusted,' shouted Jurojin.

'Trust is the most powerful inventory item you can carry, man,' said Vegas, struggling to break free as the metal blade was forced tighter to his neck.

The deer tapped its hoof and the immortals turned to see Berry, smiling, and holding out her arms in welcome.

'Dr Jones? Is that you?' she smiled. 'You found me.'

Vegas looked up. 'She mean me?'

Bishamon looked to Lars, who nodded in acknowledgment. 'He's cool. Let him go.'

Bishamon loosened his sword.

'Do I know you?' asked Vegas.

Daikoku made introductions. 'Behold, the goddess of creation, Izanami.'

'Honoured I'm sure,' he smiled. 'Can I get up now?' He reached his hand out to Berry and she helped him to his feet.

The dragonfly appeared. It seemed frantic, flying over and over in a repetitive pattern to form neon Kanji symbols in the air.

天狗

The deer lifted its nose and snorted.

Fokuro realised just in time, and shouted the name of the creature that was being written. 'Tengu!'

Berry felt its hand change from cold skin to feather, as Dr Vegas shapeshifted.

67

Tengu vanished as quickly as it had appeared. A tense anticipation hung in the tropical air.

'What was that thing?' she shivered. 'Where did it go?'

'It has not gone,' replied Fokuro.

Clouds formed above with a vengeful purpose. A roar of thunder scorched the skies as a swooping mass blocked out the sun. A swirling coil flexed to reveal a mighty snake; black and red scales glistened along its armoured body. The cobra hissed, observing each of them in turn, assessing their individual threats from inside the typhoon.

'This is no Ōkami from our world,' gasped Bishamon. He clutched at his sword.

The ground trembled and collapsed to form a deep pit, trapping the immortals inside.

The snake was incredibly fast and it struck in an instant, surveying each target from multiple attack positions, moving like nothing they had seen before, never staying in one spot for more than a second.

'I got this,' shouted Berry. She threw the shawl over her shoulder and whistled. Her red gryphon darted out of the sky and spun in spirals around the snake, deadly talons raised like blades in the sunlight. It struck, slicing deep marks into the serpent's scales. The snake recoiled.

The red gryphon swooped in for a second attack, but the snake reared up to confront it, making a deep gurgling sound and showering venom in the air. The gryphon flew directly into the poisonous cloud and was blinded. The snake thrust itself up and caught the gryphon in its fangs. Feathers flew as the life was shaken from it.

Berry fell to her knees, defeated.

'It is too strong,' uttered Daikoku.

The cobra began to spin in circles, forming a figure of eight in the sky.

Lars turned to her. 'We need to do this together. We need to form a super clan.'

She smiled and nodded. 'Imperial uncle, Daikoku, can you distract it?'

He bowed deeply and swung his Jade crystal tablet. A dark mist formed around the immortals.

They felt the collective consciousness – the teaming up of players to form a single connected force much stronger than they could ever be individually – and the ancient immortals became one.

For the first time in millennia, Fokuro lifted his leg, swivelled his body to one side, and stepped down from his deer. He bowed to begin the Kata, and then lunged into a rear backflip, spinning several times before landing perfectly on one leg, his other leg raised in the air to adopt the Kung Fu stance of the Praying Mantis.

Hotei collapsed, causing Berry to gasp, but before he hit the floor he picked himself up and side stepped into the Kung Fu position of the Drunken Master.

Jurojin stuck out his fat belly, spinning his iron crutch around him as fast as a propeller.

Daikoku flung his legs in the air in frantic scissor cuts. He spun on his head, and rolled over to rotate a leg beneath him in a foot sweep, causing the ground to quake in a whirlwind.

The immortals spread out to form an attack triangle. The Ōkami took position and prepared to strike.

'Watch out for special attacks!' shouted Lars. 'We will guide you.'

'Round two – fight!' shouted Jurojin, as he spun his iron crutch and flung it at the snake. It spat in the clouds and rained venom on them.

Daikoku flew into the sky, snapping scissor cuts with his legs. The snake recoiled.

Fokuro spun, disorienting the creature, tying it in knots. He then leaped up onto the back of his deer and raced forwards to slam the snake in the neck with a series of deathly blows. The creature snapped, slicing a deep cut through Fokuro's stomach. He fell from his deer and rolled on the dirt.

The real Dr Vegas climbed up on the roof of a twisted shrine that overlooked Central Station. He had felt the ground shake and watched the skies turn black, as the Ōkami had materialised on the horizon.

He consulted his Map of Everything and calculated precisely where his old friend should emerge. The unstoppable elephant was waiting. It moved out of the shadows and lumbered in his direction.

'Hold onto your butts,' he said, as he took a leap of faith and flung himself from the roof.

The elephant tried to shake him but he managed to hold on. It ran down the quayside, moving faster than he had expected. The colourful shawl on its back began to slip and fell to the dirt to reveal two, glorious, feathered wings. The elephant flexed them and with a single flap, launched itself into the air.

'I didn't think this through,' shouted Vegas, as he was pulled skyward, narrowly missing a cherry blossom tree, his legs splaying feebly behind him.

'Heal and run,' shouted Lars. 'Dodge and build. You need more dodge.'

Hotei spun in a cartwheel, picking up Fokuro, and moving him to safety before the serpent could make its next attack. He twisted in full circle and flew back at the snake like a rotating Shuriken blade, blinding the Ōkami in one eye and leaving multiple cuts across its face.

Bishamon stood fast and repelled deadly fangs. Metal chimed with teeth as it struck his sword. He spun, using all of his weight to gain power, and hurled the sword at the Ōkami.

The snake exploded in a cloud.

'It is over,' smiled Jurojin.

But Lars and Berry knew that as with every boss battle, there was always more to come.

The cloud became a multitude of spirits that twisted in the air. They spun faster and began to take on a new form. White electricity emanated from a creature the size of a mountain. Yellow eyes saw beyond time and space, as it channelled the strength of a thousand souls.

The demon embodiment of Tadashi Finjoto appeared before them. It focused on the immortal gathering, and prepared to strike the final death blow.

'I didn't mean to do that,' bellowed Bishamon.

'Check your health,' shouted Lars. He could sense the void of darkness approaching as shadow animals began creeping into the arena, attracted from far across the afterlife.

'Back down,' screamed Berry. 'You're going to get us all killed.'

'Fokuro is hurt,' shouted Hotei. 'We cannot win this.'

'Life is short, my brother,' said Lars with a grin. 'And if there's one thing I've learned, it's never give up.'

Dr Vegas saw the Ōkami implode and reform to become the giant mountain-like boss. He hoped he wasn't too late. The sacred elephant flapped, lifting him higher, swinging wildly through the air. The demon lumbered below and lashed out an arm that shocked the earth and cracked the skies.

The immortals were scattered.

A group of objects were uniting on the horizon, darkening the sky like a flock of fat birds. The sacred elephant appeared to be heading directly for it. As they got closer, Vegas realised what it was. A wreath of winged elephants had flocked together and were approaching from all corners of the afterlife to form a herd. They returned the shrill trumpet call as they gathered. The elephant dropped to the ground and shook Vegas from its back. He spun over in the dirt and immediately reached for his glasses case.

The beast was skyward in a flash and began to loop with the herd, gaining speed, and in a single movement, they formed a mighty ball and hurled themselves like a meteor at the demon embodiment of Finjoto.

The sacred elephants landed with an incredible force that cracked the Earth. Shafts of white light broke through the fragmented dirt. The ground imploded and sucked in on itself, pulling the demon down into the depths — followed by Berry, Lars and Dr Vegas.

68

Berry could see flaming torches stretch far into the void of Tengu's cavern. The shadow of a jagged beak was cast across the sandstone walls. The hooked claw of a raven foot took a step forward, and a bony hand reached down to her.

'We meet again, Izanami.' Its voice echoed down the chamber. 'So tell me, was it worth it? Did you find the time on mortal soil as fulfilling as you had imagined?'

She was thrust up into the air until she was confronted by a single timeline etched into the stone.

'Let me reveal to you the true nature of your wasted human existence.'

She studied the ancient markings, trying to interpret its message. Looking back as far as she could see, the line seemed to twist and merge with others that preceded it, but there were no connections going forward – just a single, solitary line.

Berry felt the shocking impact of a life that had been totally unfulfilled, and one that would always remain that way. She was never going to grow beyond the here and now of her perfect isolation. She would always be alone.

Why did she continue to shut out the world in this way, making no connections, forming no emotional bonds, just hiding in the safe zone of her virtual worlds? She had found refuge in her creation, in the virtual battlefield of Atari Shock, and built an existence for herself where life could be lived as an avatar, where she was responsible for no one and had nothing real to challenge her. Despite becoming mortal, she had never even lived. She shivered at the fact that the life she had wasted, should never have existed.

'Cast off the petty insignificance of your mortal incarnation and stay with me, Izanami,' crowed Tengu. 'Live by my side and together we will create a Universe that is worthy of you.'

Berry looked at the birdman and reached out to take its feathered claw.

69

Dr Vegas studied the mess of conflicting hieroglyphic images along the sandstone wall. He was overwhelmed by the complexity of confused detail. The memories rushed back to him, and he realised that this was his timeline.

He saw the house where he grew up, where he used to draw pictures on his bedroom walls, his college years in medical school, the drunken nights playing poker and staying up until dawn, his first loves, his learned experiences, a car accident, digging holes, building sandcastles, the sadness of his father passing away, caring for his mother until she too gave up and left him alone – it all returned to him in an instant as he realised who he was – Mike Jones; the over-confident young anaesthetist who made a serious error on shift by inserting the tube from a ventilating machine into the patient's oesophagus instead of her windpipe, starving her of oxygen and causing her to go into cardiac arrest on the operating table. The scared young man who suffered the consequences of failed ambition, who falsified evidence to hide the fact that he was three times over the legal alcohol limit, who hid from the truth and disappeared into a world of on-stage regression therapy on a mystery tour of spiritual science. The man whose life completely changed when he fell in love with Sarah Clarkson, and then chose to walk out of her life altogether.

'You remember her, don't you, Michael Jones?' rasped Tengu. It flapped a wing and flames flickered. Sarah fell from the shadows.

'Sarah?'

'Not only her. There is another that you have been hiding from.'

Two women were now standing before him. He didn't recognise the other at first.

'I offer the gift of redemption.' Tengu lowered its staff, blocking physical contact. 'Only one will reincarnate. You must choose who is to be sacrificed.'

The skin of the other woman was pale and almost blue. Blood dripped from the surgical incisions that had been left open when she had passed away over ten years ago. He looked into the face of death, and into the eyes of the woman that he had killed.

'You took everything from me,' she sobbed. 'I left my husband, my son, all alone. I didn't even get to say goodbye.'

Mike felt the depth of her sadness penetrate his soul. 'I think about you every single day.' He reached out his hand.

'Don't you dare ask me for forgiveness,' she scolded. 'I trusted you with my life.'

He looked to the ground. 'I'm so sorry.'

Tengu turned its head and smirked. 'How does it feel, Dr Vegas, to wield the power of life over death?'

70

Lars saw his timeline stretch far into an infinite past, right back to the dawn of his immortal awakening. It was a maze of puzzles and patterns, just like the ones that had been carved onto his body.

He traced it forwards and it simplified to form the single line of his mortal existence; his re-birth, his infancy, the first time he walked, spoke and became hooked to the perfect isolation of the gaming screen.

Tengu clacked its beak. 'And so, we come to you, who or whatever you are,' it croaked. The creature looked to Berry. She was silent, lost in her timeline etchings. Dr Vegas was hanging his head in shame. It turned back to Lars. 'You are no one.'

'My name is Izanagi,' he said, boldly.

The birdman rustled its feathers. 'Fool.'

'I am master of the cloud chamber and reviver of the dead. I am Izanagi.'

'Where are the sacred marks? You are nothing. I carry a message from the firstborn; the Protogenoi who created the very fabric of our Universe. Your immortal reign is over.' Tengu spun its staff. 'Return to grow fat on the mortal fruit that you so love to consume. There is nothing for you here.' It cocked its head in question. 'Leave Izanami with me, and

I promise to return you to the comforting walls of mortality that you have built around yourself. You will live again, and you will die again, as a simple mortal. Do we have an accord?'

'I can't do that.'

'You choose to let down those that you love? How human you have become.' It twisted its staff and Claire fell forwards.

He reached out to her and she backed away. She didn't recognise him, but the moment he said her name it was as though a veil had been lifted between worlds.

'Claire?'

'Lars?'

'You had no right to bring her here.'

'Where am I?' she sobbed, becoming increasingly frightened.

'This has nothing to do with her.'

'Oh, but it does,' clacked Tengu. 'It has everything to do with every mortal creature, living and dead, for you have betrayed them all. You are not worthy of your former status. You will never again be master of the cloud chamber.' It waved its staff. 'Speak now, mortal. Tell him what you said to me?'

She stepped forward. 'I don't love you.'

'Claire, please?'

'You have never respected me. You wasted our life together.'

'Why are you saying this?'

'What made you so...' she stumbled, 'selfish and irresponsible?'

'Claire, listen to what you're saying?'

'All of those years that I wasted on you, waiting for you to come to your senses, but you just drifted further away.'

He looked for the wise advice of Hotei, but the immortals weren't anywhere to be seen. Lars had to confront this one alone.

Was she right? Had he taken the precious time given to him and wasted it on a life that had brought them nothing? Perhaps he hadn't been there to support her, to help make her life a happy one, instead he had retreated and left her totally alone, to sink in the depths of loneliness.

'Lars,' she hesitated. 'You never gave me the chance to tell you – we were going to be a family.' She looked at the floor. 'I hate you for leaving me.'

Tengu flexed its wings in joy and danced. 'You see. There is nothing for you here or there. You have achieved nothing. You are nothing.' It swiped its staff between them. 'The choice is made,' it cawed. 'The only real decision that you will ever make. She does not want you, pathetic mortal. You have failed her. She has suffered because of you, and she will suffer in my New World, because of you.' It snapped its beak and wielded its staff in a full circle, striking Claire and tripping her over.

'Don't touch her.'

She fell heavily, protecting her stomach. 'What about our deal?' she pleaded, reaching up to the birdman. 'You promised to save my child?'

'And save it I shall, but your timeline ends here.'

'No,' screamed Lars.

'Behold, the new master of the cloud chamber, for I am the bringer of death.' It slammed its staff into the ground and Lars was thrown across the chamber.

'All is wasted. All is gone. Your weakness speaks volumes,' laughed Tengu. 'This woman will forever walk my afterlife.

You will never see her again.' It swiped its staff over Claire and she curled into the foetal position as she vapourised into a cloud of dust.

It raised its staff and struck the wall, breaking Lars' timeline in two. 'Your unborn child will follow a different path.' It gathered the timeline together in a cosmic string. 'This belongs to me.'

Lars felt the overwhelming shock of every emotional state that he'd been denied as a mortal. A multitude of sensations radiated through him as he felt the complex depths expand his soul. Deep outlines began to trace themselves into glowing shapes on his skin. Spirals spread across his body that burst into flaming infinity symbols. He fell to the floor, clawing helplessly at his arms and chest, pain increasing in the violent heat of rage as he screamed out and a devastating pulse of energy exploded into the afterlife.

The soul trams ground to a halt. The lights of Central Station fell dark. The elephant circle scattered, flinging the beasts to the far corners of the Earth. The flaming waters on the banks of the Shozukawa subsided. The clocks at the end of Time stopped.

The force crumbled the afterlife in a shockwave of cosmic energy, and Tengu's lair imploded and collapsed to dust.

71

A fat lizard sat on a rock and basked in the sun of a new dawn. It licked its lips, having helped itself to as many moths as it could during the evolving vortex. The mists surrounding the mountain island of Hōrai had subsided to reveal a glimmering, golden palace. A solitary dragonfly hovered on the breeze.

The immortals sat in a crater and watched the dust settle. They scratched their toes and stroked their beards as they supped from their magic gourds. Their shawls flapped in the electric air.

Fokuro's deer was helping its master to stand as he stumbled, clutching his hand to his side.

Berry saw the dark stain of blood. 'You're injured? You can't be hurt. You're immortal?'

'And sometimes we bleed,' he sighed. 'The birdman, tell me, did it make you an offer?'

'It had nothing to offer that I couldn't find myself.'

Fokuro nodded. 'That is good to hear, Izanami.'

The lizard started to make a deep hacking sound. It choked and retched and poked out its tongue to cough up a single grey moth which glided inches above ground. It flew serenely over to its creator.

The immortals turned their heads to watch. The lizard guiltily cleaned its face.

'Stay very still,' stuttered Hotei. 'Hold out your hand. Welcome it.'

Berry didn't dare move. She scrunched her forehead, feeling its tiny legs tickle her as it crawled down her finger. It flicked out a long tongue and tasted the nectar of her skin. Its wings spread in the warm sunshine and burst into life with colourful patterns; vibrant blues, greens, yellows and oranges, spiralling into infinity as the grey moth transformed into a butterfly.

'Did I do that?' she asked, amazed at the transformation.

'There is no life beyond death without you,' explained Hotei. 'You bring fertility. It is the sacred power that only you hold, Izanami.'

Berry felt that she had never created anything so beautiful.

'Are you ok, my dear?' asked Fokuro.

A tear came to her eye when she realised the sad fact that she couldn't remember the last time anyone had asked. She nodded and thanked him, wiping away the tear which fell to the ground and blossomed into a meadow of bright pink lotus flowers. Grass sprouted through dry cracks.

Fokuro smiled as he watched his deer take a mouthful, feeling the soft ground underfoot for the very first time.

The butterfly launched itself, flicked and stopped, flicked and stopped, and dropped to the dust. Stretching out its tongue, it basked in the sweet scent of the afterlife, lifting its tiny legs to dance in happy circles. Colours began to spread, infecting the dry ground. Lush green grass spread across the valley. Flowers and trees flushed with swaying leaves and petals. The sound of insects and birds began to flood the air.

In the distance, bells rang harmoniously from the clocks of Central Station. The regeneration of life energised the land of the dead.

Berry watched the world around her erupt into a vibrancy of colour as the afterlife became fertile once more. She was conscious of everything. The simple breath of air on her skin. The warmth of the sun that lit the sky. The delicate insect that crawled across her bare feet. She noticed the composition of every tiny creature that scattered chaotically, moving forward and turning back on itself, constantly moving but going nowhere. At that precise moment, she felt that she understood the essence of life itself.

Fokuro held his side and winced. She carefully helped him to sit on the grass and held the old man in her arms. The deer tottered up to lick his face.

'The land of the dead has suffered in your absence,' he said, as he admired the view. 'I ask you now to bestow on me your most precious of gifts. Release me.' He smiled, uncomplaining, but she could see that he was in pain. She held him softly and allowed the energy to radiate from her immortal soul and bring liberation to her ancient brother.

'As one dies – so another is born,' whispered Fokuro. 'It is the natural cycle of the Universe.' He closed his eyes and a glow of light surrounded him as his soul was taken.

The deer spat out a mouthful of grass and began bleating.

Berry stroked its nose. 'Don't worry, little one,' she said. 'Your father hasn't left you.' She held the deer around its portly belly and gave it a comforting squeeze.

The immortals watched, solemnly feeling the new born sun on their faces, content in the knowledge that each unique ray of light now held the immortal memory of their brother. He would always be with them — in every spark of sunshine, in every drop of rain, in every flake of snow — for eternity.

The deer calmed but began to bleat incessantly as a shell-shocked old man staggered out of the dust. Professor Malcolm Van Peterson stumbled forward, his hand on his forehead, seeming dazed. The deer ran up to him and rubbed its nose on his side. 'Oh,' he laughed. 'Who are you then?' It turned its head to caress him and bleated again as Sarah appeared at the crater's edge.

'Papa? Mike? Is that you?' she laughed through tears, and ran over to embrace them.

Mike felt the sudden clarity of recognition. 'Found you,' he said, as they held each other.

She wiped away a tear. 'Just like we said, right? In the next life?'

'Sarah, what have I done?' said Van Peterson. 'You don't belong here.'

'You did what you had to do, papa,' she replied. 'You tried.' They hugged each other tightly. 'The woman in the hospital gown, what happened to her, Mike?'

He smiled, mournfully. 'We came to an arrangement.'

Berry gently launched the butterfly into the air and waved it on its way. It twisted into a spiralling vortex of colour.

The professor was transfixed.

Mike looked to the ground. 'We have to go,' he said, as he squeezed her hand tighter. He stepped into the circle and urged them to follow. Sarah held their hands, feeling safe between Mike and her father. The swirling circle increased in intensity.

As they stepped across the threshold, the vision of a woman joined with them and took the old man's hand. 'Everything will be all right,' whispered Lotus Flower. 'You are at peace now, Malcolm. Come.'

As Sarah returned to the realm of the living, she felt the grip of their hands weaken in hers.

A black raven landed on a golden rooftop that glistened in the sunshine of the new dawn. Bishamon caught its eye and unsheathed his sword, causing a shockwave to tremble the foundations of the building and the raven to lose its footing and launch itself into the air.

'I am watching you,' he bellowed.

The bird cawed and flapped lazily in the perfect sky, but not before it shot an evil look at Lars.

He gazed at the colourful morning of the afterlife and twisted the lush green grass between his toes. The scene would have been overwhelming to any mortal being, but he basked in the splendour of it. He now knew that this was just the beginning.

'I see that you have finally made your decision,' said Hotei, as he sat next to Lars.

'I have?' he laughed.

'The eyes tell all, my brother, and your soul speaks clearly now.'

They watched the spiralling vortex of bright butterflies, and Berry, who was busy counting lotus flowers.

She did the maths, listing the infinite number of creatures that now flourished in her New World. She smiled when she saw the immortals watching. 'Did I make all of this? It's so beautiful.'

'You are capable of far more beauty than you know, Izanami,' whispered Hotei.

She looked into the sky. A dark object drifted clumsily across the glowing sun.

'Who are we?' she asked.

'I am he, and you are he, as you are me, and we are all together,' said Lars, with a knowing grin.

Hotei laughed.

'I like that one too,' she sniffed. 'Wish I had a Jujyfruit.'

Was Claire still wandering the afterlife? Why didn't she tell him that they were going to be a family? Would he have acted any different if he'd known?

'Your mortal wife and child can be saved, Izanagi,' explained Hotei, as if reading his thoughts.

Lars felt the grass between his fingertips and raised his head to admire the vibrancy of colour that spread for as far as he could see. Questions and answers, truth and meaning, what had he really been searching for? He had created a fantasy world to distract himself from the mortal reality that he was born into. Was this how everyone survived, he wondered, how they found peace when confronted by the terror of life and death?

Lars finally understood that there was no programme running in the background, no secret off-switch, and no hidden code. There was only the opportunity to live in the here and now and the chance to create something beautiful if he tried — the most precious inventory items that he could carry — trust, honesty and love.

He also knew that one day, whatever distractions he used to hide from the terrifying truth, everything would be gone at a moment's notice, when he watched the people around him pass away and felt the gravitational pull of death tear the bleeding heart from his soul.

Izanagi realised that this was what it felt like to be alive.

It was time. The butterfly vortex had become an awe-inspiring whirlwind of colour.

Berry looked to the immortals as they enjoyed the fresh feeling of grass between their toes. 'Will they be ok without us?' she asked, but she already knew the answer.

Lars held the hand of his immortal wife, Izanami. Her skin felt reassuring and soft. 'Let's go,' he said, and they took a step forward into the swirling vortex.

'The sacrifice has been made,' said Hotei.

He inhaled and felt the deep rush of enlightenment as the life force of the quintillions flowed through him. He instantly knew every detail of their mortal existence; their sorrows, their loves, their heartbroken hopes and dreams. He no longer felt the yearning, the waiting for an event that would never happen, or the urge to complete a game that would never end. With each new breath, the sea of abandoned souls dissipated, and the afterlife was at peace once more.

He exhaled and he became transcendental.

Time ceased to exist, along with the memory of the mortal, Lars Nilsson.

72

Dr Vegas puffed on a mandrake cigarette.

Cows poked their heads through holes in the heavy foliage. The bath tipped over as he pulled on his stomper boots and strolled out into the lush, green glade. He embraced the new morning that glistened in the neon sunrise. A rainbow of lotus flowers blossomed across the valley.

A herd of winged elephants performed acrobatics on the horizon, lit by an orange afterglow. He whistled and a golden gryphon screeched in reply, spinning infinity symbols in the ominous and darkening sky.

73

Berry kissed her baby son on the forehead and whispered goodnight.

A small lantern flickered at his bedside, casting shadows of an infinite Universe across the nursery ceiling.

A cup of tea was waiting in the kitchen, heaped with five perfect servings of sugar.

'How's our little boy?'

'Sleeping peacefully.' She gave her husband a squeeze. 'Won't be long.'

She opened the laptop and joined the servers of Atari Shock. War was raging online. She inserted the sugar-coated USB drive and uploaded the avatar.

His Immortal legacy continued.

74

Izanagi watched over the sea of souls.

A tiny lizard nestled in the weaves of his ginger beard that was now as thick as the sands of Time. The dragonfly buzzed overhead. He drank from his ancient gourd and handed it around the magic circle, insisting on a hearty quaff from all.

The professor accepted, wiping the sweet wine from his lips. His portly belly shook as he laughed and thanked his immortal host. The deer chewed grass by his side.

Peace had been restored. The deceased were blessed with safe passage to Nirvana once more.

Izanagi held the music device in the palm of his wrinkled hand. He pressed play and indulged in the frenetic energy of rock and roll − for there were some things that the ancient immortal, who once knew what it was like to be mortal, simply could not sacrifice.

75

Finjoto crawled through a black mist. He was terrified, trapped in a typhoon that showed no sign of relenting. Clouds swirled in anger on the banks of the Shozukawa as a river of fire burned.

He begged for forgiveness. There was no one to hear him. He accepted his fate and felt his body become vacant as it was consumed by a multitude of spirits. His soul was assimilated.

He had the strength of a hundred limbs. He could see through ten thousand eyes. The earth became soft to his touch as he found a new rhythm; leaping into tall trees, gliding over the mountains and valleys of the dead, rising and falling in pockets of tropical air, scanning the ground with hawk-like penetration. He swam in the murky depths of the underworld.

He was the seeker, he was the hunter; he was the destructive yearning of millions of rejected souls deemed unfit for Nirvana.

The Oracle, Shozuka-no-baba, opened an eye. A choice had been made, but it was not the one that she had bargained for. Izanagi had been underestimated. The Tengu had failed her. She scowled at the arrogance of the immortals and the fake utopia that taunted her primordial birth right. 'The Protogenoi awaken,' she sneered.

Time held no meaning for the ancient immortals – those self-appointed guardians of the afterlife – but their time had just run out.

DR VEGAS AND THE EIGHT IMMORTALS WILL RETURN

Lightning Source UK Ltd.
Milton Keynes UK
UKHW012023090223
416719UK00005B/668/J